IN LANDS THAT NEVER WERE

Tales of Swords and Sorcery from *The Magazine of Fantasy & Science Fiction*

Edited by
Gordon Van Gelder

THUNDER'S MOUTH PRESS
NEW YORK

In Lands That Never Were

Published in the United States by:
Thunder's Mouth Press
An imprint of Avalon Publishing Group
245 W. 17th St., 11th Floor
New York, NY 10011

First U.S. printing September 2004.

Library of Congress Cataloging-in-Publication Data on file.

ISBN 1-56858-314-1
10 9 8 7 6 5 4 3 2 1

Typesetting by Pracharak Technologies (P) Ltd.
Printed in Canada by Webcom on 100% recycled paper.

Previous anthologies from F&SF

Edited by Anthony Boucher and J. Francis McComas

The Best from Fantasy & Science Fiction (1952)
The Best from Fantasy & Science Fiction: Second Series (1953)
The Best from Fantasy & Science Fiction: Third Series (1954)

Edited by Anthony Boucher

The Best from Fantasy & Science Fiction: Fourth Series (1955)
The Best from Fantasy & Science Fiction: Fifth Series (1956)
The Best from Fantasy & Science Fiction: Sixth Series (1957)
The Best from Fantasy & Science Fiction: Seventh Series (1958)
The Best from Fantasy & Science Fiction: Eighth Series (1959)

Edited by Robert P. Mills

The Best from Fantasy & Science Fiction: Ninth Series (1960)
A Decade of Fantasy and Science Fiction (1960)
The Best from Fantasy & Science Fiction: Tenth Series (1961)
The Best from Fantasy & Science Fiction: Eleventh Series (1962)

Edited by Avram Davidson

The Best from Fantasy & Science Fiction: Twelfth Series (1963)
The Best from Fantasy & Science Fiction: Thirteenth Series (1964)
The Best from Fantasy & Science Fiction: Fourteenth Series (1965)

Edited by Edward L. Ferman

The Best from Fantasy & Science Fiction: Fifteenth Series (1966)
The Best from Fantasy & Science Fiction: Sixteenth Series (1967)
The Best from Fantasy & Science Fiction: Seventeenth Series (1968)
Once and Future Tales from The Magazine of Fantasy and Science Fiction (1968)
The Best from Fantasy & Science Fiction: Eighteenth Series (1969)
The Best from Fantasy & Science Fiction: Nineteenth Series (1971)
The Best from Fantasy & Science Fiction: 20th Series (1973)
The Best from Fantasy & Science Fiction: 22nd Series (1977)
The Best from Fantasy & Science Fiction: 23rd Series (1980)
The Best from Fantasy & Science Fiction: A 30 Year Retrospective (1980)
The Best from Fantasy & Science Fiction: 24th Series (1982)
The Best Fantasy Stories from The Magazine of Fantasy & Science Fiction (1986)
The Best from Fantasy & Science Fiction: A 40th Anniversary Anthology (1989)
Oi, Robot: Competitions and Cartoons from The Best from Fantasy & Science Fiction (1995)

Edited by Edward L. Ferman and Robert P. Mills

Twenty Years of The Magazine of Fantasy & Science Fiction (1970)

Edited by Edward L. Ferman and Anne Devereaux Jordan

The Best Horror Stories from The Magazine of Fantasy & Science Fiction (1988)

Edited by Edward L. Ferman and Kristine Kathryn Rusch

The Best from Fantasy & Science Fiction: A 45th Anniversary Anthology (1994)

Edited by Edward L. Ferman and Gordon Van Gelder

The Best from Fantasy & Science Fiction: The 50th Anniversary Anthology (1999)

Edited by Gordon Van Gelder

One Lamp: Alternate History Stories from The Magazine of Fantasy & Science Fiction (2003)

Table of Contents

This book is for three Johns:
John Joseph Adams
John G. H. Oakes
John O'Neill

All brave warriors in the barbaric land
that is contemporary publishing

Introduction

ꙮ

When it comes to definitions, fantasy fiction tends to be even harder to pin down than science fiction. Science fiction is more recognizable as a fairly recent genre (with nineteenth-century origins) and has enjoyed debates about its boundaries for more than seventy years, while fantastic literature is older and more amorphous. And perhaps by its very nature of encompassing so much, fantasy fiction has not lent itself so readily to efforts at definition. When John Clute coedited The Encyclopedia of Fantasy in the mid-1990s, he found he had to create much of the vocabulary with which he could discuss and categorize the field.

In fact, the 1997 entry on "Heroic Fantasy" in The Encyclopedia of Fantasy says, "There may be a useful distinction between Heroic Fantasy and Sword and Sorcery, but no one has yet made it." For my part, I have little interest in attempting any definitions with this book-I'm looking to bring you a collection of terrific stories united by their common goal of telling a rousing good story set in a land that never was. Call 'em "heroic fantasy," call 'em "high fantasy," call 'em "Bob" if you like-I just hope you enjoy them.

Yet as I assembled the stories here, I found myself wondering about the various ways in which these stories played off each other. These stories brim with swordsplay and magic, but they vary widely in other regards. Robert E. Howard's nihilism, for instance, seems like a far cry from the romanticism of Ursula Le Guin's tale or the drawing-room type of drama seen in Ellen Kushner's story. The biggest difference I've discerned seems to fall along gender lines; men often emphasize the military aspects of heroic fantasy and treat conflict as inevitable, while women often subvert this approach by emphasizing more of the genre's romantic traditions ("romantic" as in the work of Chrétien de Troyes and the Arthurian romances). The stories' various attitudes towards death-which runs deep through this book-might highlight this notion, but I readily admit that several stories in this book disprove even this broad theory and I offer it only in hopes that it points others to more accurate observations about the genre.

Inevitably, any book of this sort must omit stories of one sort or another. I chose not to include any stories here that were set on other planets—so-called "science fantasy" stories of the sort Jack Vance writes so well-even though many such tales would go well here.

I also weighted the book heavily towards recent stories, despite a wealth of material to draw upon, especially from the late 1970s and 1980s. I think there's something interesting afoot right now; from Yoon Ha Lee's mathematical fantasy to Charlie Finlay's efforts at what he has called "New Pulp" and Rod Garcia's hip romanticism, it seems like writers these days find fantasy stories useful vehicles for saying something different. What they're saying intrigues me-I want to share it and encourage more of it, which explains why you're holding this book now.

There's a strong strand of escapism in these stories-the desire to play in worlds that never were-but with any such escape, the exit is also an entrance. In this case, the exit door seems to open onto new ways of looking at our own world, so I chose to end the book with a story set in the contemporary world.

Fantasy has changed a lot over the past century, and I hope this book reflects that fact in interesting ways. Our need for fantasy, our wish to escape into adventures in worlds that never were, is eternal. I think the writers assembled here have given us vivid, imaginative, and rousing tours of fantastic lands; I hope you like them as much as I do.

Gordon Van Gelder
April, 2004

The Hall of the Dead

ജ്ഞ

Robert E. Howard and L. Sprague de Camp

If any one name is synonymous with heroic fantasy, it's Conan, the larger-than-life creation of Robert E. Howard. The story-teller from Cross Plains, Texas, gave us an enduring figure when he published seventeen tales of the barbarian swordsman in the pages of Weird Tales *in the years of 1932-1936. One might even say that Conan is now governing the state of California in the person of Arnold Schwarzenegger, who portrayed the character in two 1980s films.*

But it's worth noting that Conan did not stride boldly across the twentieth century the way his nobly savage progenitor, Tarzan, did. Robert Howard's early death in 1936 (at the age of thirty) stunted his publishing career and through the 1940s and 1950s, Conan might best be called a cult hero. It was only in the late 1960s that Conan really began to come into his own as an icon of popular culture, due largely to the efforts of Glenn Lord, L. Sprague de Camp, and Lin Carter in reviving efforts to publish stories of the barbarian swordsman, completing unfinished Conan stories, and organizing the original tales.

"The Hall of the Dead" dates from that period, specifically early in 1967. Its original form was a 650-word outline about Conan's early life that turned up in Howard's papers. It was fleshed out by L. Sprague de Camp, whose own work in the fantasy field includes the lovely Harold Shea's "Incomplete

Enchanter" stories that first appeared in the 1940s and other classic fantasies such as The Goblin Tower *and* The Tritonian Ring. *Mr. de Camp died in 2000 at the age of 93.*

Various writers have written tales of Conan in the past twenty-five years—including Poul Anderson, Karl Edward Wagner, Roland J. Green, and Robert Jordan—but for me, Robert E. Howard's work still packs the biggest wallop. Which makes me happy to note that his original stories are being reprinted; The Coming of Conan the Cimmerian *is the first volume making these stories available again.*

Incidentally, for anyone interested in more about Robert E. Howard, I recommend Dark Valley Destiny, *the biography written by L. Sprague de Camp along with Catherine Crook de Camp and Jane Whittington Griffn. The 1996 film about Howard's romance with Novalyne Price Ellis,* The Whole Wide World, *is also recommended highly.*

The gorge was dark, although the setting sun had left a band of orange and yellow and green, along the western horizon. Against this band of color, a sharp eye could still discern, in black silhouette, the domes and spires of Shadizar the Wicked, the city of dark-haired women and towers of spider-haunted mystery—the capital of Zamora.

As the twilight faded, the first few stars appeared overhead. As if answering a signal, lights winked on in the distant domes and spires. While the light of the stars was pale and wan, that of the windows of Shadizar was a sultry amber, with a hint of abominable deeds.

The gorge was quiet save for the chirping of nocturnal insects. Presently, however, this silence was broken by the sound of moving men. Up the gorge came a squad of Zamorian soldiers—five men in plain steel caps and leather jerkins, studded with bronze buttons, led by an officer in a polished bronze cuirass and a helmet with a towering horsehair crest. Their bronze-greaved legs swished through the long, lush grass that covered the floor of the gorge. Their harness creaked and their weapons clanked and tinkled. Three of them bore bows and the other two, pikes; short swords hung at their sides and bucklers were slung across their backs. The officer was armed with a long sword and dagger.

One of the soldiers muttered: "If we catch this Conan fellow alive, what will they do with him?"

"Send him to Yezud to feed to the spider god, I'll warrant," said another. "The question is, shall we be alive to collect that reward they promised us?"

"Not afraid of him, are you?" said a third.

"Me?" The second speaker snorted. "I fear naught, including death itself. The question is, whose death? This thief is not a civilized man, but a wild barbarian, with the strength of ten. So I went to the magistrate to draw up my will—"

"It is cheering to know that your heirs will get the reward," said another. "I wish I had thought of that."

"Oh," said the first man who had spoken, "they'll find some excuse to cheat us of the reward, even if we catch the rascal."

"The prefect himself has promised," said another. "The rich merchants and nobles whom Conan has been robbing raised a fund. I saw the money—a bag so heavy with gold that a man could scarce lift it. After all that public display, they'd not dare to go back on their word."

"But suppose we catch him not," said the second speaker. "There was something about paying for it with our heads." The speaker raised his voice. "Captain Nestor! What was that about our heads—"

"Hold your tongues, all of you!" snapped the officer. "You can be heard as far as Arenjun. If Conan is within a mile, he'll be warned. Cease your chatter, and try to move without so much clangor."

The officer was a broad-shouldered man of medium height and powerful build; daylight would have shown his eyes to be gray and his hair light brown, streaked with gray. He was a

Gunderman, from the northernmost province of Aquilonia, fifteen hundred miles to the west. His mission—to take Conan dead or alive—troubled him. The prefect had warned him that, if he failed, he might expect severe punishment—perhaps even the headsman's block. The king himself had demanded that the outlaw be taken, and the king of Zamora had a short way with servants who failed their missions. A tip from the underworld had revealed that Conan was seen heading for this gorge earlier that day, and Nestor's commander had hastily dispatched him with such troopers as could be found in the barracks.

Nestor had no confidence in the soldiers that trailed behind him. He considered them braggarts who would flee in the face of danger, leaving him to confront the barbarian alone. And, although the Gunderman was a brave man, he did not deceive himself about his chances with this ferocious, gigantic young savage. His armor would give him no more than a slight edge. As the glow in the western sky faded, the darkness deepened and the walls of the gorge became narrower, steeper, and rockier. Behind Nestor, the men began to murmur again:

"I like it not. This road leads to the ruins of Larsha the Accursed, where the ghosts of the ancients lurk to devour passers-by. And in that city, 'tis said, lies the Hall of the Dead—"

"Shut up!" snarled Nestor, turning his head. "If—"

At that instant, the officer tripped over a rawhide rope stretched across the path and fell sprawling in the grass. There was the snap of a spring pole released from its lodgment, and the rope went slack.

With a rumbling roar, a mass of rocks and dirt cascaded down the left-hand slope. As Nestor scrambled to his feet, a stone the size of a man's head struck his corselet and knocked him down again. Another knocked off his helmet, while smaller stones stung his limbs. Behind him sounded a multiple scream and the clatter of stone striking metal. Then silence fell.

Nestor staggered to his feet, coughed the dust out of his lungs, and turned to see what had befallen. A few paces behind him, a rock slide blocked the gorge from wall to wall. Approaching, he made out a human hand and a foot projecting from the rubble. He called but received no reply. When he touched the protruding members, he found no life. The slide, set off by the pull on the rope, had wiped out his entire squad.

Nestor flexed his joints to learn what harm he had suffered. No bones appeared to be broken, although his corselet was dented and he bore several bruises. Burning with wrath, he found his helmet and took up the trail alone. Failing to catch the thief would have been bad enough, but if he also had to confess to the loss of his men, he foresaw a lingering and painful death. His only chance now was to bring back Conan—or at least his head.

I

Sword in hand, Nestor limped on up the endless windings of the gorge. A light in the sky before him showed that the moon, a little past full, was rising. He strained his eyes, expecting the barbarian to spring upon him from behind every bend in the ravine.

The gorge became shallower and the walls less steep. Gullies opened into the gorge to right and left, while the bottom became stony and uneven, forcing Nestor to scramble over rocks and underbrush. At last the gorge gave out completely. Climbing a short slope, the Gunderman found himself on the edge of an upland plateau, surrounded by distant mountains. A bowshot ahead, bone-white in the light of the moon, rose the walls of Larsha. A massive gate stood directly in front of him. Time had bitten scallops out of the wall, and over it rose half-ruined roofs and towers.

Nestor paused. Larsha was said to be immensely old. According to the tales, it went back to Cataclysmic times, when the forebears of the Zamorians, the Zhemri, formed an island of semi-civilization in a sea of barbarism. Stories of the death that lurked in these ruins were rife in the bazaars of Shadizar. As far as Nestor had been able to learn, not one of the many men who had invaded the ruins, searching for the treasure rumored to exist there, had ever returned. None knew what form the danger took, because no survivor had lived to carry the tale.

A decade before, King Tiridates had sent a company of his bravest soldiers, in broad daylight, into the city, while the king himself waited outside the walls. There had been screams and sounds of flight, and then—nothing. The men who waited outside had fled, and Tiridates perforce had fled with them. That was the last attempt to unlock the mystery of Larsha by main force.

Although Nestor had all the usual mercenary's lust for unearned wealth, he was not rash. Years of soldiering in the kingdoms between Zamora and his homeland had taught him caution. As he paused, weighing the dangers of his alternatives, a sight made him stiffen. Close to the wall, he sighted the figure of a man, slinking toward the gate. Although the man was too far away to recognize faces in the moonlight, there was no mistaking that panther-like stride. Conan!

Filled with rising fury, Nestor started forward. He walked swiftly, holding his scabbard to keep it from clanking. But, quietly though he moved, the keen ears of the barbarian warned him. Conan whirled, and his sword whispered from its sheath. Then, seeing that only a single foe pursued him, the Cimmerian stood his ground.

As Nestor approached, he began to pick out details of the other's appearance. Conan was well over six feet tall, and his threadbare tunic failed to mask the hard lines of his mighty thews. A leathern sack hung by a strap from his shoulder. His face was youthful but hard, surmounted by a square-cut mane of thick black hair.

Not a word was spoken. Nestor paused to catch his breath and cast aside his cloak, and in that instant Conan hurled himself upon the older man.

Two swords glimmered like lightning in the moonlight as the clang and rasp of blades shattered the graveyard silence. Nestor was the more experienced fighter, but the reach and blinding speed of the other nullified this advantage. Conan's attack was as elemental and irresistible as a hurricane. Parrying shrewdly, Nestor was forced back, step after step. Narrowly he watched his opponent, waiting for the other's attack to slow from sheer fatigue. But the Cimmerian seemed not to know what fatigue was.

Making a backhand cut, Nestor slit Conan's tunic over the chest but did not quite reach the skin. In a blinding return thrust, Conan's point glanced off Nestor's breastplate, plowing a groove in the bronze.

As Nestor stepped back from another furious attack, a stone turned under his foot. Conan aimed a terrific cut at the Gunderman's neck. Had it gone as intended, Nestor's head would have flown from his shoulders; but, as he stumbled, the blow hit his crested helm instead. It struck with a heavy clang, bit into the iron, and hurled Nestor to the ground.

Breathing deeply, Conan stepped forward, sword ready. His pursuer lay motionless with blood seeping from his cloven helmet. Youthful overconfidence in the force of his own blows convinced Conan that he had slain his antagonist. Sheathing his sword, he turned back toward the city of the ancients.

II

The Cimmerian approached the gate. This consisted of two massive valves, twice as high as a man, made of foot-thick timbers sheathed in bronze. Conan pushed against the valves, grunting, but without effect. He drew his sword and struck the bronze with the pommel. From the way the gates sagged, Conan guessed that the wood of the doors had rotted away; but the bronze was too thick to hew through without spoiling the edge of his blade. And there was an easier way.

Thirty paces north of the gate, the wall had crumbled so that its lowest point was less than twenty feet above the ground. At the same time, a pile of tailings against the foot of the wall rose to within six or eight feet of the broken edge.

Conan approached the broken section, drew back a few paces, and then ran forward. He bounded up the slope of the tailings, leaped into the air, and caught the broken edge of the wall. A grunt, a heave, and a scramble, and he was over the edge, ignoring scratches and bruises. He stared down into the city. Inside the wall was a cleared space, where for centuries plant life had been waging war upon the ancient pavement. The paving slabs were cracked and up-ended. Between them, grass, weeds, and a few scrubby trees had forced their way.

Beyond the cleared area lay the ruins of one of the poorer districts. Here the one-story hovels of mud brick had slumped into mere mounds of dirt. Beyond them, white in the moonlight, Conan discerned the better-preserved buildings of stone—the temples, the palaces, and the houses of the nobles and the rich merchants. As with many ancient ruins, an aura of evil hung over the deserted city.

Straining his ears, Conan stared right and left. Nothing moved. The only sound was the chirp of crickets.

Conan, too, had heard the tales of the doom that haunted Larsha. Although the supernatural roused panicky, atavistic fears in his barbarian's soul, he hardened himself with the thought that, when a supernatural being took material form, it could be hurt or killed by material weapons, just like any earthy man or monster. He had not come this far to be stopped from a try at the treasure by man, beast, or demon.

According to the tales, the fabled treasure of Larsha lay in the royal palace. Gripping his scabbarded sword in his left hand, the young thief dropped down from the inner side of the broken wall. An instant later, he was threading his way toward the center of the city. He made no more noise than a shadow.

Ruin encompassed him on every side. Here and there the front of a house had fallen into the street, forcing Conan to detour or to scramble over piles of broken brick and marble. The gibbous moon was now high in the sky, washing the ruins in an eerie light. On the Cimmerian's right rose a temple, partly fallen but with the portico, upheld by four massive marble columns, still intact. Along the edge of the roof, a row of marble gargoyles peered down—statues of monsters of bygone days, half demon and half beast.

Conan tried to remember the scraps of legend that he had over heard in the wineshops of the Maul, concerning the abandonment of Larsha. There was something about a curse sent by an angered god, many centuries before, in punishment for deeds so wicked that they made the crimes and vices of Shadizar look like virtues . . .

He started for the center of the city again but now noticed something peculiar. His sandals tended to stick to the shattered pavement, as if it were covered with warm pitch. The soles made sucking noises as he raised his feet. He stooped and felt the ground. It was coated with a film of a colorless, sticky substance, now nearly dry.

Hand on hilt, Conan glared about him in the moonlight. But no sound came to his ears. He resumed his advance. Again his sandals made sucking noises as he raised them. He halted, turning his head. He could have sworn that similar sucking noises came to his ears from a distance. For an instant, he thought they might be the echoes of his own footsteps. But he had passed the half-ruined temple, and now no walls rose on either side of him to reflect the sound.

Again he advanced, then halted. Again he heard the sucking sound, and this time it did not cease when he froze to immobility. In fact, it became louder. His keen hearing located it as coming from directly in front of him. Since he could see nothing moving in the street before him, the source of the sound must be in a side street or in one of the ruined buildings.

The sound increased to an indescribable slithering, gurgling hiss. Even Conan's iron nerves were shaken by the strain of waiting for the unknown source of the sound to appear.

At last, around the next corner poured a huge, slimy mass, leprous gray in the moonlight. It glided into the street before him and swiftly advanced upon him, silent save for the sucking sound of its peculiar method of locomotion. From its front end rose a pair of hornlike projections, at least ten feet long, with a shorter pair below. The long horns bent this way and that, and Conan saw that they bore eyes on their ends.

The creature was, in fact, a slug, like the harmless garden slug that leaves a trail of slime in its nightly wanderings. This slug, however, was fifty feet long and as thick through the middle as Conan was tall. Moreover, it moved as fast as a man could run. The fetid smell of the thing wafted ahead of it.

Momentarily paralyzed with astonishment, Conan stared at the vast mass of rubbery flesh bearing down upon him. The slug emitted a sound like that of a man spitting, but magnified many times over.

Galvanized into action at last, the Cimmerian leaped sideways. As he did so, a jet of liquid flashed through the night air, just where he had stood. A tiny droplet struck his shoulder and burned like a coal of fire.

Conan turned and ran back the way he had come, his long legs flashing in the moonlight. Again he had to bound over piles of broken masonry. His ears told him that the slug was close behind. Perhaps it was gaining. He dared not turn to look, lest he trip over some marble fragment and go sprawling; the monster would be upon him before he could regain his feet.

Again came that spitting sound. Conan leaped frantically to one side; again the jet of liquid flashed past him. Even if he kept ahead of the slug all the way to the city wall, the next shot would probably hit its mark.

Conan dodged around a corner to put obstacles between himself and the slug. He raced down a narrow zigzag street, then around another corner. He was lost in the maze of streets, he knew; but the main thing was to keep turning corners so as not to give his pursuer another clear shot at him. The sucking sounds and the stench indicated that it was following his trail. Once, when he paused to catch his breath, he looked back to see the slug pouring around the last corner he had turned.

On and on he went, dodging this way and that through the maze of the ancient city. If he could not outrun the slug, perhaps he could tire it. A man, he knew, could outlast almost any animal in a long-distance run. But the slug seemed tireless.

Something about the buildings he was passing struck him as familiar. Then he realized that he was coming to the half-ruined temple he had passed just before he met the slug. A quick glance showed him that the upper parts of the building could be reached by an active climber.

Conan bounded up a pile of rubbish to the top of the broken wall. Leaping from stone to stone, he made his way up the jagged profile of the wall to an unruined section facing the street. He found himself on a stretch of roof behind the row of marble gargoyles. He approached them, treading softly lest the half-ruined roof collapse beneath him and detouring around holes through which a man could fall into the chambers below.

The sound and smell of the slug came to him from the street. Realizing that it had lost his trail and uncertain as to which way to turn, the creature had evidently stopped in front of the temple. Very cautiously—for he was sure the slug could see him in the moonlight—Conan peered past one of the statues and down into the street.

There lay the great, grayish mass, on which the moon shone moistly. The eye stalks wavered this way and that, seeking the creature's prey. Beneath them, the shorter horns swept back and forth a little above the ground, as if smelling for the Cimmerian's trail.

Conan felt certain that the slug would soon pick up his trail. He had no doubt that it could slither up the sides of the building quite as readily as he had climbed it.

He put a hand against a gargoyle—a nightmarish statue with a humanoid body, bat's wings, and a reptilian head—and pushed. The statue rocked a trifle with a faint crunching noise.

At the sound, the horns of the slug whipped upward toward the roof of the temple. The slug's head came around, behind its body into a sharp curve. The head approached the front of the temple and began to slide up one of the huge pillars, directly below the place where Conan crouched with bared teeth.

A sword, Conan thought, would be of little use against such a monstrosity. Like other lowly forms of life, it could survive damage that would instantly destroy a higher creature.

Up the pillar came the slug's head, the eyes on their stalks swiveling back and forth. At the present rate, the monster's head would reach the edge of the roof while most of its body still lay in the street below.

Then Conan saw what he must do. He hurled himself at the gargoyle. With a mighty heave, he sent it tumbling over the edge of the roof. Instead of the crash that such a mass of marble would ordinarily make on striking the pavement, there floated up the sound of a moist, squashy impact, followed by a heavy thud as the forward part of the slug's body fell back to earth.

When Conan risked a glance over the parapet, he saw that the statue had sunk into the slug's body until it was almost buried. The great gray mass writhed and lashed like a worm on a fisherman's hook. A blow of the tail made the front of the temple tremble; somewhere in the interior a few loose stones fell clattering. Conan wondered if the whole structure were about to collapse beneath him, burying him in the debris.

"So much for you!" snarled the Cimmerian.

He went along the row of gargoyles until he found another that was loose and directly over part of the slug's body. Down it went with another squashing impact. A third missed and shattered on the pavement. A fourth and smaller statue he picked bodily up and, muscles cracking with the strain, hurled outward so that it fell on the writhing head.

As the beast's convulsions slowly subsided, Conan pushed over two more gargoyles to make sure. When the body no longer writhed, he clambered down to the street. He approached the great, stinking mass cautiously, sword out. At last, summoning all his courage, he slashed into the rubbery flesh. Dark ichor oozed out, and rippling motions ran through the wet, gray skin. But, even though parts might retain signs of independent life, the slug as a whole was dead.

III

Conan was still slashing furiously when a voice made him whirl about. It said:

"I've got you this time!"

It was Nestor, approaching sword in hand, with a blood-stained bandage around his head in place of his helmet. The Gunderman stopped at the sight of the slug. "Mitra! What is this?"

"It's the spook of Larsha," said Conan, speaking Zamorian with a barbarous accent. "It chased me over half the city before I slew it." As Nestor stared incredulously, the Cimmerian continued: "What do you here? How many times must I kill you before you stay dead?"

"You shall see how dead I am," grated Nestor, bringing his sword up to guard.

"What happened to your soldiers?"

"Dead in that rock slide you rigged, as you soon shall be—"

"Look, you fool," said Conan, "why waste your strength on sword strokes, when there's more wealth here than the pair of us can carry away—if the tales are true? You are a good man of your hands; why not join me to raid the treasure of Larsha instead?"

"I must do my duty and avenge my men! Defend yourself, dog or a barbarian!"

"By Crom, I'll fight if you like!" growled Conan, bringing up his sword. "But think, man! If you go back to Shadizar, they'll crucify you for losing your command—even if you took my head with you, which I do not think you can do. If one tenth of the stories are true, you'll get more from your share of the loot than you'd earn in a hundred years as a mercenary captain."

Nestor had lowered his blade and stepped back. Now he stood mute, thinking deeply. Conan added: "Besides, you'll never make real warriors of these poltroons of Zamorians!"

The Gunderman sighed and sheathed his sword. "You are right, damn you. Until this venture is over, we'll fight back to back and go equal shares on the loot, eh?" he held out his hand.

"Done!" said Conan, sheathing likewise and clasping the other's hand. "If we have to run for it and get separated, let's meet at the fountain of Ninus."

IV

The royal palace of Larsha stood in the center of the city, in the midst of a broad plaza. It was the one structure that had not crumbled with age, and this for a simple reason. It was carved out of a single crag or hillock of rock that once broke the flatness of the plateau on which Larsha stood. So meticulous had been the construction of this building, however, that close inspection was needed to show that it was not an ordinary composite structure. Lines engraved in the black basaltic surface imitated the joints between building stones.

Treading softly, Conan and Nestor peered into the dark interior. "We shall need light," said Nestor. "I do not care to walk into another slug like that in the dark."

"I don't smell another slug," said Conan, "but the treasure might have another guardian."

He turned back and hewed down a pine sapling that thrust up through the broken pavement. Then he lopped its limbs and cut it into short lengths. Whittling a pile of shavings with his sword, he started a small fire with flint and steel. He split the ends of two of the billets until they were frayed out and then ignited them. The resinous wood burned vigorously. He handed one torch to Nestor, and each of them thrust half the spare billets through his girdle. Then, swords out, they again approached the palace.

Inside the archway, the flickering yellow flames of the torches were reflected from polished walls of black stone, but underfoot the dust lay inches thick. Several bats, hanging from bits of stone carving overhead, squeaked angrily and whirred away into deeper darkness.

They passed between statues of horrific aspect, set in niches on either side. Dark hallways opened on either hand. They crossed a throne room. The throne, carved of the same black stone as the rest of the building, still stood. Other chairs and divans, being made of wood, had crumbled into dust, leaving a litter of nails, metallic ornaments, and semi-precious stones on the floor.

"It must have stood vacant for thousands of years," whispered Nestor.

They traversed several chambers, which might have been a king's private apartments, but the absence of perishable furnishings made it impossible to tell. They found themselves before a door. Conan put his torch close to it.

It was a stout door, set in an arch of stone and made of massive timbers, bound together with brackets of green-filmed copper. Conan poked the door with his sword. The blade entered easily; a little shower of dusty fragments, pale in the torchlight, sifted down.

"It's rotten," growled Nestor, kicking out. His boot went into the wood almost as easily as Conan's sword had done. A copper fitting fell to the floor with a dull clank.

In a moment they had battered down the rotten timbers in a shower of wood dust. They stooped, thrusting their torches ahead of them into the opening. Light, reflected from silver, gold, and jewels, winked back at them.

Nestor pushed through the opening, then backed out so suddenly that he bumped into Conan, "There are men in there!" he hissed.

"Let's see." Conan thrust his head into the opening and peered right and left. "They're dead. Come on!"

Inside, they stared about them until their torches burned down to their hands and they had to light a new pair. Around the room, seven giant warriors, each at least seven feet tall, sprawled in chairs. Their heads lay against the chair backs and their mouths hung open. They wore the trappings of a bygone age; their plumed copper helmets and the copper scales on their corselets were green with age. Their skins were brown and waxy-looking, like those of mummies, and grizzled beards hung down to their waists. Copper-bladed bills and pikes leaned against the wall beside them or lay on the floor.

In the center of the room rose an altar, of black basalt like the rest of the palace. Near the altar, on the floor, several chests of treasure had lain. The wood of these chests had rotted away; the chests had burst open, letting a glittering drift of treasure pour out on the floor.

Conan stepped close to one of the immobile warriors and touched the man's leg with the point of his sword. The body lay still. He murmured: "The ancients must have mummified them, as they tell me the priests do with the dead in Stygia."

Nestor looked uneasily at the seven still forms. The feeble flames of the torches seemed unable to push the dense darkness back to the sable walls and roof of the chamber.

The block of black stone in the middle of the room rose to waist height. On its flat, polished top, inlaid in narrow strips of ivory, was a diagram of interlaced circles and triangles. The whole formed a seven-pointed star. The spaces between the lines were marked by symbols in some form of writing that Conan did not recognize. He could read Zamorian and write it after a fashion, and he had smatterings of Hyrkanian and Corinthian, but these cryptic glyphs were beyond him.

In any case, he was more interested in the things that lay on top of the altar. On each point of the star, winking in the ruddy, wavering light of the torches, lay a great, green jewel, larger than a hen's egg. At the center of the diagram stood a green statuette of a serpent with upreared head, apparently carved from jade.

Conan moved his torch close to the seven great, glowing gems. "I want those," he grunted. "You can have the rest."

"No, you don't!" snapped Nestor. "Those are worth more than all the other treasure in this room put together. I will have them!"

Tension crackled between the two men, and their free hands stole toward their hilts. For a space they stood silently, glaring at each other. Then Nestor said:

"Then let us divide them."

"You cannot divide seven by two," said Conan. "Let us flip one of these coins for them. The winner takes the seven jewels, while the other man has his pick of the rest. Does that suit you?"

Conan picked a coin out of one of the heaps that marked the places where the chests had lain. Although he had acquired a good working knowledge of coins in his career as a thief, this was entirely unfamiliar. One side bore a face, but whether of a man, a demon, or an owl he could not tell. The other side was covered with symbols like those on the altar.

Conan showed the coin to Nestor. The two treasure hunters grunted agreement. Conan flipped the coin into the air, caught it, and slapped it down on his left wrist. He extended the wrist, with the coin still covered, toward Nestor. "Heads," said the Gunderman.

Conan removed his hand from the coin. Nestor peered and growled: "Ishtar curse the thing! You win. Hold my torch a moment."

Conan, alert for any treacherous move, took the torch. But Nestor merely untied the strap of his cloak and spread the garment on the dusty floor. He began shoveling handfuls of gold and gems from the heaps on the floor into a pile on the cloak.

"Don't load yourself so heavily that you can't run," said Conan. "We are not out of this yet, and it's a long walk back to Shadizar."

"I can handle it," said Nestor. He gathered up the corners of the cloak, slung the improvised bag over his back, and held out a hand for his torch.

Conan handed it to him and stepped to the altar. One by one he took the great, green jewels and thrust them into the leathern sack that hung from his shoulder.

When all seven had been removed from the altar top, he paused, looking at the jade serpent. "This will fetch a pretty price," he said. Snatching it up, he thrust it, too, into his booty bag."

"Why not take some of the remaining gold and jewels, too?" asked Nestor. "I have all I can carry."

"You've got the best stuff," said Conan. "Besides, I don't need any more. With these I can buy a kingdom! Or a dukedom, anyway, and all the wine I can drink and women I—"

A sound caused the plunderers to whirl, staring wildly. Around the walls, the seven mummified warriors were coming to life. Their heads came up, their mouths closed, and air hissed into their ancient, withered lungs. Their joints creaked like rusty hinges as they picked up their pikes and bills and rose to their feet.

"Run!" yelled Nestor, hurling his torch at the nearest giant and snatching out his sword.

The torch struck the giant in the chest, fell to the floor, and went out. Having both hands free, Conan retained his torch while he drew his sword. The light of the remaining torch flickered feebly on the green of the ancient copper harness as the giants closed in on the pair.

Conan ducked the sweep of a bill and knocked the thrust of a pike aside. Between him and the door, Nestor engaged a giant who was moving to block their escape. The Gunderman parried a thrust and struck a fierce, backhanded blow at his enemy's thigh. The blade bit, but only a little way; it was like chopping wood. The giant staggered, and Nestor hewed at another. The point of a pike glanced off his dented cuirass.

The giants moved slowly, or the treasure hunters would have fallen before their first onset. Leaping, dodging, and whirling, Conan avoided blows that would have stretched him senseless on the dusty floor. Again and again his blade bit into the dry, woody flesh of his assailants. Blows that would have decapitated a living man only staggered these creatures from another age. He landed a chop on the hand of one attacker, maiming the member and causing the giant to drop his pike.

He dodged the thrust of another pike and put every ounce of strength into a low forehand cut at the giant's ankle. The blade bit half through, and the giant crashed to the floor.

"Out!" bellowed Conan, leaping over the fallen body.

He and Nestor raced out the door and through halls and chambers. For an instant Conan feared they were lost, but he caught a glimpse of light ahead. The two dashed out the main portal of the palace. Behind them came the clatter and tramp of the guardians. Overhead, the sky had paled and the stars were going out with the coming of dawn.

"Head for the wall," panted Nestor. "I think we can outrun them."

As they reached the far side of the plaza, Conan glanced back. "Look!" he cried.

One by one, the giants emerged from the palace. And one by one, as they came out into the growing light, they sank to the pavement and crumbled into dust, leaving their plumed copper helmets, their scaled cuirasses, and their other accouterments in heaps on the ground.

V

"Well, that's that," said Nestor. "But how shall we get back into Shadizar without being arrested? It will be daylight long before we get there."

Conan grinned. "There's a way of getting in that we thieves know. Near the northeast corner of the wall stands a clump of trees. If you poke around among the shrubs that mask the wall, you will find a kind of culvert—I suppose to let the water out of the city in heavy rains. It used to be closed by an iron grating, but that has rusted away. If you are not too fat, you can worm your way through it. You come out in a lot where people dump rubbish from houses that have been torn down."

"Good," said Nestor. "I'll—"

A deep rumble cut off his words. The earth heaved and rocked and trembled, throwing him to the ground and staggering the Cimmerian.

"Look out!" yelled Conan.

As Nestor started to scramble up, Conan caught his arm and dragged him back towards the center of the plaza. As he did so, the wall of a nearby building fell over into the plaza. It smashed down just where the two had been standing, but its mighty crash was lost in the thunder of the earthquake.

"Let's get out of here!" shouted Nestor.

Steering by the moon, now low in the western sky, they ran zigzag through the streets. On either side of them, walls and columns leaned, crumbled, and crashed. The noise was deafening. Clouds of dust arose, making the fugitives cough.

Conan skidded to a halt and leaped back to avoid being crushed under the front of a collapsing temple. He staggered as fresh tremors shook the earth beneath him. He scrambled over piles of ruin, some old and some freshly made. He leaped madly out from under a falling column drum. Fragments of stone and brick struck him; one laid open a cut along his jaw. Another glanced from his shin, making him curse by the gods of all the lands he had visited.

At last he reached the city wall. It was a wall no longer, having been shaken down to a low ridge of broken stone.

Limping, coughing, and panting, Conan climbed the ridge and turned to look back. Nestor was no longer with him. Probably, he thought, the Gunderman had been caught under a falling wall. Conan listened but could hear no cry for help.

The rumble of quaking earth and falling masonry died away. The light of the low moon glistened on the vast cloud of dust that covered the city. Then a dawn breeze sprang up and slowly wafted the dust away.

Sitting on the crest of the ridge of ruin that marked the site of the wall, Conan stared back across the site of Larsha. The city bore an aspect entirely different from when he had entered it. Not a single building remained upright. Even the monolithic palace of black basalt, where he and Nestor had found their treasure, had crumbled into a heap of broken blocks. Conan gave up thoughts of going back to the palace on some future occasion to collect the rest of the treasure. An army of workmen would have to clear away the wreckage before the valuables could be salvaged.

All of Larsha had fallen into heaps of rubble. As far as he could see in the growing light, nothing moved in the city. The only sound was the belated fall of an occasional stone.

Conan felt his booty bag, to make sure that he still had his loot, and turned his face westward, towards Shadizar. Behind him, the rising sun shot a spear of light against his broad back.

VI

The following night, Conan swaggered into his favorite tavern, that of Abuletes, in the Maul. The low, smoke-stained room stank of sweat and sour wine. At crowded tables, thieves and murderers drank ale and wine, diced, argued, sang, quarreled, and blustered. It was deemed a dull evening here when at least one customer was not stabbed in a brawl.

Across the room, Conan sighted his sweetheart of the moment, drinking alone at a small table. This was Semiramis, a strongly built, black-haired woman several years older than the Cimmerian.

"Ho there, Semiramis!" roared Conan. "I've got something to show you! Abuletes! A jug of your best Kyrian! I'm in luck tonight!"

Had Conan been older, caution would have stopped him from openly boasting of his plunder, let alone displaying it. As it was, he strode up to Semiramis's table and up-ended the leathern sack containing the seven green gems.

The jewels cascaded out of the bag, thumped the wine-wet table top—and crumbled instantly into fine green powder, which sparkled in the candle light. Conan dropped the sack and stood with his mouth agape, while nearby drinkers burst into raucous laughter.

"Crom and Mannanan!" the Cimmerian breathed at last. "This time, it seems, I was too clever for my own good." Then he bethought him of the jade serpent, still in the bag. "Well, I have something that will pay for a few good carousals, anyway."

Moved by curiosity, Semiramis picked up the sack form the table. Then she dropped it with a scream.

"It's—it's alive!" she cried.

"What—" began Conan, but a shout from the doorway cut him off:

"There he is, men! Seize him!"

A fat magistrate had entered the tavern, followed by a squad of the night watch, armed with bills. The other customers fell silent, staring woodenly into space as if they knew nothing of Conan or of any of the other riff-raff who were Abuletes's guests.

The magistrate pushed toward Conan's table. Whipping out his sword, the Cimmerian put his back against the wall. His blue eyes blazed dangerously, and his teeth showed in the candle light.

"Take me if you can, dogs!" he snarled. "I've done nothing against your stupid laws!" Out of the side of his mouth, he muttered to Semiramis: "Grab the bag and get out of here. If they get me, it's yours."

"I—I'm afraid of it!" whimpered the woman.

"Oh-ho!" chortled the magistrate, coming forward. "Nothing, eh? Nothing but to rob our leading citizens blind! There's evidence enough to lop your head off a hundred times over! And then you slew Nestor's soldiers and persuaded him to join you in a raid on the ruins of Larsha, eh? We found him earlier this evening, drunk and boasting of his feat. The villain got away from us, but you shan't!"

As the watchmen formed a half-circle around Conan, bills pointing toward his breast, the magistrate noticed the sack on the table. "What's this, your latest loot? We'll see—"

The fat man thrust a hand into the sack. For an instant he fumbled. Then his eyes widened; his mouth opened to emit an appalling shriek. He jerked his hand out of the bag. A jade-green snake, alive and writhing, had thrown a loop around his wrist and had sunk its fangs into his hand.

Cries of horror and amazement arose. A watchman sprang back and fell over a table, smashing mugs and splashing liquors. Another stepped forward to catch the magistrate as he tottered and fell. A third dropped his bill and, screaming hysterically, broke for the door.

Panic seized the customers. Some jammed themselves into the door, struggling to get out. A couple started fighting with knives, while another thief, locked in combat with a watchman, rolled on the floor. One of the candles was knocked over; then another, leaving the room but dimly lit by the little earthenware lamp over the counter.

In the gloom, Conan caught Semiramis's wrist and hauled her to her feet. He beat the panic-stricken mob aside with the flat of his sword and forced his way through the throng to the door. Out in the night, the two ran, rounding several corners to throw off pursuit. Then they stopped to breathe. Conan said:

"This city will be too cursed hot for me after this. I'm on my way. Good-bye, Semiramis."

"Would you not care to spend a last night with me?"

"Not this time. I must try to catch that rascal Nestor. If the fool hadn't blabbed, the law would not have gotten on my trail so quickly. He has all the treasure a man can carry, while I ended up with naught. Maybe I can persuade him to give me half; if not—" He thumbed the edge of his sword.

Semiramis sighed. "There will always be a hideout for you in Shadizar, while I live. Give me a last kiss."

They embraced briefly. Then Conan was gone, like a shadow in the night.

VII

On the Corinthian Road that leads west from Shadizar, three bowshots from the city walls, stands the fountain of Ninus. According to the story, Ninus was a rich merchant who suffered from a wasting disease. A god visited him in his dreams and promised him a cure if he would build a fountain on the road leading to Shadizar from the west, so that travelers could wash and quench their thirst before entering the city. Ninus built the fountain, but the tale does not tell whether he recovered from his sickness.

Half an hour after his escape from Abuletes's tavern, Conan found Nestor, sitting on the curbing of Ninus's fountain.

"How did you make out with your seven matchless gems?" asked Nestor.

Conan told what had befallen his share of the loot. "Now," he said, "since—thanks to your loose tongue—I must leave Shadizar, and since I have none of the treasure left, it would be only right for you to divide your remaining portion with me."

Nestor gave a barking, mirthless laugh. "My share? Boy, here is half of what I have left." From his girdle he brought out two pieces of gold and tossed one to Conan, who caught it. "I owe it to you for pulling me away from that falling wall."

"What happened to you?"

"When the watch cornered me in the dive, I managed to cast a table and bowl a few over. Then I picked up the bright stuff in my cloak, slung it over my back, and started for the door. One who tried to halt me I cut down, but another landed a slash on my cloak. The next thing I knew, the whole mass of gold and jewels spilled out on the floor, and everybody—watchmen, magistrate, and customers—joined in a mad scramble for them." He held up the cloak, showing a two-foot rent in the fabric. "Thinking that the treasure would do me no good if my head were adorning a pike over the West Gate, I left while the leaving was good. When I got outside the city, I looked in my mantle, but all I found were those two coins, caught in a fold. You're welcome to one of them."

Conan stood scowling for a moment. Then his mouth twitched into a grin. A low laugh rumbled in his throat; his head went back as he burst into a thunderous guffaw. "A fine pair of treasure-seekers we are! Crom, but the gods have had sport with us! What a joke!"

Nestor smiled wryly. "I am glad you see the amusing side of it. But after this I do not think Shadizar will be safe for either of us."

"Whither are you bound?" asked Conan.

"I'll head east, to seek a mercenary post in Turan. They say King Yildiz is hiring fighters to whip his raggle-taggle horde into a real army. Why not come with me, lad? You're cut out for a soldier."

Conan shook his head. "Not for me, marching back and forth on the drill ground all day while some fathead officer bawls: 'Forward, *march*! Present, *pikes*!' I hear there are good pickings in the West; I'll try that for a while."

"Well, may your barbarous gods go with you," said Nestor. "If you change your mind, ask for me in the barracks at Agrapur. Farewell!"

"Farewell!" replied Conan. Without further words, he stepped out on the Corinthian Road and soon was lost to view in the night.

A Hedge Against Alchemy

ꕥ

John Morressy

After the intensity of the preceding story, it seems like a good idea to give you a lighter one, something more sympathetic to wizards than barbarians. Enter John Morressy, whose sprightly stories of the curmudgeonly wizard Kedrigern have graced our pages for nearly a quarter of a century. "A Hedge Against Alchemy" was the first Kedrigern story, published back in 1981. Kedrigern's latest caper, "The Unpleasantness at Le Château Malveillant," ran in our April 2004 issue.

Kedrigern took his wizardly studies seriously, but he was a sensible man withal. On a beautiful morning in early spring he saw greater wisdom in sitting comfortably in his dooryard, soaking up the sunshine, than in conning ancient lore in his dim, cobwebby study.

He sprawled back in pillowed comfort, feet up on a cushion, and rang with languid gesture a little silver bell. From within-doors came the sound of sudden motion, and soon the slapping of huge feet on the flagstones. A small, hideous creature appeared at Kedrigern's side.

It was almost all head, and a very ugly head, too, with its bulging eyes and tangled brows and scarcity of forehead; with its great hook of nose, like a drinking horn covered with warts; with its ledge of chin and hairy ears like wide-flung shutters.

Two great dirty flat feet splayed at the ends of the creature's tiny legs, and great hands like sails jutted out from its sides. The top of its mottled, warty, scurfy head reached just to the level of Kedrigern's footstool, and there the creature shuddered to a halt, trembling with the eager will to serve.

"Ah, there you are," Kedrigern said.

The creature wildly nodded its monstrous head, spraying saliva about in generous quantities, and said, "Yah! Yah!"

"Good fellow, Spot. Listen carefully, now."

"Yah! Yah!" said Spot, bouncing up and down excitedly.

"I will have, I think, a small mug of very cold ale. Bring the pitcher, in case my thirst is greater than I anticipate. And bring with it a morsel of cheese just of a size to cover the lid of the pitcher, and a loaf of bread. And ask Princess if she'd care to join me."

"Yah! Yah!" said Spot, and windmilled off about his duties.

Kedrigern looked after him affectionately. Trolls were a bad lot, it was true, but if one got them young and trained them properly, they could be devoted servants. Excellent mousers, as well. They were hopeless when it came to good table manners, but one could not have everything.

He settled back among the cushions, closed his eyes, and emitted a sigh of quiet pleasure. This was the life for a sensible man, he thought snugly. Not like your damned alchemy.

Kedrigern could not understand the fascination of alchemy. It was all the rage these days, everyone was talking it up, but to him it was nothing more than a lot of smoke and stink and a horrible mess and pompous jargon about things no one understood but everyone felt obliged to speak of with solemn authority. Yet it seemed to be catching on. The bright young people were not interested in traditional wizardry anymore. It was alchemy or nothing for them.

Just one more sign of the times, he believed, and bad times they were, with barbarians sweeping in from the east and burning the churchmen, churchmen issuing anathemas and burning the alchemists, and alchemists burning everything they could lay their hands on in their wild desire to turn lead into gold. Smoke and howling and destruction, that's all anyone cared about these days.

Except for Kedrigern, who was learning more and more about temporal magic and becoming rather good at it. He had reached into the future several times and established solid linkage with a specific time-point, though he was not quite certain just what point it was. He had even managed to pluck curious artifacts from that unformed age and retain them for study. There was much yet to learn, of course . . . but there would be time for that . . . much to learn. . . .

Kedrigern fell into a light doze, awakening with a frown when a shadow fell upon him. He opened his eyes and saw a great hulking figure standing before him, blocking out the sun.

It took his eyes a moment to accustom themselves to the light, and his wits another moment to reconvene in the here-and-now, and then Kedrigern saw that the creature before him was a man of a kind he had hoped never to encounter.

He was twice the wizard's height and four times his bulk. Bare arms like the trunks of aged hornbeams hung from his beetling shoulders. Torso and thick legs were encased in coarse furs. A tiny head was centered between the bulging shoulders with no sign of a neck intervening. About him hung an effluvium of rancid animal fat and venerable perspiration. He was a barbarian, no doubt, and barbarians were no friends of wizards. Or of anyone else, for that matter.

"This road to Silent Thunder Peak?" the barbarian asked. His voice was like a fall of stone deep within a cave.

"Yes, it is," Kedrigern said politely. He pointed to his left. "Just follow the uphill track. If you hurry, you can reach the peak by sunset. Marvelous view on a day like this. I'd offer you a drop of some cool refreshment but I'm—"

"You wizard?" the barbarian rumbled.

That was the sort of question one did not rush to answer. Far too many people were wandering about these days with the notion that slaying a wizard was somehow a deed of great merit. It was the churchmen put them up to that, Kedrigern knew. Churchmen never had a good word for anyone. Barbarians, alchemists, and wizards were condemned alike, in outbursts of chilling zeal and remarkably poor judgment. All the same, this specimen did not look like someone who took his orders from a holy man.

"Wizard?" Kedrigern asked, squinting up. "Do I understand that you're inquiring after the whereabouts of a wizard?"

"You wizard?" the barbarian asked once more, exactly as before.

An uneasiness came over Kedrigern. It was not at the barbarian's great size and ugliness, nor even at his sudden appearance here in this isolated retreat where Kedrigern had withdrawn from worldly affairs to concentrate on his studies and enjoy Princess's companionship. It was intangible, a sense of wrong presence. He had the eerie sensation that a member of his brotherhood was near, and that was manifestly absurd. This creature was no wizard.

"It's interesting that you should ask," said Kedrigern thoughtfully. "It suggests an inquiring turn of mind not immediately evident in your manner and appearance." As he spoke, he slipped his hand behind him to work the figures necessary to a spell for the deflection of edged weapons. "Most people expect a wizard to go about in a long robe covered with cabalistic symbols, and wear a conical cap, and have a long white beard flapping down around his knees. I, as you can see, am plainly dressed in good homespun tunic and trousers, wear no headgear of any kind, and am clean-shaven. Consequently, a casual passer-by might easily assume that I am some honest tradesman or artisan who has chosen to live apart from his fellows when I am in fact an adept in the rare and gentle arts." He hoped earnestly that this great brute would not decide to smash him flat with a club before he could proceed to a further protective spell. Even with the assistance of magic, it was difficult to be prepared for all contingencies when dealing with people such as this.

The barbarian's tiny black eyes, set closely on either side of a shapeless smudge of nose, peered at Kedrigern from behind a fringe of lank, greasy hair. In those eyes shone no glimmer of understanding.

"You wizard?" he repeated.

"Me wizard," Kedrigern said resignedly. "Who you?"

"Me Buroc," said the barbarian, thumping his chest proudly.

"Oh, dear me," Kedrigern murmured.

Buroc was the barbarian's barbarian. He was known through the land as Buroc the Depraved and had added to his name such epithets as Flayer of God's Earth, Fist of Satan, and Torch of Judgment, as well as other titles emblematic of mayhem and savagery. It was said of Buroc that he had divided the human race into two parts: enemies and victims. Enemies he slew at once. Victims he slew when he had no further use for them. He recognized no third category.

Looking into that flat expressionless face crisscrossed with pale scars, Kedrigern believed all he had ever heard of Buroc. The barbarian's face reminded him of a cheap clay vessel shattered to bits and hastily glued together. The chief difference, in Kedrigern's estimation, was that the vessel of clay would radiate a higher spirituality.

"You come with Buroc," said the barbarian.

"Oh, I think not. The offer raises some unusual possibilities, but I'm afraid murder, rape, and pillage aren't my line of work, Buroc. I'm more the bookish sort. And I'm not so nimble as I used to be. Thoughtful of you to ask, though. Now it might be best if you were running along." Kedrigern said as he hurried through a backup spell against indeterminate violence. With that done, he felt secure against any of Buroc's bloodthirsty caprices.

"Buroc find golden mountain. Need wizard."

"Oh?"

"Mountain of gold. Spell hide mountain. You break spell. Split forty-forty," said Buroc in an outburst of eloquence.

"Fifty-fifty," Kedrigern corrected him.

Buroc's eyes glazed, and for a moment he seemed immobilized. Then he nodded his tiny head and repeated, "Fifty-fifty."

"Where is this golden mountain, Buroc?" Kedrigern asked, spacing his words and enunciating carefully.

Again the barbarian's eyes glazed over, and Kedrigern realized with a start that this was evidence of a reasoning process going on in the recesses of that little head. "You come. Me show."

"Is it far away?"

After a time, Buroc said, "Sun. Sun. Golden mountain."

"Three days from here, I take it. Not bad. Not bad at all," said Kedrigern, his interest growing.

This was a rare opportunity. It would set the alchemists on their ears and put them in their proper place once and for all. Let them stink up the countryside with their furnaces and fill the peaceful silence with their babble of Philosopher's Egg and Emerald Table and such pseudo-magical rot in their feeble attempts to create a pinch of third-rate gold dust. Kedrigern, using only his magic, would possess a golden mountain. Well, half a golden mountain. Whatever the dangers, magical or physical, this was too good to let pass.

"You're not the ideal client, Buroc, nor are you my first choice as a partner. And I'm sure that somewhere in that miniature sconce of yours lurks an inchoate notion of mincing me small once we've achieved our goal . . . but I can't resist your offer," he said.

"You come?"

"I come."

At this moment Princess made her appearance, approaching on delicate and silent feet. She bore a silver tray on which stood a frosty pitcher, two gleaming silver mugs, a fist-sized chunk of golden cheese, and a loaf of pale brown bread. Seeing Buroc, she stopped abruptly.

Princess was a woman of spectacular beauty, with a tumble of glistening raven hair cascading to her hips, eyes the color of a midday August sky, and sculpture-perfect features. Her dress of emerald green clung to her slender form, and a circlet of gold ringed her brow. Buroc's eyes gleamed at the sight of her, with a light that betokened single-minded lust. She moved close to Kedrigern and glanced at him, wide-eyed, in frightened appeal.

Inwardly, Kedrigern cursed Spot and promised the troll a sound thrashing at the earliest opportunity. He did not like the idea of Princess's being ogled by this brute, nor did he anticipate pleasant consequences from Buroc's all too patent interest. But what was done could not be undone, except at the cost of more magic than he could presently spare.

"No need to be nervous, Princess. This fellow and I have business," he said.

"Brereep," she replied softly.

"Lady talk funny," Buroc said.

"Spoken like a true connoisseur of linguistic elegance. Carp if you will, Buroc, I'm very fond of Princess," Kedrigern said, extending his hand to her. She set the tray down. He took her hand and raised it to his lips, and she blushed prettily. "I know that somewhere out in the ponds and marshes I was bound to find her. They couldn't all be enchanted princes. But I certainly wasn't going to go around kissing every toad I saw. Time-consuming, for one thing, and not my idea of a good time, for another. So I used my magic. About ninety-eight percent successful, I'd say. Princess has been a charming companion, and I'm very fond of her. Very fond, indeed."

"Brereep," Princess said, with a shy smile.

"Talk like frog," Buroc said, obviously disapproving.

Princess looked hurt. She pouted in a most fetching way. Kedrigern squeezed her hand and said, "Not that it's any of your business, Buroc, but we manage to communicate quite effectively. Don't we, Princess?"

She raised a hand to stroke his cheek and murmured, "Brereep."

"Sweet of you to say so," he responded. Turning to the barbarian, he said, "I think Princess, by her very presence, attests to my abilities. Now, do you have horses for us?"

"Lady come?"

Kedrigern weighed that for a moment. He could leave her here, protected by a spell. But if anything befell him, Princess would be alone and helpless, and unaware of her helplessness. That was unthinkable. Much as he disliked subjecting her to Buroc's hungry eyes, he felt it the better course.

"The lady comes," he said.

Buroc's eyes again glazed over in thought, then he lifted one columnar arm and pointed down the road. "Horses wait."

"We'll pack some food and be with you shortly," Kedrigern said. His glance lighted on the tray Princess had brought. "Meanwhile, be my guest. Eat. Drink," he said, presenting the tray.

Impressed by the speed with which bread, cheese, and ale vanished, Kedrigern decided to use Buroc in an experiment. Leaving Princess to pack the food for the journey, he filled a sack with objects captured in one of his blind gropings into the future. They were small cylindrical things of bright metal wound in bands of colored paper marked with symbols and pictures. At first he had assumed that they were talismans of some unintelligible magic, but he had learned, quite by accident, that they were actually foodstuffs, protected by a near-impenetrable metal shell. He could not imagine how this had been done, or why, nor could he conceive of who, or what, would eat such things, or how they might go about it. If Buroc could manage to deal with the cylinders, that might explain something about them.

Kedrigern glanced about his study. It was cluttered with paraphernalia retrieved in the course of his temporal magic exercise, which had linked him with a remote future age. He had learned very little about that age so far, aside from the fact that it contained a great variety of mysterious metal objects and was very noisy. But his investigations were still in their infancy.

Outside, he pulled a metal cylinder from his bag and tossed it to Buroc. "Food, Buroc. Good. Eat," he said, rubbing his stomach in illustrative gesture.

Buroc bit down on the cylinder, frowned, and took it from his mouth. After staring at it for a time, he laid it on a stump, drew a huge, heavy dagger, and brought the blade down hard, splitting the object in two. He picked up one half, sucked at it, tossed it aside, and did the same with the other half. "More," he said.

Kedrigern tossed him the sack, and Buroc treated himself to a dozen more, leaving the dooryard littered with glinting metal and shreds of colored paper. "Skin tough. Meat good," the barbarian said.

So that was how one enjoyed the contents of those metal cylinders. A dark thought came to Kedrigern. This remote age into which his magic had extended might be peopled by barbarians like Buroc. He pictured a landscape littered from horizon to horizon with shards of scrapped metal trodden by huge barbarian feet, and shuddered. Perhaps it was a sign that the alchemists would triumph in the end. That was the kind of world that would gladden their tiny hearts.

Buroc led the way to where two shaggy horses stood tethered, grazing complacently on the spring grass. He mounted the larger one, leaving the smaller for the wizard and the lady. Kedrigern mounted and reached down to swing Princess up before him. The saddle was quite roomy enough for the two of them.

They traveled in silence for some time. Kedrigern was absorbed in his troubled speculations, Princess was fascinated by the unfamiliar sights and sounds, and Buroc was completely occupied with keeping to the trail. The way led through open countryside for a time, across flowery meadows and down a fragrant woodland trail, then through a wide valley to the outskirts of a cathedral town. Kedrigern, still deep in thought, grunted in surprise as Princess squeezed his waist tightly and clung to him.

The town was a grisly scene. Smoke hung in the air, rank and sickly-smelling, only now beginning to dissipate on a gentle breeze. Doorways and windows gaped, and the great cathedral was open to the skies. Above wheeled flights of crows, and Kedrigern saw a wolf start from their path. When he saw the first bodies, he raised his hand to caress Princess's head, buried in his shoulder, and worked a small concealing magic to hide the carnage form her. He could feel her trembling.

"It's all right now, Princess," he whispered. "We're out in a meadow covered with flowers. Daffodils, as far as the eye can see."

"Brereep," she said faintly, not moving her head.

Buroc reined his mount to a halt and made a sweeping gesture that encompassed the scene. "Buroc do all," he announced.

"Why?"

The barbarian turned his little eyes on the wizard, held his gaze for a long moment, then pointed to the ruins of the cathedral. "Me burn." Swinging his hand to indicate a heap of sprawled corpses, he said, "Me kill." Jerking his horse's head aside, he rode on, erect and proud in the saddle.

At the sound of Buroc's voice, Princess clung more tightly to Kedrigern. "Odd, how barbarians seem to have no knowledge whatsoever of the nominative singular pronoun, Princess," he said by way of diversion. "It's always *me* this and *me* that, particularly when they're being boastful. Your typical barbarian's grasp of syntax seems to be on a par with his grasp of other people's rights to life and property."

"Brereep," Princess said softly.

"Well, yes, I know that your acquaintance with barbarians is slight, my dear. One would hardly expect a well-bred lady to mingle with the likes of Buroc, much less chat with him. You'll just have to take my word for it. I do, though, sometimes wonder if it's all an affectation."

"Brereep?"

"No, truly I do," Kedrigern said. He fell silent for a time, then smiled, then laughed softly to himself. "Can't you just picture them, off by themselves somewhere, hairy and rank, dropping all pretense and cutting loose with compound-complex sentences and sophisticated constructions in the subjective?"

She laughed at the suggestion, and from time to time, as they went on, she glanced at Buroc, then at Kedrigern, and the two of them smothered laughter as children do at a solemn ceremony. They passed no further scenes of devastation and Princess showed no further signs of fear.

ꕥ

Kedrigern relaxed somewhat in his concern for Princess, but he saw much to cause him concern about other matters. He had traveled not at all in recent years, content to live on his quiet hillside with Princess and his magic and loyal Spot to wait on them. The world he saw now was a far worse place than the world he had forsaken. Nature was as lovely as ever; but where the hand of man had fallen, all was blight and death and ruin. The barbarians were overrunning everything. What little they left intact, the alchemists pounded, and boiled, and burned in their hunger for gold.

He became increasingly certain that the alchemists were going to triumph in the end. They would persist until they had turned every bit of lead into gold, and their work would precipitate an age of chaos. The future world that Kedrigern had reached with his magic might well be a place of horrors, if he read the indications correctly. It was a troubling prospect, and he sank into gloom.

Their journey was relatively quiet. They passed three villages which lay in ruins, and at each one, Buroc stopped to point out the carnage and destruction and loudly claim credit for it. He evidenced a growing attentiveness to Princess's reaction, and that disturbed Kedrigern. But at night, when they camped, the barbarian behaved himself. All the same, Kedrigern cast a protective spell around the tent which he and Princess shared.

They came on the third day to a sunless valley where nothing grew. Carrion birds watched with interest from the twisted white limbs of dead trees as the riders picked their way across this place of muck and stone toward a low hill that rose in its center. Only as they approached did Kedrigern determine that the bristling outline of the hill was not caused by the remains of a forest but by bare poles thrust into the ground at disturbing angles. He felt the tingling of magic in the air, and reined in his horse, calling sharply to Buroc.

"No farther! That place is protected!"

Buroc jerked his horse to a halt and turned to face the wizard. "Golden mountain," he said.

Kedrigern was annoyed with himself. He should have known. There were few better ways to keep people far distant than to give a place the appearance of a burying ground of the Old Race. He dismounted, and cautioning Princess to stay behind with the restless horse, he walked closer. The sensation of enchantment grew.

With his back to Buroc, he reached into his tunic and drew out a silver disc about a hand's breadth in diameter which hung on a chain about his neck. It was the medallion of his brotherhood and contained great virtue. Running his first two fingers over certain of the symbols inscribed thereon, he raised the medallion to his eye and sighted through the tiny aperture at its center.

Before him rose a mound of gold. It was not a mountain, not even a fair-sized hill. But it would do. It was pure, glittering gold, flooding the gloomy valley with its light.

Kedrigern slipped the medallion inside his tunic and rubbed his eyes wearily; using the Aperture of True Vision was a strain. When he looked again, the mound rose as before, like the trodden corpse of a giant hedgehog. He turned in time to see a flash of silver in Buroc's hand, which the barbarian quickly removed from before his eye and dropped inside his furs. Kedrigern recognized the silver object, and a chill went through him.

"How did you learn about the golden mountain, Buroc?" he asked off-handedly.

"Man tell Buroc."

"Freely and cheerfully, I'm sure. Did the man give you anything?"

The barbarian paused before replying, "Do magic. Buroc share gold."

"There's no hurry, Buroc. Did you take anything from this helpful man?"

"Do magic," Buroc said, and his voice was hard.

"Just now, I don't want gold. I want the silver medallion that's hanging around your filthy neck. You took it from a brother wizard."

The barbarian reached inside his fur tunic. He hesitated, then he withdrew his empty hand. "Wizard give to Buroc. Mine."

"No wizard gives away his medallion. You came upon a brother when his force was spent, and you killed him. That's how you found the golden mountain. But you don't know how to penetrate the enchantment, and you never will." Kedrigern folded his arms and gazed scornfully up at the mounted barbarian. "So, you great greasy heap of ignorant boastful brutality, you can look until your greedy heart consumes itself, but you can never possess."

With an angry growl, Buroc dropped to the ground, drawing his long curving sword with smooth and practiced swiftness and charging at Kedrigern. The wizard stood his ground. The blade hummed down, then rebounded with the sharp crack of splintering crystal. Fragments of glinting steel spun through the air, and Buroc howled in pain and wrung his hands.

Kedrigern moved his lips silently, extending his hands before him. With a shout, he flung a bolt of shriveling force at the raging barbarian. It struck, and burst in a shower of light, and it was Kedrigern's turn to cry out and nurse his hands. But worse than the pain of rebounded magic was the shock of realization—the power that protected him from Buroc, protected the barbarian from him.

The medallion had a twofold purpose: to signify fellowship in the company of wizards, and to protect whoever wore it against unfriendly magic. It knew no loyalty but to its current wearer.

They faced one another, Kedrigern standing his ground, Buroc circling warily, each eager to strike but cautious from the first shock. Buroc, snarling like a hungry dog, wrenched a jagged stone the size of a cauldron from the muddy ground. Raising it high overhead, he flung it squarely at the wizard's chest. It shattered into gravel and fell like hard rain around them.

"No use, Buroc. You can't hurt me."

The barbarian, panting as much with rage as with exertion, glared at him, motionless, eyes glazing in a furious attempt at thought. After a time, a malicious grin cut across his face.

"Buroc no hurt wizard. Wizard no hurt Buroc. No can hurt."

"I'll think of something."

"Wizard not hurt Buroc!" the barbarian repeated triumphantly.

With unnerving speed, Buroc turned and raced to Princess's side. He seized her wrist in one huge hand and clutched her hair with the other. "Buroc hurt lady!" he roared. "Wizard no hurt Buroc, and Buroc hurt lady!"

Kedrigern felt his stomach flutter at the thought of Princess in Buroc's hands. In desperation, he aimed a bolt at the barbarian's tiny head. The recoiling force staggered him, and he heard Buroc's laughter through a haze of pain. Princess's shriek brought him to his senses.

"I can't reach him, Princess!" he cried. "The medallion protects him, just as it protects me. I'm helpless!"

She turned her terrified eyes on him. Buroc forced her head around, to confront his ugly face.

One recourse remained. His magic was useless against the barbarian, but it would work on Princess. It was dangerous for anyone to be subjected a second time to shape-changing enchantment, but anything was better than ravishment and mutilation at Buroc's hands. She would understand, he was certain.

"Be brave, Princess. There's still a chance," he said. And shaking his head to clear it, Kedrigern began to recite the necessary words, spurred by the sight of Princess's vain struggle.

Buroc pulled her to him. She clawed at his face, and he struck her hands aside. She tore at his tunic, while he laughed and lifted her off her feet. Still she clawed at him. Then, with a bright flash, the silver medallion flew through the air. Kedrigern broke off his spell to dash forward and snatch the medallion before it touched the ground. He dangled it by its broken chain, then swung it around his head, laughing aloud.

"Come, Buroc. Fetch," he said.

Buroc did not hesitate. He flung Princess aside and hurled himself at the wizard, clawing for the medallion. Kedrigern raised a hand, and Buroc froze in mid air, then crashed to the ground with a loud *splap* and a splash of mud. He was rigid as stone.

Kedrigern ran to Princess, raised her up and held her tightly in his arms, speaking soft consoling words until she had stopped shaking. He led her, half carrying her, to the horse and drew from the saddlebag a heavy cloak, which he threw over her shoulders.

"You're a brave woman, Princess. And quicker with your wits than either of us. Buroc never knew what you were up to," he said.

"Brereep?" she asked.

He glanced at Buroc. Already, the clarity of his outline was fading and graying as the petrifaction spell did its work. Soon the Flayer of God's Earth would be no more than a curiously formed pile of stone. The general barbarity would, no doubt, continue; but Buroc's contribution would be missing.

"Quick and painless, Princess," said Kedrigern. "Better than he deserved, but under the circumstances I wanted something quick and dependable. Anything more appropriate would have required more time than either of us could spare." A glint of gold caught his eye. He stooped and took up the golden circlet, wiping it free of mud before placing it on her brows. "We'll leave with no more gold than we brought, if you have no objection."

"Brereep," she said decisively.

"I didn't think you would." He gestured vaguely toward the bristling gravemound. "We know how to get back, and I doubt that anyone will stumble on this and carry it off in the meantime. I'd like to give this whole affair some thought," he said, swinging her up into the saddle.

He mounted Buroc's horse, and side by side they started back. He was silent for a time, deeply preoccupied, but when he became aware of her curious gaze on him, he explained himself.

"I might as well tell you now, Princess," he said, sighing, "that pile of gold is probably close to worthless. Well, maybe not completely worthless. Not just yet. But by the time we get all the wagons we need, and undo the enchantment that's been placed on it—a mighty powerful one—and get it all to a trustworthy buyer, it's sure to be too late. It's all these alchemists, you see. They're frauds, and charlatans, a pack of jargon-spouting pseudo-magicians, I know all that, but they're always *busy*, and there are so *many* of them. . . ." he sighed again, and shook his head sadly. "They're bound to find what they're after. And once they can turn lead into gold, our golden mountain will be worthless. They'll turn all the lead in the world into gold. There'll be gold everywhere."

She laid her hand on his, to console him. He smiled bravely, but could not keep up a façade. Twice that day she heard him murmur, "All the lead into gold," and sigh, and say no more. At night, he said it in his sleep, and gnashed his teeth.

The second day he was silent. On the third morning, he said, "It's not as if I sought it out. I mean, it was just handed to me, and to have it taken away before we even have a chance . . . it isn't fair, Princess." He moped along for a time, then turned his mind to sending orders ahead to Spot. He wanted the house tidy and dinner ready for their return, and that required concentration. When instructing Spot, one had to be precise. Spot could not be left any margin for initiative. Telling it to prepare dinner meant risking the sight of a heap of dead moles on one's platter.

When they reached the foot of the trail to Silent Thunder Mountain, Kedrigern, who had been leading his horse, gazing dejectedly on the ground, let out a sudden yell of exultation. He clapped his hands and shouted for joy. Princess, unable to resist his gaiety, laughed along with him, but looked at him in silent appeal.

"I've solved it, Princess! We'll beat those alchemists at their own game!" he cried, beaming. "Once they've turned all the lead into gold, lead will be rare and precious. So—" and he stopped to laugh and clap his hands and cut a caper on the path— "we'll turn the golden mountain into lead! It's a brilliant idea. Brilliant! Isn't it, my love?"

"Brereep," she said.

Ill Met in Lankhmar

ᘏᘖ

Fritz Leiber

While it's hard to overestimate Robert E. Howard's influence on the genre of heroic fantasy, Fritz Leiber's stories strike me as being almost as influential, while not quite so widely known.

The first such story—Fritz Leiber's first published story, in fact—was "Two Sought Adventure," published in Unknown *magazine back in 1939. It combined a tall Nordic swordsman by the name of Fafhrd with a short tricky thief known as the Gray Mouser into a combination who are to heroic fantasy what Hope and Crosby are to buddy movies: the paradigmatic pair. You'll see their influence several times in this volume, particularly in "After the Gaud Chrysalis" and "King Rainjoy's Tears."*

More than anything, what Fritz Leiber brought to heroic fantasy is a sense of irony, a lighter spirit that helps counterbalance the nihilism and gloom that often permeates the genre. The world of Newhon in which these stories are set is not as rich in myth as is Conan's Cimmeria, but its more Byzantine sense of urban life strikes me as having had a big impact on many another writer, especially British novelists Michael Moorcock and M. John Harrison, whose respective Elric and Viriconium stories are closer in spirit to Leiber than to Howard. (Leiber, incidentally, is generally credited with having coined the term "swords and sorcery.")

Over the course of his long career, Fritz Leiber wrote many classics of horror (Conjure Wife) *and science fiction* (The Big Time) *in addition to his fantasy stories, and he was a frequent contributor to our pages. He died in 1992. "Ill Met in Lankhmar" was first published in our April 1970 issue.*

Silent as specters, the tall and the fat thief edged past the dead, noose-strangled watch-leopard, out the thick, lock-picked door of Jengao the Gem Merchant, and strolled east on Cash Street through the thin black night-smog of Lankhmar.

East on Cash it had to be, for west at Cash and Silver was a police post with unbribed guardsmen restlessly grounding and rattling their pikes.

But tall, tight-lipped Slevyas, master thief candidate, and fat, darting-eyed Fissif, thief second class, with a rating of talented in double-dealing, were not in the least worried. Everything was proceeding according to plan. Each carried thonged in his pouch a smaller pouch of jewels of the first water only, for Jengao, now breathing stentoriously inside and senseless from the slugging he'd suffered, must be allowed, nay, nursed and encouraged to build up his business again and so ripen it for another plucking. Almost the first law of the Thieves' Guild was never to kill the hen that laid eggs with a ruby in the yolk.

The two thieves also had the relief of knowing that they were going straight home now, not to a wife, Aarth forbid!—or to parents and children, all gods forfend!—but to Thieves' House, headquarters and barracks of the all-mighty Guild, which was father to them both and mother too, though no woman was allowed inside its ever-open portal on Cheap Street.

In addition there was the comforting knowledge that although each was armed only with his regulation silver-hilted thief's knife, they were nevertheless most strongly convoyed by three reliable and lethal bravoes hired for the evening from the Slayers' Brotherhood, one moving well ahead of them as point, the other two well behind as rear guard and chief striking force.

And if all that were not enough to make Slevyas and Fissif feel safe and serene, there danced along soundlessly beside them in the shadow of the north curb a small, malformed or at any rate somewhat large-headed shape that might have been a very small dog, a somewhat undersized cat, or a very big rat.

True, this last guard was not an absolutely unalloyed reassurance. Fissif strained upward to whisper softly in Slevyas's long-lobed ear, "Damned if I like being dogged by that familiar of Hristomilo, no matter what security he's supposed to afford us. Bad enough that Krovas did employ or let himself be cowed into employing a sorcerer of most dubious, if dire, reputation and aspect, but that—"

"Shut your trap!" Slevyas hissed still more softly.

Fissif obeyed with a shrug and employed himself in darting his gaze this way and that, but chiefly ahead.

Some distance in that direction, in fact just short of Gold Street, Cash was bridged by an enclosed second-story passageway connecting the two buildings which made up the premises of the famous stone-masons and sculptors Rokkermas and Slaarg. The firm's buildings themselves were fronted by very shallow porticoes supported by unnecessarily large pillars of varied shape and decoration, advertisements more than structural members.

From just beyond the bridge came two low, brief whistles, a signal from the point bravo that he had inspected that area for ambushes and discovered nothing suspicious and that Gold Street was clear.

Fissif was by no means entirely satisfied by the safety signal. To tell the truth, the fat thief rather enjoyed being apprehensive and even fearful, at least up to a point. So he scanned most closely through the thin, sooty smog the frontages and overhangs of Rokkermas and Slaarg.

On this side the bridge was pierced by four small windows, between which were three large niches in which stood—another advertisement—three life-size plaster statues, somewhat eroded by years of weather and dyed varyingly tones of dark gray by as many years of smog. Approaching Jengao's before the burglary, Fissif had noted them. Now it seemed to him that the statue to the right had indefinably changed. It was that of a man of medium height wearing cloak and hood, who gazed down with crossed arms and brooding aspect. No, not indefinably quite—the statue was a more uniform dark gray now, he fancied, cloak, hood, and face; it seemed somewhat sharper featured, less eroded; and he would almost swear it had grown shorter!

Just below the niches, moreover, there was a scattering of gray and raw white rubble which he didn't recall having been there earlier. He strained to remember if during the excitement of the burglary, the unsleeping watch-corner of his mind had recorded a distant crash, and now he believed it had. His quick imagination pictured the possibility of a hole behind each statue, through which it might be given a strong push and so tumbled onto passersby, himself and Slevyas specifically, the right-hand statue having been crashed to test the device and then replaced with a near twin.

He would keep close watch on all the statues as he and Slevyas walked under. It would be easy to dodge if he saw one start to overbalance. Should he yank Slevyas out of harm's way when that happened? It was something to think about.

His restless attention fixed next on the porticoes and pillars. The latter, thick and almost three yards tall, were placed at irregular intervals as well as being irregularly shaped and fluted, for Rokkermas and Slaarg were most modern and emphasized the unfinished look, randomness, and the unexpected.

Nevertheless it seemed to Fissif, that there was an intensification of unexpectedness, specifically that there was one more pillar under the porticoes than when he had last passed by. He couldn't be sure which pillar was the newcomer, but he was almost certain there was one.

The enclosed bridge was close now. Fissif glanced up at the right-hand statue and noted other differences from the one he'd recalled. Although shorter, it seemed to hold itself more strainingly erect, while the frown carved in its dark gray face was not so much one of philosophic brooding as sneering contempt, self-conscious cleverness, and conceit.

Still, none of the three statues toppled forward as he and Slevyas walked under the bridge. However, something else happened to Fissif at that moment.

One of the pillars winked at him.

The Gray Mouser turned round in the right-hand niche, leaped up and caught hold of the cornice, silently vaulted to the flat roof, and crossed it precisely in time to see the two thieves emerge below.

Without hesitation he leaped forward and down, his body straight as a crossbow bolt, the soles of his ratskin boots aimed at the shorter thief's fat-buried shoulder blades, though leading him a little to allow for the yard he'd walk while the Mouser hurtled toward him.

In the instant that he leaped, the tall thief glanced up over-shoulder and whipped out a knife, though making no move to push or pull Fissif out of the way of the human projectile speeding toward him.

More swiftly than one would have thought he could manage, Fissif whirled round then and thinly screamed, "Slivikin!"

The ratskin boots took him high in the belly. It was like landing on a big cushion. Writhing aside from Slevyas's thrust, the Mouser somersaulted forward, and as the fat thief's skull hit a cobble with a dull *bong* he came to his feet with dirk in hand, ready to take on the tall one.

But there was no need. Slevyas, his eyes glazed, was toppling too.

One of the pillars had sprung forward, trailing a voluminous robe. A big hood had fallen back from a youthful face and long-haired head. Brawny arms had emerged from the long, loose sleeves that had been the pillar's topmost section. While the big fist ending one of the arms had dealt Slevyas a shrewd knockout punch on the chin.

Fafhrd and the Gray Mouser faced each other across the two thieves sprawled senseless. They were poised for attack, yet for the moment neither moved.

Fafhrd said, "Our motives for being here seem identical."

"Seem? Surely must be!" the Mouser answered curtly, fiercely eyeing this potential new foe, who was taller by a head than the tall thief.

"You said?"

"I said, 'Seem? Surely must be!'"

"How civilized of you!" Fafhrd commented in pleased tones.

"Civilized?" the Mouser demanded suspiciously, gripping his dirk tighter.

"To care, in the eye of action, exactly what's said," Fafhrd explained. Without letting the Mouser out of his vision, he glanced down. His gaze traveled from the pouch of one fallen thief to that of the other. Then he looked up at the Mouser with a broad, ingenuous smile.

"Fifty-Fifty?" he suggested.

The Mouser hesitated, sheathed his dirk, and rapped out, "A deal!" He knelt abruptly, his fingers on the drawstrings of Fissif's pouch. "Loot you Slivikin," he directed.

It was natural to suppose that the fat thief had been crying his companion's name at the end.

Without looking up from where he knelt, Fafhrd remarked, "That . . . ferret they had with them. Where did it go?"

"Ferret?" the Mouser answered briefly. "It was a marmoset!"

"Marmoset," Fafhrd mused. "That's a small tropical monkey, isn't it? Well, might have been—I've never been south—but I got the impression that—"

The silent, two-pronged rush which almost overwhelmed them at that instant really surprised neither of them. Each had unconsciously been expecting it.

The three bravoes racing down upon them in concerted attack, all with swords poised to thrust, had assumed that the two highjackers would be armed at most with knives and as timid in weapons-combat as the general run of thieves and counter-thieves. So it was they who were thrown into confusion when with the lightning speed of youth the Mouser and Fafhrd sprang up, whipped out fearsomely long swords, and faced them back to back.

The Mouser made a very small parry in carte so that the thrust of the bravo from the east went past his left side by only a hair's breadth. He instantly riposted. His adversary, desperately springing back, parried in turn in carte. Hardly slowing, the tip of the Mouser's long, slim sword dropped under that parry with the delicacy of a princess curtsying and then leapt forward and a little upward and went between two scales of the bravo's armored jerkin and between his ribs and through his heart and out his back as if all were angelfood cake.

Meanwhile Fafhrd, facing the two bravoes from the west, swept aside their low thrusts with somewhat larger, downsweeping parries in seconde and low prime, then flipped up his sword, as long as the Mouser's but heavier, so that it slashed through the neck of his right-hand adversary, half decapitating him. Then dropping back a swift step, he readied a thrust for the other.

But there was no need. A narrow ribbon of bloodied steel, followed by a gray glove and arm, flashed past him from behind and transfixed the last bravo with the identical thrust the Mouser had used on the first.

The two young men wiped their swords. Fafhrd brushed the palm of his open right hand down his robe and held it out. The Mouser pulled off right-hand gray glove and shook it. Without word exchanged, they knelt and finished looting the two unconscious thieves, securing the small bags of jewels. With an oily towel and then a dry one, the Mouser sketchily wiped from his face the greasy ash-soot mixture which had darkened it.

Then, after only a questioning eye-twitch east on the Mouser's part and a nod from Fafhrd, they swiftly walked on in the direction Slevyas and Fissif and their escort had been going.

After reconnoitering at Gold Street, they crossed it and continued east on Cash at Fafhrd's gestured proposal.

"My woman's at the Golden Lamprey," he explained.

"Let's pick her up and take her home to meet my girl," the Mouser suggested.

"Home?" Fafhrd inquired politely.

"Dim Lane," the Mouser volunteered.

"Silver Eel?"

"Behind it. We'll have some drinks."

"I'll pick up a jug. Never have too much juice."

"True. I'll let you."

Fafhrd stopped, again wiped right hand on robe, and held it out. "Name's Fafhrd."

Again the Mouser shook it. "Gray Mouser," he said a touch defiantly, as if challenging anyone to laugh at the sobriquet.

"Gray Mouser, eh?" Fafhrd remarked. "Well, you killed yourself a couple of rats tonight."

"That I did." The Mouser's chest swelled and he threw back his head. Then with a comic twitch of his nose and a sidewise half-grin he admitted, "You'd have got your second man easily enough. I stole him from you to demonstrate my speed. Besides, I was excited."

Fafhrd chuckled. "You're telling me? How do you suppose I was feeling?"

Once more the Mouser found himself grinning. What the deuce did this big fellow have that kept him from putting on his usual sneers?

Fafhrd was asking himself a similar question. All his life he'd mistrusted small men, knowing his height awakened their instant jealousy. But this clever little chap was somehow an exception. He prayed to Kos that Vlana would like him.

On the northeast corner of Cash and Whore a slow-burning torch shaded by a broad, gilded spiral cast a cone of light up into the thickening black night-smog and another cone down on the cobbles before the tavern door. Out of the shadows into the second cone stepped Vlana, handsome in a narrow black velvet dress and red stockings, her only ornaments a silver-hilted dagger in a silver sheath and a silver-worked black pouch, both on a plain black belt.

Fafhrd introduced the Gray Mouser, who behaved with an almost fawning courtesy. Vlana studied him boldly, then gave him a tentative smile.

Fafhrd opened under the torch the small pouch he'd taken off the tall thief. Vlana looked down into it. She put her arms around Fafhrd, hugged him tight and kissed him soundly. Then she thrust the jewels into the pouch on her belt.

When that was done, he said, "Look, I'm going to buy a jug. You tell her what happened, Mouser."

When he came out of the Golden Lamprey he was carrying four jugs in the crook of his left arm and wiping his lips on the back of his right hand. Vlana frowned. He grinned at her. The Mouser smacked his lips at the jugs. They continued east on Cash. Fafhrd realized that the frown was for more than the jugs and the prospect of stupidly drunken male revelry. The Mouser tactfully walked ahead.

When his figure was little more than a blob in the thickening smog, Vlana whispered harshly, "You had two members of the Thieves' Guild knocked out cold and you didn't cut their throats?"

"We slew three bravoes," Fafhrd protested by way of excuse.

"My quarrel is not with the Slayers' Brotherhood, but that abominable guild. You swore to me that whenever you had the chance—"

"Vlana! I couldn't have the Gray Mouser thinking I was an amateur counter-thief consumed by hysteria and blood lust."

"Well, he told me that *he'd* have slit their throats in a wink, if he'd known I wanted it that way."

"He was only playing up to you from courtesy."

"Perhaps and perhaps not. But you knew and you didn't—"

"Vlana, shut up!"

Her frown became a rageful glare, then suddenly she laughed widely, smiled twitchingly as if she were about to cry, mastered herself and smiled more lovingly. "Pardon me, darling," she said. "Sometimes you must think I'm going mad and sometimes I believe I am."

"Well, don't," he told her shortly. "Think of the jewels we've won instead. And behave yourself with our new friends. Get some wine inside you and relax. I mean to enjoy myself tonight. I've earned it."

She nodded and clutched his arm in agreement and for comfort and sanity. They hurried to catch up with the dim figure ahead.

The Mouser, turning left, led them a half square north on Cheap Street to where a narrower way went east again. The black mist in it looked solid.

"Dim Lane," the Mouser explained.

Vlana said, "Dim's too weak—too *transparent* a word for it tonight," with an uneven laugh in which there were still traces of hysteria and which ending in a fit of strangled coughing.

She gasped out, "Damn Lankhmar's night-smog! What a hell of a city!"

"It's the nearness here of the Great Salt Marsh," Fafhrd explained.

And he did indeed have part of the answer. Lying low betwixt the Marsh, the Inner Sea, the River Hlal, and the southern grain fields watered by canals fed by the Hlal, Lankhmar with its innumerable smokes was the prey of fogs and sooty smogs.

About halfway to Carter Street, a tavern on the north side of the lane emerged from the murk. A gape-jawed serpentine shape of pale metal crested with soot hung high for a sign. Beneath it they passed a door curtained with begrimed leather, the slit in which spilled out noise, pulsing torchlight, and the reek of liquor.

Just beyond the Silver Eel the Mouser led them through an inky passageway outside the tavern's east wall. They had to go single file, feeling their way along rough, slimily bemisted brick.

"Mind the puddle," the Mouser warned. "It's deep as the Outer Sea."

The passageway widened. Reflected torchlight filtering down through the dark mist allowed them to make out only the most general shape of their surroundings. Crowding close to the back of the Silver Eel rose a dismal, rickety building of darkened brick and blackened, ancient wood. From the fourth story attic under the ragged-guttered roof, faint lines of yellow light shone around and through three tightly latticed windows. Beyond was a narrow alley.

"Bones Alley," the Mouser told them.

By now Vlana and Fafhrd could see a long, narrow wooden outside stairway, steep yet sagging and without a rail, leading up to the lighted attic. The Mouser relieved Fafhrd of the jugs and went up it quite swiftly.

"Follow me when I've reached the top," he called back. "I think it'll take your weight, Fafhrd, but best one of you at a time."

Fafhrd gently pushed Vlana ahead. She mounted to the Mouser where he now stood in an open doorway, from which streamed yellow light that died swiftly in the night-smog. He was lightly resting a hand on a big, empty, wrought-iron lamp-hook firmly set in a stone section of the outside wall. He bowed aside, and she went in.

Fafhrd followed, placing his feet as close as he could to the wall, his hands ready to grab for support. The whole stairs creaked ominously and each step gave a little as he shifted his weight onto it. Near the top, one step gave way with the muted crack of half-rotted wood. Gently as he could, he sprawled himself hand and knee on as many steps as he could get, to distribute his weight, and cursed sulphurously.

"Don't fret, the jugs are safe," the Mouser called down gaily.

Fafhrd crawled the rest of the way and did not get to his feet until he was inside the doorway. When he had done so, he almost gasped with surprise.

It was like rubbing the verdigris from a cheap brass ring and revealing a rainbow-fired diamond of the first water. Rich drapes, some twinkling with embroidery of silver and gold, covered the walls except where the shuttered windows were—and the shutters of those were gilded. Similar but darker fabrics hid the low ceiling, making a gorgeous canopy in which the flecks of gold and silver were like stars. Scattered about were plump cushions and low tables, on which burned a multitude of candles. On shelves against the walls were neatly stacked like small logs a vast reserve of candles, numerous scrolls, jugs, bottles, and enameled boxes. In a large fireplace was set a small metal stove, neatly blacked, with an ornate firepot. Also set beside the stove was a tidy pyramid of thin, resinous torches with frayed ends—fire-kindlers—and other pyramids of small, short logs and gleamingly black coal.

On a low dais by the fireplace was a couch covered with cloth of gold. On it sat a thin, pale-faced, delicately handsome girl clad in a dress of thick violet silk worked with silver and belted with a silver chain. Silver pins headed with amethysts held in place her high-piled black hair. Round her shoulders was drawn a wrap of snow-white serpent fur. She was leaning forward with uneasy-seeming graciousness and extending a narrow white hand which shook a little to Vlana, who knelt before her and now gently took the proffered hand and bowed her head over it, her own glossy, straight, dark-brown hair making a canopy, and pressed its back to her lips.

Fafhrd was happy to see his woman playing up properly to this definitely odd, though delightful situation. Then looking at Vlana's long, red-stockinged leg stretched far behind her as she knelt on the other, he noted that the floor was everywhere strewn—to the point of double, treble, and quadruple overlaps—with thick-piled, close-woven , many-hued rugs of the finest quality imported from the Eastern Lands. Before he knew it, his thumb had shot toward the Gray Mouser.

"You're the Rub Robber!" he proclaimed. "You're the Carpet Crimp!—and the Candle Corsair too!" he continued, referring to two series of unsolved thefts which had been on the lips of all Lankhmar when he and Vlana had arrived a moon ago.

The Mouser shrugged impassive-faced at Fafhrd, then suddenly grinned, his slitted eyes a-twinkle, and broke into an impromptu dance which carried him whirling and jigging around the room and left him behind Fafhrd, where he deftly reached down the hooded and long-sleeved huge robe from the latter's stooping shoulders, shook it out, carefully folded it, and set it on a pillow.

The girl in violet nervously patted with her free hand the cloth of gold beside her, and Vlana seated herself there, carefully not too close, and the two women spoke together in low voices, Vlana taking the lead.

The Mouser took off his own gray, hooded cloak and laid it beside Fafhrd's. Then they unbelted their swords, and the Mouser set them atop folded robe and cloak.

Without those weapons and bulking garments, the two men looked suddenly like youths, both with clear, close-shaven faces, both slender despite the swelling muscles of Fafhrd's arms and calves, he with long red-gold hair falling down his back and about his shoulders, the Mouser with dark hair cut in bangs, the one in brown leather tunic worked with copper wire, the other in jerkin of coarsely woven gray silk.

They smiled at each other. The feeling each had of having turned boy all at once made their smiles embarrassed. The Mouser cleared his throat and, bowing a little, but looking still at Fafhrd, extended a loosely spread-fingered arm toward the golden couch and said with a preliminary stammer, though otherwise smoothly enough, "Fafhrd, my good friend, permit me to introduce you to my princess. Ivrian, my dear, receive Fafhrd graciously if you please, for tonight he and I fought back to back against three and we conquered."

Fafhrd advanced, stooping a little, the crown of his red-gold hair brushing the be-starred canopy, and knelt before Ivrian exactly as Vlana had. The slender hand extended to him looked steady now, but was still quiveringly a-tremble, he discovered as soon as he touched it. He handled it as if it were silk woven of the white spider's gossamer, barely brushing it with his lips, and still felt nervous as he mumbled some compliments.

He did not sense that the Mouser was quite as nervous as he, if not more so, praying hard that Ivrian would not overdo her princess part and snub their guests, or collapse in trembling or tears, for Fafhrd and Vlana were literally the first beings that he had brought into the luxurious nest he had created for his aristocratic beloved—save the two love birds that twittered in a silver cage hanging to the other side of the fireplace from the dais.

Despite his shrewdness and cynicism, it never occurred to the Mouser that it was chiefly his charming but preposterous coddling of Ivrian that was making her doll-like.

But now as Ivrian smiled at last, the Mouser relaxed with relief, fetched two silver cups and two silver mugs, carefully selected a bottle of violet wine, then with a grin at Fafhrd uncorked instead one of the jugs the Northerner had brought, and near-brimmed the four gleaming vessels and served them all four.

With no trace of stammer this time, he toasted, "To my greatest theft to date in Lankhmar, which willy-nilly I must share fifty-fifty with—" he couldn't resist the sudden impulse "—with this great, long-haired, barbarian lout here!" And he downed a quarter of his mug of pleasantly burning wine fortified with brandy.

Fafhrd quaffed off half of his, then toasted back, "To the most boastful and finical little civilized chap I've ever deigned to share loot with," quaffed off the rest, and with a great smile that showed white teeth, held out his empty mug.

The Mouser gave him a refill, topped off his own, then set that down to go to Ivrian and pour into her lap from their small pouch the gems he'd filched from Fissif. They gleamed in their new, enviable location like a small puddle of rainbow-hued quicksilver.

Ivrian jerked back a-tremble, almost spilling them, but Vlana gently caught her arm, steadying it. At Ivrian's direction, Vlana fetched a blue-enameled box inlaid with silver, and the two of them transferred the jewels from Ivrian's lap into its blue velvet interior. Then they chatted on.

As he worked through his second mug in smaller gulps, Fafhrd relaxed and began to get a deeper feeling of his surroundings. The dazzling wonder of the first glimpse of this throne room in a slum faded, and he began to note the ricketiness and rot under the grand overlay.

Black, rotten wood showed here and there between the drapes and loosed its sick, ancient stinks. The whole floor sagged under the rugs, as much as a span at the center of the room. Threads of night-smog were coming through the shutters, making evanescent black arabesques against the gilt. The stones of the large fireplace had been scrubbed and varnished, yet most of the mortar was gone from between them; some sagged, others were missing altogether.

The Mouser had been building a fire there in the stove. Now he pushed in all the way the yellow flaring kindler he'd lit from the fire-pot, hooked the little black door shut over the mounting flames, and turned back into the room. As if he'd read Fafhrd's mind, he took up several cones of incense, set their peaks a-smolder at the fire-pot, and placed them about the room in gleaming, shallow brass bowls. Then he stuffed silken rags in the widest shutter-cracks, took up his silver mug again, and for a moment gave Fafhrd a very hard look.

Next moment he was smiling and lifting his mug to Fafhrd, who was doing the same. Need of refills brought them close together. Hardly moving his lips, the Mouser explained, "Ivrian's father was a duke. I slew him. A most cruel man, cruel to his daughter too, yet a duke, so that Ivrian is wholly unused to fending for herself. I pride myself that I maintain her in grander state than her father did with all his servants."

Fafhrd nodded and said amiably, "Surely you've thieved together a charming little palace."

From the couch Vlana called in her husky contralto, "Gray Mouser, your Princess would hear an account of tonight's adventure. And might we have more wine?"

Ivrian called, "Yes, please, Mouse."

The Mouser looked to Fafhrd for the go-ahead, got the nod, and launched into his story. But first he served the girls wine. There wasn't enough for their cups, so he opened another jug and after a moment of thought uncorked all three, setting one by the couch, one by Fafhrd where he sprawled now on the pillowy carpet, and reserving one for himself. Ivrian looked apprehensive at this signal of heavy drinking ahead, Vlana cynical.

The Mouser told the tale of counter-thievery well, acting it out in part, and with only the most artistic of embellishments—the ferret-marmoset before escaping ran up his body and tried to scratch out his eyes—and he was interrupted only twice.

When he said, "And so with a whish and a snick I bared Scalpel—" Fafhrd remarked, "Oh, so you've nicknamed your sword as well as yourself?"

The Mouser drew himself up. "Yes, and I call my dirk Cat's Claw. Any objections? Seem childish to you?"

"Not at all. I call my own sword Graywand. Pray continue."

And when he mentioned the beastie of uncertain nature that had gamboled along with the thieves (and attacked his eyes!), Ivrian paled and said with a shudder, "Mouse! That sounds like a witch's familiar!"

"Wizard's," Vlana corrected. "Those gutless Guild-villains have no truck with women, except as fee'd or forced vehicles for their lust. But Krovas, their current king, is noted for taking *all* precautions, and might well have a warlock in his service."

"That seems most likely; it harrows me with dread," the Mouser agreed with ominous gaze and sinister voice, eagerly accepting any and all atmospheric enhancements of his performance.

When he was done, the girls, eyes flashing and fond, toasted him and Fafhrd for their cunning and bravery. The Mouser bowed and eye-twinklingly smiled about, then sprawled him down with a weary sigh, wiping his forehead with a silken cloth and downing a large drink.

After asking Vlana's leave, Fafhrd told the adventurous tale of their escape from Cold Corner—he from his clan, she from an acting troupe—and of their progress to Lankhmar, where they lodged now in an actors' tenement near the Plaza of Dark Delights. Ivrian hugged herself to Vlana and shivered large-eyed at the witchy parts of his tale.

The only proper matter he omitted from his account was Vlana's fixed intent to get a monstrous revenge on the Thieves' Guild for torturing to death her accomplices and harrying her out of Lankhmar when she'd tried freelance thieving in the city before they met. Nor of course did he mention his own promise—foolish, he thought now—to help her in this bloody business.

After he'd done and got his applause, he found his throat dry despite his skald's training, but when he sought to wet it, he discovered that his mug was empty and his jug too, through he didn't feel in the least drunk—he had talked all the liquor out of him, he told himself, a little of the stuff escaping in each glowing word he'd spoken.

The Mouser was in like plight and not drunk either—though inclined to pause mysteriously and peer toward infinity before answering question or making remark. This time he suggested, after a particularly long infinity-gaze, that Fafhrd accompany him to the Eel while he purchased a fresh supply.

"But we've a lot of wine left in *our* jug," Ivrian protested. "Or at least a little," she amended. It did sound empty when Vlana shook it. "Besides, you've wine of all sorts here."

"Not this sort, dearest, and first rule is never mix'em," the Mouser explained, wagging a finger. "That way lies unhealth, aye, and madness."

"My dear," Vlana said, sympathetically patting her wrist, "at some time in any good party all the men who are really men simply have to go out. It's extremely stupid, but it's their nature and can't be dodged, believe me."

"But, Mouse, I'm scared. Fafhrd's tale frightened me. So did yours—I'll hear that familiar a-scratch at the shutters when you're gone, I know I will!"

"Darlingest," the Mouser said with a small hiccup, "there is all the Inner Sea, all the Land of the Eight Cities, and to boot all the Trollstep Mountains in their skyscraping grandeur between you and Fafhrd's Cold Corner and its silly sorcerers. As for familiars, pish!—they've never in the world been anything but the loathy, all-too-natural pets of stinking old women and womanish old men."

Vlana said merrily, "Let the sillies go, my dear. 'Twill give us chance for a private chat, during which we'll take 'em apart from wine-fumey head to restless foot."

So Ivrian let herself be persuaded, and the Mouser and Fafhrd slipped off, quickly shutting the door behind them to keep out the night-smog, and the girls heard their light steps down the stairs.

Waiting for the four jugs to be brought up from the Eel's cellar, the two newly met comrades ordered a mug each of the same fortified wine, or one near enough, and ensconced themselves at the least noisy end of the long serving counter in the tumultuous tavern. The Mouser deftly kicked a rat that thrust black head and shoulders from his hole.

After each had enthusiastically complimented the other on his girl, Fafhrd said diffidently, "Just between ourselves, do you think there might be anything to your sweet Ivrian's notion that the small dark creature with Slivikin and the other Guild-thief was a wizard's familiar, or at any rate the cunning pet of a sorcerer, trained to act as go-between and report disasters to his master or to Krovas?"

The Mouser laughed lightly. "You're building bugbears—formless baby ones unlicked by logic—out of nothing, dear barbarian brother, if I may say so. How could that vermin make useful report? I don't believe in animals that talk—except for parrots and such birds, which only . . . parrot.

"Ho, there, you back of the counter! Where are my jugs? Rats eaten the boy who went for them days ago? Or he simply starved to death while on his cellar quest? Well, tell him to get a swifter move on and brim us again!

"No, Fafhrd, even granting the beastie to be directly or indirectly a creature of Krovas, and that it raced back to Thieves' House after our affray, what would that tell them there? Only that something had gone wrong with the burglary at Jengao's."

Fafhrd frowned and muttered stubbornly, "The furry slinker might, nevertheless, somehow convey our appearances to the Guild masters, and they might recognize us and come after us and attack us in our homes."

"My dear friend," the Mouser said condolingly, "once more begging your indulgence, I fear this potent wine is addling your wits. If the Guild knew our looks or where we lodge, they'd have been nastily on our necks days, weeks, nay, months ago. Or conceivably you don't know that their penalty for freelance thieving within the walls of Lankhmar is nothing less than death, after torture, if happily that can be achieved."

"I know all about that, and my plight is worse even than yours," Fafhrd retorted, and after pledging the Mouser to secrecy, told him the tale of Vlana's vendetta against the Guild and her deadly serious dreams of an all-encompassing revenge.

During his story the four jugs came up from the cellar, but the Mouser only ordered that their earthenware mugs be refilled.

Fafhrd finished, "And so, in consequence of a promise given by an infatuated and unschooled boy in a southern angle of the Cold Waste, I find myself now as a sober—well, at other times—man being constantly asked to make war on a power as great as that of Lankhmar's overlord, for as you may know, the Guild has locals in all other cities and major towns of this land. I love Vlana dearly and she is an experienced thief herself, but on this one topic she has a kink in her brains, a hard knot neither logic nor persuasion can even begin to loosen."

"Certes t'would be insanity to assault the Guild direct, your wisdom's perfect there," the Mouser commented. "If you cannot break your most handsome girl of this mad notion, or coax her from it, then you must stoutly refuse e'en her least request in that direction."

"Certes I must," Fafhrd agreed with great emphasis and conviction. "I'd be an idiot taking on the Guild. Of course, if they should catch me, they'd kill me in any case for freelancing and highjacking. But wantonly to assault the Guild direct, kill one Guild-thief needlessly—lunacy entire!"

"You'd not only be a drunken, drooling idiot, you'd questionless be stinking in three nights at most from that emperor of diseases, Death. Malicious attacks on her person, blows directed at the organization, the Guild requites tenfold what she does other rule-breaking, freelancing included. So, no least giving-in to Vlana in this one matter."

"Agreed!" Fafhrd said loudly, shaking the Mouser's iron-thewed hand in a near crusher grip.

"And now we should be getting back to the girls," the Mouser said.

"After one more drink while we settle the score. Ho, boy!"

"Suits."

Vlana and Ivrian, deep in excited talk, both started at the pounding rush of footsteps up the stairs. Racing behemoths could hardly have made more noise. The creaking and groaning were prodigious, and there were the crashes of two treads breaking. The door flew open and their two men rushed in through a great mushroom top of night-smog which was neatly sliced off its black stem by the slam of the door.

"I told you we'd be back in a wink," the Mouser cried gaily to Ivrian, while Fafhrd strode forward, unmindful of the creaking floor, crying, "Dearest heart, I've missed you sorely," and caught up Vlana despite her voiced protests and pushings-off and kissed and hugged her soundly before setting her back on the couch again.

Oddly, it was Ivrian who appeared to be angry at Fafhrd then, rather than Vlana, who was smiling fondly if somewhat dazedly.

"Fafhrd, sir," she said boldly, her little fists set on her narrow hips, her tapered chin held high, her dark eyes blazing, "my beloved Vlana has been telling me about the unspeakably atrocious things the Thieves' Guild did to her and to her dearest friends. Pardon my frank speaking to one I've only met, but I think it quite unmanly of you to refuse her the just revenge she desires and fully deserves. And that goes for you too, Mouse, who boasted to Vlana of what you would have done had you but known, all the while intending only empty ingratiation. You who in like case did not scruple to slay my very own father!"

It was clear to Fafhrd that while he and the Gray Mouser had idly boozed in the Eel, Vlana had been giving Ivrian a doubtless empurpled account of her grievances against the Guild and playing mercilessly on the naïve girl's bookish, romantic sympathies and high concept of knightly honor. It was also clear to him that Ivrian was more than a little drunk. A three-quarters empty flask of violet wine of far Kiraay sat on the low table next the couch.

Yet he could think of nothing to do but spread his big hands helplessly and bow his head, more than the low ceiling made necessary, under Ivrian's glare, now reinforced by that of Vlana. After all, they *were* in the right. He *had* promised.

So it was the Mouser who first tried to rebut.

"Come now, pet," he cried lightly as he danced about the room, silk-stuffing more cracks against the thickening night-smog and stirring up and feeding the fire in the stove, "and you too, beauteous Lady Vlana. For the past month Fafhrd has by his highjackings been hitting the Guild-thieves where it hurts them most—in their purses a-dangle between their legs. Come, drink we up all." Under his handling, one of the new jugs came uncorked with a pop, and he darted about brimming silver cups and mugs.

"A merchant's revenge!" Ivrian retorted with scorn, not one whit appeased, but rather enangered anew. "At the least you and Fafhrd must bring Vlana the head of Krovas!"

"What would she *do* with it? What *good* would it be except to spot the carpets?" the Mouser plaintively inquired, while Fafhrd, gathering his wits at last and going down on one knee, said slowly, "Most respected Lady Ivrian, it is true I solemnly promised my beloved Vlana I would help her in her revenge, but if Mouse and I should bring Vlana the head of Krovas, she and I would have to flee Lankhmar on the instant, every man's hand against us. While you infallibly would lose this fairyland

Mouser has created for love of you and be forced to do likewise, be with him a beggar on the run for the rest of your natural lives."

While Fafhrd spoke, Ivrian snatched up her new-filled cup and drained it. Now she stood up straight as a soldier, her pale face flushed, and said scathingly, "*You count the cost*! You speak to me of *things*—" She waved at the many-hued splendor around her "—of mere property, however costly—when honor is at stake. You gave Vlana *your word*. Oh, is knighthood wholly dead?"

Fafhrd could only shrug again and writhe inside and gulp a little easement from his silver mug.

In a master stroke, Vlana tried gently to draw Ivrian down to her golden seat again. "Softly, dearest," she pleaded. "You have spoken nobly for me and my cause, and believe me, I am most grateful. Your words revived in me great, fine feelings dead these many years. But of us here, only you are truly an aristocrat attuned to the highest proprieties. We other three are naught but thieves. Is it any wonder some of us put safety above honor and word-keeping, and most prudently avoid risking our lives? Yes, we are three thieves and I am outvoted. So please speak no more of honor and rash, dauntless bravery, but sit you down and—"

"You mean they're both *afraid* to challenge the Thieves' Guild, don't you?" Ivrian said, eyes wide and face twisted by loathing. "I always thought my Mouse was a nobleman first and a thief second. Thieving's nothing. My father lived by cruel thievery done on rich wayfarers and neighbors less powerful than he, yet he was an aristocrat. Oh, you're *cowards*, both of you! *Poltroons*!" she finished, turning her eyes flashing with cold scorn first on the Mouser, then on Fafhrd.

The latter could stand it no longer. He sprang to his feet, face flushed, fists clenched at his sides, quite unmindful of his down-clattered mug and the ominous creak his sudden action drew from the sagging floor.

"*I am not a coward*!" he cried. "I'll dare Thieves' House and fetch you Krovas's head and toss it with blood a-drip at Vlana's feet. I swear by my sword Graywand here at my side!"

He slapped his left hip, found nothing there but his tunic, and had to content himself with pointing tremble-armed at his belt and scabbarded sword where they lay atop his neatly folded robe—and then picking up, refilling splashily, and draining his mug.

The Gray Mouser began to laugh in high, delighted, tuneful peals. All stared at him. He came dancing up beside Fafhrd, and still smiling widely, asked, "*Why not*? Who speaks of fearing the Guild-thieves? Who becomes upset at the prospect of this ridiculously easy exploit, when all of us know that all of them, even Krovas and his ruling clique, are but pygmies in mind and skill compared to me or Fafhrd here? A wondrously simple, foolproof scheme has just occurred to me for penetrating Thieves' House, every closet and cranny. Stout Fafhrd and I will put it into effect at once. Are you with me, Northerner?"

"Of course I am," Fafhrd responded gruffly, at the same time frantically wondering what madness had gripped the little fellow.

"Give me a few heartbeats to gather needed props, and we're off!" the Mouser cried. He snatched from shelf and unfolded a stout sack, then raced about, thrusting into it coiled ropes, bandage rolls, rags, jars of ointment and unction and unguent, and other oddments.

"But you can't go *tonight*," Ivrian protested, suddenly grown pale and uncertain-voiced. "You're both . . . in no condition to."

"You're both *drunk*," Vlana said harshly. "Silly drunk—and that way you'll get naught in Thieves' House but your deaths. Fafhrd! Control yourself!"

"Oh, no," Fafhrd told her as he buckled on his sword. "You wanted the head of Krovas heaved at your feet in a great splatter of blood, and that's what you're going to get, like it or not!"

"Softly, Fafhrd," the Mouser interjected, coming to a sudden stop and drawing tight the sack's mouth by its strings. "And softly you too, Lady Vlana, and my dear princess. Tonight I intend but a scouting expedition. No risks run, only the information gained needful for planning our murderous strike tomorrow or the day after. So no head-choppings whatsoever tonight, Fafhrd, you hear me? Whatever may hap, hist's the word. And don your hooded robe."

Fafhrd shrugged, nodded, and obeyed.

Ivrian seemed somewhat relieved. Vlana too, though she said, "Just the same you're both drunk."

"All to the good!" the Mouser assured her with a mad smile. "Drink may slow a man's sword-arm and soften his blows a bit, but it sets his wits ablaze and fires his imagination, and those are the qualities we'll need tonight."

Vlana eyed him dubiously.

Under cover of this confab Fafhrd made quietly yet swiftly to fill once more his and the Mouser's mugs, but Vlana noted it and gave him such a glare that he set down mugs and uncorked jug so swiftly his robe swirled.

The Mouser shouldered his sack and drew open the door. With a casual wave at the girls, but no word spoken, Fafhrd stepped out on the tiny porch. The night-smog had grown so thick he was almost lost to view. The Mouser waved four fingers at Ivrian, then followed Fafhrd.

"Good fortune go with you," Vlana called heartily.

"Oh, be careful, Mouse," Ivrian gasped.

The Mouser, his figure slight against the loom of Fafhrd's, silently drew shut the door.

Their arms automatically gone around each other, the girls waited for the inevitable creaking and groaning of the stairs. It delayed and delayed. The night-smog that had entered the room dissipated and still the silence was unbroken.

"What can they be doing out there?" Ivrian whispered. "Plotting their course?"

Vlana impatiently shook her head, then disentangled herself, tiptoed to the door, opened it, descended softly a few steps, which creaked most dolefully, then returned, shutting the door behind her.

"They're gone," she said in wonder.

"I'm frightened!" Ivrian breathed and sped across the room to embrace the taller girl.

Vlana hugged her tight, then disengaged an arm to shoot the door's three heavy bolts.

In Bones Alley the Mouser returned to his pouch the knotted line by which they'd descended from the lamp hook. He suggested, "How about stopping at the Silver Eel?"

"You mean and just *tell* the girls we've been to Thieves' House?" Fafhrd asked.

"Oh, no," the Mouser protested. "But you missed your stirrup cup upstairs—and so did I."

With a crafty smile Fafhrd drew from his robe two full jugs.

"Palmed 'em, as 'twere, when I set down the mugs. Vlana sees a lot, but not all."

"You're a prudent, far-sighted fellow," the Mouser said admiringly. "I'm proud to call you comrade."

Each uncorked and drank a hearty slug. Then the Mouser led them west, they veering and stumbling only a little, and then north into an even narrower and more noisome alley.

"Plague Court," the Mouser said.

After several preliminary peepings and peerings, they staggered swiftly across wide, empty Crafts Street and into Plague Court again. For a wonder it was growing a little lighter. Looking upward, they saw stars. Yet there was no wind blowing from the north. The air was deathly still.

In their drunken preoccupation with the project at hand and mere locomotion, they did not look behind them. There the night-smog was thicker than ever. A high-circling nighthawk would have seen the stuff converging from all sections of Lankhmar in swift-moving black rivers and rivulets, heaping, eddying, swirling, dark, and reeking essence of Lankhmar from its branding irons, braziers, bonfires, kitchen fires, and warmth fires, kilns, forges, breweries, distilleries, junk, and garbage fires innumerable, sweating alchemists' and sorcerers' dens, crematoriums, charcoal burners' turfed mounds, all those and many more . . . converging purposefully on Dim Lane and particularly on the Silver Eel and the rickety house behind it. The closer to that center it got, the more substantial the smog became, eddy-strands and swirl-tatters tearing off and clinging like black cobwebs to rough stone corners and scraggly surfaced brick.

But the Mouser and Fafhrd merely exclaimed in mild, muted amazement at the stars and cautiously zigzagging across the street of the Thinkers, called Atheist Avenue by moralists, continued up Plague Court until it forked.

The Mouser chose the left branch, which trended northwest. "Death Alley."

After a curve and recurve, Cheap Street swung into sight about thirty paces ahead. The Mouser stopped at once and lightly threw his arm against Fafhrd's chest.

Clearly in view across Cheap Street was the wide, low, open doorway of Thieves' House, framed by grimy stone blocks. There led up to it two steps hollowed by the treadings of centuries. Orange-yellow light spilled out from bracketed torches inside. There was no porter or guard in sight, not even a watchdog on a chain. The effect was ominous.

"Now how do we get into the damn place?" Fafhrd demanded in a hoarse whisper. "That doorway stinks of traps."

The Mouser answered, scornful at last, "Why, we'll walk straight through that doorway you fear." He frowned. "Tap and hobble, rather. Come on, while I prepare us."

As he drew the skeptically grimacing Fafhrd back down Death Alley until all Cheap Street was again cut off from view, he explained, "We'll pretend to be beggars, members of their guild, which is but a branch of the Thieves' Guild and reports in to the Beggarmasters at Thieves' House. We'll be new members, who've gone out by day, so it'll not be expected that the Night Beggarmaster will know our looks."

"But we don't look like beggars," Fafhrd protested. "Beggars have awful sores and limbs all a-twist or lacking altogether."

"That's just what I'm going to take care of now," the Mouser chuckled, drawing Scalpel. Ignoring Fafhrd's backward step and wary glance, the Mouser gazed puzzledly at the long tapering strip of steel he'd bared, then with a happy nod unclipped from his belt Scalpel's scabbard furbished with ratskin, sheathed the sword and swiftly wrapped it up, hilt and all, spirally, with the wide ribbon of a bandage roll dug from his sack.

"There!" he said, knotting the bandage ends. "Now I've a tapping cane."

"What's that?" Fafhrd demanded. "And why?"

The Mouser laid a flimsy black rag across his own eyes and tied it fast behind his head.

"Because I'll be blind, that's why." He took a few shuffling steps, tapping the cobbles ahead with wrapped sword—gripping it by the quillons, or cross guard, so that the grip and pommel were up his sleeve—and groping ahead with his other hand. "That look all right to you?" he asked Fafhrd as he turned back. "Feels perfect to me. Bat-blind!—eh? Oh, don't fret, Fafhrd—the rag's but gauze. I can see through it—fairly well. Besides, I don't have to convince anyone inside Thieves' House I'm actually blind. Most Guildbeggars fake it, as you must know. Now what to do with you? Can't have you blind also—too obvious, might wake suspicion." He uncorked his jug and sucked inspiration. Fafhrd copied this action, on principle.

The Mouser smacked his lips and said, "I've got it! Fafhrd, stand on your right leg and double up your left behind you at the knee. Hold!—don't fall on me! Avaunt! But steady yourself by my shoulder. That's right. Now get that left foot higher.

We'll disguise your sword like mine, for a crutch cane—it's thicker and'll look just right. You can also steady yourself with your other hand on my shoulder as you hop—the halt leading the blind. But higher with that left foot! No, it just doesn't come off—I'll have to rope it. But first unclip your scabbard."

Soon the Mouser had Graywand and its scabbard in the same state as Scalpel and was tying Fafhrd's left ankle to his thigh, drawing the rope cruelly tight, though Fafhrd's wine-numbed nerves hardly registered it. Balancing himself with his steel-cored crutch cane as the Mouser worked, he swigged from his jug and pondered deeply.

Brilliant as the Mouser's plan undoubtedly was, there did seem to be drawbacks to it.

"Mouser," he said, "I don't know as I like having our swords tied up, so we can't draw 'em in emergency."

"We can still use 'em as clubs," the Mouser countered, his breath hissing between his teeth as he drew the last knot hard. "Besides, we'll have our knives. Say, pull your belt around until your knife is behind your back, so your robe will hide it sure. I'll do the same with Cat's Claw. Beggars don't carry weapons, at least in view. Stop drinking now, you've had enough. I myself need only a couple swallows more to reach my finest pitch."

"And I don't know as I like going hobbled into that den of cutthroats. I can hop amazingly fast, it's true, but not as fast as I can run. Is it really wise, think you?"

"You can slash yourself loose in an instant," the Mouser hissed with a touch of impatience and anger. "Aren't you willing to make the least sacrifice for art's sake?"

"Oh, very well," Fafhrd said, draining his jug and tossing it aside. "Yes, of course I am."

"Your complexion's too hale," the Mouser said, inspecting him critically. He touched up Fafhrd's features and hands with pale gray greasepaint, then added wrinkles with dark. "And your garb's too tidy." He scooped dirt from between the cobbles and smeared it on Fafhrd's robe, then tried to put a rip in it, but the material resisted. He shrugged and tucked his lightened sack under his belt.

"So's yours," Fafhrd observed, and crouching on his right leg got a good handful of muck himself. Heaving himself up with a mighty effort, he wiped the stuff off on the Mouser's cloak and grey silken jerkin too.

The small man cursed, but, "Dramatic consistency," Fafhrd reminded him. "Now come on, while our fires and our stinks are still high." And grasping hold of the Mouser's shoulder, he propelled himself rapidly toward Cheap Street, setting his bandaged sword between cobbles well ahead and taking mighty hops.

"Slow down, idiot," the Mouser cried softly, shuffling along with the speed almost of a skater to keep up, while tapping his (sword) cane like mad. "A cripple's supposed to be *feeble*—that's what draws the sympathy."

Fafhrd nodded wisely and slowed somewhat. The ominous empty doorway slid again into view. The Mouser tilted his jug to get the last of his wine, swallowed awhile, then choked sputteringly. Fafhrd snatched and drained the jug, then tossed it over shoulder to shatter noisily.

They hop-shuffled across Cheap Street and without pause up the two worn steps and through the doorway, past the exceptionally thick wall. Ahead was a long, straight, high-ceilinged corridor ending in a stairs and with doors spilling light at intervals and wall-set torches adding their flare, but empty all its length.

They had just got through the doorway when cold steel chilled the neck and pricked a shoulder of each of them. From just above, two voices commanded in unison, "Halt!"

Although fired—and fuddled—by fortified wine, they each had wit enough to freeze and then very cautiously look upward.

Two gaunt, scarred, exceptionally ugly faces, each topped by a gaudy scarf binding back hair, looked down at them from a big, deep niche just above the doorway. Two bent, gnarly arms thrust down the swords that still pricked them.

"Gone out with the noon beggar-batch, eh?" one of them observed. "Well, you'd better have a high take to justify your tardy return. The Night Beggarmaster's on a Whore Street furlough. Report above to Krovas. Gods, you stink! Better clean up first, or Krovas will have you bathed in live steam. Begone!"

The Mouser and Fafhrd shuffled and hobbled forward at their most authentic. One niche-guard cried after them, "Relax, boys! You don't have to put it on here."

"Practice makes perfect," the Mouser called back in a quavering voice. Fafhrd's fingerends dug his shoulder warningly. They moved along somewhat more naturally, so far as Fafhrd's tied-up leg allowed. Truly, thought Fafhrd, Kos of the Dooms seemed to be leading him direct to Krovas and perhaps headchopping would be the order of the night. And now he and the Mouser began to hear voices, mostly curt and clipped ones, and other noises.

They passed some doorways they'd liked to have paused at, yet the most they dared do was slow down a bit more.

Very interesting were some of those activities. In one room young boys were being trained to pick pouches and slit purses. They'd approach from behind an instructor, and if he heard scuff of bare foot or felt touch of dipping hand—or, worst, heard *clunk* of dropped leaden mock-coin—that boy would be thwacked.

In a second room, older student thieves were doing laboratory work in lock picking. One group was being lectured by a grimy-handed graybeard, who was taking apart a most complex lock piece by weighty piece.

In a third, thieves were eating at long tables. The odors were tempting, even to men full of booze. The Guild did well by its members.

In a fourth, the floor was padded in part and instruction was going on in slipping, dodging, ducking, tumbling, tripping, and otherwise foiling pursuit. A voice like a sergeant-major's rasped, "Nah, nah, nah! You couldn't give your crippled grandmother the slip. I said duck, not genuflect to holy Arth. Now this time—"

By that time the Mouser and Fafhrd were halfway up the end stairs, Fafhrd vaulting somewhat laboriously as he grasped curving banister and swaddled sword.

The second floor duplicated the first, but was as luxurious as the other had been bare. Down the long corridor lamps and filigreed incense pots pendent from the ceiling alternated, diffusing a mild light and spicy smell. The walls were richly draped, the floor thick-carpeted. Yet this corridor was empty too and, moreover, *completely* silent. After a glance at each other, they started off boldly.

The first door, wide open, showed an untenanted room full of racks of garments, rich and plain, spotless and filthy, also wig stands, shelves of beards and such. A disguising room clearly.

The Mouser darted in and out to snatch up a large green flask from the nearest table. He unstoppered and sniffed it. A rotten-sweet gardenia-reek contended with the nose-sting of spirits of wine. The Mouser sloshed his and Fafhrd's fronts with this dubious perfume.

"Antidote to muck," he explained with the pomp of a physician, stoppering the flask. "Don't want to be parboiled by Krovas. No, no, no."

Two figures appeared at the far end of the corridor and came toward them. The Mouser hid the flask under his cloak, holding it between elbow and side, and he and Fafhrd continued boldly onward.

The next three doorways they passed were shut by heavy doors. As they neared the fifth, the two approaching figures, coming on arm-in-arm, became distinct. Their clothing was that of noblemen, but their faces those of thieves. They were frowning with indignation and suspicion, too, at the Mouser and Fafhrd.

Just then, from somewhere between the two man-pairs, a voice began to speak words in a strange tongue, using the rapid monotone priests employ in a routine service, or some sorcerers in their incantations.

The two richly clad thieves slowed at the seventh doorway and looked in. Their progress ceased altogether. Their necks strained, their eyes widened. They paled. Then of a sudden they hastened onward, almost running, and bypassed Fafhrd and the Mouser as if they were furniture. The incantatory voice drummed on without missing a beat.

The fifth doorway was shut, but the sixth was open. The Mouser peeked in with one eye, his nose brushing the jamb. Then he stepped forward and gazed inside with entranced expression, pushing the black rag up onto his forehead for better vision. Fafhrd joined him.

It was a large room, empty so far as could be told of human and animal life, but filled with most interesting things. From knee-height up, the entire far wall was a map of the city of Lankhmar. Every building and street seemed depicted, down to the meanest hovel and narrowest court. There were signs of recent erasure and redrawing at many spots, and here and there little colored hieroglyphs of mysterious import.

The floor was marble, the ceiling blue as lapis lazuli. The side walls were thickly hung, the one with all manner of thieves' tools, from a huge, thick, pry-bar that looked as if it could unseat the universe, to a rod so slim it might be an elf-queen's wand and seemingly designed to telescope out and fish from a distance for precious gauds on milady's spindle-legged, ivory-topped vanity table. The other wall had padlocked to it all sorts of quaint, gold-gleaming and jewel-flashing objects, evidently mementos chosse for their oddity from the spoils of memorable burglaries, from a female mask of thin gold, breathlessly beautiful in its features and contours but thickly set with rubies simulating the spots of the pox in its fever stage, to a knife whose blade was wedge-shaped diamonds set side by side and this diamond cutting-edge looking razor-sharp.

In the center of the room was a bare round table of ebony and ivory squares. About it were set seven straight-backed but well-padded chairs, the one facing the map and away from the Mouser and Fafhrd being higher backed and wider armed than the others—a chief's chair, likely that of Krovas.

The Mouser tiptoed forward, irresistibly drawn, but Fafhrd's left hand clamped down on his shoulder.

Scowling his disapproval, the Northerner brushed down the black rag over the Mouser's eyes again and with his crutch-hand thumbed ahead, then set off in that direction in most carefully calculated, silent hops. With a shrug of disappointment the Mouser followed.

As soon as they had turned away from the doorway, a neatly black-bearded, crop-haired head came like a serpent's around the side of the highest-backed chair and gazed after them from deep-sunken yet glinting eyes. Next a snake-supple, long hand followed the head out, crossed thin lips with ophidian forefinger for silence, and then finger-beckoned the two pairs of dark-tunicked men who were standing to either side of the doorway, their backs to the corridor wall, each of the four gripping a curvy knife in one hand and a dark leather, lead-weighted bludgeon in the other.

When Fafhrd was halfway to the seventh doorway, from which the monotonous yet sinister recitation continued to well, there shot out through it a slender, whey-faced youth, his narrow hands clapped over his mouth, under terror-wide eyes, as if to shut in screams or vomit, and with a broom clamped in an armpit, so that he seemed a bit like a young warlock about to take to the air. He dashed past Fafhrd and the Mouser and away, his racing footsteps sounding rapid-dull on the carpeting and hollow-sharp on the stairs before dying away.

Fafhrd gazed back at the Mouser with a grimace and shrug, then squatting one-legged until the knee of his bound-up leg touched the floor, advanced half his face past the doorjamb. After a bit, without otherwise changing position, he beckoned the Mouser to approach. The latter slowly thrust half his face past the jamb, just above Fafhrd's.

What they saw was a room somewhat smaller than that of the great map and lit by central lamps that burnt blue-white instead of customary yellow. The floor was marble, darkly colorful and complexly whorled. The dark walls were hung with astrological and anthropomantic charts and instruments of magic and shelved with cryptically labeled porcelain jars and also with vitreous flasks and glass pipes of the oddest shapes, some filled with colored fluids, but many gleamingly empty. At the foot of the walls, where the shadows were thickest, broken and discarded stuff was irregularly heaped, as if swept out of the way and forgotten, and here and there opened a large rathole.

In the center of the room and brightly illuminated by contrast was a long table with thick top and many stout legs. The Mouser thought fleetingly of a centipede and then of the bar at the Eel, for the table top was densely stained and scarred by many a spilt elixir and many a deep black burn by fire or acid or both.

In the midst of the table an alembic was working. The lamp's flame—deep blue, this one—kept a-boil in the large crystal cucurbit a dark, viscid fluid with here and there diamond glints. From out of the thick, seething stuff, strands of a darker vapor streamed upward to crowd through the cucurbit's narrow mouth and stain—oddly, with bright scarlet—the transparent head and then, dead black now, flow down the narrow pipe from the head into a spherical crystal receiver, larger even than the cucurbit, and there curl and weave about like so many coils of living black cord—an endless, skinny, ebon serpent.

Behind the left end of the table stood a tall, yet hunchbacked man in black robe and hood, which shadowed more than hid a face of which the most prominent features were a long, thick, pointed nose with out-jutting, almost chinless mouth. His complexion was sallow-gray like sandy clay. A short-haired, bristly, gray beard grew high on his wide cheeks. From under a receding forehead and bushy gray brows, wide-set eyes looked intently down at an age-browned scroll, which his disgustingly small clubhands, knuckles big, short backs gray-bristled, ceaselessly unrolled and rolled up again. The only move his eyes ever made, beside the short side-to-side one as he read the lines he was rapidly intoning, was an occasional glance at the alembic.

On the other end of the table, beady eyes darting from the sorcerer to the alembic and back again, crouched a small black beast, the first glimpse of which made Fafhrd dig fingers painfully into the Mouser's shoulder and the latter almost gasp, but not from the pain. It was most like a rat, yet it had a higher forehead and closer-set eyes, while its forepaws, which it constantly rubbed together in what seemed restless glee, looked like tiny copies of the sorcerer's clubhands.

Simultaneously yet independently, Fafhrd and the Mouser each became certain it was the beast which had gutter-escorted Slivikin and his mate, then fled, and each recalled what Ivrian had said about a witch's familiar and Vlana about the likelihood of Krovas employing a warlock.

The tempo of the incantation quickened; the blue-white flames brightened and hissed audibly; the fluid in the cucurbit grew thick as lava; great bubbles formed and loudly broke; the black rope in the receiver writhed like a nest of snakes; there was an increasing sense of invisible presences; the supernatural tension grew almost unendurable, and Fafhrd and the Mouser were hard put to keep silent the open-mouthed gapes by which they now breathed, and each feared his heartbeat could be heard cubits away.

Abruptly the incantation peaked and broke off, like a drum struck very hard, then instantly silenced by palm and fingers outspread against the head. With a bright flash and dull explosion, cracks innumerable appeared in the cucurbit; its crystal became white and opaque, yet it did not shatter or drip. The head lifted a span, hung there, fell back. While two black nooses appeared among the coils in the receiver and suddenly narrowed until they were only two big black knots.

The sorcerer grinned, let the end of the parchment roll up with a snap, and shifted his gaze from the receiver to his familiar, while the latter chattered shrilly and bounded up and down in rapture.

"Silence, Slivikin! Come now *your* time to race and strain and sweat," the sorcerer cried, speaking pidgin Lankhmarese now, but so rapidly and in so squeakingly high-pitched a voice that Fafhrd and the Mouser could barely follow him. They did, however, both realize they had been completely mistaken as to the identity of Slivikin. In moment of disaster, the fat thief had called to the witch-beast for help rather than to his human comrade.

"Yes, master," Slivikin squeaked back no less clearly, in an instant revising the Mouser's opinions about talking animals. He continued in the same fifelike, fawning tones, "Harkening in obedience, Hristomilo."

Hristomilo ordered in whiplash pipings, "To your appointed work! See to it you summon an ample sufficiency of feasters!—I want the bodies stripped to skeletons, so the bruises of the enchanted smog and all evidence of death by suffocation will be vanished utterly. But forget not the loot! On your mission, now—depart!"

Slivikin, who at every command had bobbed his head in manner reminiscent of his bouncing, now squealed, "I'll see it done!" and gray lightninglike, leaped a long leap to the floor and down an inky rathole.

Hristomilo, rubbing together his disgusting clubhands much as Slivikin had his, cried chucklingly, "What Slevyas lost, my magic has re-won!"

Fafhrd and the Mouser drew back out of the doorway, partly for fear of being seen, partly in revulsion from what they had seen and heard, and in poignant if useless pity for Slevyas, whoever he might be, and for the other unknown victims of the ratlike and conceivable rat-related sorcerer's death spells, poor strangers already dead and due to have their flesh eaten from their bones.

Fafhrd wrested the green bottle from the Mouser and, though almost gagging on the rotten-flowery reek, gulped a large, stinging mouthful. The Mouser couldn't quite bring himself to do the same, but was comforted by the spirits of wine he inhaled.

Then he saw, beyond Fafhrd, standing before the doorway to the map room, a richly clad man with gold-hilted knife jewel-scabbarded at his side. His sunken-eyed face was prematurely wrinkled by responsibility, overwork, and authority, and framed by neatly cropped black hair and beard. Smiling, he silently beckoned them with a serpentine gesture.

The Mouser and Fafhrd obeyed, the latter returning the green bottle to the former, who recapped it and thrust it under his left elbow with well-concealed irritation.

Each guessed their summoner was Krovas, the Guild's Grandmaster. Once again Fafhrd marveled, as he hobbledehoyed along, reeling and belching, how Kos or the Fates were guiding him to his target tonight. The Mouser, more alert and more apprehensive too, was reminding himself that they had been directed by the niche-guards to report to Krovas, so that the situation, if not developing quite in accord with his own misty plans, was still not deviating disastrously.

Yet not even his alertness, nor Fafhrd's primeval instincts, gave them forewarning as they followed Krovas into the map room.

Two steps inside, each of them was shoulder-grabbed and blugdeon-menaced by a pair of ruffians further armed with knives tucked in their belts.

"All secure, Grandmaster," one of the ruffians rapped out.

Krovas swung the highest-backed chair around and sat down, eying them coolly.

"What brings two stinking, drunken beggar-guildsmen into the top-restricted precincts of the masters?" he asked quietly.

The Mouser felt the sweat of relief bead his forehead. The disguises he had brilliantly conceived were still working, taking in even the head man, though he had spotted Fafhrd's tipsiness. Resuming his blind-man manner, he quavered, "We were directed by the guard above the Cheap Street door to report to you in person, great Krovas, the Night Beggarmaster being on furlough for reasons of sexual hygiene. Tonight we've made a good haul!" And fumbling in his purse, ignoring as far as possible the tightened grip on his shoulders, he brought out a golden coin and displayed it tremble-handed.

"Spare me your inexpert acting," Krovas said sharply. "I'm not one of your marks. And take that rag off your eyes."

The Mouser obeyed and stood to attention again insofar as his pinioning would permit, and smiling the more seeming carefree because of his reawakening uncertainties. Conceivably he wasn't doing quite as brilliantly as he'd thought.

Krovas leaned forward and said placidly yet piercingly, "Granted you were so ordered, why were you spying into a room beyond this one when I spotted you?"

"We saw brave thieves flee from that room," the Mouser answered pat. "Fearing that some danger threatened the Guild, my comrade and I investigated, ready to scotch it."

"But what we saw and heard only perplexed us, great sir," Fafhrd appended quite smoothly.

"I didn't ask you, sot. Speak when you're spoken to," Krovas snapped at him. Then, to the Mouser, "You're an overweening rogue, most presumptuous for your rank. Beggars claim to protect thieves indeed! I'm of a mind to have you both flogged for your spying, and again for your drunkenness, aye, and once more for your lies."

In a flash the Mouser decided that further insolence—and lying, too—rather than fawning, was what the situation required. “I am a most presumptuous rogue indeed, sir,” he said smugly. Then he set his face solemn. “But now I see the time has come when I must speak darkest truth entire. The Day Beggarmaster suspects a plot against your own life, sir, by one of your highest and closest lieutenants—one you trust so well you’d not believe it, sir. He told us that! So he set me and my comrade secretly to guard you and sniff out the verminous villain.”

“More and clumsier lies!” Krovas snarled, but the Mouser saw his face grow pale. The Grandmaster half rose from his seat. “Which lieutenant?”

The Mouser grinned and relaxed. His two captors gazed sidewise at him curiously, loosing their grip a little. Fafhrd’s pair seemed likewise intrigued.

The Mouser then asked coolly, “Are you questioning me as a trusty spy or a pinioned liar? If the latter, I’ll not insult you with one more word.”

Krovas’ face darkened. “Boy!” he called. Through the curtains of an inner doorway, a youth with the dark complexion of a Kleshite and clad only in a black loincloth sprang to kneel before Krovas, who ordered, “Summon first my sorcerer, next the thieves Slevyas and Fissif,” whereupon the dark youth dashed into the corridor.

Krovas hesitated a moment in thought, then shot a hand toward Fafhrd. “What do you know of this, drunkard? Do you support your mate’s crazy tale?”

Fafhrd merely sneered his face and folded his arms, the still-slack grip of his captors permitting it, his sword-crutch hanging against his body from his lightly gripping hand. Then he scowled as there came a sudden shooting pain in his numbed, bound-up left leg, which he had forgotten.

Krovas raised a clenched fist and himself wholly from his chair, in prelude to some fearsome command—likely that Fafhrd and the Mouser be tortured, but at that moment Hristomilo came gliding into the room, his feet presumably taking swift, but very short steps—at any rate his black robe hung undisturbed to the marble floor despite his slithering speed.

There was a shock at his entrance. All eyes in the map room followed him, breaths were held, and the Mouser and Fafhrd felt the horny hands that gripped them shake just a little. Even Krovas's tense expression became also guardedly uneasy.

Outwardly oblivious to his reaction to his appearance, Hristomilo, smiling thin-lipped, halted close to one side of Krovas' chair and inclined his hood-shadowed rodent face in the ghost of a bow.

Krovas asked sharply yet nervously, gesturing toward the Mouser and Fafhrd, "Do you know these two?"

Hristomilo nodded decisively. "They just now peered a befuddled eye each at me," he said, "whilst I was about that business we spoke of. I'd have shooed them off, reported them, save such action would have broken my spell, put my words out of time with the alembic's workings. The one's a Northerner, the other's features have a southern cast—from Tovilyis or near, most like. Both younger than their now-looks. Freelance bravoes, I'd judge 'em, the sort the Brotherhood hires as extras when they get at once several big guard and escort jobs. Clumsily disguised now, of course, as beggars."

Fafhrd by yawning, the Mouser by pitying headshake tried to convey that all this was so much poor guesswork. The Mouser even added a warning glare, brief as lightning, to suggest to Krovas that the conspiring lieutenant might be the Grandmaster's own sorcerer.

"That's all I can tell you without reading their minds," Hristomilo concluded. "Shall I fetch my lights and mirrors?"

"Not yet." Krovas faced the Mouser and said, "Now speak truth, or have it magicked from you and then be whipped to death. Which of my lieutenants were you set to spy on by the Day Beggarmaster? But you're lying about that commission, I believe?"

"Oh, no," the Mouser denied it guilelessly. "We reported our every act to the Day Beggarmaster and he approved them, told us to spy our best and gather every scrap of fact and rumor we could about the conspiracy."

"And he told me not a word about it!" Krovas rapped out. "If true, I'll have Bannat's head for this! But you're lying, aren't you?"

As the Mouser gazed with wounded eyes at Krovas, a portly man limped past the doorway with help of a gilded staff. He moved with silence and aplomb.

But Krovas saw him. "Night Beggarmaster!" he called sharply. The limping man stopped, turned, came crippling majestically through the door. Krovas stabbed a finger at the Mouser, then Fafhrd. "Do you know these two, Flim?"

The Night Beggarmaster unhurriedly studied each for a space, then shook his head with its turban of cloth of gold. "Never seen either before. What are they? Fink beggars?"

"But Flim wouldn't know us," the Mouser explained desperately, feeling everything collapsing in on him and Fafhrd. "All our contacts were with Bannat alone."

Flim said quietly, "Bannat's been abed with the swamp ague this past ten-day. Meanwhile I have been Day Beggarmaster as well as Night."

At that moment Slevyas and Fissif came hurrying in behind Flim. The tall thief bore on his jaw a bluish lump. The fat thief's head was bandaged above his darting eyes. He pointed quickly at Fafhrd and the Mouser and cried, "There are the two that slugged us, took our Jengao loot, and slew our escort."

The Mouser lifted his elbow and the green bottle crashed to shards at his feet on the hard marble. Gardenia-reek sprang swiftly through the air. But more swiftly still the Mouser, shaking off the careless hold of his startled guards, sprang toward Krovas, clubbing his wrapped-up sword.

With startling speed Flim thrust out his gilded staff, tripping the Mouser, who went heels over head, midway seeking to change his involuntary somersault into a voluntary one.

Meanwhile Fafhrd lurched heavily against his left-hand captor, at the same time swinging bandaged Graywand strongly upward to strike his right-hand captor under the jaw. Regaining his one-legged balance with a mighty contortion, he hopped for the loot-wall behind him.

Slevyas made for the wall of thieves' tools, and with a muscle-cracking effort wrenched the great pry-bar from its padlocked ring.

Scrambling to his feet after a poor landing in front of Krovas's chair, the Mouser found it empty and the Thief King in a half-crouch behind it, gold-hilted dagger drawn, deep-sunk eyes coldly battle-wild. Spinning around, he saw Fafhrd's guards on the floor, the one sprawled senseless, the other starting to scramble up, while the great Northerner, his back against the wall of weird jewelry, menaced the whole room with wrapped-up Graywand and with his long knife, jerked from its scabbard behind him.

Likewise drawing Cat's Claw, the Mouser cried in trumpet-voice of battle, "Stand aside, all! He's gone mad! I'll hamstring his good leg for you! And racing through the press and between his own two guards, who still appeared to hold him in some awe, he launched himself with flashing dirk at Fafhrd, praying that the Northerner, drunk now with battle as well as wine and poisonous perfume, would recognize him and guess his stratagem.

Graywand slashed well above his ducking head. His new friend not only guessed, but was playing up—and not just missing by accident, the Mouser hoped. Stooping low by the wall, he cut the lashings on Fafhrd's left leg. Graywand and Fafhrd's long knife continued to spare him. Springing up, he headed for the corridor, crying overshoulder to Fafhrd, "Come on!"

Hristomilo stood well out of his way, quietly observing. Fissif scuttled toward safety. Krovas stayed behind his chair, shouting, "Stop them! Head them off!"

The three remaining ruffian guards, at last beginning to recover their fighting-wits, gathered to oppose the Mouser. But menacing them with swift feints of his dirk, he slowed them and darted between—and then just in the nick of time knocked aside with a downsweep of wrapped-up Scalpel Flim's gilded staff, thrust once again to trip him.

All this gave Slevyas time to return from the tools-wall and aim at the Mouser a great swinging blow with the massive pry-bar. But even as that blow started, a very long, bandaged and scabbarded sword on a very long arm thrust over the Mouser's shoulder and solidly and heavily poked Slevyas high on the chest, jolting him backwards, so that the pry-bar's swing was short and sung past harmlessly.

Then the Mouser found himself in the corridor and Fafhrd beside him, though for some weird reason still only hopping. The Mouser pointed toward the stairs. Fafhrd nodded, but delayed to reach high, still on one leg only, and rip off the nearest wall a dozen yards of heavy drapes, which he threw across the corridor to baffle pursuit.

They reached the stairs and started up the next flight, the Mouser in advance. There were cries behind, some muffled.

"Stop hopping, Fafhrd!" the Mouser ordered querulously. "You've got two legs again."

"Yes, and the other's still dead," Fafhrd complained. "Ahh! Now feeling begins to return to it."

A thrown knife whished between them and dully clinked as it hit the wall point-first and stone-powder flew. Then they were around the bend.

Two more empty corridors, two more curving flights, and then they saw above them on the last landing a stout ladder mounting to a dark, square hole in the roof. A thief with hair bound back by a colorful handkerchief—it appeared to be the door guards' identification—menaced the Mouser with drawn sword, but when he saw that there were two of them both charging him determinedly with shining knives and strange staves or clubs, he turned and ran down the last empty corridor.

The Mouser, followed closely by Fafhrd, rapidly mounted the ladder and vaulted up through the hatch into the star-crusted night.

He found himself near the unrailed edge of a slate roof which slanted enough to have made it look most fearsome to a novice roof-walker, but safe as houses to a veteran.

Turning back at a bumping sound, he saw Fafhrd prudently hoisting the ladder. Just as he got it free, a knife flashed up close past him out of the hatch.

It clattered down near them and slid off the roof. The Mouser loped south across the slates and was halfway from the hatch to that end of the roof when the faint chink came of the knife striking the cobbles of Murder Alley.

Fafhrd followed more slowly, in part perhaps from a lesser experience of roofs, in part because he still limped a bit to favor his left leg, and in part because he was carrying the heavy ladder balanced on his right shoulder.

"We won't need that," the Mouser called back.

Without hesitation Fafhrd heaved it joyously over the edge. By the time it crashed in Murder Alley, the Mouser was leaping down two yards and across a gap of one to the next roof, of opposite and lesser pitch. Fafhrd landed beside him.

The Mouser led them at almost a run through a sooty forest of chimneys, chimney pots, ventilators with tails that made them always face the wind, black-legged cisterns, hatch covers, bird houses, and pigeon traps across five roofs, until they reached the Street of the Thinkers at a point where it was crossed by a roofed passageway much like the one at Rokkermas and Slaarg's.

While they crossed it at a crouching lope, something hissed close past them and clattered ahead. As they leaped down from the roof of the bridge, three more somethings hissed over their heads to clatter beyond. One rebounded from a square chimney almost to the Mouser's feet. He picked it up expecting a stone, and was surprised by the greater weight of a leaden ball big as two doubled-up fingers.

"They," he said jerking thumb overshoulder, "lost no time in getting slingers on the roof. When roused, they're good."

Southeast then through another black chimney-forest toward a point on Cheap Street where upper stories overhung the street so much on either side that it would be easy to leap the gap. During this roof-traverse, an advancing front of night-smog, dense enough to make them cough and wheeze, engulfed them and for perhaps sixty heartbeats the Mouser had to slow to a shuffle and feel his way, Fafhrd's hand on his shoulder. Just short of Cheap Street they came abruptly and completely out of the smog and saw the stars again, while the black front rolled off northward behind them.

"Now what the devil was that?' Fafhrd asked and the Mouser shrugged.

A nighthawk would have seen a vast thick hoop of black night-smog blowing out in all directions from a center near the Silver Eel.

East of Cheap Street the two comrades soon made their way to the ground, landing back in Plague Court.

Then at last they looked at each other and their trammeled swords and their filthy faces and clothing made dirtier still by roof-soot, and they laughed and laughed and laughed, Fafhrd roaring still as he bent over to massage his left leg above and below knee. This hooting self-mockery continued while they unwrapped their swords—the Mouser as if his were a surprise package—and clipped their scabbards once more to their belts. Their exertions had burnt out of them the last mote and atomy of strong wine and even stronger stenchful perfume, but they felt no desire whatever for more drink, only the urge to get home and eat hugely and guzzle hot, bitter gahveh, and tell their lovely girls at length the tale of their mad adventure.

They loped on side by side.

Free of night-smog and drizzled with starlight, their cramped surroundings seemed much less stinking and oppressive than when they had set out. Even Bones Alley had a freshness to it.

They hastened up the long, creaking, broken-treaded stairs with an easy carefulness, and when they were both on the porch, the Mouser shoved at the door to open it with surprise-swiftness.

It did not budge.

"Bolted," he said to Fafhrd shortly. He noted now there was hardly any light at all coming through the cracks around the door, nor had any been noticeable through the lattices—at most, a faint orange-red glow. Then with sentimental grin and in fond voice in which only the ghost of uneasiness lurked, he said, "They've gone to sleep, the unworrying wenches!" He knocked loudly thrice and then cupping his lips called softly at the door crack, "Hola, Ivrian! I'm home safe. Hail, Vlana! Your man's done you proud, felling Guild-thieves innumerable with one foot tied behind his back!"

There was no sound whatever from inside—that is, if one discounted a rustling so faint it was impossible to be sure of it.

Fafhrd was wrinkling his nostrils. "I smell vermin."

The Mouser banged on the door again. Still no response.

Fafhrd motioned him out of the way, hunching his big shoulder to crash the portal.

The Mouser shook his head and with a deft tap, slide, and a tug removed a brick that a moment before had looked to be a firm-set part of the wall beside the door. He reached in all his arm. There was the scrape of a bolt being withdrawn, then another, then a third. He swiftly recovered his arm and the door swung fully inward at touch.

But neither he nor Fafhrd rushed in at once, as both had intended to, for the indefinable scent of danger and the unknown came puffing out along with an increased reek of filthy beast and a slight, sickening sweet scent that though female was no decent female perfume.

They could see the room faintly by the orange glow coming from the small oblong of the open door of the little, well-blacked stove. Yet the oblong did not sit properly upright but was unnaturally a-tilt—clearly the stove had been half overset and now leaned against a side wall of the fireplace, its small door fallen open in that direction.

By itself alone, that unnatural angle conveyed the entire impact of a universe overturned.

The orange glow showed the carpets oddly rucked up with here and there ragged black circles a palm's breadth across, the neatly stacked candles scattered about below their shelves along with some of the jars and enameled boxes, and—above all—two black, low, irregular, longish heaps, the one by the fireplace, the other half on the golden couch, half at its foot.

From each heap there stared at the Mouser and Fafhrd innumerable pairs of tiny, rather widely set, furnace-red eyes.

On the thickly carpeted floor on the other side of the fireplace was a silver cobweb—a fallen silver cage, but no love birds sang from it.

There was the faint scrape of metal as Fafhrd made sure Graywand was loose in his scabbard.

As if that tiny sound had beforehand been chosen as the signal for attack, each instantly whipped out sword and they advanced side by side into the room, warily at first, testing the floor with each step.

At the screech of the swords being drawn, the tiny furnace-red eyes had winked and shifted restlessly, and now with the two men's approach they swiftly scattered pattering, pair by red pair, each pair at the forward end of a small, low, slender, hairless-tailed black body, and each making for one of the black circles in the rugs, where they vanished.

Indubitably the black circles were ratholes newly gnawed up through the floor and rugs, while the red-eyed creatures were black rats.

Fafhrd and the Mouser sprang forward, slashing and chopping at them in a frenzy, cursing and human-snarling besides.

They sundered few. The rats fled with preternatural swiftness, most of them disappearing down holes near the walls and the fireplace.

Also Fafhrd's first frantic chop went through the floor and on his third step, with an ominous crack and splintering, his leg plunged through the floor to his hip. The Mouser darted past him unmindful of further crackings.

Fafhrd heaved out his trapped leg, not even noting the splinter-scratches it got and as unmindful as the Mouser of the continuing creakings. The rats were gone. He lunged after his comrade, who had thrust a bunch of kindlers into the stove, to make more light.

The horror was that, although the rats were all gone, the two longish heaps remained, although considerably diminished and, as now shown clearly by the yellow flames leaping from the titled black door, changed in hue—no longer were the heaps red-beaded black, but a mixture of gleaming black and snow-serpent white, and the reds of stockings and blood and bloody flesh and bone.

Although hands and feet had been gnawed bone-naked, and bodies tunneled heart-deep, the two faces had been spared. But that was not good, for they were the parts purple-blue from death by strangulation, lips drawn back, eyes bulging, all features contorted in agony. Only the black and very dark brown hair gleamed unchanged—that and the white, white teeth.

As each man stared down at his love, unable to look away despite the waves of horror and grief and rage washing higher and higher in him, each saw a tiny black strand uncurl from the black depression ringing each throat and drift off, dissipating, toward the open door behind them—two strands of night-smog.

With a crescendo of crackings the floor sagged three spans more in the center before arriving at a new temporary stability.

Edges of centrally tortured minds noted details: that Vlana's silver-hilted dagger skewered to the floor a rat, which, likely enough, overeager had approached too closely before the night-smog had done its magic work. That her belt and pouch were gone. That the blue-enameled box inlaid with silver, in which Ivrian had put the Mouser's share of the highjacked jewels, was gone too.

The Mouser and Fafhrd lifted to each other white, drawn faces which were quite mad, yet completely joined in understanding and purpose. No need for Fafhrd to explain why he stripped off his robe and hood, or why he jerked up Vlana's dagger, snapped the rat off it with a wrist-flick, and thrust it in his belt. No need for the Mouser to tell why he searched out a half dozen jars of oil and after smashing three of them in front of the flaming stove, paused, thought, and stuck the other three in the sack at his waist, adding to them the remaining kindlers and the fire-pot, brimmed with red coals, its top lashed down tight.

Then, still without word exchanged, the Mouser reached into the fireplace and without a wince at the burning metal's touch, deliberately tipped the flaming stove forward, so that it fell door-down on oil-soaked rugs. Yellow flames sprang up around him.

They turned and raced for the door. With louder crackings than any before, the floor collapsed. They desperately scrambled their way up a steep hill of sliding carpets and reached door and porch just before all behind them gave way and the flaming rugs and stove and all the firewood and candles and the golden couch and all the little tables and boxes and jars—and the unthinkably mutilated bodies of their first loves—cascaded into the dry, dusty, cobweb-choked room below, and the great flames of a cleansing or at least obliterating cremation began to flare upward.

They plunged down the stairs which tore away from the wall and collapsed in the dark as they reached the ground.

They had to fight their way over the wreckage to get to Bones Alley.

By then flames were darting their bright lizard-tongues out of the shuttered attic windows and the boarded-up ones in the story just below. By the time they reached Plague Court, running side by side at top speed, the Silver Eel's fire alarm was clanging cacophonously behind them.

They were still sprinting when they took the Death Alley fork. Then the Mouser grappled Fafhrd and forced him to a halt. The big man struck out, cursing insanely, and only desisted—his white face still a lunatic's—when the Mouser cried panting, "Only ten heartbeats to arm us!"

He pulled the sack from his belt and keeping tight hold of its neck, crashed it on the cobbles—hard enough to smash not only the bottles of oil, but also the fire-pot, for the sack was soon flaming at its base.

Then he drew gleaming Scalpel and Fafhrd Graywand, and they raced on, the Mouser swinging his sack in a great circle beside him to fan its flames. It was a veritable ball of fire burning his left hand as they dashed across Cheap Street and into Thieves' House, and the Mouser, leaping high, swung it up into the great niche above the doorway and let go of it.

The niche-guards screeched in surprise and pain at the fiery invader of their hidey-hole.

Student thieves poured out of the doors ahead at the screeching and foot-pounding, and then poured back as they saw the fierce point of flames and the two demon-faced on-comers brandishing their long, shining swords.

One skinny little apprentice—he could hardly have been ten years old—lingered too long. Graywand thrust him pitilessly through, as his big eyes bulged and his small mouth gaped in horror and plea to Fafhrd for mercy.

Now from ahead of them there came a weird, wailing call, hollow and hair-raising, and doors began to thud shut instead of spewing forth the armed guards Fafhrd and the Mouser prayed would appear to be skewered by their swords. Also, despite the long, bracketed torches looking newly renewed, the corridor was darkening.

The reason for the last became clear as they plunged up the stairs. Strands of night-smog appeared in the stairwell, materializing from nothing, or the air.

The strands grew longer and more tangible. They touched and clung nastily. In the corridor above they were forming from wall to wall and from ceiling to floor, like a gigantic cobweb, and were becoming so substantial that the Mouser and Fafhrd had to slash them to get through, or so their two maniac minds believed. The black web muffled a little a repetition of the eerie, wailing call, which came from the seventh door ahead and this time ended in a gleeful chittering and cackling as insane as the emotions of the two attackers.

Here, too, doors were thudding shut. In an ephemeral flash of rationality, it occurred to the Mouser that it was not he and Fafhrd the thieves feared, for they had not been seen yet, but rather Hristomilo and his magic, even though working in defense of Thieves' House.

Even the map room whence counterattack would most likely erupt, was closed off by a huge oaken, iron-studded door.

They were now twice slashing the black, clinging, rope-thick spiderweb for every single step they drove themselves forward. While midway between the map and magic rooms, there was forming on the inky web, ghostly at first but swiftly growing more substantial, a black spider as big as a wolf.

The Mouser slashed heavy cobweb before it, dropped back two steps, then hurled himself at it in a high leap. Scalpel thrust through it, striking amidst its eight new-formed jet eyes, and it collapsed like a daggered bladder, loosing a vile stink.

Then he and Fafhrd were looking into the magic room, the alchemist's chamber. It was much as they had seen it before, except some things were doubled, or multiplied even further.

On the long table two blue-boiled cucurbits bubbled and roiled, their heads shooting out a solid, writhing rope more swiftly than moves the black swamp-cobra, which can run down a man—and not into twin receivers, but into the open air of the room (if any of the air in Thieves' House could have been called open then) to weave a barrier between their swords and Hristomilo, who once more stood tall though hunchbacked over his sorcerous, brown parchment, though this time his exultant gaze was chiefly fixed on Fafhrd and the Mouser, with only an occasional downward glance at the text of the spell he drummingly intoned.

While at the other end of the table, in web-free space, there bounced not only Slivikin, but also a huge rat matching him in size in all members except the head.

From the ratholes at the foot of the walls, red eyes glittered and gleamed in pairs.

With a bellow of rage Fafhrd began slashing at the black barrier, but the ropes were replaced from the cucurbit heads as swiftly as he sliced them, while the cut ends, instead of drooping slackly, now began to strain hungrily toward him like constrictive snakes or strangle-vines.

He suddenly shifted Graywand to his left hand, drew his long knife and hurled it at the sorcerer. Flashing toward its mark, it cut through three strands, was deflected and slowed by a fourth and fifth, almost halted by a sixth, and ended hanging futilely in the curled grip of a seventh.

Hristomilo laughed cacklingly and grinned, showing his huge upper incisors, while Slivikin chattered in ecstasy and bounded the higher.

The Mouser hurled Cat's Claw with no better result—worse, indeed, since his action gave two darting smog-strands time to curl hamperingly around his sword-hand and strangling around his neck. Black rats came racing out of the big holes at the cluttered base of the walls.

Meanwhile other strands snaked around Fafhrd's ankles, knees and left arm, almost toppling him. But even as he fought for balance, he jerked Vlana's dagger from his belt and raised it over his shoulder, its silver hilt glowing, its blade brown with dried rat's-blood.

The grin left Hristomilo's face as he saw it. The sorcerer screamed strangely and importuningly then, and drew back from his parchment and the table, and raised clawed clubhands to ward off doom.

Vlana's dagger sped unimpeded through the black web—its strands even seemed to part for it—and betwixt the sorcerer's warding hands, to bury itself to the hilt in his right eye.

He screamed thinly in dire agony and clawed his face.

The black web writhed as if in death spasm.

The cucurbits shattered as one, spilling their lava on the scarred table, putting out the blue flames even as the thick wood of the table began to smoke a little at the lava's edge. Lava dropped with *plops* on the dark marble floor.

With a faint, final scream Hristomilo pitched forward, hands clutched to his eyes above his jutting nose, silver dagger-hilt protruding between his fingers.

The web grew faint, like wet ink washed with a gush of clear water.

The Mouser raced forward and transfixed Slivikin and the huge rat with one thrust of Scalpel before the beasts knew what was happening. They too died swiftly with thin screams, while all the other rats turned tail and fled back down their holes swift almost as black lightning.

Then the last trace of night-smog or sorcery-smoke vanished, and Fafhrd and the Mouser found themselves standing alone with three dead bodies amidst a profound silence that seemed to fill not only this room but all Thieves' House. Even the cucurbit-lava had ceased to move, was hardening, and the wood of the table no longer smoked.

Their madness was gone and all their rage, too—vented to the last red atomy and glutted to more than satiety. They had no more urge to kill Krovas or any other thieves than to swat flies. With horrified inner-eye Fafhrd saw the pitiful face of the child-thief he'd skewered in his lunatic anger.

Only their grief remained with them, diminished not one whit, but rather growing greater—that and an ever more swiftly growing revulsion from all that was around them: the dead, the disordered magic room, all Thieves' House, all of the city of Lankhmar to its last stinking alleyway.

With a hiss of disgust the Mouser jerked Scalpel from the rodent cadavers, wiped it on the nearest cloth, and returned it to its scabbard. Fafhrd likewise sketchily cleansed and sheathed Graywand. Then the two men picked up their knife and dirk from where they'd dropped to the floor when the web had dematerialized, though neither glanced at Vlana's dagger where it was buried. But on the sorcerer's table they did notice Vlana's black velvet, silver-worked pouch and belt, and Ivrian's blue-enameled box inlaid with silver. These they took.

With no more word than they had exchanged back at the Mouser's burnt nest behind the Eel, but with a continuing sense of their unity of purpose, their identity of intent, and of their comradeship, they made their way with shoulders bowed and with slow, weary steps which only very gradually quickened out of the magic room and down the thick-carpeted corridor, past the map room's wide door now barred with oak and iron, and past all the other shut, silent doors, down the echoing stairs, their footsteps speeding a little; down the bare-floored lower corridor past its closed, quiet doors, their footsteps resounding loudly no matter how softly they sought to tread; under the deserted, black-scorched guard-niche, and so out into Cheap Street, turning left and north because that was the nearest way to the Street of the Gods, and there turning right and east—not a waking soul in the wide street except for one skinny, bent-backed apprentice lad unhappily swabbing the flagstones in front of a wine shop in the dim pink light beginning to seep from the east, although there were many forms asleep, a-snore and a-dream in the gutters and under the dark porticoes—yes, turning right and east down the Street of the Gods, for that way was the Marsh Gate, leading to Causey Road across the Great Salt Marsh; and the Marsh Gate was the nearest way out of the great and glamorous city that was now loathsome to them, a city of beloved, unfaceable ghosts—indeed, not to be endured for one more stabbing, leaded heartbeat than was necessary.

Counting the Shapes

ꝏ

Yoon Ha Lee

Yoon Ha Lee was born in 1979 and sold her first story to F&SF *in 1999. Most of her stories have been science fiction of a military sort, but her first foray into the realms of fantasy proved so successful that it needs to be included here. Ms. Lee graduated from Cornell University with a degree in Mathematics and received a Master's Degree in Math Education from Stanford University—and you'll soon see that mathematics figures prominently in her current work. She and her husband recently moved from Boston to a small town in the middle of the state of Washington.*

How many shapes of pain are there?
Are any topologically equivalent?
And is one of them death?

I

Biantha woke to a heavy knocking on the door and found her face pressed against a book's musty pages. She sat up and brushed her pale hair out of her face, trying to discern a pattern to the knocking and finding that the simplest one was impatience. Then she got to her feet and opened the door, since her warding spell had given her no warning of an unfriendly presence outside. Besides, it would be a little longer before the demons reached Evergard.

"Took your time answering the door, didn't you, Lady Biantha?" Evergard's gray-haired lord, Vathré, scowled at her. Without asking for permission, which he never did anyway, he strode past her to sweep his eyes over the flurry of papers that covered her desk. "You'd think that, after years of glancing at your work, I might understand it."

"Some of the conjectures are probably gibberish anyway." She smiled at him, guessing that what frustrated him had little to do with her or the theorems that made her spells possible. Vathré visited her quarters when he needed an ear detached from court intrigues. "What troubles you this time, my lord?"

He appropriated her one extra chair and gestured for her to sit at the desk, which she did, letting her smile fade. "We haven't much longer, Biantha. The demons have already overrun Rix Pass. No one agrees on when they'll get here. The astrologer refused to consult the stars, which is a first—claimed he didn't want to see even an iffy prediction—" Vathré looked away from her. "My best guess is that the demons will be here within a month. They still have to march, overwhelming army or no."

Biantha nodded. Horses barely tolerated demon-scent and went mad if forced to carry demons. "And you came to me for battle spells?" She could not keep the bitterness from her voice. The one time she had killed with a spell had been for a child's sake. It had not helped the child, as far as she knew.

"Do you have any battle spells?" he asked gravely.

"Not many." She leaned over and tapped the nearest pile of paper. "I was in the middle of this proof when I discovered that I'd have to review one of Yverry's theorems. I fell asleep trying to find it. Give me a few days and I can set up a battle spell that will kill any demons you've already managed to wound."

Biantha saw the weariness in the lord's green eyes and flushed. "It isn't much, I know."

"That helps, but it isn't what I came for."

Dread opened at the pit of her stomach. "The Prophecy."

Vathré inclined his head.

"I've tried to pry some sense out of it ever since I learned of it, you know." She rubbed her eyes. "The poetry translates into shapes and equations that are simply intractable. I've tried every kind of analysis and transformation I know. If there's any hope in the rhymes, the rhythms, the ambiguities, don't ask me to show you where it is. You'd do better consulting the minstrels for a lecture on symbolism."

"I don't *trust* the minstrels." His brows drew together. "And any time I consult the other magicians, I get too many uncertainties to untangle. The seers and healers are hopeless. The astrologer gets headaches trying to determine where to start. The cartomancer gives me a dozen different *possibilities* each time she casts the cards. As far as the Prophecy is concerned, yours is the only kind of magic I can trust."

Biantha smiled wanly. "Which is why, of course, it's so limited." Sometimes she envied the astrologer, the cartomancer, the enchanters, the healers, the seers—magicians whose powers were less reliable but more versatile. "I'll work on it, my lord."

"A month," he reminded her.

She hesitated. "Have you declared your heir yet?"

Vathré eyed her. "Not you, too?"

She swallowed. "If you die, my lord, someone must carry on. Don't leave the succession in doubt. A problem may have several solutions, but some solutions can still be wrong."

"We've been over this before," he said. "Considering the current state of affairs, I'd have to declare a chain of succession down to the apprentice cook. If anyone survives, they can argue over it. My advisors can rule by council until then."

Biantha bowed her head and watched him leave.

II

Usually Biantha avoided Evergard's great hall. It reminded her of her former home, the demon emperor's palace, though the scents of lavender and lilacs drifted through the air, not the smell of blood; people smiled at her instead of bowing or curtsying rigidly. Musicians played softly while nobles chattered, idle soldiers gambled for pittances, and children scampered in and out, oblivious to the adults' strained voices. A few of the boys were fair-haired, like herself. Biantha closed her eyes briefly before turning along the walls, partly to avoid thinking about a particular fair-haired boy, partly because she had come to study the tapestries for inspiration.

The tapestries' colors remained as vibrant as they had been when she first swore fealty to Lord Vathré upon the Blade Fidora. Biantha had long ago determined the logic by which the tapestries had been arranged, and did not concern herself with it now. Instead, she inspected the scenes of the Nightbreak War.

Here was the Battle of Noiren Field, where webs of starlight blinded a thousand soldiers and angular silhouettes soared above, ready for the massacre. Here was General Vian on a blood bay destrier, leading a charge against a phalanx of demons. Here was amber-eyed Lady Chandal weeping over a fallen young man whose closed eyes might also have been amber, flowers springing up where her tears splashed onto the battlefield. Biantha swallowed and quickened her steps. One by one she passed the tapestries until she found what she sought.

Unlike the other Nightbreak tapestries, its border had been woven in rust rather than Evergard's colors, blue and black: rust for betrayal. She stared at the dispassionate face of Lord Mière, enchanter and traitor to Evergard. His had been a simpler magic than her own, drawing upon ritual and incantation. With it he had almost defeated the Watchlanders; only his daughter's knife had saved them.

Symmetry, she sighed. The one thing she had pried from the Prophecy was that it possessed a twisted symmetry. It hinted at two wars between the demons' empire and the Watchlands, and because records of the first war—the Nightbreak War—were scant, Biantha had yet to understand certain cantos, certain equations, that dealt with it. Hours with Evergard's minstrels and historians hadn't helped. Other than herself, only Vathré knew there might be a second traitor among them.

Or that, because they had won the first war, they might lose the second, in a cruel mirroring transformation of history.

"Lady Biantha."

She turned. "Yes?"

The captain—she did not know his name—bowed slightly. "It isn't often that we see you down here, my lady."

Biantha smiled wryly. "A bit too much noise for my work, and on occasion I test spells that might go wrong, sometimes fatally so. My chambers are shielded, but out here. . . "

In the demon emperor's court, her words would have been a veiled threat. Here, the captain nodded thoughtfully and gestured at the tapestry. "I was wondering why you were looking at this. Most people avoid it."

"I was thinking about the Prophecy," she said, retracing the intractable equations in her mind. There had to be a way to balance term against term, solve the system and read Evergard's future, but it continued to escape her. "I'm worried."

"We all are."

Biantha paused. "You said 'most people.' Does that include yourself?"

His mouth twisted. "No. It's a useful reminder. Do you ever wish you had stayed at the demon emperor's palace?"

She read honest curiosity in the captain's expression, not innuendo. "Never." She breathed deeply. "I started learning mathemagic there because magicians, even human magicians, are protected unless they do something foolish. Otherwise I would have been a slave or a soldier; I had no wish for the former and no heart, no talent, for the latter."

Such a small word, *foolish*, when the penalty it carried had given Biantha nightmares for years. She had seen the demon emperor touch his serpent-eyed scepter to a courtesan's perfumed shoulder, as if in blessing; had been unable to avert her gaze before she saw the woman's eyes boiling away and splinters of bone erupting through the rouged skin.

The captain looked down. "I'm sorry to have reminded you, my lady."

"A useful reminder," she echoed. "And what does this portrait of Lord Mière remind you of, if I may ask?"

"Honor, and those who lose it," he said. "Lord Mière was my great-grandfather."

Biantha blinked and saw that there was, indeed, a resemblance in the structure of his face. Her eyes moved to the tapestry's rust border. What had driven Mière to betrayal? It occurred to her, not for the first time, that she herself had fled the demon emperor's court—but the symmetry here seemed incomplete. "Do you think there's hope for us?" she asked the captain.

He spread his hands, studying Biantha's face as she had his just a moment before. "There are those who say we must have a chance, or you would have returned to the demons."

She felt herself flush—and then laughed, though that laughter came perilously close to tears. "I have rarely known demons to forgive. Neither have they forgiven Evergard their defeat in the Nightbreak War."

"More's the pity," said the captain, frowning thoughtfully, and took his leave.

For us or the demons? Biantha thought.

III

Symmetry. The word haunted Biantha through the days and nights as she struggled with the Prophecy. She had wondered, after meeting the captain, if it meant something as simple as her flight from the demons, the fact that one of Lord Mière's descendants survived here. The ballads said Mière had but a single daughter, named Paienne, but they made no mention of her after she saved the Watchlands.

The secret eluded her, slipped away from her, sent her into dreams where dizzying shifts in perspective finally drove her to awaken. Biantha turned to her tomes, seeking clues in others' mathemagical speculations; when she tired of that, she memorized her battle spells, bowing to the heartless logic of war. And went back to the tomes, their treasury of axioms and theorems, diagrams and discussions.

She was leafing through Athique's *Transformations* when someone imitated thunder on her door. Biantha put down the book and opened the door. "Yes?"

The herald bowed elaborately. "A meeting of the court, my lady. Lord Vathré wishes you to attend."

"I'll be there." Firmly, she shut the door and changed into her formal robes as swiftly as she could. Biantha had attended few court meetings: at first, because Vathré had still been uncertain of her loyalties, then because of her awkwardness as a foreigner, and finally because she rarely had anything to contribute to matters of state and found her time better spent working on her magic. That Vathré should summon her now was unusual.

She was right. For once the attendants and servants had been cleared out, and the court had arrayed itself along the sides of the throne room while Vathré and his advisers sat at the head. She took her place between the astrologer and Lady Iastre. The astrologer wore his habitual frown, while the lady's face was cool and composed, revealing nothing. Biantha knew better, after playing draughts or rithmomachia against Iastre once a week in less hectic times: Iastre's face only went blank when she anticipated trouble.

"We have a guest today," said Vathré at his driest. His eyes might have flicked to Biantha, too briefly for her to tell for certain.

On cue, the guards led in a man who wore black and red and gold, stripped of his sword—she knew there had been a sword, by the uniform. The style of his clothing spoke of the demons' realm, and the only one besides the emperor who dared appear in those colors was his champion. The emperor's champion, her son.

A challenge? Biantha thought, clenching her hands so they would not shake. *Has Marten come to challenge Vathré*? But surely the emperor knew Evergard held different customs and would hardly surrender the Watchlands' fate to a duel's outcome.

Hopelessly, she studied the man who had so suddenly disrupted her memories of the child who hid flowers and leaves between the pages of her books, who climbed onto her desk to look out the window at the soldiers drilling. He had her pale hair, a face very like hers. His hands, relaxed at his sides, were also hers, though deadlier; Biantha knew of the training an emperor's champion underwent and had little faith that the guards could stop him from killing Vathré if he wished. But Marten's eyes belonged to a man Biantha had tried to forget, who had died attempting to keep her from leaving the palace with their child.

Silence descended upon the throne room. Vathré's court noted the resemblance, though Marten had yet to spot his mother. He looked straight ahead at Evergard's lord.

Vathré stood and drew the Blade Fidora from its sheath. It glimmered like crystal, like the first light of morning, like tears. The lords and ladies glanced at each other but did not set whispers spinning through the room. Biantha, too, kept silent: a word spoken false in the unsheathed sword's presence would cause it to weep or bleed; the magic had driven men and women mad, and no lord of Evergard used it lightly.

"I am trying to decide whether you are very thoughtless or very clever," Vathré said softly. "Who are you and why are you here?"

"I was the sword at the emperor's side," he answered, "and that sword was nameless." The pale-haired man closed his eyes, opened them. "My name is Marten. I came because the emperor has thousands of swords now, to do his bidding; and I no longer found that bidding to my taste."

Vathré glanced down at the Blade Fidora. Its color remained clear and true. "An interesting time to change your loyalties—if, indeed, they've changed. You might have found a better way to leave than by showing up here in full uniform, scaring the guards out of their wits."

"I left when the demons were . . . subduing a village," Marten said flatly. "I don't know the village's name. I hardly had time to find more suitable attire, my lord, and on campaign one dresses in uniform as a matter of course. To do otherwise would have aroused suspicion."

"And you weren't afraid of being caught and killed on the spot?" one of the advisers demanded.

He shrugged. "I was taught three spells in my training. One allowed me to walk unharmed through the palace wards. One calls fire from blood. And the last lets me pass by like the dream of a ghost."

Biantha glanced at the Blade Fidora and its unwavering light.

Lady Iastre coughed. "Forgive me if I'm less well-informed than I ought to be," she said, "and slow to react as well—but you mentioned being 'on campaign.' Is this a common thing, that 'the sword at the emperor's side' should be out in the field?"

Marten's eyes moved toward the source of the voice, and so he caught sight of Biantha. He inhaled sharply. Biantha felt her face freeze, though she longed to smile at the stranger her son had become. *Answer*, she wished him. *Say you've come to me after so many years—*

Marten gathered himself and said, “I came to warn you, if nothing else; death is a price I have taken from many.” His voice shook, but he continued to face Vathré squarely. “The demon emperor has come, and your battles will be the harder for it.” Then the whispers began, and even Iastre cast troubled eyes toward Biantha; the light of the Blade Fidora reflected all the shades of fear, all the colors of despair, that were voiced. “Please,” Marten said, raising his voice but slightly, “let me help. My lord, I may be slow in learning that there is more to war than following orders. That there are people who die for their homes or their families—”

“Families,” Biantha repeated, tasting bitterness. So calm, his face, like polished metal. She felt Iastre’s hand on her arm and forced a smile.

The whispers had died down, and Marten faltered. “I know how the emperor thinks,” he said at last. “Let me help you there, my lord, or have me killed. Either way, you will have taken the emperor’s champion from him.”

So pale, his face, like Fidora’s light. Biantha caught her breath, waiting for Vathré to speak.

Lines of strain etched the lord’s face as he left the throne to stand before Marten. “Will you swear fealty to the Watchlands and their lord, then?”

Marten did not flinch. “Yes.”

Yes, echoed Biantha, doubt biting her heart. She had not known, when she first came to Evergard, what powers the Blade Fidora possessed. A magician-smith had died in its forging, that there might never again be a traitor like Lord Mière. Vathré had questioned Biantha, as he had just questioned Marten, and the first part of the sword’s virtue had been plain to her, a mirror of spoken minds.

Only later had Vathré told her the second part, that a false oath sworn upon the sword killed the oath-taker. Once an heir to Evergard had sworn guardianship to the Watchlands and their people and fallen dead. Once a weary soldier had woken

Evergard's lady three hours before dawn to confess a betrayal planned, and then committed suicide. Biantha had no desire to find her son the subject of another story, another song. How had Paienne felt, she wondered suddenly, when her father's treachery became part of the Nightbreak War's history?

Marten laid his hand upon the glass-clear blade. "I swear it." Then, swallowing, he looked directly at Biantha.

She could not bring herself to trust him, even after the long years, when he wore a uniform like his father's. This time, she did turn away.

IV

"There's something sinful," said Iastre, fingers running round and round a captured draughts piece, "in sitting here playing a game when our world is falling apart."

Biantha smiled uncertainly and considered her options. "If I stayed in my room and fretted about it all the time, I should go mad." She nudged one of her pieces to a new square, musing on how the symmetry of the game—red on black, black on black—had soon been spoiled by their moves.

"I hear it was Marten's planning that kept the demons from overrunning Silverbridge so far."

She looked up and saw Iastre's worried expression. "A good thing, I suppose—especially considering that the emperor now has a personal reason for wanting to humble the Watchlands."

"Surely you don't think he should have stayed in the emperor's service," Iastre protested.

Oh, but he did once, Biantha did not say. "It's your move."

A snort. "Don't change the subject on me now. You fled the emperor's palace, too, if you'll recall."

"Too well," she agreed. She had slept poorly the first few years at Evergard, hearing danger in the footfalls that passed by her door and dreaming of the emperor's serpent-eyed scepter upon her own shoulder. "But I left in a time of peace, and as terrible a crime as I had committed, I was only a human mathemagician. Besides,"—and Biantha drew in a shaky breath—"they knew they had my son: punishment enough."

Iastre shook her head and finally made her move. "He's here now, and he may be our only hope."

"That," she said, "is what worries me."

Even here, playing draughts, Biantha found no escape from Marten. She had spotted him once in the courtyard, sparring against Evergard's best soldiers while a healer and several enchanters looked on, lest the former champion seek a life instead of a touch. At mealtimes in the great hall she took to eating at the far end of the high table; yet over the clinking glasses and silverware, the tense voices and rustling clothes, Biantha heard Marten and Vathré speaking easily with each other. Evergard's lord trusted Marten—they all trusted Marten now, while she dared not.

Like a pendulum, her thoughts swung between her son and Paienne, her son and Lord Mière. Late at night, when she walked the battlements listening vainly for the footfalls of marching soldiers, feeling betrayal's cold hand in every tremor of the wind, she remembered tales of the Nightbreak War. Biantha had never put much faith in the minstrels' embellished ballads, but the poetry preyed upon her fears.

Working with fragments of history and the military reports that came in daily, she attempted to map past onto future, battle onto battle . . . betrayal onto betrayal. And failed, over and over. And cursed the Prophecy, staring at the worn and inscrutable pages, alone in her room. It was during one of those bouts that a familiar knocking startled her from her work.

Marten? thought Biantha involuntarily. But she had learned the rhythm of Vathré's tread, and when she opened the door she knew who waited behind it. The twin edges of relief and disappointment cut her heart.

The gray-haired man looked her up and down, and scowled. “I thought you might be overworking yourself again.”

She essayed a smile, stepping aside so he could enter. “Overwork, my lord? Tell that to the soldiers who train, and fight, and die for it, or see their friends die for it. Tell that to the cook or the servants in the keep.”

“There are ways and ways of work, my dear.” He paced around the chamber, casting a curious eye over her bookcase and her cluttered desk, then rested a hand on her shoulder. “Perhaps I should come back later, when you’ve rested—and I do mean rest, not sitting in bed to read your books rather than sitting at your desk.”

Biantha craned her head back to glance at him. “At least tell me why you came.”

“Marten,” he said bluntly, releasing her shoulder.

She flinched.

“You’re hurting the boy,” Vathré said. “He’s been here quite a while and you haven’t said a word to him.”

She arched an eyebrow. “He’s not the boy I left behind, my lord.” Her voice nearly broke.

“I’m old enough to call you a girl, Lady Biantha. Don’t quibble. Even I can’t find cause to mistrust him, and the years have made me paranoid.”

“Oh?” She ran her fingers over her copy of the Prophecy, worn smooth by years of on-and-off study. By all accounts, Marten’s advice was sound—but the demons kept coming.

“I’m sending him to command at Silverbridge.” Vathré shook his head. “We’ve held out as long as we can, but it looks like our efforts have been no more than a delaying action. I haven’t told the council yet, but we’re going to have to withdraw to Aultgard.” He exhaled softly. “Marten will keep the demons occupied while the bulk of the army retreats.”

Biantha stared at him.

“The soldiers are coming to trust him, you know,” he remarked. “He’s perhaps the best tactician Evergard has seen in the past couple generations, and I want to see if that trust is justified."

She closed her eyes and said, "A gamble, my lord. Wouldn't you do better to put someone else in charge?"

Vathré ignored her question. "I thought you should know before I announce it."

"Thank you, my lord." Biantha paused, then added, "Do you know where Marten might be at the moment?"

He smiled sadly. "Haunting the battlements, hoping you will stop by."

She bowed her head and, after he had left, went to search for her son. Biantha found him by the southern tower, a sword sheathed at his back. Even now it disconcerted her to see him in the dress of Evergard's soldiers, as if her mind refused to surrender that first image of Marten standing before the court in red and black and gold.

"Mother," he said, clasping his hands behind his back.

Slowly, reluctantly, she faced him. "I'm here."

Moonlight pooled in his eyes and glittered in the tears that streaked his face. "I remember," he said without accusation. "I was seven years old and you told me to pack. You were arguing with Father."

Biantha nodded. Marten had nearly reached the age where he would have to begin training as either a magician or a soldier, or forfeit what little protection his parents' status gave him. Over the years, as their son grew older, she spoke to her husband of leaving the demons' empire to seek refuge in the Watchlands or the realms further east. He always treated her kindly, without ever turning an eye to the courtesans—demon and human both—who served those the emperor favored.

Yet Biantha had never forgotten her husband's puzzlement, molting slowly into anger, that she should wish to leave a court that sheltered them, though it did nothing to shelter others. She could not reconcile herself to the demons' casual cruelty: One of the emperor's nieces sent, after an ill-advised duel, to redeem her honor by riding a horse to the mines of Sarmont and back, five days and back forcing a terrified beast to carry her. The pale-eyed assassin who had fallen from favor after killing the rebellious lady of Reis Keep, solely because he had left evidence of his work. Children drowned after a plague blinded them and clouded their wits. If nothing else, the demons were as cruel to each other as to the humans who lived among and below them, but Biantha had found less and less comfort in that knowledge.

"I stood in the doorway," Marten went on, "trying to understand. Then Father was weeping—"

She had said to her husband, *If you will not come, then I must go without you.*

"—and he drew his sword against you."

"And I killed him," Biantha said, dry-mouthed. "I tried to get you to come with me, but you wouldn't leave him. You started to cry. I had little time, and there were ever guards nearby, listening for anything amiss. So I went alone. It would have been my death to stay after murdering one of the emperor's officers. In the end, the emperor's trust meant more to him than you or I."

"Please don't leave me again," Marten whispered. He stood straight-backed in the darkness, the hilt of the sword at his back peering over his shoulder like a sleepy eye, but his face was taut. "I am leaving for Silverbridge tomorrow."

"Will you be at the forefront?"

"It would be unwise." His mouth tightened for a moment. "I will be giving orders."

"To kill." *And, perhaps, be killed*, she wanted to say, but the words fluttered in her throat.

Marten met her gaze calmly. "It is war, Mother."

"It is now," she agreed, "but it wasn't before. I know what it is to be the emperor's champion. 'The sword at the emperor's side,' you said. The others heard the words only; they have never lain awake and sleepless for memory of bloodstains on a pale rug, or because of the sudden, silenced cries at night. How many fell to your blade, Marten?"

"I came to follow you when I started losing count." His eyes were dry, now, though Biantha saw the shapes of pain stirring behind them. "When the numbers started slipping out of my grasp."

Biantha held silence before her like a skein of threads that wanted words to untangle it.

He lifted a hand, hesitated, let it drop. "I wanted to talk to you once, if never again. Before I go to Silverbridge where the demons await."

She smiled at him, then. But always the suspicion remained that he had some way of breaking his oath to Vathré, that the demon emperor had sent him to ensure the Watchlands' downfall through some subtle plan—or, more simply, that he had come to betray the mother he had abandoned, who had abandoned him; she no longer knew which.

"Go, then," said Biantha, neither promise nor peril in her voice, and left him to await dawn, alone.

V

Four days later, Biantha stood before her bookcase, eyes roaming aimlessly over her collection of mathemagical works, some in the tight, angular script of the demon empire, others in the ornate writing common to the Watchlands' scholars. *There has to be something useful*, she told herself, even after having scoured everything that looked remotely relevant. Now, more than ever, she wished she had talent for another of the magical disciplines, which did not rely on memorized proofs or the vagaries of inspiration, though none of them had ever seemed to get far with the Prophecy.

Would that it were a straightforward problem—

Biantha froze. The Prophecy did not describe the idealized spaces with which she had grown accustomed to dealing, but the tangles of truth, the interactions of demons and humans, the snarls of cause and effect and relation. Even the astrologer admitted privately that his predictions, on occasion, failed spectacularly where people were involved. She had been trying to linearize the cantos: the wrong approach.

Evergard's treasurer had once teased her about the cost of paper, though she took care to waste as little as possible. She located a pile of empty sheets in a drawer and set them on her desk, opening her copy of the Prophecy to the first page. After a moment, Biantha also retrieved Sarielle's *Speculations, Spells and Stranger Sets*, sparing a glance for the 400-line poem in the back; Sarielle of Rix had fancied herself a poet. She had passed evenings lingering over the book's carefully engraved figures and diagrams, curves that Sarielle had labeled "pathological" for their peculiarities.

Symmetry. That which remained changeless. Red pieces upon black and black upon black at the start of a draughts match. A ballad that began and ended with the same sequence of measures; and now that Biantha turned her thoughts in this direction, she remembered a song that traveling minstrels had performed before the court, voice after voice braiding into a whole that imitated each part. Her image in the mirror. And now, Sarielle's pathological curves, where a segment of the proper proportion spawned yet more such segments.

Methodically, she went through the Prophecy, searching for these other symmetries, for the solution that had eluded her for so long. Late into the night, throat parched because she had drained her pitcher and dared not break her concentration by fetching another or calling a servant, Biantha placed *Speculations, Spells and Stranger Sets* to one side and thumbed through the appendix to Athique's *Infinities*. Athique and Sarielle, contemporaries, had been opposites as far as titles went. She reached the approximations of various shapes, sieves and flowers, ferns and laces, that no mortal hand could craft.

One page in particular struck her: shapes built from varying polygons and with various "pathologies," as Athique dubbed them in what Biantha suspected had been a jab at Sarielle's would-be wordsmithing, repeating a procedure to the borders of infinity. The Prophecy harbored greater complexities, but she wondered if her solution might be one of many algorithms, many possibilities. Her eyes flooded: a lifetime's work that she had uncovered, explored briefly by mathemagicians before her, and she had little time in which to seek a solution that helped the Watchlands.

Even after she had snuffed the lamp and curled into bed, a headache devouring her brain, words still burned before her eyes: *Symmetry. Pathologies. Infinity.*

VI

Only a few weeks later, Biantha found herself walking aimlessly down a corridor, freeing her mind from the Prophecy's tyrannous grip, when Lady Iastre shook her shoulder. "They're back, Biantha," she said hurriedly. "I thought you'd like to be there to greet them."

"Who's back?"

"Your son. And those who survived Silverbridge."

Those who survived. Biantha closed her eyes, shaking. "If only the demons would leave us alone—"

The other woman nodded sadly. "But it's not happening. The emperor will soon be at Evergard itself, is the news I've been hearing. Come on."

"I can't," she said, and felt as though the keep were spinning around her while pitiless eyes peered through the walls. "Tell him—tell Marten—I'm glad he's back." It was all she could think to say, a message for her son—a message that she would not deliver in person, because the urgency of the situation had jarred her thoughts back to the Prophecy.

"Biantha!" Iastre cried, too late to stop her.

In bits and pieces she learned the rest of the story, by eavesdropping benignly on dinner conversations and the servants' gossip. The emperor had indeed forsaken his court for the battlefield, perhaps because of Evergard's stubborn resistance. None of this surprised her, except when a curly-haired herald mentioned the serpent-eyed scepter. To her knowledge that scepter had never left the empire—unless, and the thought sickened her, the demons had begun to consider Evergard part of their empire. It had turned Silverbridge, the shining bridge of ballad, into rust and tarnish, and even now the demons advanced.

Vathré gave a few permission to flee further east with their families, those whose presence mattered little to the coming siege. Others prepared to fight, or die, or both; the mock-battles that Biantha sometimes watched between the guards grew more grim, more intent. She and Iastre agreed that the time for draughts and rithmomachia had passed, as much as she would have welcomed the distraction.

As for Marten—she saw almost nothing of him except the terrible weariness that had taken up residence in his face, as though he had survived a torture past bearing. Biantha grieved for him as a mother; as a mathemagician, she had no comfort to offer, for her own helplessness threatened to overwhelm her. Perhaps he in his turn sensed this, and left her alone.

Day by day the demons came closer, to the point where she could stand on the battlements and see the baleful lights in the distance: the orange of campfires, the gold and silver of magefires. Day by day the discussions grew more frantic, more resigned.

At last, one morning, the horns blazed high and clear through the air, and the siege of Evergard began. Biantha took her place on the parapets without saying any farewells, though some had been said to her, and watched while archers fired into the demons' massed ranks. Not long after, magefire rolled over their hastily raised shields, and she prepared her own spells. Only when the demons began to draw back and prepare a second attack did she call upon powers that required meticulous proofs, held in her mind like the memory of a favorite song—or a child in her arms.

She gathered all the shapes of pain that afflicted the demons and twisted them into death. Red mists obscured her vision as the spell wrenched her own soul, sparing her the need to watch the enemy falling. Yet she would have to use the spell again and again before the demons' mathemagicians shaped a ward against it. Those who shared her art rarely ventured into battle, for this reason: it often took too long to create attacks or adapt to them. A theorem needed for a spell might take years to discover, or turn out to be impossible; and inspiration, while swift, was sometimes unreliable. She had seen mathemagicians die from careless assumptions in spellcasting.

By midday Biantha no longer noticed the newly fallen corpses. She leaned against the wall's cold stone—and glimpsed black and red and gold in the distance: the demon emperor, carrying the serpent-eyed scepter that she remembered too clearly. For a moment she thought of the Blade Fidora and cursed the Prophecy's inscrutable symmetry. "No," she whispered. Only if the emperor were certain of victory would he risk himself in the front lines, and a cold conviction froze her thoughts.

Marten. He's counting on Marten to help him.

She had to find Vathré and warn him. She knew where he would be and ran, despite the archers' protests that she endangered herself. "My lord!" she cried, grieving already, because she saw her fair-haired son beside gray-haired Vathré, directing the defense. "My lord! The emperor—" Biantha nearly tripped, caught herself, continued running.

Vathré turned, trusting her, and then it happened.

The emperor raised his scepter, and darkness welled forth to batter Evergard's walls. In the darkness, colors moved like the fire of dancing prisms; silence reigned for a second, strangely disturbing after the clamor of war. Then the emperor's spell ended, leaving behind more dead than the eye could count at a glance. Broken shapes, blood, weapons twisted into deadly metal flowers, a wind like the breath of disease.

Biantha stared disbelievingly over the destruction and saw that the demons who had stood in the spell's path had died as well; saw that the emperor had come forward to spare his own soldiers, not—she hoped not—because he knew he had a traitor in the Watchlanders' ranks. So much death, and all they had been able to do, she and the other magicians, was watch.

"Mercy," Vathré breathed.

"The scepter," Marten said harshly. "Its unspoken name is Decay."

She looked across at the gates and sneezed, dust stinging her nostrils. Already those who had fallen were rotting, flesh blackening and curling to reveal bone; Evergard's sturdy walls had become cracked and mottled.

Marten was shouting orders for everyone to abandon that section of wall before it crumbled. Then he looked at her and said, "We have to get down. Before it spreads. You too, my lord."

Vathré nodded curtly and offered Biantha his arm; Marten led the way down, across footing made newly treacherous. The walls whispered dryly behind them; she flinched at the crash as a crenel broke off and plummeted.

"—use that scepter again?" she heard the lord asking Marten as she concentrated on her footing.

"No," she and her son both said. Biantha continued, "Not so far from the seat of his power and without the blood sacrifices. Not against wood or stone. But a touch, against living flesh, is another matter."

They had reached safety of sorts with the others who had fled the crumbling section of wall. "What of the Prophecy?" Vathré asked her, grimacing as he cast his gaze over the morning's carnage.

"Prophecy?" Marten repeated, looking at them strangely.

Perhaps he had not heard, or failed to understand what he heard, in the brief time he had been at Evergard. Biantha doubted he had spent much time with the minstrels. At least he was not—she prayed not—a traitor, as she had thought at first. Breath coming hard, she looked around, listened to the cries of the wounded, and then, all at once, the answer came to her, one solution of several.

Perspective. Time and again she had brooded over the Prophecy and the second war it foretold. *The rhymes, the rhythms, the ambiguities*, she had said to Vathré not long ago. She had thought about the strange symmetry, the Nightbreak War's traitor—but failed to consider that, in the Prophecy's second war, the corresponding traitor might betray the demons. The demons, not the Watchlands.

Last time, Lord Mière had betrayed the Watchlands, and died at Paienne's hand—father and daughter, while Biantha and Marten were mother and son. But the mirror was imperfect, as the twisted symmetry already showed her. Marten did not have to die, and there was still hope for victory.

"The emperor is still down there," said Vathré quietly. "It seems that if someone were to stop him, we could hold the keep. Hold the keep, and have a chance of winning."

"A challenge," Biantha breathed, hardly aware that those around them were listening avidly, for on this hung Evergard's fate. "Challenge the emperor. He has his honor, strange as it may seem to us. He lost his champion; will he turn down an opportunity to slay, or be slain by, that champion?"

Had there been such a challenge in the Nightbreak War? The ballads, the histories, failed to say. No matter. They were not living a ballad, but writing their own lines to the song.

Vathré nodded, seeing the sense in her words; after all, she had lived in the demons' realm. Then he unfastened the sheath of his sword from his belt and held it out to Marten. "Take the sword," he said.

If she was wrong, giving the Blade Fidora to him was unrivaled folly. But they no longer had a choice, if they meant to take advantage of the Prophecy's tangled possibilities.

He blanched. "I can't. I don't even know who the heir is—" probably because Vathré *still* had not declared the succession. "I haven't the right."

Biantha gazed at the gates, now twisted into rusty skeins. The captain of the guard had rallied the remaining troops and was grimly awaiting the demons' advance.

The lord of Evergard said, exasperated, "I *give* you the right. This isn't the time for questions or self-recriminations. *Take the sword.*"

Resolutely, Marten accepted the Blade Fidora. He grasped the sword's hilt, and it came clear of the scabbard, shining faintly. "I'm sorry for what I have done in the past," he whispered, "even though that doesn't change what was done. Help me now."

"Hurry," said Biantha, guessing the battle's shape. "The emperor will soon come to claim his prize, *our* home, and you must be there to stop him." She stood on her toes and kissed him on the cheek: a mother's kiss, which she had not given him for too many years. She called to mind every protective spell she could think of and forged them together around him despite her exhaustion. "Go with my blessing." *And please come back to me.* After losing him once, Biantha did not mean to lose him again.

"And go with mine," Vathré echoed.

He ducked his head and moved away at a run. Shivering, Biantha tried to gather the strength for more magic against the demons, to influence the Prophecy in their favor. She felt as if she were a formula in an old book, a creature of faded ink and yellowed paper.

As she and Vathré watched, Marten shoved through the soldiers at the gate, pausing only to exchange a few words with some of his comrades. They parted for him, wondering that he and not Vathré held the Blade Fidora; Vathré waved at them in reassurance. Past the gates were the emperor and his elites, dressed in rich colors, standing in near-perfect formation.

"Traitor," said the emperor to Marten in the cool voice that never revealed anything but mockery; demon and human both strained to hear him. "Do you think Evergard's blade will protect you?"

In answer Marten swung the sword toward the emperor's exposed throat, where veins showed golden through the translucent skin. The elites reacted by moving to surround him while the emperor brought his serpent-eyed scepter up in a parry. The soldiers of Evergard, in their turn, advanced in Marten's defense. Biantha felt a hysterical laugh forming: the soldiers of both sides looked as though they had choreographed their motions, like dancers.

Now, straining to see what was happening, she realized why the emperor had chosen her son for his champion. Several of the elites saw clearly the blows that would kill them, yet failed to counter in time. Yet her eyes were drawn to the emperor himself, and she sucked in her breath: the emperor appeared to be aiming at a woman who had crippled one of the elites, but Biantha saw the twist in the scepter's trajectory that would bring it around to strike Marten. Even a traitor champion could not survive a single touch of the scepter; it would weaken him beyond his ability to recover.

"Marten!" she screamed. He was all she had left of her old home and its decadent intrigues; of a man with gentle hands who had loved her within the narrow limits of court life; of her family. The emperor had stolen him from her for so long—

Mathemagical intuition launched her past the meticulous lemmas and lines of a proof, panic giving her thoughts a hawk's wings. Biantha spun one more spell. Symmetry: the emperor's attack became Marten's, in spaces too strange for the mind to imagine. The Blade Fidora went true to its target, while the scepter missed entirely, and it was the emperor's golden blood that showered Marten's hands.

I'm sorry for everything, Marten, thought Biantha, and folded out of consciousness.

VII

The minstrels who survived the Siege of Evergard made into song the deaths, the desperation, the duel between the demon emperor and he who was now heir to the Watchlands. Biantha, for her part, listened and grieved in her own way for those who had died . . . for Mière's great-grandson. There was more to any story, she had learned, than what the minstrels remembered; and this was as true of herself, her husband, her son.

Biantha wrote only two lines in the margin of an unfinished book—a book of her own theorems.

VIII

There are too many shapes of love to be counted.
One of them is forgiveness.

IX

It was a conjecture, not a proof, but Biantha knew its truth nonetheless. After the ink had dried, she left her room with its well-worn books and went to the great hall where Vathré and Iastre, and most especially Marten, expected her for dinner.

—for Ch'mera, and for those who teach math

Firebird

ꙮ

R. Garcia y Robertson

Rod Garcia grew up in California but he has lived in Mt. Vernon, Washington, for many years. He is the author of several novels, including The Sprial Dance, American Woman, *and most recently a series of "timeslip" stories about a modern woman going back in time,* Knight Errant *and* Lady Robyn. *His science fiction and fantasy stories tend to be lush, baroque, and very imaginative. They also tend to exhibit a strong historical background, which is perhaps unsurprising given that Mr. Garcia used to teach history. His story "The Iron Wood" in our August 2000 issue was one of his first fantasy stories that did not use an actual historical venue as its setting, but instead blended various elements from the Middle Ages to form the fascinating world of Markovy, a world he has continued to explore. "Firebird" is the second such story, a rich adventure concerning a witch and a knight. A novel based on this story is due to be published next year.*

Witch-girl

Deep in the Woods, gathering fungus for the Bone Witch's supper, Katya heard the firebird call her name. "Katea-katea-katea . . ." Brushing tangled black hair from sea-green eyes, she searched for the bird, seeing only tall pine trunks and blue bars of sky. Her bright homespun dress had the red-orange firebird embroidered on the bodice, done in silk from Black

Cathay, and the Barbary cloth called Crimson. She had stitched it herself on sunless winter days. Katya called out, "Here I am. Come tell what you see."

She listened. Insects hummed in hot pine-scented air. Farther off she heard a woodpecker knocking. She called again, "Come to me. Come to me. Come tell what you see."

Now that she was fully grown, Katya never feared the woods by daylight. Leopards, troll-bears, lycanthropes, and forest sprites lurked between the trees, waiting to make a meal of the unwary. But by day the woods had a hundred eyes alert for any suspicious movement. No lynx or leopard could stir a foot without birds calling and squirrels chattering. All Katya need do was listen. Night was another matter. But the Bone Witch did not let her out at night. Nor would the Witch let her leave the hut without her slave collar and protective rune. Each morning she made Katya repeat her invisibility spell. She was valuable property, the Witch told her. "I have not raised you to feed some hungry troll-bear—not when you are finally becoming useful."

Katya saw things differently. She began life as a girl-child thrown away in time of war and famine. Survival taught her to make the best of today, for tomorrow was bound to be worse. It taught her to lie instinctively, and never to shit where she meant to sleep. And to trust in her luck, which had kept her from the fate of hundreds like her. Death had had ample chance to take her, making Katya think she was being saved for something special. Like to be a princess.

At nine she was given to the Witch for two handfuls of salt and a cattle pox cure. The family feeding her figured they were doing everyone a favor. "The Witch can better provide for you. We are poor," the father informed her—as if she had somehow not noticed, sleeping on straw between the hearth and the hogs—"while you are stubborn and willful." His wife agreed. "Getting you to obey is like trying to teach a cat to fetch." Had Katya been a boy, it would have been different. But she was a girl, naturally wanton, unruly, frivolous and amoral, a growing threat to their son's virtue. They were duty-bound to keep her chaste and ignorant, then give her to some man in marriage—a dead loss to the family. Better by far to give her to the Bone Witch.

Only their lazy son objected. Not the least threatened, he wanted her around. Without her, who would do his chores? Who would he spy on in the bath? He had promised to rape her when they got bigger.

Katya herself had said nothing. Even at nine, she had a stubborn sense of self-worth that regularly got her whipped. People called her changeling and worse, with her pert ways and wicked green eyes—a girl switched at birth for a defiant demon-child. Bundling up her straw doll and wooden spoon, she took a seat in the father's cart. They lurched off, crossing the Dys at Byeli Zamak, headed for the Iron Wood. All she could think was that she was to become a witch-girl. And witches were burned.

But that was years ago. And she had not been burnt—not yet at least. By now she had spent half her life in the woods. She knew which mushrooms were food, and which sent you on flights of fancy. Which berries were sweet and which were deadly nightshade, which herbs cured and which herbs killed. Having nothing of her own, she happily appropriated all of nature, making these her woods. Every screech and cry in the trees spoke to her. When it was safe, she spoke back.

"Katea-katea-katea . . ." The call came closer. Like her, the firebird was a curious soul, and could be coaxed with low soft calls. He hated to think of anything happening in his woods without him telling the world about it.

Picking up her bark basket, she headed for the sound, fording a shallow stream to enter a fern-choked glade ringed by stands of slim silver birch. Birches loved the light and fought to fill any sort of clearing. At the far end of the glade she skirted a pond frequented by red deer and herons. On the bare bank she saw pug marks.

Kneeling amid the bracken, she felt the tracks with her fingers. The ground was hard, and the claw prints worn and splayed with age. Three nights ago, after the rain when the moon was full, an old female leopard came from the same direction she had, stopped to drink, then headed up the ridge, aiming for the thickly wooded crest separating the forest from the cultivated lands beyond. Any leopard with business beyond the ridge could easily be a stock thief or man-eater.

Not a cat she cared to meet. Stomach tensed, she looked about. Mossy patches shone like polished jade. The protective rune on her armlet shielded Katya from magic—but not from fang or claw. Straightening up, she set out again, keeping the breeze at her back. Leopards did not know humans have no sense of smell, and never stalked from upwind—so she need only worry about what lay ahead. These were her woods. Let some old leopard scare her, and she would never go out at all.

"Katea-katea-katea . . ." She spotted a flash of orange among the pine trunks. The bird waited at the crest of the ridge.

And not just the firebird, but a fire as well. Black oily smoke billowed from beyond the ridge crest, smearing clear blue sky. Hairs rose at the nape of her neck. She had not smelled the smoke because the wind was behind her—but she knew where it came from. Byeli Zamak was burning.

Topping the ridge, she stopped to stare. This was as far as the slave collar allowed her to go. Below her the forest ended. Rolling steppe spread out from the foot of the ridge, broken by loops of river, dark patches of ploughland, and the onion domes of village churches. Between her and the steppe, guarding the fords of the Dys, stood a huge round tower seven stories tall with walls twenty feet thick—Byeli Zamak, the White Castle. Smoke poured from the tower. Katya pictured the inferno inside, fed by grain and oil stored in the basement, burning up though the wooden floors, feeding on gilt furniture, Barbary tapestries, Italian paintings, and canopied beds. A cornerstone of her world was consumed in flames.

She came from these settled lands. Somewhere out there she had been born. Somewhere out there her family was massacred—for the black earth beyond the woods was sown with bones and watered by blood. Constant strife had consumed her family, and almost made an end to her. She had begged in those villages, and slept in the painted doorways of those churches, waking to find crows and ravens waiting to make a meal of her.

When she was given to the Witch, all that changed. Her slave collar kept her penned in the woods—where the worst she need fear was leopards and troll-bears. Even when old King Demitri died, Byeli Zamak remained, towering over the fords of the Dys—the gatehouse to the Iron Wood. King and gold-domed capital were the stuff of faerie tales, but Byeli Zamak was solid and real, part of Katya's landscape, built by earth giants from native stone. And now it burned. Her first thought was to tell the Bone Witch.

"Katea-katea . . ." the firebird called again, this time from right overhead. Looking up, she saw the flame-colored jay perched on the limb of a tall larch, scoffing and chuckling. Clown prince of the bird clan, the fire orange jay was a wickedly mischievous trickster, a merciless nest robber and accomplished mimic. Katya had heard him perfectly imitate the screaming whistle of a hawk, just to see what havoc he could wreak.

"Is this what you saw?" Katya tilted her head toward the inferno below. Just like a jay to revel in someone else's misfortune. He squawked back at her, this time giving the man call. Jays greeted every predator with a different call. Warnings did little good if you did not know whether to look out for a leopard, or a hawk, or a lynx. The man call was totally distinct. Jays did not use it for her or the Witch.

Hearing a waxwing whistle, Katya turned to see a roe deer bound up the slope and disappear over the ridge. Something was coming. Something alarming enough to flush a doe from cover. The firebird flew off, still making the man call.

From below came the weighty clump of slow hoofbeats climbing the ridge. A horse was coming up from the fords, carrying something heavy and clanking. She whispered her invisibility spell. So long as she remained still and silent, no one could see her. Or so the Witch said. So far it had never failed.

She watched the rider top the ridge. Bareheaded, he rode slumped forward, eyes half shut, his soot-stained blue and white surcoat covering a body encased in steel—a man-at-arms, maybe even a knight, just managing to stay atop a big gray charger. Her heart went out to him. He looked so hurt and handsome, his long elegant eyelashes wet with tears. Bloody clots in his fashionable pudding-basin haircut dripped red streaks down proud cheekbones, past genteel lips. His beardless face made him look young, marking him as a foreigner. Or a eunuch.

Here was her storm petrel: strong and beautiful, but a sure sign of the whirlwind to come. So long as Byeli Zamak had held for the King, only unarmed serfs crossed the fords into the forest, to gather sticks and snare squirrels, stripping bark for their shoes and stealing honey from the bees. On May Day they came singing, their arms full of flowers, celebrating the return of spring, slipping off in pairs to make love upon the forest floor—while she watched, invisible and intrigued. In summer the forest rang with their axes—the nearest thing they had to weapons. It was a flogging offense for a serf to have a bow, or a boar spear. Death to be caught with a sword.

But this stranger had a huge sword slung across his back, and his torn surcoat bore the embattled blue bend of the King's Horse Guards. His crested helm hung from his saddle bow, alongside an ugly saw-toothed war hammer. Hunched forward, he carried something heavy in the crook of his shield arm, wrapped in silk embroidery, tucked against his armored breast. She stood stock-still, letting him rattle past, close enough to touch.

When he had gotten far enough ahead of her, she set off after him, slipping silently from tree to tree, following the bird calls down the ridge onto the forest floor. Tiny red flecks of blood shone on green fern fronds, marking his trail for her.

Now the breeze was full in her face, which she did not like. A leopard could come up behind her, stalking her as easily as she trailed this knight. Worse yet, the breeze brought the foul scent of a troll-bear's lair, faint but growing stronger. The rotting corpse smell of discarded carcasses, mixed with the rank odor of the troll-bear's droppings, was unmistakable, like smelling a long dead lizard on a hot day. Only the image of the knight's hurt face kept her going.

She nearly caught up with her knight beneath a cool coppice of oaks. Leaves rustled like water overhead and the rattle of armor had ceased—but the smell of horse droppings, followed by a nervous whinny, warned her she was getting too close. Sinking to all fours, she wriggled through the undergrowth, curious to see why he had stopped. Had he smelled the troll-bear?

Her knight had dismounted. Kneeling in the bracken beside his horse, he attacked the ground with a big saxe knife, digging a hole in the dark earth. She watched patiently. When he had dug down the length of his arm, he sheathed the knife, and reached for an embroidered bundle lying beside him. Gently he lowered the bundle into the hole. Whatever it was had to be something precious—she could tell by how he handled it. A gold icon perhaps. Or a great crystal goblet. Or a dead baby.

He carefully covered over the hole, hiding his work with fallen leaves. Then he looked up, sensing he was watched, staring straight at her. But she stayed still as a fawn, and the spell held. Drained by the simple act of digging, he heaved himself onto his horse, no mean feat in full armor. Then he lurched off upwind, headed for the troll-bear's lair. Unless she did something the troll-bear would savage both horse and rider, cracking her knight's armor like a badger breaking open a snail.

When the carrion odor got unbearable, his horse stopped again, refusing to go on. She waited for her knight to turn or dismount, but he stayed slumped in his saddle, eyes closed, his horse nervously cropping the bracken. Warning calls died away and the woods grew still. A good sign. Either the troll-bear was gorged senseless, or away from its den. Shrugging off her spell, she stepped out from between the trees, slowly walking toward her knight. His horse saw her first, snorting and shying. Speaking softly, she reached out and took the reins, "Have no fear. I will take you to good grass and water."

Her knight opened his eyes, which were blue and alert. He smiled at what he saw, saying, "*Mon Dieu*, I am dead." He did not look very dead, clinging stubbornly to his saddle. "And here is an angel to take me to Heaven." "I am no angel," she told him. She was a witch-child, willful, disobedient, and hopelessly damned.

His smile widened. "Then a forest sprite, young and beautiful. What more could a vagabond want?" He spoke with a funny foreign accent, but his tone told her he was friendly. Gently turning the tired horse's head, she led him slowly downwind away from the troll-bear's lair. Her knight swayed alarmingly in the saddle. "Fair nymph," he called down to her. "Where are you taking us?"

She smiled over her shoulder. "To water." He was by far the most marvelous thing she had ever found in the woods, and she wanted to see him with his face washed.

Leading the horse back to the base of the ridge—to where a spring burst from beneath tall triangular rocks—she helped her knight dismount. Sitting him down, she wet a cloth and wiped his wincing face. He cleaned up nicely. She liked his handsome beardless face, firm and manly, but smooth to the touch. His scalp wound was bloody but not deep, and merely needed to be cleaned, then sewn shut. Luckily she knew which plants produced natural antibiotics, had been gathering them for the Witch.

He watched as she worked, smiling ruefully. "Just when you wonder what you are fighting for, Heaven sends a reminder."

"What reminder is that?" She searched through her bark basket for the right leaves.

"You really do not know, do you?"

"No. That is why I asked." Her knight had a funny way of talking, even for a foreigner. She crushed the leaves with a rock, mixing them with water from the spring.

"I have had a most damnable day," he told her, "trying to hold Byeli Zamak for your infant Prince Ivan. Besieged by the boy's own uncle, upholding the honor of your dead king, and being badly beaten for my pains. Just when I think I cannot go on—that there is nothing in this benighted land worth saving—you come along. Proving me completely wrong."

"This will hurt," she warned him, parting his hair to expose the wound.

"*Certainement*; so far today, everything has." Taking that as assent, she poured her makeshift potion onto the bloody gash. He shouted in protest, raising a steel-gloved hand to shield his head. "*Merde*! Does *Mademoiselle* mean to murder me too?"

She grabbed his gauntlet to keep it away from the wound. "No. This will help you. I swear." She found her embroidery needle with her free hand.

He relaxed. "*C'est bien, c'est bien. Mademoiselle* merely took me by surprise." He sat stoically while she poured potion on the needle, then began sewing his scalp back together, wincing when she tightened a stitch, but otherwise acting as if she were clipping his curls. Asking, "What may I call Mademoiselle?"

"Katya," she replied shyly, resisting the impulse to invent. She wanted him to know her name.

"*Enchanté*. Sir Roy d'Roye, Chevalier de l'Étoile, et le Baron d'Roye. At your service." He winced again, as her needle went in. "What does *Mademoiselle* do when not torturing wounded knights?"

She pulled the stitch tight, saying softly, "I serve the Bone Witch."

"A Witch? But of course. And a wicked one too, from the way that potion burned me. . . ."

"But she is merely my foster mother. My real mother was a queen. And I am a princess." Not knowing who her parents were, she felt free to invent royal ones.

Baron d'Roye raised an eyebrow. "Princess in disguise, I presume?"

"Of course," she replied scornfully. "Why else would I be dressed like a peasant?"

"Your majesty carries off her masquerade amazingly well."

"Shush!" she whispered. From atop the ridge came the firebird's man call. She listened harder. The call came again, fading as the bird took flight. Someone was coming. She asked, "Are there men after you?"

"Indeed, though for no good reason."

She hastily finished her stitching, saying, "I must hide you." She had no fear for herself, but the thought of seeing her newfound knight hurt or killed was too much to bear. Helping him to his feet, she guided him up the rocks to a protruding shelf where two boulders formed a tiny cave between them, too high up to be seen from the spring. She shoved him inside, saying, "Stay here."

"Only if your majesty promises to come for me," he replied.

"I will." She truly wanted to see more of him, only not right now. Not with men coming.

"Promise?"

"I swear." She pushed him further into the cave, where there was no chance of him being seen from below.

"Bring food," he begged.

"I will," she hastily agreed.

"And wine."

She did not bother to answer, scrambling back down the rocks to the spring. Taking his mount's reins, she turned the horse away from the spring.

"Good wine. If your highness has it."

Still thirsty, the horse balked at being led off by a stranger. She had to heave on the reins to get him pointed back the way she wanted to go. Her knight called down to her, "And what about my horse?"

"I will hide him too," she promised, pulling harder, hauling the unwilling animal away from the spring.

"*Au revoir*," he called out.

"Silence, please," she shouted back, mortified to be making so much noise with strangers in the woods. Dragging the weary charger away from rest and water, she doubled back on their original tracks. Anyone seeing the return prints would have no reason to search out the cave, and would follow the trail she was making. Katya felt confident she could lose them—these were her woods.

When she had put distance between herself and the spring, she found a swift brook and splashed along it, letting the running water hide their trail. Spotting a good place to leave the stream—a rock shelf that would not take hoof prints—she deliberately passed it by. Downstream from the rock shelf she let the horse stray, making tracks on the bank, then leading him back into the water, and up onto the opposite bank. When she was satisfied with her false trail, she carefully retreated upstream, leading the horse out over the rocks, trying her utmost not to leave tracks.

She stayed on hard ground until she was well out of sight of the stream, and could no longer hear its rippling. Then she tied the horse to a tree and went back alone. Walking as lightly as she could, she covered up any sign of the horse's passing, smoothing over stray prints, and sprinkling dust where they had wet the rocks. When she reached the stream, she whispered her spell, lying down to watch.

She waited, her heart beating against the hard stone. On the far side of the stream she saw a splendid spider web, shot with rainbows. Worth coming back for when she was not so busy. In the meantime she thought about her knight. He had a funny foreign way of talking, but that only made him more special. He had a good heart as well, she knew by the way he spoke to her. He even seemed to like her, though that was a lot to hope for.

First she heard warning calls—the indignant chatter of a red squirrel, the rasping cry of a frightened pine tit. Followed by the voices of men, and the neighing of their horses. They came slowly downstream, searching both banks, looking for the spot where she left the water.

One huge fellow in half-armor and big bucket-topped riding boots urged his mount up onto the rock shelf, coming so close she could count the flanges on the heavy steel mace hanging from his saddle bow. Matted hair and flecks of blood clung to the sharp steel. He wore his sallet tipped back, searching the ground for tracks. His hard bearded face could not compare to the clean elegant features of Sir Roy d'Roye, Chevalier de l'Étoile. But his surcoat had the same embattled blue bend as her knight's—charged with a sable crescent, the badge of Prince Sergey Mikhailovich, Grand Duke of Ikstra. Crown Prince Ivan's belligerent uncle. She held her breath as he studied the spot where she led the charger out of the stream. Did he see something? A crushed leaf or overturned stone? The scrape mark of a steel shoe?

Calls came from downstream. They had found her false trail. Prince Sergey's man-at-arms turned his horse about, splashing back into the stream. She was safe—for now. When the calls faded into the forest, she slid back off the rocks, and carefully made her way to where she had tethered the horse. The Witch would scold her if she did not return soon with her bark basket full of herbs and fungus.

As she set out, clouds of little white butterflies whirled up from patches of sunlight, fluttering between the horse's legs, then darting off between the trees. The deeper she went into the woods, the less she worried about hiding her trail. The only warning calls were for her. At the head of Long Lake, she saw wild swans swimming on clear water fringed by pines.

Beyond the lake the pine wood ended. On the far side stood a forest of black iron trunks with stark metal branches—the Iron Wood—a cold dark barrier reeking of magic, stretching over the hills to the east, lifeless and forbidding. She led the reluctant horse into the black leafless wood. Spiked branches closed around her, and forest sounds faded. No woodpeckers beat at the hard metal bark. No squirrels ran along the blade-like limbs. No living beasts made their home in the Iron Wood—just trolls and siren spirits, witches and the walking dead.

Happy to be nearly home, she threaded her way through the thorny metal maze. Finally a clearing appeared ahead, a white patch amid the black tangle. She led the big war horse up to a tall white hut made entirely of bones, long white thigh bones as big as a man, stacked one atop the other like grisly logs. Serfs called them dragon bones, but Katya knew better. They came from a long-haired, elephant-trunked monster that once roamed the northern tundra, bigger by far than any Barbary elephant. She had seen their great curved tusks in a forest bone pit, along with bits of the hairy hide.

Huge antlers from an ancient giant elk hung above the Bone Hut's leather door. Swallows nested in nooks beneath the eves. Little chestnut-throated birds peered out of the mud nests at her. Their parents flew back and forth, chattering at her, then streaking off in the direction of Long Lake, coming back with ants, gnats, wasps, and assassin bugs to feed their young.

Slowly the skin door swung open, and the Bone Witch emerged. Older than sin, and grim as death, the Witch wore a knuckle bone necklace and a linen winding sheet for a dress. White hair hung down to bare skeletal feet. Around her thin waist was a wormwood belt, supporting the thief-skin bag that held her charms. The horse backed and snorted at the sight of her.

She muttered a charm and the shying charger relaxed. "A beautiful beast," the Bone Witch declared. "Where did you find him?"

"In the woods." Katya had always brought lost or strayed animals out of the woods. Fallen eagle chicks. Little lame squirrels. Orphaned leopard cubs. This war horse was by far her most impressive find. She made no mention of his master. The Bone Witch had warned her not to bring men into the Iron Wood. Abandoned cubs and a weary war horse were one thing—but no stray knights. No matter how handsome and helpless they looked.

She held out her basket to show she had not wasted the whole morning, saying, "Byeli Zamak has been burned."

The Witch nodded, "I smelled it on the wind." It was impossible to surprise the Bone Witch.

"And a leopard drank from the pond beneath the ridge."

The Witch nodded again. "Three nights ago, when the moon was full." Accepting the fungus, the Witch told her to give the gray charger a rubdown, "And see he has grass and water. You cannot bring things home unless you care for them."

"I will, I will," she assured the Witch. And went to work at once, taking the horse around to the paddock behind the bone hut, rubbing him down, giving him water and barley. Filling a bark basket with food, she got out the Witch's steel sickle, saying she would go cut grass at Long Lake. Nothing a horse could live on grew in the Iron Wood.

The Witch sniffed her basket. "And you will take food to the knight hiding in the cave by the spring?"

She gave a guilty nod.

"You are free to play with whatever you find in the woods, so long as your chores do not go wanting."

"Oh, no! I will gather more fungus, and webs for spinning. See, I am taking my spindle."

The Witch shook her head. "Your youth will be the death of me. Always rushing life along."

"No! Never." She kissed the Witch's cold wrinkled lips. "You will always be here." The Bone Witch had been in the Iron Wood forever.

"Of course, but what has that to do with it?" The Witch shooed her out of the hut.

As the Witch predicted, she went straight to the cave, fearing she would find it empty. Nearing the spring, she stopped to listen. And heard nothing. Maybe he had obeyed her and stayed in the cave. More likely he was long gone.

She was thrilled to find herself wrong. "*Bonjour*," he greeted her with a grin when she stuck her head into the cave. Heaving himself upright, he peered at her basket. "What is this? Food, how wonderful! Did you bring wine as well?" She admitted she had not, having never so much as seen a grape. "Alas, too bad. But this is magic enough. Is there meat?"

"*Kalbasa*." She doled out a length of smoked sausage.

"Excellent, good old *kalbasa*, and bread too. What a wonderful wood sprite. Would there be caviar to go with it?"

"There is." She showed him the gleaming fish roe wrapped in a cool leaf. Long Lake teemed with sturgeon.

"Caviar! Fantastic. What a feast!"

"And myot also." She showed him the comb.

"Honey. How delightful."

"And yogurt."

"Ah yes, Markovy's answer to sour milk."

"And *diynya*."

"*Diynya*?" He looked puzzled.

She lifted the melon from the bottom of the basket, holding it out to him. "*Diynya*."

"Of course. Diynya. How utterly delicious." Taking the melon, he kissed her. "*Merci beaucoup, Mademoiselle* wood sprite."

Her lips tingled from her first kiss by a grown man. The lumpish son of the family she lived with once held her down and tried to kiss her, but she bit his tongue. This was completely different. Delicious shivers shot through her, raising goosebumps from nipples to her groin. That he did it quickly and casually did not matter. Nor did it matter that he had clearly forgotten her name. It was enough that she remembered his, Sir Roy d'Roye, Chevalier de l'Étoile, et le Baron d'Roye. She felt utterly ecstatic, having her first real kiss come from someone so special. Not just a knight, but a lord. And hers to feed and care for.

Making her worry all the more for him. "Why do they want to harm you?"

"Rank prejudice," he replied, spreading caviar with his thumb. "Pure silly superstition."

She broke open the melon, sipped the juice, and passed it to him. "But why would Prince Ivan's uncle attack Byeli Zamak?"

He heaved a sigh. "*Mademoiselle* does not live in a nation. Markovy is a collection of family quarrels with vague boundaries, whose preferred form of government is civil war. Being a foreign heretic, I do not give a lead sou who wins—but I swore an oath to your king, to uphold his honor and his heir. Not that noble oaths mean a lot when you are having your head beat in."

Getting over her goosebumps, she took her spindle from the basket, and started to spin spider's thread from a web she had found on the way. Working the tiny threads relaxed her.

"Markovites are the most superstitious folk in creation," he complained between bites. "Believing in all manner of faeries, imps, djinn, witches, and whatnot. Byeli Zamak supposedly held a magic treasure—the Firebird's Egg. A marvelous tale. And Prince Sergey is an utterly gullible Grand Duke, who thinks this mythical egg will make him master of Markovy. But I held Byeli Zamak for Prince Ivan, and King Demitri before him. As Castellan I would know if Byeli Zamak held such an egg. And it does not."

Katya herself absolutely believed in the Firebird's Egg. King Demitri had stolen the Egg from its nest deep in the Iron Wood, and kept it locked in a cool deep basement vault beneath Byeli Zamak—where it would not hatch and would always be his. It had been King Demitri's greatest treasure, and his greatest curse. Making his life tragic and miserable. The curse cost him both his wives, and all his children, except for Ivan, his heir. Why Ivan's uncle would want the ill-fated egg was totally beyond her—but that did not mean it did not exist.

Her knight told more stories, of far-off Gascony where he was born, and how he lost everything and ended up in exile. "I possess an astounding ability to choose the losing side. Counting this latest debacle at Byeli Zamak, I have been in half a dozen pitched fights—and have always come out a loser. A remarkable record, not easily achieved. When I sided with the English they lost to the King of France. When I switched my allegiance to the King, he lost to the English. Scots in the French service call me 'Tyneman' in tribute to my many defeats. An honor really. Any lout with a bit of ability can run off a string of victories. But to lose every time—that requires not just talent, but uncanny luck as well."

"I cannot believe your luck could be so bad." She did not want to believe anything bad about him.

"Bad luck?" He laughed. "Not in the least, my luck is excellent. Could not be better."

"Really? But is it not better to win than lose?"

"Better perhaps—but not always easier. Anyone can survive a victory, just stay to the back and shout loudly. But surviving six defeats is a rare feat. Requiring more than a swift horse. Twice—at Lipan and St. Jacob-on-Bris—I was the only one not killed or taken. That is phenomenal luck."

"I mean, I do not believe you must always lose."

He scoffed at her innocence. "Tell it to the Swiss. They were near unbeatable until I sided with them."

By now dusk was settling outside the cave. Shafts of golden light slanted between the trees, slicing deep into the forest. Having seen her knight fed and cared for, she needed to get back and cut grass for his horse, then see to the Witch's supper, making the most of the long summer twilight. Sadly she took her leave, fairly sure he would not wander off in the short night, and meaning to be back by morning. D'Roye declared himself devastated to see her go, cheering her immensely. She finally had her knight in armor. Who cared if he was a foreigner, and somewhat the worse for wear—a footloose loser from some far-off land?

Before returning to the Witch, she had one more thing to do. Cautiously she snuck up on the troll-bear's lair, hoping her own scent would be hidden by the carrion stink. When she found the spot she sought, she dug down into the deep forest loam, using the Witch's steel sickle. She glanced repeatedly over her shoulder, uncomfortably aware that she had watched her knight dig in this exact spot without him knowing it.

Setting aside the sickle, she dug the last few inches with her hands, not wanting to harm what lay hidden in the hole. Finally she felt something soft and warm beneath her fingers. Brushing aside the last of the dirt, she recognized the embroidered tapestry her knight had kept next to his armored breast. Unwrapping the tapestry, she felt the smooth hard surface underneath, the warm, living Firebird's Egg.

She folded the tapestry back over the Egg, then refilled the hole, happy her knight had not lied to her. He claimed that as Castellan he would have known if Byeli Zamak held such a magical egg—and it did not. But that was because he had escaped Byeli Zamak with it, and buried it here by the troll-bear's lair. Being a born romancer, she took such truthful misdirection as a sign of true love.

I

Prince Sergey

She meant to see her knight right after morning chores, before he could wander away from the cave—but the Bone Witch had a dozen things for her to do. For no apparent reason the Witch wanted the swallows' nests taken from under the eves, and her pet rats turned loose, then her favorite fetishes hung on branches in the Iron Wood. So many pointless tasks that she suspected the Witch of trying to keep her from seeing D'Roye. The Bone Witch's motives were as obscure as her methods.

The rats seemed happy to be set free, but the swallows complained bitterly, chattering shrilly and darting at her head. It was useless to tell them that the Witch ordered the mass removal. While she battled indignant swallows, the Witch sat at her bone table writing on thin strips of Chinese paper in her little cramped script. Tying these tiny messages to the feet of her carrier pigeons, the Witch released the pigeons one by one, sending them off into the blue summer sky.

Katya asked what was so important that the Witch must tell the world. The Bone Witch shushed her. "Be patient. In time all comes clear."

So the Witch always said. Katya returned to her tasks, working until the Bone Hut looked positively bare. Since the day she arrived the chaos of her new home had fascinated her—fetishes decorating bone rafters, swallows darting in and out, pigeons cooing in the eves, rats peering from wicker cages, all lit by tulip-shaped paper lanterns. It took her mind off the terror of belonging to a witch. She fully expected to be cooked and eaten, unless the Witch chose to have her raw. Soon Katya realized that she would have to do the cooking—but by then chores and boredom made her treasure the hut's distractions. Now it chilled her to see her home so neat. All the animals were gone, except for her knight's horse in the paddock out back. She hoped this latest mad impulse did not last.

Finally the Witch agreed to let her go. "There is nothing else for you to do here. Now go and make your way in the world. Be smart. Be brave. Think of me now and again. And if you ever need help, call on me. No matter how far you go, or what you become, I will be with you."

Katya told her she was only going to take breakfast to her knight. And her slave collar kept her from going much farther—but the Witch had a way of seeing grand drama in the most mundane things, like the song of a lark, or the first buds of spring. "Do not worry, I will be back in the afternoon."

"No, you won't," the Bone Witch replied. "Always remember, I tried to care for you and teach you trollcraft. Now recite your spell."

She recited her invisibility spell, grabbed up her basket and headed for the Iron Wood, happy to be free of the Witch—if only for a while.

She did not get far. There were no warning cries in the Iron Wood. No birds or squirrels to keep watch for her. She was concentrating on the winding trail through the metal trunks, when she caught a whiff of horses on the wind. Horses meant men. She froze, whispered her spell, and waited—hoping her heart was not banging too loud.

Hearing the clip-clop of iron-shod hooves, she realized they were riding down the crooked trail toward the Bone Witch's hut—coming in twos, to save getting slashed by spiked branches. In a moment they would be riding right over her, invisible or not. She turned and dashed back the way she had come. Byeli Zamak had been gone for only a day, and already men were coming farther than she ever thought possible. At the clearing in the metal wood, the Bone Witch stood waiting by her skin door, a grim smile on her wrinkled face. Katya told the sorceress she had heard horsemen coming, but the Witch merely nodded. Had the Witch known about these horsemen? Probably. The Bone Witch had sent her off with her basket and spell, knowing full well that she would not get far.

Hoofbeats grew louder as the column of riders neared the clearing. She waited alongside the Witch, curious to see what sort of horsemen dared come into the Iron Wood. But the first figure to appear was not on horseback—and only half a man. Man-shaped and naked, he strolled lithely into the clearing, covered head to foot with soft brown hair. His eyes were wolf's eyes. Canine fangs protruded from thin smiling lips.

Lycanthrope. She had never seen one like this before—few had and lived. He was not the harmless sort who totally shed human form to run with the wolves and mate with the bitches. He was a soulless demon from deep in the Iron Wood—the absolute worst of wolf and man. Or so the Witch always told her.

Behind him rode an incongruous pair. The taller of the two was a steel-helmeted horse archer wearing a blue Horse Guard's brigandine studded with silver nail heads. He had a huge dead swan hanging from his high saddle. Riding at his side was a dwarf mounted on a pony, wearing a parti-colored tunic and a fool's cap. More horsemen filed into the clearing behind them, spreading out from their column of two's—horse archers, knights, and men-at-arms, followed by squires and valets, even a steward and a butler in their uniforms of office. And an Ensign, holding up a grand duke's banner, with a black crescent and the lightning stroke sign of Ikstra. Beneath the banner rode Prince Sergey himself. Katya had never seen a prince of the blood before, but there was no mistaking this one. Grand Duke Sergey was a prince from the bootheels up, wearing silver-chased armor and a gold coronet on his old-fashioned great helmet. He had his visor tipped back and she could see the hard cold sheen in his pale blue eyes, glinting like dangerous ice in the spring.

He stared evenly at the aged Bone Witch—two of the most feared people in Markovy were meeting for the first time. Totally different, yet each in their own way absolutely terrifying. Prince Sergey, Grand Duke of Ikstra, broke the frosty silence, "Good morrow, grandmother, we are trailing a mounted knight, riding a gray war horse and wearing a blue-and-white surcoat. He is most likely wounded. Have you seen him?"

"No, my lord," replied the Bone Witch. "Not him, nor anyone like him."

"Strange," mussed Prince Sergey, "our wolfman trailed his horse straight to this clearing." The Lycanthrope stood waiting, a hideous look on his fanged face, clearly hoping to make a meal out of someone. "He was Castellan of Byeli Zamak, and claims to be a baron."

"And yet I have not seen him," the Witch insisted.

Prince Sergey looked to the dwarf sitting on his pony. Rising in his saddle, the dwarf took a deep breath through his nose. Two more sniffs, and the dwarf settled back in the saddle, saying, "She is telling the truth."

Prince Sergey nodded. Then his gaze turned to Katya, staring at her like she had failed to pay her squirrel tax. "What about the girl? Has she seen him?"

The "girl" gulped. "No, my lord, never." She shook her head vigorously, shrinking back beside the Witch.

Prince Sergey looked again at the dwarf. This time the little man swung off his pony, and walked over to her. His head came up to Katya's waist. Lifting his nose, he sniffed her belly, then ran his nostrils down her thigh. He stepped back, saying, "She is lying."

Sergey raised an eyebrow. "Has she seen the Castellan?" His dwarf shrugged. The little man was a lie sniffer, not a mind reader. His majesty turned back to her, "Have you seen a knight wearing blue and white?"

She had no good answer, caught between her need to lie, and knowing the dwarf would sniff her out. Anything she said would put her at the mercy of these men. The wolfman leered at her. He was the one who had found her. Without him, this clumsy crowd of horsemen could not have trailed her from the stream—but a Lycanthrope can track a mouse on a moonless night.

"Well, have you seen him?" the Grand Duke demanded.

Before she could think of some truthful misdirection, a shout of triumph came from the back of the Bone Hut. A couple of squires came around the corner proudly leading her knight's horse. Someone called out, "That's his horse. The big gray that belongs to the Castellan."

Prince Sergey stared hard at the horse, then looked back at her. "Have you seen the knight who rode this horse?"

She nodded dumbly, unable to come up with anything but the truth, though she knew it would doom her.

"Good," the Grand Duke concluded, "we are at last getting somewhere. Do you know where he is?"

"Not for certain." He could be long gone from the cave. In fact she fervently hoped he was.

Prince Sergey smiled, a chilling, terrible sight. "Nothing in life is certain—but I wager this will be sure enough." He turned to his Ensign, saying, "Pay her for the girl."

Taking his reins in his banner hand, the Ensign fished a gold coin out of his purse, tossing it at the naked feet of the Witch. The Bone Witch made no attempt to pick up the coin. "That is for the girl," the Ensign explained.

"She is not for sale," replied the Witch.

"Give her the whole purse," the Grand Duke ordered impatiently. His Ensign tossed the purse down beside the coin—but the Witch ignored it as well. "What do you want, grandmother?" Grand Duke Sergey seemed astonished that the Bone Witch refused his generosity.

"For you to leave." There was a hint of warning in the Witch's answer.

"We will," Sergey agreed, "when we have the girl."

"She is under my protection," the Witch insisted.

Grand Duke Sergey glared at her. Katya could feel the tension in the clearing. Two dozen armed men sat loafing in the saddle, backed by valets, pages, a steward, and butler. Horses looked on with equine curiosity. The Lycanthrope stood waiting, aching to use his fangs and claws. "By rights I could have you burned," Prince Sergey pointed out.

"Do it if you dare," replied the Witch, unworried by the prince's power.

Sergey motioned for his archers to dismount, saying, "Seize the girl."

Horrified, Katya stepped back toward the skin door. This was all her fault. She had brought the horse to the Bone Hut. An archer tried to brush past the Witch to grab her—but the Bone Witch shoved him sideways, landing him in a heap. Two archers seized the Witch's arms, but she whirled about, faster than the eye could follow, sending the armored pair flying to opposite ends of the clearing. Another archer tried to draw his sword, but the Witch reached out and grabbed his wrist, twisting it until it snapped. His blade dropped from limp fingers.

Archers fell back, appalled by the old woman's strength. The Lycanthrope dropped to a crouch, prepared to spring. Prince Sergey shouted, "Use your bows—but do not hit the girl. I will flay the man that misses."

A half dozen arrows leaped from their bows, striking the Witch in the chest and hip. She hardly even winced, standing between Katya and the men. Katya clung to the skin door, her fist jammed in her mouth, stifling a scream, aghast at what she had done.

More arrows thudded into the Witch. Painfully the old woman turned to face her. The Bone Witch's chest looked like a bloody pin cushion. Arrows continued to hit her from behind. Staggering from the impact, the Witch opened her mouth as if she meant to speak. All that came out was a horrible gargling sound, followed by a great gout of blood. Shocked and sickened, Katya watched the Witch sink slowly to her knees.

"Stop shooting! Stop shooting!" Sergey cried. "You will hit the girl." Silence settled over the clearing as tears poured down Katya's cheeks. Half a dozen bows were pointed at her, arrows knocked and ready. She could see their gleaming chiseled steel points aimed at her chest. The Witch lay at her feet, feathered with arrows. Katya too expected to die—if not now, then soon.

Prince Sergey broke the silence, spurring his mount to put himself between her and the archers, shouting, "Down bows! Damn you! Down bows!"

Hurriedly his men obeyed. Wiping her tears away, Katya seized the Prince's stirrup. "Why did you kill her?" she wailed. "I am the one who lied."

Startled, Prince Sergey stared down in disbelief, as if astonished she could speak. "The Witch did not know where he was. You did." So the Witch died, and she lived—for now. "You do know where the Castellan is?" Sergey wanted to be sure.

She nodded. Any other answer would be her death warrant.

"And you can take us to him?"

She nodded again.

"Good." Prince Sergey pulled his boot from his stirrup, planted the heel on her shoulder, and shoved, sending her sprawling. He waved to his men, "Burn the place. Burn the Witch's body. Burn it all."

Prince Sergey cantered off. For a moment she lay looking up at blue sky framed by black iron tree tops, her breath coming in ragged gasps. Without warning, a big bearded archer took the Prince's place. Looking down at her, he laughed, saying, "Here's a cute young case of the clap. And already on her back."

"Give your middle leg a rest," another archer advised.

"What do you mean?" the man asked indignantly. "I've not been fucked in a fortnight."

"Small wonder." The second archer helped her to her feet, brushing the dirt off her dress, which was spattered with the Bone Witch's blood.

Someone called out, "Does she have a name?"

"Do you?" asked the archer.

Of course, she thought—but all she said was, "Katya."

"She calls herself Katya." The horse archer was speaking to a huge man in an oversized suit of plate armor. Mounted on a big black Frisian, he towered over everything, seeming to reach right to the ridgepole of the Bone Hut. He wore the same blue-white surcoat as her knight, but many times bigger, and marked with the sword-and-shield badge of a Master-at-arms. Tipping back the visor on his German sallet, he asked her in a big booming voice, "Where do you come from, girl?"

Scared senseless, she still had the presence of mind to lie. "I am the daughter of a Kazak hetman, Kaffa Khan. Harm me, and he will come with a *tumen* of horse archers to hunt you all to death."

He laughed, saying, "Have knee-high give her a sniff."

She had forgotten about the Dwarf. Too much had happened since she last saw the little man. He walked over and took a deep sniff, then turned to the Master-at-arms, saying, "She lies."

The Master-at-arms did not look surprised—her lie had been feeble at best. "Come, my little khanum, give us the truth. Or I will see you suffer."

She admitted she did not know who her parents were, saying, "I was raised here, by the Witch." Mentioning the Bone Witch made her want to cry, but she stopped herself.

"Are you virtuous?" asked the Master-at-arms.

She stared dumbly up at him. What a stupid question to ask a witch-child. How could anyone be both damned and virtuous?

"There's your answer," the lecherous horse archer chuckled. "She does not even know what you are asking."

The Master-at-arms grinned, "Well, it is bad luck to execute a virgin. . . ."

"Especially for the virgin," a horse archer added, getting a laugh from his fellows.

The Master-at-arms signaled for silence. "But in your case we will risk it. Stop your lying, and lead us to the Castellan. Otherwise we will have you flayed and left to fry in the sun. Unlucky or not. Do you understand?"

She understood.

He turned to the squires and archers, telling them to get busy, "Drag the Witch into the hut, and set it on fire." None too happy with their task, archers dragged the Witch's body into the Bone Hut. Katya watched them pile the straw beds atop the Witch, then throw on firewood, furniture, and the contents of the winter clothes chests. Dousing the pile with cooking oil, they set it alight. Soon the Bone Hut was blazing away. She saw her life going up in smoke and flames—just like Byeli Zamak.

"Mount up," the Master-at-arms ordered. Squires hoisted her aboard D'Roye's gray charger. One of them handed her the reins, and something to go with them. Looking down, she saw it was her straw doll—the one she had brought with her when she first came to live with the Witch. The young squire who had given it to her looked embarrassed. Of all these men—from Grand Duke Sergey down to the lowest valet—this boy alone seemed ashamed for what they had done.

The Master-at-arms gave her a grin that was all beard and teeth, saying, "Now lead us to the Castellan." She nodded, clutching the straw doll to her belly. Somehow, some way, she meant to come out of this alive and whole. But how that would happen, Heaven alone knew.

II

The Firebird's Egg

Mounted on her knight's gray charger, she led the whole cavalcade along the winding trail out of the Iron Wood. The Master-at-arms rode beside her, with the dwarf mounted pillion behind him, and the Lycanthrope loping on ahead. Boxed in by armed ruthless men, she could neither lose them nor lie to them—not so long as they had the wolfman to track her, and the dwarf to sniff out her lies. Only a stroke of monumental good fortune could save her, and she had long ago learned she had to make her own luck.

Whenever the Master-at-arms questioned her directions, the dwarf made sure she told only the truth, putting a heavy burden on someone who always relied on lies. Whatever saved her now had to be the Lord's honest truth. At the head of Long Lake, hot perfumed pine scent replaced the cold metal odor of the Iron Wood. Swans clumped at the center of the lake, already learning to be wary of the archers. She turned west, straight for the ridge line separating the forest from the steppe. The Master-at-arms looked askance. "You are leading us back toward Byeli Zamak?"

"That is where I left him, in a cave by the spring at the base of the ridge."

"Is that so?" he asked the dwarf riding behind him.

"She is telling the truth," replied the dwarf, looking pleased that she had learned not to lie.

The Master-at-arms turned back to her. "And this is the shortest way there?"

"Absolutely," she assured him. The dwarf confirmed her. An east wind had blown all morning, and she was determined to lead them straight downwind, avoiding the roundabout way she came the day before. No need now to hide her tracks. "If I take you right to him, will you let me go?"

"Of course, of course," the big man answered affably. But she was looking behind him at the dwarf, who glanced sharply up, saying nothing. Having a lie-sniffer riding on your horse's rump worked both ways. She had seen that same look of contempt on the dwarf's face when she tried to lie. The Master-at-arms did not mean to let her go. None of them did. Once she had served her purpose they would burn her as a witch. If they had not already promised her to the Lycanthrope.

As they plunged into the living wood, with its green trees and countless eyes, she heard a squirrel chatter, followed by the firebird's cry. It was not the flame jay's man call. She kept her eyes fixed on the path ahead, making sure the Master-at-arms got no warning from her. As the firebird's cry faded behind her, she strained her ears, trying to tell what was happening at the back of the column. All she could hear was the horse archers, laughing and joking behind her. They had a seemingly endless stock of sacrilegious stories to keep their spirits up.

Suddenly a scream rang out. The Master-at-arms grabbed her reins, looking back down the column. They waited. The story tellers fell silent. She watched little white butterflies dance in the sunlight. Presently a horse archer on a bay mare came galloping up. "What happened?" demanded the Master-at-arms.

"A leopard," the horse archer gasped.

"A leopard?" The Master-at-arms looked shocked.

"Yes, it dropped out of a tree on the last man in the column—Vasily, from Suzdal. He stopped to tighten his stirrup and take a piss. Before he could remount the cat was on him. By the time we got back to him, he was dead and the beast was gone."

"That makes no sense," complained the Master-at-arms. "A leopard attacking an armed man in daylight?" And from upwind, Katya added to herself, carefully searching the trees. A wood tit stared back at her. "No cat could be that hungry," insisted the Master-at-arms.

The horse archer shrugged. "The cat did not act hungry. It just broke Vasily's neck, then went on its way."

The Master-at-arms snorted, "Which makes even less sense. Sling his body over a horse, and tell Prince Sergey we are ready to move." The archer turned his bay mare about and went trotting back down the column.

Again they waited. Katya sat listening to the pines murmuring overhead. A woodpecker started to hammer, then stopped suddenly. Had it seen something? Slowly the profane stories reappeared—"A nun, a bishop, and a brothel keeper are in a boat. The bishop says to the nun . . ." She kept her ears tuned to the trees, listening for the woodpecker, and wondering why it was taking so long to get started again.

Finally Prince Sergey's Ensign trotted up, asking the same question, "Are you ready to move on? His highness means to be back at Byeli Zamak by dusk." Rolling his eyes, the Master-at-arms told him, "I sent a man back saying we were ready to ride."

"What man?" asked the Ensign.

This provoked another commotion. A search failed to find the messenger, but did discover his bay mare, nervously cropping bracken in a nearby clearing. Fresh blood shone on her saddle. The Master-at-arms exploded, "This is absurd. We cannot sit here waiting to be eaten. Tell His Highness we are setting out—unless the leopard gets you first."

She started up again at a brisk trot. No one complained. Not with bloodthirsty leopards stalking the column. Men kept twisting in their saddles, glancing over their shoulders, looking everywhere but ahead. She saw a familiar break in the pines, backed by a tall stand of oaks. Since they were headed downwind there was no warning but the cry of a crossbill, which the men ignored. Only the Lycanthrope looked uneasy, padding silently along, ears cocked forward, claws extended.

Suddenly the werewolf froze, hairs quivering. She braced herself. This was it. The next seconds would decide if she lived or died. The Lycanthrope spun about and vanished into the undergrowth. An archer called out, "What scared the wolfman? Why has he run off?"

As if to answer him, the troll-bear burst from his hidden lair, bellowing defiance at the intruders. Twice the size of a normal bear, with steel-hard hide and razor claws, the beast roared into the column, scattering men and horses. Rolling out of her saddle, Katya dropped to a crouch and whispered her spell. Instantly she vanished.

From her invisible crouch she got a close-up view of the swift horrific conflict. The troll-bear's forepaws flailed about, mace-headed battering rams slashing through plate armor like parchment. The Master-at-arms seized a lance from a squire, slapped down his visor, and charged the monster full tilt. His lance shattered on the troll-bear's hornlike hide. The enraged beast backhanded him out of the saddle, crushed him with a hind foot, then bit his horse's head off.

None of the other heroes who captured her tried to stop the troll-bear. The whole column—six lances of Horse Guards, with their attendant squires, valets, and archers, along with Prince Sergey's entourage of pages, Ensign, steward, and butler—vanished in an eyeblink, as if they too knew an invisibility spell. The troll-bear went howling after them, snapping pine saplings and uprooting boulders.

Which was why sensible woods creatures avoided a troll-bear's lair. The carrion stink was like a viper's hiss, a warning to unwary neighbors. Silence settled on the forest. Clutching her straw doll, she surveyed the new made clearing out the corner of her eyes. The worst part of being invisible was the inability to turn her head. Absolutely maddening when you wanted to know if it was safe to be seen. She was frozen in place staring at the armored leg of the Master-at-arms, sticking out from beneath a headless horse. She saw no sign of the dwarf who had been riding behind him.

Finally she made herself close her eyes, trusting in her ears to see behind her. Nothing. No warning cries, no rustle of leaves. No smell but the stink of troll-bear from somewhere upwind. She was free.

And alive. From the moment the Witch had died, she counted herself dead as well. Her demise seemed certain. She had let herself be tracked, and had gotten the Witch killed. And she was in the hands of men who meant to dispose of her in some grotesque fashion once she did their bidding. Now her life had been saved by a troll-bear. Few indeed could make that claim.

So what to do with her newfound freedom? Her first thought was for her knight. He was at the heart of this. He and the Firebird's Egg. She did not believe Prince Sergey would risk the Iron Wood just to put an end to some foreign born Castellan of Byeli Zamak. Love did not make her that blind. Her knight was not nearly as important as the Egg he had carried.

Moving stealthily downwind, ears tuned to the slightest sound, she crept up on the rocks and spring. She did not think any of the men could have caught up with her, even if they escaped the troll-bear. But having gotten her life back, she did not mean to let down her guard. Hot afternoon air hung heavy and expectant. And unnaturally quiet. Beyond the bubbling spring, the forest seemed to be holding its breath.

Suddenly she heard the firebird's shrill cry. She froze against a big boulder speckled with bird lime, whispering her spell. This was the second time today she had heard the bird's warning. It was as if the jay were watching over her. This cry was different than any she had heard before, the man-call mixed with an unfamiliar trill.

As she strained to survey the rocks without moving her head, a heavy form dropped on her from atop the boulder. Hairy arms seized her waist, and vice-hard thighs gripped her hips. Her struggles broke the invisibility spell, which had been no match for the Lycanthrope's supernatural senses. She was merely an unarmed young woman, fighting immensely strong arms, while the man-beast's fanged hairy face leered into hers.

Horrified, she struggled harder. Keeping her arms pinned, the Lycanthrope dragged her back away from the spring—but did nothing else to harm her. No clawing. No fangs in the neck. Not reassuring in the least, with his steel-like erection digging into the small of her back.

Then she felt the Lycanthrope relax. Looking up, she saw horsemen staring down at her. Prince Sergey sat bareheaded on his charger, having lost his gold-crowned helmet. His Ensign was beside him, along with a single horse archer, several frightened squires, and a bedraggled looking butler—all that was left of the proud cavalcade that had ridden boldly into the Iron Wood. The Lycanthrope must have been stalking ahead of them. Coming on her scent trail, he had gone up the backside of the boulder and dropped down onto her.

Prince Sergey trotted over to where she stood, glaring down at her. "Did you know we were riding into a troll-bear's lair?"

Her immediate impulse to lie died on her lips, when she spotted the dwarf riding behind the butler. She shook her head instead. "I will not tell you anything unless you let me go."

"Be cooperative," Prince Sergey warned. "I have only to say the word, and the beast holding you will savage you on the spot."

"You will not learn a lot from that," she pointed out.

"Yes," Sergey admitted, "but I might very much enjoy it." Nonetheless he waved to the wolfman. "Let her go."

The Lycanthrope let go of her, a little victory, and likely to be her last. Katya took a deep breath, wishing she could just disappear right here. What had she done to deserve all this? Not a thing so far as she could see. Prince Sergey leaned forward in the saddle. "Now, tell us what we want to know."

"If I do, will you let me go?" She stared past the prince at the dwarf seated behind his butler.

"Just tell the truth, and you have nothing to fear."

The dwarf's nose wrinkled, as if he whiffed something foul. So much for honesty. Prince Sergey had no intention of freeing her. She closed her eyes, taking another slow breath, prolonging the inevitable. "What do you wish to know?"

"Tell where the Castellan is," Prince Sergey demanded, royally impatient.

"Right here," came the cheerful reply. Her eyes flew open. There was her knight, standing tall and nonchalant, sword in hand, a wry smile on his handsome face. Seeing him appear out of nowhere was like suddenly getting her life back. He made a mocking bow to Prince Sergey. "Baron Roy d'Roye, Chevalier de l' Étoile, and until late Castellan of Byeli Zamak. At your service."

Sergey sat up in the saddle. "My God! You! Why did you not open Byeli Zamak to me?"

Her knight shrugged armored shoulders. "You did not say *s'il vous plait*. King Demitri gave me Byeli Zamak to hold for his heir."

"I am Prince Ivan's uncle. Byeli Zamak should have come to me."

"And it has," D'Roye reminded him, smiling at his latest defeat.

Prince Sergey leaned forward again. "But not the Firebird's Egg."

"That is what brings us here." Her knight looked smug.

"So you have the Egg?"

"Not on me. But I know where it is."

"Where?" Sergey demanded.

"What will you pay to know?"

"Half my kingdom?" Sergey suggested sarcastically.

"I will give it up cheaper than that. Set this wood sprite free. Her and me, alive and ahorsed—that is all I ask."

Katya fought back tears. Her knight had given up his hiding place, and the Egg he protected, all to save her. A foolish impetuous gesture that would probably get them both killed. Still, she was touched.

"Almost too cheap," Sergey mused. "Generosity from an enemy is always suspect—but perhaps you are merely a fool."

"Obviously. Pray indulge me nonetheless."

"You, the girl, and two horses—easy enough." Sergey lifted a steel-gloved finger. "After I have the Egg."

"As you wish." Keeping his big two-handed sword drawn, her knight turned to her. "*Mademoiselle*, I must go with these men—hopefully I will be coming back with a pair of horses."

"She comes with us," Sergey insisted.

D'Roye rolled his eyes apologetically. "Alas, *Mademoiselle*, I fear this Grand Duke means it. Fortunately, it is but a short way into the forest. . . ."

"By a stand of big oaks," she reminded him.

His eyes lit up. "I see you know the place."

She nodded excitedly. She knew better than he did. And the deeper they got into her woods, the safer they would be. Get far enough into the forest, and she and her knight were more than a match for any number of killers on horseback. But she did not say that aloud, for fear the killers would hear. She had to rely on him reading it in her smile.

He did seem to understand, setting out happily, not the least worried by the armed men around them, laughing, and making light of things. She wanted to tell him about the Bone Witch, but that too must wait. This time they approached the troll-bear's lair from downwind—by far the safest direction. So long as you stayed out of the beast's hearing you had little to fear. But as soon as they whiffed the carrion scent, Prince Sergey's men revolted, none of them wanting a rematch with the monster. Their horses too refused to go any farther, shying and whinnying at the fearful stench.

Sergey immediately demanded that the dwarf sniff her knight for a lie. D'Roye submitted with good grace, for once having nothing to hide. But the dwarf went right up to him, sniffing vigorously. Katya could guess why. The little man desperately hoped to smell a lie. If her knight was telling the truth, they would have to march straight back toward the troll-bear's lair.

Finally, the dwarf admitted D'Roye smelled sincere. Sergey was forced to leave the horses and squires behind, but he bullied the Ensign, horse archer, and butler into accompanying him on foot. Katya did not fear any of these men half so much as she feared the Lycanthrope.

The dwarf did not get a choice. Like her, he was too valuable to leave behind, and would come whether he willed it or not. She went out of her way to comfort the little man, whose only concern was for the truth. He and the Witch were the only ones she had never been able to lie to, which she very much respected. "Stay close to me," she told him, "and I will try to see you are safe."

He looked warily up at her, "Is that so?"

"I thought you would know." He was the one with the supremely educated nose. As they set out walking, she slid her hand inside her dress, stroking the straw doll hidden next to her breast, just for luck.

When they got to the oak grove, the butler had to go down on his beribboned knees and dig for the Egg with his bare hands. Prince Sergey would not let him use so much as a toothpick, for fear of harming the Egg. Her knight stood watching calmly, leaning on his big two-handed sword. She motioned for the dwarf to get behind her. Which he immediately did, backing away toward the bushes. A bad sign—the little man who knew his master best was expecting the worst.

Reaching his hands into the hole, the butler drew forth the Firebird's Egg. As he unwrapped the dirty tapestry, everyone stared in awe at Markovy's greatest wonder. Except for the Lycanthrope, who kept his hungry eyes fixed on her. What had he been promised when Prince Sergey had the Egg?

Her knight spoke first. "*Excusez-moi*, this may be exceptionally foolish of me, but I beg you to listen to the advice of your late king."

"What advice?" Sergey looked suspiciously at her knight, as if he was an insect with an especially annoying hum.

"King Demitri sent a deathbed message to me, ordering that this Egg be returned safely to its Nest. Not an easy task, but one I heartily endorse. There is a terrible curse on this Egg. How many lives has that damned Egg cost in the last two days alone?" Her knight was right, Byeli Zamak had been burned. And so had the Bone Hut. Prince Sergey's proud company had been reduced to a scared handful, standing around the magical Egg.

Prince Sergey gave a snort of contempt. "We need no lessons from the loser."

"There are worse things than losing," her knight pointed out. "My own fortunes have improved mightily since I put that ill-fated Egg in the ground."

"Really?" Prince Sergey arched an eyebrow.

"Absolutely." Her knight smiled at her. "I was beaten and bleeding, fleeing yet another defeat. But as soon as I parted from that Egg, there came this delightful forest nymph, stitching my wounds and serving me caviar."

"How lucky for you," Sergey laughed. "My own ambitions are a bit higher."

Her knight shrugged, "To each their own. Hopefully, King Demitri will know I tried. Now if I may depart with my own prize." He reached a steel-gloved hand out to her.

"You may inform Demitri in person." Prince Sergey nodded to the Lycanthrope. "Kill him and the girl is yours."

Faster than thought, the Lycanthrope leaped at D'Roye's throat, claws extended. But her knight had expected treachery. His blade came up in a terrific backhand swipe. Only the wolfman's supernatural agility saved him from being cut in two. Twisting in midair, the beast managed to evade the blade, landing on all fours.

All eyes were on her knight, so Katya stepped back against a tree, whispering her spell. The dwarf had already vanished into the undergrowth. Holding her breath, she stood rigid, smelling sap sweating from the pine behind her, watching the fight and wanting to help, but not knowing how.

D'Roye kept his sword between himself and the werewolf, feinting and slashing. Despite his speed and cunning, the Lycanthrope could not get past the flashing blade. Twice he tried to duck under the sword, and got nicked in the shoulder and the ear. But the wolfman moved too fast for D'Roye to land a killing blow. Stalking sideways, he searched for an opening.

"Help the beast," Prince Sergey commanded. "Take him from behind."

His butler just stood there, stupidly holding the Egg—but the Ensign and horse archer obeyed, drawing their swords and trying to slide around behind D'Roye. So long as the Lycanthrope kept him busy in front, it would only be a matter of time before one of the others got at his back.

Being the bolder of the two, the Ensign was first to get in position. As D'Roye aimed a slash at the werewolf, the Ensign raised his own sword, stepping in to strike.

Seeing the Ensign lunge past her, Katya leaped forward, seizing the man's sword arm. Coming out of nowhere, she took the Ensign by surprise. As he struggled to shake her off, D'Roye spun about, hitting him a wicked two-handed blow just beneath the breastplate. Groaning, the Ensign went down, rattling like a pile of dropped pans.

Instantly the Lycanthrope bounded at D'Roye. But her knight seemed to know what was coming. Ignoring the downed Ensign, he let his momentum spin him completely about. This time his backhand caught the Lycanthrope between the neck and collarbone, severing the beast's jugular in a hideous spray of blood. The werewolf landed in a gory heap at his feet.

Strong arms grabbed her from behind. The horse archer had not dared to take on D'Roye, but he seized her to use as a living shield. Prince Sergey whipped his sword out, and she felt the sharp point at her throat. "Stop," the Grand Duke commanded. "Drop your sword or I will kill her."

Her knight let his point drop, saying, "Come now, Your Highness, that is hardly sporting. All we want is to be on our way."

"Drop your sword," Prince Sergey demanded. "Or I swear by God Almighty I shall slit her throat."

With a sigh, D'Roye jammed his sword point first into the ground beside the dead Lycanthrope. Then he stepped back, away from the blade, folding his arms. "I warn you, this will bring nothing but grief."

"Perhaps," Sergey admitted with a grin. "But you will not be there to see it." Katya's heart sank. Her knight would die—merely for showing mercy—and she would have to watch. Sergey stepped toward D'Roye, hefting his sword.

As he did, a black and amber body dropped on him from the branches above. Prince Sergey gasped as the leopard sank her fangs into his neck. Staggering beneath the weight of the leopard the Grand Duke dropped to his knees, then pitched forward onto his face. Katya watched in astonishment as the big cat continued to bite down on the Grand Duke, making sure he never got up.

D'Roye jerked his sword out of the ground, saying to the horse archer holding her, "Let the girl go, if you want to live." The arms holding her vanished, and she heard footfalls behind her as the horse archer took off into the forest. Her knight turned to Prince Sergey's butler, who still held the Firebird's Egg, a sick look on his horrified face. "Carefully set down that Egg, and you too may go."

Placing the Egg gently on the ground, the butler backed slowly through the bracken, bumped into a tree, then turned and ran for his life. All that remained of Prince Sergey's expedition into the Iron Wood was a trio of bodies, lying around the Firebird's Egg. "*Mon Dieu*," D'Roye muttered, "that went far better than I could ever have imagined."

Slowly the leopard rose up, changing as she did, becoming a withered naked old woman with wrinkled skin and bone white hair. And not a single arrow mark on her. The Bone Witch smiled at Katya. "I told you I would be here if you needed me."

Her knight lowered his point and looked over at her. "This I suppose is your witch?"

She hastened to introduce the Bone Witch to her knight, proud of the way he went down on one knee before the withered old woman, saying, "*Madame* Witch, Baron Roy d'Roye, at your service."

"Is that just a gallantry," asked the Witch, "or are you really at my service?"

"Absolutely. *Madame* has saved my life, and I owe her anything that honor allows."

"Good," the Bone Witch declared, "I have need of your honor." Then the Witch turned to her. "Come here, my daughter."

She walked happily over, grateful to be free of Prince Sergey's killers and glad to see the Witch alive—but utterly ecstatic to have someone finally call her "daughter."

Giving her a wrinkled kiss, the Witch took the slave collar from around her neck. "Now I have one last chore for you."

"Whatever you wish." For once she truly meant it.

"Return the Firebird's Egg to its proper nest, so it may hatch and the curse on Markovy can be lifted."

"But how will I get there?" She felt surprised the Witch would give her a task so important, and so seemingly impossible.

"These will take you there." The Witch snapped her bony fingers and a trio of horses ambled into the clearing—the knight's war horse, a black mare with a horse archer's bow and quiver hanging from her saddle, and a big bay palfrey laden with supplies. D'Roye's eyes lit up, seeing the gray charger he had clearly given up for lost.

"I mean, how will I find the Nest?" All Katya knew of the Firebird's Nest was that it lay deep in the Iron Wood.

The Witch gave a low call, holding out her finger, and the flame jay flew down to land on it. Stroking the bird's breast, the crone cooed, "You can take them there, can you not?" Throwing back his head, the jay gave a confident raucous reply, flying over to land on the black mare's saddle. "See," the Witch told her, "he is more than ready. Are you?"

Katya nodded solemnly, seeing that this is what the Witch had been training her for—how she would finally be "useful."

When she had the Egg safely tucked into the palfrey's pack saddle, Katya kissed the Bone Witch good-bye, and climbed onto the black mare. She watched her knight bow good-bye to the Witch, then mount his gray charger, grinning merrily. Her whole life led her to this point. As an orphan growing up, she invented royal parents and a magical future for herself. Just when puberty and poverty were about to lay waste her fantasies, she was given to the Bone Witch, making the magical part real. Now the rest was coming to pass—she had a horse beneath her, a charming knight at her side, and a quest ahead with the kingdom's future at stake. She took her straw doll out of her dress, putting it in the black mare's saddle bag.

Only one thing made her uneasy: her knight was a foreigner, not required to care if there was a curse on Markovy. And he was a real baron to boot, who did not need her royal dreams and extravagant lies. She asked softly and sincerely, "Are you sure you want to do this? You are free to go your own way if you wish."

"Heavens no, *Mademoiselle*." He grinned happily. "Not when my lady has at long last landed me on the winning side."

Dragon's Gate

ꕥ

Pat Murphy

What sort of compilation of heroic fantasy stories would this be if it didn't have a dragon story in it? Tales of brave knights and fierce dragons have been a staple of adventure fiction for centuries. F&SF *has done its best to contribute to the tradition over the years, and this most recent effort is a fine adventure that also explores the nature of storytelling itself. It ran in our August 2003 issue.*

Pat Murphy is the author of several novels, including The Falling Woman, The City, Not Long After, The Shadow Hunter, *and* Nadya. *Her most recent books,* Wild Angel, There and Back Again, *and* Adventures in Time and Space with Max Merriwell, *play with varying perspectives on different fantasy and science fiction traditions. Ms. Murphy also collaborates on a regular science column for* F&SF *with Paul Doherty, one of her colleagues at the Exploratorium museum in San Francisco, where she works.*

My name is Alita, which means "girl to be trusted." My mother calls me Al. If anyone asks, I tell them it's short for Alonzo, a solid masculine name. At fifteen years of age, I can pass for a boy on the verge of manhood. I dress in men's clothing, preferring tunic and breeches to petticoats and skirts.

My mother plays the harp and sings ballads; I am a storyteller. I know common folk stories (rife with bawdy asides and comic characters), heroic tales favored by the nobility (usually involving handsome princes, beautiful princesses, and courtly love), and morality tales (favored by the clergy, but not by many others). I know how a story should go.

The story that I tell you now is unruly and difficult. It refuses to conform to any of the traditional forms. This story wanders like sheep without a shepherd. It involves a prince and a dragon, but not until later. There will be magic and wishes and . . . well, I'll get to all that presently.

I begin my story in the mountain town of Nabakhri, where shepherds and weavers gather each fall. The shepherds come down from the mountains to sell their wool; the weavers come up from the lowlands to buy. My mother and I come to the festival to entertain the lot of them.

Twilight was falling when my mother and I reached the town. We had been traveling for two days, beginning our journey in the warm valley where the Alsi River ran. There, people grew rice and millet and wore bright colorful clothing. In Nabakhri, people grew barley and potatoes, herded goats and sheep, and wore heavy woolen clothing.

The trail that led to town was steep, better suited for goats than for our pony. The evening breeze blew from the great glacier that filled the valley to the west of Nabakhri. Our pony's breath made clouds in the cold, crisp air.

At the edge of town, we waited for a flock of sheep to cross the main path. The sheep bleated in protest as dogs nipped at their heels. One of the shepherds, an older man in a ragged cloak, glanced at us. He smiled as he noted my mother's harp, slung on the side of our pony's pack. "Musicians!" he said. "Are you looking for an inn?"

I nodded. After the long summer alone in the mountains, shepherds are eager for music and good company.

"The inns in the center of the village are full," he said. "Try Sarasri's place. West side of the village, overlooking the glacier. Good food, good drink."

Someone shouted from the direction in which the man's flock was disappearing. The man lifted a hand in farewell and hurried after his sheep.

Sarasri's was a sprawling, ramshackle inn on the edge of town. We hitched the pony by the open door to the tavern, where the air was rich with the scent of lamb stew and fried bread. The barmaid called for Sarasri, the innkeeper.

Sarasri, a stout, round-faced woman, hurried from the kitchen, drying her hands on her apron. In the lowlands, it's unusual for a woman to run an inn, but women from the mountain tribes often go into business for themselves.

"We're looking for a room," I said, but she was shaking her head before the words were out of my mouth.

"Alas, young fellow, there are too many travelers this year," she said. "I don't know that there's a room left anywhere in town."

My mother was not listening. She was looking past Sarasri into the tavern. "What do you think I should play tonight, Al?" she asked me. "It looks like there'll be quite a crowd." She smiled at Sarasri—my mother has a smile that could melt the snow on a mountaintop ten miles distant. "You have such a lovely inn," she said warmly and sincerely.

My mother is warm-hearted and guileless—traits that serve her in good stead. When my father read fortunes with the Tarot cards, my mother was always represented by the Fool, a young man in motley who is about to dance over the edge of a cliff. The Fool is a divine innocent, protected by angels. If he tripped over the cliff's edge, he would fall into a haystack.

Sarasri glanced at my mother. "You are musicians? It would be nice to have music in the tavern tonight." She frowned, thinking hard. "I do have one small room . . . ."

The room was used for storage—burlap sacks of potatoes and baskets filled with wool were stacked against one wall. The remaining space was barely big enough for a bed and a table. The window overlooked the glacier—at least we would not wake in the morning to the clamor of the village.

"Good enough?" I asked my mother.

"This is just wonderful." My mother would be comfortable in a stable stall, as long as she had her harp to play.

My father, a conjurer skilled at illusions and fortune telling, had died three years ago, when I was a girl of twelve. After his death, it fell to me to attend to practical details of life, as my mother was ill-suited to such a task. I did my best to take care of her.

When the weather was warm, we traveled from town to town. Wherever there was a festival, we performed in the taverns, passing the hat for our keep. In the cold months, we stayed in the lowlands, in the small village where my mother was born.

That evening, in Sarasri's tavern, my mother sang for an appreciative (and drunken) crowd of shepherds. Following my mother's performance, I told the tale of King Takla and the ice woman. With the glacier so near, I thought it appropriate to tell a story about the ice women.

Ice women are, of course, cousins of the river women. River women, as every lowlander knows, are magical creatures that take the form of beautiful maidens with green eyes and long hair the color of new leaves. Ice women are just as beautiful, but their eyes are as blue as the ice in the deep glacial caves and their hair is as white as new snow. Just as the river women inhabit the rivers, the ice women live in the high mountain glaciers.

King Takla, the ruler of a small kingdom high in the mountains, was hunting for mountain goats when he found a woman sleeping in a hollow in the glacier. She lay on the bare ice, covered with a white shawl woven of wool as fine and delicate as the first splinters of winter frost on the stones of the mountain. Only her beautiful face was exposed to the cold mountain air.

Takla recognized that she was not an ordinary woman. He knew, as all the hill folks know, that taking an ice woman's shawl gave a man power over her. He snatched up the shawl, revealing the ice woman's naked body. Ah, she was beautiful.

Her skin was as smooth and pale as the ice on which she rested. Her face was that of a sleeping child, so innocent and pure.

Takla hid the shawl in his hunting pack. Then, captivated by the woman's beauty, Takla lay beside her on the ice, kissing her pale face, caressing her naked breasts, stroking her thighs.

When she woke and stared at him with cool blue eyes, he spoke to her, saying, "You will be my queen, beautiful one." Though she struggled to escape, he grasped her arms and pulled her close to him. Overcome with passion for this pale maiden, he forced himself upon her.

Then Takla wrapped her in his hunting cloak and took her back to his castle to become his queen. He dressed her in fine clothing and adorned her with glittering gems. Her beauty surpassed that of any mortal woman, but she never smiled and she seldom spoke. When she did, her voice was as soft as the sound of wind-blown ice crystals whispering over the snow.

"I must go home," she told Takla. "My mother will miss me. My sisters will miss me."

"You have a husband now," he told her. "Your mother will get over it. And if your sisters are as beautiful as you are, they must come to court and find husbands here." He kissed her pale face.

There are different ways one could tell this tale. In the tavern, I told it from King Takla's point of view, describing the ice woman's beauty, the allure of her naked body. A magical being captivates a man against his will. She is a lovely temptress. Unable to control his passion, the man takes possession of her.

In this version of the story, King Takla is helpless, a strong man stricken by love. In this version, Takla is an honest man in his way—he marries the ice woman, takes her for his queen. What more could any woman want?

I think that the ice woman would tell a very different version of the story. She was sleeping peacefully, bothering no one, when the king raped and abducted her, taking her away from her home and her sisters.

This version of the story would not be as popular in the tavern, but I think about it often, particularly when we perform in a tavern filled with soldiers. I am aware that my mother is a beautiful woman and that the soldiers admire more than her music. Because I dress as a young man, I avoid the soldiers' leers.

Of course, the tale of King Takla does not end with his capture of the ice woman. A man who takes a magical creature to his bed must face the consequences of his action.

After Takla brought the ice woman to his castle, blue-white lights flickered over the ice fields at night. The glacier moaned and creaked as the ice shifted and people said that the ice women were talking among themselves. A year passed and the ice woman bore King Takla a son—a sturdy child with his father's red hair and his mother's piercing blue eyes.

Not long after his son's birth, King Takla went hunting alone in the mountains. While following a path that led beside the glacier, he saw a white mountain goat, standing a hundred yards away on the ice. He shot an arrow, and the beast fell.

Takla made his way across the ice to where the goat had stood. But when he reached the place where the goat had fallen, he found nothing but ice. A trick of the ice women, he thought, and turned to retrace his steps to the rocky mountain slope. A tall woman with white hair blocked his way.

"King Takla," she said. "You must set my daughter free."

Takla studied the woman. This woman was older than his wife, but just as beautiful. The same fair features, the same piercing blue eyes, the same beautiful body.

"Your daughter is my wife and the mother of my son," he said.

"I will reward you handsomely if you let her go," said the woman. She held out a silver hunting horn. "Release my daughter and sound the horn—and I will come and grant you a wish. Three times I will come when the horn is sounded and three wishes I will grant." She held the instrument up so that the king could admire its fine workmanship and contemplate what wishes he might make.

Takla studied the horn and considered the woman's offer. He had, over the passing year, grown weary of his wife's unsmiling silence. Yes, she was beautiful, but he had begun to admire one of his wife's ladies-in-waiting, a fiery beauty with auburn hair and dark brown eyes. If he accepted the ice woman's offer, his wife would return to her people, leaving him free to marry again. With the ice woman's help, he could become more powerful.

Takla smiled and took the horn from the woman's hand. She stepped aside and he returned to his castle.

He took his wife's white shawl from the trunk where it had been hidden for the past year. When he entered his wife's chambers, she was suckling his infant son. She saw the shawl in his hands and her blue eyes widened. She handed the baby to her lady-in-waiting, the beauty who had captured the king's attention.

"What have you brought me?" the king's wife asked softly.

"Your mother gave me a gift." The king lifted the horn. "Three wishes will be mine, in exchange for one wish of hers. Her wish is that I set you free."

The king's wife took the shawl from his hands and wrapped it around her shoulders. Without a word, she left the room, running through the corridor, down the stairs, and out to the glacier. She was never seen again.

Takla smiled at the lady-in-waiting, then kissed his son on the forehead. Since the lady held his son cradled in her arms, bestowing this sign of fatherly affection afforded the king an opportunity to admire her bosom.

Filled with joy and thoughts of continuing power, Takla took the hunting horn and left the castle, climbing to a rock outcropping that overlooked the glacier, the castle, the pass, and the valley.

The Sun was dipping toward the horizon in the west. Takla looked out over his kingdom and thought of his first wish.

He put the horn to his lips and blew. A blue light flickered in the glacier below, then the ice woman stood before him. "What is your wish?" she asked.

"I wish that I may remain above all others as I am now and that my reign will last as long as the stones of the mountain."

The ice woman smiled and lifted her hand. The silver horn fell from the king's hand as a transformation took place. The king became stone, a royal statue gazing over the kingdom.

"As you wish, you will stay here, above all others," the ice woman said. "Your reign will last as long as the stones of the mountain. Until the wind and the weather wear you away, you will reign over this place."

Among the mountain people, there is a saying. "Like a gift of the ice women," they say about presents that end up costing the recipient dearly. It is best not to meddle in magical matters. One must not trust a gift of the ice women.

I had just reached the end of the story when the wind blew the tavern door open. At the time, I thought that was a stroke of good luck; the blast of cold air made my listeners shiver and appreciate the story all the more. "A gift of the ice women," I said, and the crowd laughed.

I passed among the shepherds, gathering coins from those who had enjoyed the tale. When I walked near the kitchen door, I saw that Sarasri was frowning. She spoke to me as I passed. "That's not a good tale to tell so close to the glacier. You'd best keep your shutters closed tonight. The ice women won't like it that you're talking about them."

I was a humble storyteller, far beneath the notice of magical creatures. I didn't think that the ice women would concern themselves with my doings. Still, I followed Sarasri's advice that night. I closed the shutters—not to keep out the ice women, but rather to keep out the cold. Unfortunately, the wooden shutters were warped. Though I closed them as tightly as I could, a cold draft blew through the gap between them.

I did not sleep well. I could hear the glacier groaning and creaking as the ice shifted and moved. I was glad when the first light of dawn crept through the gap in the shutters, casting a bright line on my mother, who slept soundly beside me.

Quietly, I dressed and went down to the street. The weather had grown colder and the rocky paths were slick with frost. At a baker's shop I bought sweet buns for our breakfast. The buns were warm against my hands as I carried them back to our room.

When I entered the room, I called to my mother to wake her, but she did not move. I shook her, and still she did not wake. "Mother," I called to her. "Mother?"

She would not wake up. I found Sarasri in the kitchen and she sent a boy to find a healer. I sat by my mother's side, breakfast forgotten.

The healer, an old woman with white hair, sat on the edge of my mother's bed and felt my mother's cheek. She held a silver spoon beneath my mother's nose and watched to see that my mother's breath fogged the silver. She stroked my mother's hand and called to her. Then she shook her head and said, "Ice sickness."

I stared at her. "What do you mean?"

"It comes from the wind off the glacier," Sarasri said. She frowned unhappily. "That's what comes of telling tales about the women of the ice."

"Those who get the ice sickness sleep peacefully until they waste away," the healer said.

I stared at my mother. Her face was so calm and peaceful in sleep. It was hard to believe that anything was amiss. "What can I do?"

"There is one cure," the healer said.

"What is it?" I asked.

"Three drops of dragon's blood. Place them in her mouth and they'll warm her back to life." The healer shrugged. "But we have no dragon's blood and no hero to fetch it for us."

Sarasri shook her head sorrowfully. "As if a hero would help," she said. "How many have journeyed to Dragon's Gate, filled with pride and noble plans? Not a one has returned."

"Do you have to be a hero to fetch dragon's blood?" I asked. "We only need three drops of blood. The dragon doesn't have to die to give up three drops."

Sarasri frowned but the old healer nodded. "That's true," she said. "Slaying the dragon is not necessary, if you can get a bit of blood by some other means." She studied me. Her eyes were a brilliant blue, unfaded by her years. "Do you know anything about dragons?" she asked me.

"Only what I have learned from heroic tales," I said. "And that's not much. The dragon usually dies as soon as the prince shows up."

The old woman nodded. "Those tales are about princes, not about dragons. Those stories describe a dragon as a fire-breathing lizard with wings."

"Is that wrong?" I asked.

"It is not so much wrong as it is incomplete. The essence of a dragon is not in its appearance, but in its nature."

"What is its nature?"

"A dragon is an inferno of anger, blazing with fury, exploding with pain. A dragon is a beast of fire and passion, feeding on fear and hatred." The old woman stood and drew her woolen cloak around her shoulders. "Approached with fear, a dragon responds with fire."

"What if one does not approach with fear?" I asked.

She shrugged. "A difficult task to accomplish," she said. "But if it could be done, you might manage to start a conversation. I have heard that dragons like to talk. But they can smell a liar and that awakens their anger. Never lie to a dragon."

I

Perhaps this is where the story really begins. With my realization that I had to go to Dragon's Gate and return with three drops of blood from the dragon who had guarded the pass for the past hundred years.

I arranged for Sarasri to care for my mother. I left the pony in Sarasri's stables, since the way ahead was too rough and steep for the animal. Then I followed a footpath that led high into the hills.

Dragon's Gate was once known as Takla's Pass, named after King Takla, who married the ice woman. This mountain pass offered the shortest route from the lowlands to the trading cities on the Northern Sea. Long ago, caravans laden with carpets and spices and gems made their way through the mountains along this road. King Takla—and after him Takla's son, King Rinzen—charged merchants for safe passage.

All that changed a hundred years ago when good King Belen of the lowlands had, at the urging of rich merchants, sought to overthrow King Rinzen and put an end to his tolls. King Belen's army invaded the mountain kingdom. But a dragon released by some black magic drove back his army and closed the pass.

The dragon laid waste to the land. What had once been a thriving kingdom became a barren deserted land. Merchants from the lowlands banded together to offer a reward to any who could slay the dragon and open the road through the pass. But all the heroes who tried to win the reward perished in the attempt: burned by the dragon's fire, slashed by the dragon's claws.

Now merchants sent their goods through the desert and around the mountains to the south, a long and perilous journey. In the desert, bandits preyed on caravans and kidnapped merchants for ransom. But the possibility of being waylaid by bandits was better than the certainty of being killed by the dragon.

The path I took to Dragon's Gate was little better than a goat path. Winter avalanches had covered sections of the old trade route. Prickly shrubs had grown over the old road, and no one had cleared them away.

From Nabakhri, it was three days' hard travel to Dragon's Gate. The villages grew smaller and meaner as I traveled. People along the way asked me where I was going—and shook their heads grimly when they heard of my mission. "Turn back, young man," they said. "You haven't a chance of succeeding."

The last village before the dragon's pass was little better than a collection of grimy huts clinging to the side of the mountain. There a tiny teahouse doubled as an inn. Three shepherds sat by the fire in the common room, dining on lentil stew, fried bread, and tea.

The innkeeper was a stout man with an impressive mustache and a head of hair as thick as the wool on the mountain sheep. "Are you lost?" he asked me. "There is nowhere to go on this trail."

I explained my mission. He served me dinner and sat with me while I ate.

"You say you must approach the dragon without fear," he said. "How can you do that? Only a fool would not fear the dragon."

It was a good question. As I climbed the mountain trails, I had been thinking about how to quell my fear.

"Some of the stories that I tell are very frightening," I told the innkeeper. "But I am not afraid when I tell these tales because I know they will end well. What I am doing now is worthy of a story. If I think of this as a story I am telling, I will not be afraid."

The innkeeper frowned. "But you don't know that there will be a happy ending to this story of yours."

"Of course there will be," I said. "I am telling the story, remember? Why would I tell my own story with an unhappy ending?"

The innkeeper shook his head. "It sounds like you are just fooling yourself."

I nodded. "Indeed I am. What better way to keep away fear?"

The innkeeper shook his head and poured me another cup of tea. He spent the rest of the evening telling me of heroes who went to slay the dragon and never returned.

When I left the village the next morning, I did my best to put this conversation out of my mind. It wasn't easy. Above me loomed the barren crags of Dragon's Gate. Black rocks, like pointed teeth, made sharp silhouettes against the blue sky. One outcropping bore a resemblance to a standing man. That, it was said, was all that remained of King Takla.

Late in the afternoon, I reached the ice field that surrounded the castle where the dragon lived. Over the years, the glacier had flattened the walls that surrounded the castle gardens and had engulfed the outbuildings. The castle's outer walls had collapsed under the pressure of the ice, but the castle keep, the structure's central fortress, still stood. One tall tower rose from the ice field. From where I stood, the tower was as big as my thumb, held at arm's length.

Cautiously I started across the ice fields toward the tower. I used my walking stick to test each patch of ice before trusting my weight to it. Once, the ice collapsed beneath my stick, sending up a spray of snow as it fell. At my feet, where my next step would have taken me, was a crevasse so deep that the bottom was lost in blue light and shadows. The crash of the ice shelf hitting the bottom of the crevasse reverberated through the glacier.

The wind cut through my cloak; I could not stop shivering. At first, my feet ached with the cold. After a time, they became numb. I thought about how it would feel to lie down on the ice, like the ice woman in the story of King Takla. It would be painful at first, but then I would grow numb. I could rest, sleeping as peacefully as my mother slept.

The sky darkened to a deep blue. The light that reflected from cracks deep in the ice was the same beautiful blue. In my weariness, I grew dizzy. Looking up at the sky seemed much the same as gazing down into the ice. My walking stick slipped and I stumbled, falling full length onto the ice. I turned over on my back to look up at the blue sky, grateful to be resting.

I thought about staying there, just for a while. But that would not do. No tavern crowd would pay good money to hear about a hero who gave up and lay down in the snow. So I got up and kept walking on feet that felt like wood.

At last, I reached the tower and circled it, looking for a way in. Halfway around, I discovered a gap in the tower wall. I ducked through the gap and found myself on an ice-slicked stairway. Narrow slits in the walls let in just enough light to reveal the stone steps. Beneath the layers of ice, I could see sconces that had once held torches. The walls were marked with soot where flames had licked the stone.

Though the castle walls blocked the wind, it was even colder in the castle than it had been outside. My teeth chattered; I could not stop shivering. I climbed the stairs slowly, taking care not to slip on the icy steps.

At the top of the stairs was a wide corridor. The walls were clear of ice and the air felt a little warmer. Looking down the corridor, I could see a glimmer of golden light, spilling from an open doorway. I walked toward it.

In the doorway, I stopped and stared, my heart pounding. I could feel fear scratching at the edges of my awareness, but I reminded myself that there would be a happy ending. There had to be a happy ending.

The dragon slept in the center of the great hall. The beast lay on what had once been a fine carpet—now tattered and scorched. The air stank of ashes and smoke. I could feel heat radiating from the beast, like the warmth from a banked fire.

To hold fear at bay, I stared at the dragon and imagined how I might describe the monster when I told this story. The dragon's body was like that of a terrible lizard, a lizard as large as a warhorse. Its wings—great leathery wings—stretched over its back. Its eyes were closed. Its mighty head rested on its front talons. I did not stare for too long at the dragon's jaws and powerful talons. Instead, I considered the rest of the room and decided how best to describe it when I was telling this story in a tavern.

This had once been a magnificent hall. The walls were dark with soot, but I could see paintings beneath the layer of grime. More than a hundred years ago, artists had decorated these walls. On the wall to my left, two men in hunting garb shot arrows at mountain goats, which were bounding away up the mountain. On the far side of the room, the wall was painted with mountain landscape— the same mountain that lay outside the castle. But the artist had worked in a warmer and happier time. In the painting, wildflowers grew among the gray stones.

In the painting, the stones of the mountain formed a natural cave at the level of the floor. The rocks of the painted cave blended with the very real rocks of a great fireplace, large enough to hold a roasting ox.

Beside that fireplace, a skeleton sat slumped in a carved oak chair. A golden crown rested on the skull. Tatters of rich fabric clung to the bones. They fluttered in the breeze that blew through a large break in the wall to my right.

That wall had been shattered and its painting with it. I tried to imagine the blow that had shattered the wall, sending the stones tumbling inward and leaving a hole big enough to let the dragon pass through. Through the gap, I could see the glacier far below. The first stars of evening were appearing in the darkening sky. I shivered in the cool breeze.

"I smell an enemy," a voice growled.

I looked at the dragon. The beast had not moved, but its eyes were open now. They glowed like the embers of a fire. Colors shifted and flickered in their depths: gold and red and blue. "I know you are an enemy because you stink of the lowlands. You aren't a prince. You aren't a hero. What are you, and why have you come here?"

Be honest, I thought. Dragons can spot a liar. "A humble storyteller," I said.

"A storyteller?" The dragon lifted its head and studied me with glowing eyes. "How unusual. For the past hundred years, all my visitors have come to kill me. They march up the road from the lowlands with their soldiers following behind and their fear wakes me. I feel the shivering in their souls, the hatred in their hearts. I feel it burning and my own fire flares in response. And I shake off sleep and rise to do battle."

The dragon yawned, revealing a terrifying array of teeth. The beast stretched slowly, shaking out its great golden wings with a leathery rustle. Then the monster regarded me once again. "But you're not a hero. You are dressed as a boy, but I know by your smell that you are a girl. You are afraid, but not so very afraid. And you want something from me. What is it you want? Tell me, girl of the lowlands, why I shouldn't roast your bones with a single breath?"

As a storyteller, I have learned that everyone has a story. Not only that, but everyone has a story that they think should be told.

"I have a few reasons for coming here," I said carefully. "As a storyteller, I know many tales in which there are dragons. But those are stories about princes. And in every one of them, the dragon dies at the end of the tale. That doesn't seem right. I thought you might help me to tell a new sort of tale about dragons."

"Very tricky," said the dragon. "You hope to appeal to my vanity. And I notice that you said you had a few reasons and then you told me only one. You hope to intrigue me so that I'll decide you are interesting enough to spare."

When an audience catches you out, I have found it is best to acknowledge that they are right. If you deny it, they'll turn against you. "Have I succeeded?" I asked.

"Perhaps." The dragon continued to study me. "As long as I find you interesting, I will let you live. If I grow bored, I will roast you before I return to sleep. For now, I will spare you because you remind me of a wild girl I once knew." The dragon blinked slowly. "Would you like to hear about that wild girl? She was a lovely princess, until I destroyed her."

Not an entirely promising start. I reminded the dragon of a princess that it had destroyed. But at least the beast was not going to roast me immediately.

Though the heat radiated by the dragon had warmed me, my legs were trembling with weariness. I took a chance and asked, "Might I come in and sit while you tell the tale?"

The dragon stared at me, and for a moment I thought all was lost. Then the monster opened its jaws in a terrible grin. "Of course. I have forgotten the duties of a host. Come in. Sit down. There." The dragon lifted a talon and gestured to a bench beside the chair where the skeleton sat.

I crossed the room and sat on the bench, putting my pack on the stone floor beside me.

"You look cold," the dragon said. "Let me kindle a fire."

The beast opened its mouth and a blast of fire shot into the fireplace beside me. The half-burned logs, remnants of a long-dead fire, blazed.

"Alas, I have no food and drink to offer you," the dragon said. "The kitchens were crushed by the glacier long ago."

I opened my pack and took out a metal flask filled with brandy. "I have a bit of brandy. It's not the best, but I would be happy to share."

The dragon's toothy grin widened. " You drink and I will talk. I will tell the storyteller a story."

I sipped from the flask and felt the warmth of the brandy fill my throat and my chest.

"The wild girl was a princess," the dragon said. "A wild mountain princess more likely to be found hunting bandits than working her embroidery." The beast cocked its head, regarding me thoughtfully. "Tell me, what do you know of this castle, this kingdom?"

I chose my words carefully. "I know of King Takla, who built this castle and captured an ice woman for his queen."

"Very good," the dragon said. "Then you recognize that horn?"

I followed the dragon's gaze and saw a silver hunting horn, lying on the stone floor beside the royal skeleton. "King Takla's horn?" I asked.

"The very same. Blow it and the ice woman will grant your wish. But you must be very careful what you wish for."

I stared at the instrument in amazement. Though I had often told the story of King Takla, I had never thought about what happened to the horn.

"The wild princess of my story was the granddaughter of King Takla. Her father, King Rinzen, was the ruler of this mountain kingdom. He was a good king, noble and wise. Do you know of him?"

"I have heard of him," I admitted. The stories that I knew all emphasized the wealth of King Rinzen and how unfair his tolls had been.

"What have you heard?"

"Far less than I wish to know. Far less than you could tell me."

"An evasive answer," the dragon said, studying me with those great glowing eyes. "You know, I have heard that storytellers are all liars."

"Not necessarily liars," I said. "But careful in choosing the right audience for a tale."

"And I am not the right audience for the lowland tales of King Rinzen," the dragon said.

I nodded.

"Very well. Then I will tell you a tale that you don't hear in the lowlands."

I tipped back my flask and took a swallow of brandy, grateful to have survived this long.

"The men and women of King Rinzen's court hunted in the hills—sometimes for wild goat for the king's table, and sometimes for the bandits who sought to prey on merchant caravans. Decades before, King Takla had driven away the worst of the bandit gangs. But keeping the pass free of robbers and rogues required constant vigilance. You know of all this, of course."

I shook my head. None of the stories told in the lowlands talked about the bandits that King Takla and King Rinzen had driven off. In the lowland tales, these two kings were accounted as no better than bandits themselves.

"I could tell you many fine stories about bandits, about their hidden treasures, their secret caves. But that will have to wait. Just now, I was telling you about King Rinzen's court. The king was fond of musicians and storytellers. Many came to the castle to perform for the court. In this very hall, minstrels played and bards told tales of adventure, while the king listened and rewarded them handsomely for their art."

The dragon paused and I thought the beast might have lost the thread of the story. "What about the princess?" I asked.

The dragon turned its gaze back to me, eyes narrowing. "I suggest that you let me tell this story in my own way," the beast growled.

"Of course," I said hastily. "As you wish. I just wondered about the princess."

"Yes, Princess Tara. One summer evening, Princess Tara came home late from an afternoon of hawking. She knew that a troupe of performers from the lowlands had come to entertain the king. They had come from the court of King Belen, sent by him to King Rinzen. That evening, there was to be a gala performance, but Tara was weary from the hunt. She sent her apologies to her father the king and she did not go to the court that evening. She dined on bread and cheese in her chambers, and went to her bed early.

"That night she woke to the screams of women and the clash of steel." The dragon's eyes were wide open now, glowing more brightly than before. "She pulled on her clothes and ran into the corridor. It was dark except for the glow of smoldering straw. A torch had fallen, igniting the straw that was strewn on the stone floor."

"What did she do?" I asked.

"She listened in the darkness. Someone was running toward her, scattering the burning straw beneath his feet. In the dim light, she recognized a young bard who had come to the castle a week before. His eyes were wild; he was bleeding from a cut over his eye.

"'What is happening?' Tara called to him."

"'Treachery,' he gasped. 'Belen's men are in the castle. There is fighting in the great hall.' Then he ran on, and he was gone.

"Tara rushed through the darkness, hurrying toward the great hall. There, the torches cast a crimson light over a terrible scene. The air was thick with the stench of newly spilled blood. Her father was slumped in the big oak chair by the fire. He had been stabbed in the back. By the door were more dead men—some were castle guards, some were men clad in minstrel garb. The festive cloak of one of the minstrels had been torn by a sword stroke, and Tara could see armor beneath the velvet."

The dragon fell silent. I stared at the skeleton in the chair by the fireplace. King Rinzen, still wearing his crown in death.

"What had happened?" I asked at last.

"Belen's troupe of performers was a troop of assassins. They had killed the king, fought the guard, and opened the gates to the soldiers outside.

"Tara ran to her father's side. She kissed his cold cheek and vowed that she would take revenge for what had happened that night. On the wall above the fireplace hung King Takla's great silver hunting horn, the gift of the ice woman. It had fallen from King Takla's hand when he turned to stone. No one had been bold enough to risk blowing it again. An object of beauty, power, and danger, it hung on the wall above the fireplace.

"Tara could hear the tramping of boots and the rattle of armor in the corridor. Her father was dead and Belen's men had taken the castle. Tara pushed a bench to a spot near the fire and stood on the bench to take down the horn."

I nodded, realizing with a shiver that I was sitting on that very bench.

The dragon continued, its voice low. "Tara put the horn to her lips and blew, sounding a high clear note that echoed from the stone walls. The wall of the tower cracked and crumbled. A wind from the ice fields blew through the breach in the wall. Through the opening, Tara could see the dark sky above and the pale ice below. A blue light rose from the glacier and flew to the tower. A tall woman with flowing white hair appeared before Tara. ' Why have you awakened me?' the woman asked."

"The ice woman," I said.

"Tara's great-grandmother, the mother of the maiden that Takla had stolen," the dragon said. "Tara met the woman's icy gaze. 'I need your aid,' the princess said. 'Belen's men have killed my father.'

"'What do you want of me?' the ice woman said.

"'I want the power to kill my enemies and drive them from our land. I want the strength to avenge my father.'

"'Power and strength and passion,' the woman murmured. 'Death and vengeance. These are dangerous things and you are so young.'

"'Tara fell to her knees before the woman. 'You must help me.'

"The woman touched Tara's cheek. Tara could feel her tears freezing at the ice woman's touch.

"'I will grant your wish,' the ice woman said. 'Your heart will become ice; your passion, fire. And then you will have the power you need. But it troubles me to cast this spell on one so young. So I will also tell you how to break the spell and return to yourself. When the tears of your enemy melt the ice of your heart, you will become yourself once again. Until then, you will have your wish.'

"The woman's cold touch moved to Tara's breast, a searing chill that took her breath away. The woman stepped back. 'Now you will take the shape you need. You are filled with fire and passion, anger and pain. Let those dictate your form. You will have the power you seek and I will return to sleep.'

"The sorrow that had filled Tara at her father's death left her when her heart froze at the woman's touch. Rage and the desire for vengeance filled her.

"Transformation came with burning pain—a searing at her shoulders as wings formed; a blazing spasm as her back stretched, the bones creaking as they changed shape. Her jaws lengthened; her teeth grew sharp. Hands became claws." The dragon stretched its wings. Its claws flexed, making new tears in the carpet on which it lay. "Tara became a dragon," the beast said.

I stared at the dragon.

"Her breath was flame," Tara said. "Her scales shone like the coals of a fire, shifting and changing with each passing breeze. Now deep red, brighter than fresh blood; now flickering gold; now shining blue-white, like the heart of a flame." As the dragon spoke, her scales flickered and glowed.

"She spread her wings and flew, swooping low over the soldiers in the road. She opened her terrible jaws and her rage became a blast of fire. The men broke and ran. The horses, mad with fear, trampled the men as they fled. The soldiers died—so many died. In her rage, she did not distinguish between one fleeing figure and another. Belen's men burned in her flames, but so did people of her own castle. Stableboys and chambermaids, peasants and noblemen, fleeing Belen's men, fleeing the monster in the sky."

The dragon fell silent for a moment, then continued softly. "Now I live here in the castle. For a hundred years, I have lived here. Sometimes, heroes come to slay me—and I kill them instead." The dragon studied me with glowing eyes. I stared back, imagining what it would be like to be imprisoned in the body of a monster.

"Sometimes, my rage dies down, like a fire that is banked. But then someone filled with hate and fear stirs those ashes and the fire returns, as hot as ever.

"Now it is your turn, humble storyteller. Tell me a story and I will decide what to do with you."

I met the dragon's steady gaze. "I will tell you why I am here," I said. "This is not a story I would ordinarily tell, since most audiences favor stories about princes and dragons over stories about storytellers. But I think you will find it interesting. This story begins in a mountain town, one week ago. The town was having its harvest festival, and I traveled there with my mother."

I told her the story that you have already heard—about the inn on the edge of the glacier, about my mother's illness, about the healer who explained that three drops of dragon's blood would cure my mother of the illness inflicted by the ice woman. "Hope is what brings me here," I said. "Hope is what keeps me from fear and hatred."

The dragon's glowing eyes did not waver. "So you hope to slay me and take my blood?" the dragon rumbled.

"Slay you?" I laughed. The dragon stared at me, but it had been a long night. I had finished the flask of brandy and the dragon hadn't killed me yet. The idea that I planned to slay the dragon was so ridiculous that I couldn't help laughing. I pulled my dagger from my belt. The blade was half as long as one of the dragon's talons. "I suppose I planned to chop off your head with this?" I shook my head. "I'm no dragon slayer."

I thought of my mother's warm smile, of her honest heart. If only she could be here instead of me. She would smile and the dragon would know that this was a woman worth helping. "I had hoped that you might help my mother. That was all I hoped."

"Hope," the dragon repeated, her voice softening. "I remember feeling hope when I was human." The dragon's gaze moved from my face to the gap in the wall. "As a lowlander, you are my enemy. But it has been interesting talking with you this long night. It has reminded me of much that I had forgotten, over the passing years."

I glanced through the breach in the wall. A thin crescent Moon had risen over the glacier. The crackling fire in the fireplace beside me had burned to embers. While drinking brandy and talking with the dragon, I had lost track of time. It was nearly dawn.

"You came to me for help," she said. "What more will you do to save your mother? What will you give me in return for three drops of precious blood?"

I spread my hands. "What would you have me do?"

The dragon did not blink. "In memory of the wild girl that I once was, I will give you three drops of blood. But you must return after you take my blood to your mother. You must come back and keep me company for a time. Will you do that?"

"Yes," I said, without hesitation. "It's a bargain. As soon as my mother is well, I will return."

"Very well then," the dragon said, holding out a taloned paw.

I took a small metal vial from my pack. I reached out and took the dragon's talon in my hand. The scales burned against my skin. With my dagger, I pierced the scaly hide and let three drops of blood fall into the vial. They sizzled as they struck the metal.

"You have a long journey ahead of you," the dragon said. "You'd do well to rest before you begin."

As if I could sleep with a dragon at my side. Still, it did not seem wise to argue. I lay down on the carpet between the dragon and the embers of the fire. I pillowed my head on my pack, and closed my eyes. Weary from my long journey, drunk with brandy and success, I slept for a time.

When I woke, the Sun had risen over the glacier. The dragon was sleeping. As quietly as I could, I left the great hall and headed down the mountain.

I will spare you the account of my journey back to my mother's side. Suffice it to say that everyone along the trail was startled to see me, amazed to hear that I had succeeded in my quest.

At last, I reached the inn where my mother slept. Sarasri was astonished to see me. Though she had never believed that I would return, the good woman had been true to her promise. She had taken care of my mother. Pale and thin, my mother slept peacefully in the room where she had been stricken with the ice sickness.

Sarasri summoned the healer, and the old woman came to my mother's chambers. The healer smiled when she saw me.

"Three drops of dragon's blood," I said, holding out the vial.

"Very good," she said.

"Did you slay the dragon?" Sarasri asked, her eyes wide.

I shook my head. "The dragon told me a story and I told the dragon a story. The dragon gave me this blood on the condition that I return to Dragon's Gate when my mother is well."

The healer nodded. "Ah," she said, "you may very well have slain the dragon then."

I stared at the old woman. "I did not. She gave me this blood freely."

"Indeed—she gave it to you as an act of friendship. And that itself may slay the dragon. Dragons feed on hatred and fear. Acting out of love will weaken the beast."

"This act of kindness weakened the dragon?" I said. "That's not fair."

"Hate and fear nourish and strengthen a dragon. Love and friendship erode that strength. Fair or not, it's the way things work." She shrugged. "The next hero may find an easy kill. I have heard that Prince Dexter of Erland will soon be going to Dragon's Gate. But that is no concern of yours."

The old woman took the vial of blood. Her touch was cold on my hand. Gently, she stroked my mother's hair, then wet my mother's lips with the dragon's blood.

As I watched, the color returned to my mother's cheeks. My mother parted her lips, sighed, then opened her eyes and blinked at me. "Al," she murmured. "It must be past breakfast time. I'm ravenous."

Sarasri clapped her hands together and hurried off to fetch food. I held my mother's hands, cold in my grip at first, then warming—and I told her all that had happened. She feasted on scones and fresh milk. And when I thought to look around for the healer, the old woman was gone.

My mother recovered quickly. By the evening, she was out of bed. By the next morning, she was asking what we would do next.

I knew that I had to return to the dragon's castle as soon as possible. The healer's words had left me uneasy. My mother was captivated by the dragon's story, and she said that she would go with me. With some effort, I persuaded her that it was more important that she write a ballad that told Tara's tale.

At last I prevailed. But not before I found out more information about Prince Dexter and his plans.

Erland was a kingdom to the north—a small, cold, barren place. Its population lived by fishing and hunting the great whales that lived in the Northern Seas. Princes were as common as fish heads in Erland. (The king of Erland was a virile man.) Prince Dexter, the youngest of the king's eight sons, had left Erland to seek his fortune.

A group of merchants in the lowlands had offered Dexter a great reward if he would slay the dragon. From the merchants' point of view, it was a very sensible move. If the prince failed, it cost them nothing. If he succeeded, the dragon's death opened an easy route to the trading ports—and Dexter's reward would be nothing compared to the fortunes they would make.

From the prince's point of view—well, I confess, I do not understand the prince's point of view. It seems to me that there are easier ways to make your fortune than attempting to slay a dragon that has killed many heroes. But princes are raised on stories in which the dragon always dies. Like me, the prince believed in a happy ending.

Knowing that the prince would soon be going to Dragon's Gate, I set out on the trail. It was a long, difficult journey—though not as difficult as it had been the first time. It was not as cold as it had been before. As I climbed the pass to reach the castle, I saw a few wildflowers blooming among the gray stones of the mountain. They seemed like a good sign, until I looked down from my high vantagepoint and saw soldiers riding up the trail below me. Their banner was green and white, the colors of Erland.

I climbed the ice-slicked stairs of the castle and made my way to the great hall. The dragon lay where I had seen her last, stretched out on the tattered rug. But her scales were dull and lusterless.

"Tara!" I said. "Wake up!"

The dragon did not move. I threw myself on her great scaly neck. "Wake up!" I shouted again. "There is danger here."

I could feel the barest warmth through the scaly hide. The dragon's breathing was low and shallow.

I could hear the tramping of boots and the rattle of armor in the corridor. Prince Erland and his men had caught up with me. "Can you hear them?" I said. "Can you feel their fear? Can you feel the hatred in their hearts? They have come to kill you. You must wake up."

The dragon did not move.

The prince stepped into the room. His sword was drawn. For a moment I could not help but see the scene as I might have described it in a tale for the tavern crowd. A handsome prince lifted his sword against a terrible monster. But I could see the scene in another way as well: a beast of unearthly beauty, an enchanted princess enslaved and transformed by her own passion, dying for a kindness that had sapped her strength.

I pulled my dagger and stood between the prince and the dragon. The prince looked startled to see me. I could tell by his expression that this was not the way he expected the story to go. I have never heard a story in which anyone tries to protect a dragon.

"You must not kill this dragon," I told him. "She is an enchanted princess. She was weakened because she acted with great kindness. You must not slay her."

"Enchanted princess?" The prince frowned, staring at the sleeping dragon. "I'm not likely to kiss that. A woman capable of laying waste to a kingdom and driving soldiers before her like sheep is no wife for me."

Clearly he had heard too many stories of princes and enchanted princesses. I had suggested neither a kiss nor a royal wedding.

"I think I'd better just kill the beast," the prince was saying. "If you do not step aside, I will have to remove you."

I've told enough stories about princes to know that is what they are trained to do—slay monsters and marry princesses. This prince, like others of his kind, was not a man inclined to change direction quickly.

"I will not step aside," I said, holding out my dagger.

The prince was, however, trained to fight. I was not. With a flick of his sword, the prince struck my dagger aside, stepped in, twisted it from my hands, and tossed it into the corner. Then he lifted his sword.

I fell on the dragon's neck so that the prince could not strike the sleeping dragon without striking me. "Wake up," I murmured to Tara, my eyes filling with tears. It was too much; it was not fair. "You must save yourself." My tears spilled over, dropping onto the beast's neck, trickling over the dull scales.

Where the tears touched, the scales shone with a new brilliance, a blue-white light so bright it dazzled my eyes. The dragon shuddered beneath me. I released my hold on her neck, scrambling away.

The brilliant light—ten times brighter than sunlight on the ice fields—enveloped the dragon. I squinted through my tears at the light. I could see a shadow in the glare, a dark shape that changed as I strained to see what it was.

The light faded, and I blinked, my eyes still dazzled. A woman stood on the tattered rug. Her eyes were as blue as glacial ice. Her hair was the color of flames. She was dressed in an old-fashioned hunting tunic and breeches. Her hand was on the sword at her belt, and I was certain that she knew how to use it. Much experience with bandits, I suspected.

II

Tara sat by the fire that the soldiers had built, watching the flames. "Of course, you can claim your reward," I told the prince. "The merchants asked that you do away with the dragon—and you achieved that end. Your men can testify to it: The dragon is gone."

"That's true," the prince agreed.

"It is the way the story had to go," I explained to the prince. "My tears melted the ice in her heart and she returned to her true form."

"And now what happens?" The prince was studying Tara thoughtfully.

Tara turned from contemplating the fire and met his gaze. "Now I return my kingdom to its former glory. With the dragon gone, my people will return." She smiled. "It will take time, but there's no rush."

"You will need help," the prince said. "Such a lovely princess should not rule alone. Perhaps. . . ."

"Perhaps you should remember your own thoughts, as you prepared to slay a dragon," Princess Tara said, still smiling. "A woman capable of laying waste to a kingdom and driving soldiers before her like sheep is no wife for you."

She turned her gaze back to the fire. "My people will return, and so will the bandits. We will hunt the bandits in the hills and the merchants will pay a toll to pass this way."

"Perhaps you'd best not tell the merchants that part just yet," I advised the prince.

III

Is the story done yet? Not quite. There is still King Takla's horn to account for. That evening, I stood by the glacier and I blew that horn. I saw a flash of blue light over the ice, and then a beautiful woman wrapped in a white shawl stood before me. Her eyes looked familiar—a beautiful, piercing blue. Her hair was white, and she smiled with recognition when she saw me.

"You have called me," the ice woman said. "What do you wish?"

I held out the horn. "Only to return this horn," I said. "Nothing more."

The ice woman studied me. "No other wishes? You do not wish for wealth or fame or glory?"

I smiled and shook my head.

"You dress as a man, yet you are a woman. Would you wish to be a man?"

I thought about Princess Tara, a woman who hunted for bandits and claimed her own kingdom, and shook my head. "I have no wish to make," I said. Then I asked, "How is your daughter?"

"Very well," she said. "She was pleased to return to her home."

I nodded. "Of course she would be."

"How is your mother?" the ice woman asked.

"Doing well. Writing a ballad about Tara."

She took the horn from my extended hand. "You did very well," she said then. "I am glad that you could help my great-granddaughter, Tara."

I bowed to her. "I am grateful to have been of service." When I looked up, she was gone.

IV

I returned to Sarasri's inn in Nabakhri, where my mother waited. I reached the inn early in the afternoon. I went looking for my mother and found her in the kitchen. Sarasri was kneading bread and my mother was playing the harp and keeping her company.

The kitchen was warm. A pot of lamb stew bubbled on the fire. The yeasty scent of bread filled the air. "Al is back!" Sarasri shouted when she saw me. My mother abandoned her music and hugged me. Sarasri heaped lamb stew in a bowl and insisted that I eat it all.

"My wonderful child," my mother said. "You must tell us all that has happened since you left here."

I shook my head, my mouth filled with stew. "Tonight," I said. "I will tell the tale tonight."

The tavern was full that night. People had heard of my mother's illness, of my trip to Dragon's Gate and my return with dragon's blood, of my return to Dragon's Gate to keep my promise.

I smiled at the crowd. Dressed in tunic and breeches, returning in triumph from Dragon's Gate, I knew the story that they expected. It was the story of Al, a heroic young man who confronts a monster.

"My name is Alita," I said. "And that means 'a girl to be trusted.' Some of you know me as Al and think that I am a young man. But the world is filled with illusions—as I learned when I met the dragon. Let me tell you my story."

After the Gaud Chrysalis

ꟸꟹ

Charles Coleman Finlay

Here's a recent story that testifies to the enduring influence of Fritz Leiber's adventure-seeking duo. Charlie Finlay introduced us to Vertir and Kuikin in our March 2003 issue with "For Want of a Nail." Their second adventure bears all the marks that we're coming to expect from this writer: a taut adventure story with moral complexity to it, featuring characters who are pushed to their limits. Mr. Finlay referred to "the New Pulp" in a recent interview and it will be interesting to see whether this term sticks around and helps lead a movement that produces more stories as interesting as this one. "After the Gaud Chrysalis" first appeared in our June 2004 issue.

The nun in the lizard-scale robes stood taller than either of the men, not a remarkable thing in itself since they were both of average height or a bit shorter; but she was also wider than the stocky one and swaggered with a more martial bearing than the professional soldier.

The nub of her chin jutted out as she shook her round head. "I can't do it, Kuikin. I've taken the seven sacred vows."

Kuikin, the stocky man in drab clothes, folded his hands in front of him in an aspect of prayer. He opened them like two halves of a shell, as if to indicate the smallness of her vow. Or perhaps that it should be treasured like a pearl. Deliberately ambiguous. The last time he'd seen her was years ago, just before she'd taken her vows, and there had been things left unspoken and unsettled even then.

"I know," he said. "But please. Elizeh."

At the mention of her name, she raised her fist to his bent, oft-broken nose. "No."

A grin smeared across his face. "What about your vow to follow the path of righteous peace, Sister?"

"We all stray from the path sometimes," she said, quickly dropping her fist. "Don't parse logic with me. I've packed those days away in storage. I won't do it."

Vertir, the professional soldier, lean and dark-haired, shifted his scabbard and looked into the blossom-heavy trees of the convent garden.

"You wanted to come fetch her," he said. "If she won't come willingly, let's go speak to the Abbess. Or leave her behind."

Kuikin and Elizeh stared at each other, waiting for the other to blink. He opened the ink-stained fingers of one hand and gestured for her to go first.

I

The Abbess sat at her desk, the lemony walls around her imprinted with the shapes of living leaves in countless hues of green.

Vertir produced the seal, which was not that of the Dynast, but of the Notary-General of Implements and Roads; nor yet his seal of office, but his private mark.

Her ancient skin as smooth and unblemished as a child's, the diminutive Abbess looked at the seal and genuflected quickly toward the Dynast's distant palace.

"Mother Abbess," said Elizeh. "Let me tell you what they—"

The old woman tapped the leafy plaster with her fingertip, then touched her ear.

Kuikin exchanged a glance with Vertir. Even the convent walls had ears. But then, what walls did not?

Covering her head with a scaly cowl, the Abbess took up her walking staff and left the room. She thumped out a hasty cadence as she skirted the switchback trail that led to the terraced vineyards on the mountainside and chose instead the paved way downward into the Vale of Lesser Gods.

They passed graceful patios of pitted limestone where the dragon godlings crawled about, flicking their forked tongues at the air and flaring the fan-shaped ruffs about their necks. Cloaked novices slowly moved about, whisking the patios clean; one of them swept in the direction of the small party.

The Abbess paused, shook her head, then hurried on to an elegant bridge that spanned a stony gorge. The air there held the crisp, empty fragrance of early spring. Her cane thunked out to the middle of the bridge and stopped.

Kuikin glanced around. The fortress gate was barely visible through the tress at the bottom of the road. A host of purple birds congregated noisily in the treetops closer by, but the grasses below were empty except for a few logs and boulders.

No walls, no ears.

"Why," asked the Abbess, "does the Dynast's spymaster and arranger of assassinations send his lackeys after Sister Renn?"

Elizeh had become Renn when she joined the convent, Kuikin reminded himself. "We wish to borrow her experience."

"It's impossible," Elizeh said. "I can't—"

The Abbess's cane thumped on the bridge. "I will decide what is and is not possible for you." Then to Kuikin, "You have one chance to sway me. Explain this unusual request."

He opened his mouth to state—diplomatically—that the Dynast did not need to explain his demands. But Vertir said, "A gaud chrysalis is found in the Valley of Divinrifft."

The Abbess scoffed. "Gaud is dead. That age has passed."

"There are sorcerers who live to see it return," Kuikin said.

She curled her lip and drew a sharp breath. "So this is a rumor, mere wishful thinking on their part."

"Even if it is—" Kuikin hedged, unwilling to give specifics.

But Vertir said, "The Bey of Desmeé has sent soldiers and his archsorcerer to collect it, to bring it in state to the Temple of Gaud in his beyant."

The Abbess scowled. "He cannot. The Bey's oath of fealty requires him to render service to the Dynast. Whatever his faith."

"Just," Kuikin said, "as the convent's charter and grant requires you to render service to the Dynast when he requests it."

"But the Dynast's own code of laws promises every one a choice of worship and interference with no deity."

"Just as the path of your faith holds abhorrent the doctrine of Transfiguration and the marriage to the life of the flesh."

Her scowl deepened. "But why do you need her to go after that . . . that *thing*?"

"We don't," Vertir said.

"Elizeh—" Kuikin began, and saw her tense at the mention of her name, but the Abbess cut him off.

"Sister Renn."

Kuikin accepted the rebuke with a smile. "Yes. Forgive me. Sister Renn has boated down the Rifft River before, all the way to the dead city of Khorpis Kharn." He hesitated before continuing: the convent had a sister house located in Desmeé. "We believe the chrysalis is there."

The Abbess stared at Elizeh, who fidgeted with the end of her waist-long, dingy blonde braid. It amused Kuikin to see her quail. "Surely she's not the only one to have ever done so," the Abbess said.

Vertir tapped the hilt of his sword, but didn't answer.

"She's the only one we know who's done it and survived," Kuikin said.

"I don't wish to return," Elizeh said.

The birds fell through the branches in a violet rain to forage on the ground for food, commencing a raucous chatter so loud it momentarily halted all conversation. One landed on the end of the log. A mouth opened, a head twisted, and the bird disappeared in a shower of feathers as the others screeched alarm and scattered. The godling, chewing its meal, rose to its feet and stutter-stepped forward.

One of the boulders shifted and stood. It was a sister in gray robes. She trailed after the godling.

The Abbess lowered her voice. "What is your objection?"

Fear glimmered in Elizeh's eyes. "I went into that valley in search of riches and when I came out, I went in search of faith. I do not wish to return there, not for any reason. My life has turned aside on a different path."

"That new path includes a vow of obedience," the Abbess reminded her. She looked at Vertir. "Why do you reject her?"

He turned his back to the sister in the trees. "It's a fool's errand: the more fools with me, the more errors."

"It is neither foolish nor in error to despise gaud." To Kuikin, "And you want her because?"

"We will need a guide through the valley, someone we can trust. She and I have sojourned together before. We have a—"

"Mother," Elizeh protested.

"Silence! Gaud is vile and repugnant, against the reason of nature." She tilted her head heavenward, squeezed her eyes shut as if saying a prayer. When she opened them again, she glared at Elizeh. "I order you to go with them, to aid in any way you can this venture they pursue, and to not return at peril of your soul's torment for a span of three lives until you see that abomination, if it exists, *dead*!"

Elizeh's back stiffened. "I will not do murder, Mother. Not any more. That vow comes before that of obedience."

The Abbess pointed her staff at Kuikin and Vertir. "That's why you have them with you."

"He won't do murder either," Vertir said. "He's a scribe."

The Abbess stared at Kuikin. "Ah. So you have some useful training as a sorcerer then?"

"No," he replied honestly; one could not lie about sorcering. "I sparked no talent for it."

"You're scruffy for a scribe. Look more like a knee-capper, a back-alley man, with those shoulders and that face." She shook her tiny fist at Vertir and spoke in a harsh whisper. "Kill it."

The Abbess turned her back on them, staff thumping along the trail like a sexton's hammer pounding nails.

II

A cart loaded with casks waited outside the convent's storehouse. Vertir patted the horse's flank and spoke to it. Kuikin climbed onto the cart's seat, taking hold of the reins. "Every third face here is from the southern provinces."

"Doesn't mean they're from Desmeé," Vertir said.

The beyant of Desmeé on the empire's southern frontier had long ruled itself. There were those, the current Bey among them, who would do anything to restore that independence. Kuikin and Vertir had been in Desmeé within the past year to steal the Bey's aegis and murder the sorcerer who'd created it. That should have checked the Bey's ambitions, but it hadn't.

"All it takes is one more loyal to family than faith to send off a warning," Kuikin said.

Vertir held his palms out in exasperation. "What warning? The Bey's men pursue the gaud chrysalis already! You're the one who wished to come here and it's cost us days."

"She'll help us."

Vertir thrust his palms down. "You. Not us, you. Maybe. I don't know. I don't think she'll keep you warm at night, no matter what was once between—"

Elizeh swaggered around the corner of the building next to them, causing Vertir to fall silent and Kuikin to hold his reply. She had changed into traveling clothes. She shoved her bedroll in the back, checked the horses' harness and whispered to them, then climbed on to the cart seat. The wood creaked under her weight.

"Talking about me, huh?" she said to their silence. She bumped Kuikin aside and snatched the reins from his hands.

"I'll drive," he said.

She sneered at him. "If you do, it'll take us a week just to reach the front gate."

Vertir clambered onto the sideboard. "So you *have* traveled with him before."

"I don't know that you could call it traveling," she said. "He never got anywhere."

"We go way back," Kuikin insisted gruffly.

"Git!" Elizeh snapped the reins and the big shaggy horses started, pausing at the limit of the yoke until the whole cart lurched forward. The wheels rolled loudly over the stone pavement and down toward the fortress wall. They were picking up speed as they approached the narrow gate.

Kuikin gripped the seat. "Slow down!"

Vertir slid from the sideboard onto the seat. "Told you. It's easier to give him the reins."

"If you just ignore him, he shuts up after a while," she said and cracked the reins again. The horses were up to a quick trot and the wagon rolled easily over the smooth road.

"Watch out!" Kuikin covered his head as they rushed toward the wall. There wasn't enough room—

—but then the cart shot through the narrow gate with barely a foot to spare on either side. The guard yelled as he dived out of the way.

"Nicely done," Vertir said, smiling in spite of himself.

Elizeh shrugged her big shoulders. "A foot or a mile, what's the difference? If you're clear you're clear."

Kuikin twisted around. The guard was just picking himself up, staring back through the gate to see that no more carts were coming. "*Sister* Renn," Kuikin said.

"Yes?" The corner of her mouth twitched.

"Don't ever do that again!"

Vertir laughed at him.

The road dipped around a hill and they passed out of sight of the convent. A long range of scaly gray crags rose above the pine forest like a godling nested in the grass.

A pair of messenger pigeons flew over their heads from the direction of the convent. "It's likely nothing to do with us," Elizeh said, anticipating Kuikin's question.

The cart bucked hard as the dirt road grew uneven. She reined in the horses. Already they had to slow their pace.

III

Twilight fell long before they reached the imperial waystation for travelers, so Elizeh pulled the horses over in a clearing beside the road.

Vertir jumped from the wagon and set off on a circuit through the woods. Elizeh stepped down a little stiffly, walking over to look at the coal pit. "There hasn't been a fire in these stones for weeks."

While she unhitched the horses and rubbed them down, Kuikin unloaded their packs and supplies from the back of the wagon. He looked at the marks on the casks.

"Does the convent send more guards when it ships something other than vinegar?"

Elizeh hesitated. "That's not vinegar. The cask marks will be changed—the new imprint burned over that one—once we reach the sister house in Finis Opor. But I didn't tell you that."

His fingertips traced the glyph burned into the wood. His mouth had started to water. The convent's wines were famous. "That's an amazing transformation. True sorcery."

"Don't even think about tapping one."

By the time she finished and hobbled the horses where they could graze, Kuikin had started a fire. Vertir returned from the woods. "It's all clear close by."

Elizeh tossed her bedroll down by Kuikin's fire. Something in it chimed—metal ringing on metal.

"Doesn't that make it hard to sleep?" Vertir asked.

"Do you sleep easier unarmed?"

"I'm never unarmed." He cracked his knuckles, looked at Kuikin, and rolled his eyes.

Kuikin shrugged in reply, fed larger sticks into the flame.

Each layer of wool that Elizeh folded back revealed another blade, each a different type. Vertir hunkered down to look at them. "May I?" he asked.

She nodded in permission.

He poked at some small knives. "You use these for throwing?"

"Could," she said, "though I was never good at that. Preferred close work, and they're easy to hide. Some are decoys, but a couple of these can escape even a determined search."

He frowned doubtfully and picked up a nasty looking weapon as long as Kuikin's forearm. "That's an excellent ranger knife."

"I bought that in Osten years ago. It's more useful than your legion sword," she said, with a nod at the slightly curved sword in the scabbard at his waist. When he didn't say anything, she laughed. "Sure, your sword parries better and is more useful for slashing in a crowd, but I never went toe to toe against more than two hands at a time if I could help it."

"You don't have the luxury of choosing your enemies," he said. He set the ranger knife down and lifted a poniard, bending the long, thin blade. "That's superb Ferronian steel, but it's loose in the hilt, eh?"

She snatched it away from him and folded it back into the blanket. "And what if? May I never need to use it again."

"Well, if you brought them along to sell instead of use, I can help you get a fair price," Vertir said, stretching.

Kuikin waited for Elizeh to answer that but she didn't. Probably hadn't made up her own mind yet. His fingers were greasy with the fat he'd spread on the skillet. He rubbed them over the stubble on his cheeks and chin. Taking out the only knife he carried, a small thing for paring, he lifted it to scrape his face smooth.

"Don't do that," Elizeh said.

"You never liked my beard."

"You're right, I hated it. Those bare patches on your cheeks look like mange. But if you let it grow, you'll look more like an adventurer when we reach Finis Opor and less like a constipated minor bureaucrat."

"That's not true—" Vertir interjected.

"Thank you!" Kuikin said.

"—he'll just look like a mangy, constipated bureaucrat."

Elizeh's laughter pealed across the glade.

Vertir grinned, then fell serious again. "The Bey's factors have been in Finis Opor for more than a month, gathering supplies and outfitting a small army."

"They'll need it," she said, nodding, "if they plan to go overland through the valley to Khorpis Kharn." She shuddered. "But were I planning that trip again, I'd go overland too. If they've been there a month, it'll be almost impossible to catch them. We'll need to wring every extra mile out of the day."

It was Vertir's turn to nod.

"Why not intercept them with a larger army on their return?"

"One's being gathered," Vertir answered.

"But by then the gaud will have full powers," Kuikin added. The smell of frybread rose up from the skillet as he flipped the batter. Elizeh's vows precluded her from eating any meat. "It'll be impossible to stop without great bloodshed."

"But it won't be ours," Elizeh said.

"Exactly," Vertir replied.

Kuikin had no answer to that.

IV

The wagon sat motionless, just in sight of the waystation's bannered watchtower standing like a sentinel beside the road. Wasteland stretched out around them, all the way to the bandit-hiding hills, with the caravan to Finis Opor strung like a belt of jewels across its belly. The unrelenting sun above them made Kuikin's scraggly beard itch like lice.

"It's no wonder you've got bare patches on your cheeks," Elizeh said, "the way you keep scratching at them."

"It's no wonder you could never keep your lovers," Kuikin said, and regretted it at once even before she tensed and drew away from him.

They were all on edge and had been for days as they'd traveled southward. As fast as they could go was not fast enough. Only the horses seemed to be happy standing still.

Vertir ran back along the rutted trail, returning from a small group of northbound travelers. Kuikin reached out a hand and pulled him up onto the sideboard. "So what's the delay?"

"Here it comes," Vertir said.

A minor bureaucrat made his way along the caravan, followed by a small gang of men who were as bow-legged and rangy-looking as bandits. The horses caught wind of them and fidgeted nervously.

The bureaucrat's face was red and straining. He looked at Kuikin like someone recognizing a wayward brother, then examined the casks in back. "We'll take four of these for the road tax."

"*What*?" Elizeh bellowed.

Kuikin put a hand on her arm. "That's unreasonable."

The bandit-types snickered. The bureaucrat swept his hand toward the watchtower. "I'm helpless in the matter. I have to collect my yearly quota when I can. The Dynast's army moves one direction, word of the Bey of Desmeé's sorcery comes another. Anyone can see that there will be war and no travel or trade for the rest of the year."

"Perhaps there won't be a war," Elizeh said.

The bureaucrat shrugged. "Who will prevent it?"

Who, indeed. Kuikin pulled out a small bag of coins. It clinked in his palm. "How much is the tax in gold?"

The bureaucrat rapped a knuckle on one of the casks and sniffed the wood. "It sometimes happens that the sisters mistakenly mark wine as vinegar."

When he looked up at them hopefully, Kuikin tossed the man a golden peacock. "For your personal trouble."

The bureaucrat named a more reasonable amount in coin, then added, "And one barrel of the vinegar. If you don't wish to pay, the notary-captain will be here within the month. You are welcome to wait and appeal your case to him."

His gang of assistants chuckled greedily. It would take them less than a month to relieve the travelers of their horses, coin, even the clothes from their backs.

"That'll be fine," Kuikin said, placing a restraining hand on Elizeh's arm. He counted the coins while the bureaucrat beckoned two of his men to come unload the cask.

Vertir, who had been silent the whole time, jumped to the back of the wagon to help. As he selected the cask to unload, it slipped through his hands and fell on one man's foot. The second bent to lift it just as Vertir did the same and they knocked heads hard. The two bandits cursed angrily, but Vertir staggered backward, holding his head and swaying dizzily. The rest of the bureaucrat's gang laughed at them and carried the cask away.

"Why didn't you show the seal, the one you showed the Abbess?" Elizeh asked.

"Then we would have had to wait until the notary-captain arrived to verify it," Kuikin replied. He glanced at Vertir's grim face as he climbed back up to the front of the wagon. "Sometimes you have to compromise."

"I know that," Vertir told him. He had a red mark on his forehead where he'd hit the other man. "I wanted to hurt those two men much worse. But I compromised."

"You did give them a cask of vinegar?" Elizeh asked.

"One of the two you showed me." He looked at Kuikin. "We were planning on tricking you into tapping it."

Kuikin frowned at him. "That group you were talking to—"

"Mercenaries from Shin, caravan guards." Shin was Vertir's original home, an independent suzerainty on the empire's cold northern border. "They've heard rumors of the gaud incarnate."

"That's not possible," Kuikin said. "It's too soon!"

"Mercenaries hear all the news first," Elizeh said. "Especially if it means war. But this means we're too late!"

"Nah." Vertir shook his head. "From their descriptions, it sounds like they were talking of the last gaud to walk the earth, Bahl-the-Gaud, who ruled from the Temple on Trembeull mound."

"I've been by Trembuell mound and didn't see any Temple," she said.

"That's because it was destroyed when Pence-the-Martyr murdered the gaud his master," Kuikin explained. "Later, the people of that region came and hauled away even the rubble so that no sign of that time remained."

"I didn't know that's where Pence was martyred," she said. "Still, you're sure it wasn't the Temple in Desmeé?"

"I'm sure," Vertir said. "They spoke of a gaud perched atop the spire and that was at Trembuell."

Kuikin exhaled in relief. "Yes, had to be. Desmeé is a domed Temple, built during the very last years of the Interdynastum for a gaud chrysalis that it never received. There's no way the gaud could be there yet."

A cloud of blue butterflies, each a foot wide, caught his eye as they floated over the caravan and across the brown prairie in search of flowers elsewhere.

Vertir watched the butterflies pass too, then jerked his thumb toward the mercenaries. "Even the rumor of a new gaud is enough to send them running. They told me it's the end of the world we know. I've been invited to return with them to Shin, to rejoin my family and wait out this next winter of an age."

Elizeh nodded at the wedding bracelet on Vertir's wrist—a bead for each year, the colors showing only one bad year in more than a dozen. "So your wife is in Shin then?"

Instead of answering her, he tilted his head back and sang:

> "She ruled in a castle carved of ice,
> But her heart was colder still
> She summoned me once, she summoned me twice,
>   But away I had run
>   To the land of the sun,
> And today I'm running still."

He jumped off the wagon, pointing to another group coming the opposite direction. "I'll go see what else I can learn."

When he had gone Elizeh said, "That was very odd."

Kuikin shrugged. "He never speaks of his family when we're traveling on behalf of the notary-general."

"I thought wedding beads were a Pyune custom."

"His wife's from Pyune. He took it up because of her."

"Ah."

The tail end of the northbound caravan was passing by. The wagons ahead of them surged forward again. Kuikin put his arm around Elizeh, to point this out, but she knocked his hand out of the way as she picked up the reins.

"Our habits change with our circumstances," she said. "You should know that."

V

The unwalled and undefended city of Finis Opor (which its citizens called Tyrn, though nomads from the desert called it The Golden Threshold or sometimes Stench) straggled like a scab across a rocky knee of hills. Jagged roads scarred the landscape north to the Empire, south and east into the desert, and west around the valley of Divinrifft over the mountains to the sea.

A spring flowed out of the hills and streamed along a low bank beside the city's marketplace. Children serpented through the umbrella'd carts, pointing at Kuikin's beard and dashing away.

The boatman had only a few curly hairs on his dark chin. He ignored Kuikin and resumed dragging his small craft away from the water's edge.

"Wait, wait," Kuikin repeated in the merchant pidgin. "Buy boat."

The scrawny boatman shook his head. "Buy boat not." He shifted his netbag full of fish to his back and tilted his pole downstream. "You treasure to hunt, yes? In go to valley, yes?"

"Yes," Kuikin said. "Yes, exactly."

"In go to valley not, come back not!" He resumed his walk.

An uneven row of low, discolored buildings with gaps between them like bad teeth stood opposite the market. Kuikin saw Vertir pause at the corner of one, look both directions, then come over and stand in the boatman's way.

"What's the news?" Kuikin asked.

"The Bey has soldiers gathered in a rented villa on the heights above the city. Few hundred maybe, with a carriage to escort the gaud." The boatman stepped one way, then the other, trying to get around Vertir. "Is this our boat?"

"Not yet. Have they departed into the valley?"

The boatman spewed a fountain of vile-sounding words in his own incomprehensible tongue before switching back to the pidgin. "Move you, yes!"

He attempted to pass, but Vertir stepped in front of him again. "Sell you fish, yes? Sell fish?"

The man named a price. Vertir pulled out a string of coins and counted off an amount ten times too high. The man's eyes widened. He held his netbag out eagerly.

Vertir extended the coins, then retracted them from the other man's reach. "Fish to come with boat, yes? Boat we to throw fish back. Fish swim away."

"Fish dead, crazy you!" the man said, but they commenced a serious set of negotiations. The late morning sun washed over the rooftops and trees, and a new wave of people swam through the marketplace. Kuikin watched the groups form and split around the islands of carts; across the way, Elizeh appeared in a gap between the houses and scanned the crowd. He lifted his hand and she hurried over to him.

A small man paused at the corner of another building. "I couldn't give him the slip," she said. "Is that our boat?"

"Not yet," Kuikin said. "Who is he?"

"One of the honey climbers from the valley. They," she hesitated, "helped me the last time I was here."

"How so?"

"By showing me the path out of the valley and by offering not to kill me if I departed immediately and left everything behind."

The man stepped out into the open, shielding the light from his eyes. He was small and slender, clad only in a loincloth, with large flat feet, webbed hands, and the ridge-lines of vestigial gills along his ribcage. He stepped toward them, hesitated, and disappeared into the shadows again.

Kuikin caught his breath. "If he was tattooed, I'd take him for one of the sea folk in a second."

"That's what I thought too, the first time I saw them," Elizeh said. "Once you cross the mountains, it's not that far to the coast. But they live in the trees as far as I could tell, speak a language wholly unlike the sea folk's. They hunted with blowguns. The darts were tipped with poison taken from the bees."

"Do you think they'd rather help or hinder a gaud?"

"The honey climbers? I have no idea. They let no one take anything from the valley that can't be replaced. Honey's the only thing they bring up to the city to trade. They," she hesitated again, "treated me well the last time, considering the state I was in. But they promised to kill me if I returned."

"They probably say that to everyone," Vertir interjected as he joined them. He held the bag of fish, and dragged the lightweight boat beside him. "It's bark and branches. Not much. He'll build himself a newer one to replace this before we're a day downriver."

"Sure," Kuikin said, "but we'll already be a day downriver."

Elizeh examined it skeptically. "When I left the wagon at the sister house, they told me that the Bey's men had departed for the valley to welcome the gaud five days ago."

"What?" Kuikin looked toward the stream.

"Archsorceror, thirty men, and local guides?" Vertir asked.

"Yes. The Mother also told me the guides were unscrupulous men who would steal the supplies and leave before they were too deep into the valley."

"That's what I heard too. It still doesn't leave us much time to catch up with them, even by the river route. Did you hear anything about the tree folk?"

"We were just discussing them," Kuikin said.

"One followed me to the market place," Elizeh explained.

"A handful have come out of the valley lately, but nobody's sure why. The Bey's men tried to hire them for guides, but they wouldn't do it."

"They never do," Elizeh said.

They all three stood silently staring at each other for a moment. The crowd of people in the market broke on the rock of their motionlessness, staring at them as they passed.

Elizeh and Vertir bent to take hold of the boat. She said, "Kuikin, you don't need to—" at the same moment that Vertir said, "The two of you don't need to go any further."

They set the boat down again.

"You don't know what you're facing," she said. "You'll never survive the river without a guide."

"I've survived a lot of rivers without a guide," Vertir told her, "and worse than that, and all of it without you."

Kuikin grabbed the bow and dragged it to the water. They were still yammering as he shoved it out into the stream.

"The Bey's men are getting closer to their goal by the moment," he said. "I'll go on without you, if I must."

They threw their gear aboard and joined him.

"This is your last chance to turn back," Elizeh said at the same moment Vertir told him, "You could stay here, Kuikin."

He leaned into the pole, pushing off from the bank.

VI

All the rest of that day they took turns poling down the river. The banks, though far apart, grew slowly higher on either side and huge trees overhung the water, their branches draped with monkey spider webs. The spiders themselves dropped on threads to peer at the boat, chatter at it, and toss twigs at them. More disturbing were the glares of the fishermen they passed as they entered a narrow lake where the river widened before it passed a gap between twinned bluffs.

"The lake is too deep for us to pole across," Elizeh said. "And after that, the river much too swift. Over there."

Vertir followed her directions to the water's verge.

"The trees here are . . ." Kuikin faltered.

"Strange?" offered Elizeh. "Go in closer."

"Wrong," Vertir said, but he went.

Trunks dwarfed, elongated, hunchbacked, bloated; familiar barks pimpled and rent; leaves taffy-stretched, stripped, shrunken, and mottled. Everything at once looked familiar and distorted, Kuikin thought, like the sort of inbred relatives families kept locked away from strangers.

"Those," Elizeh said. "There, that one right there."

The boat bumped against half-submerged roots. Vertir raised the pole to fend off the monkey spiders nearby; as it lifted out of the water, something slithered off the end and splashed away.

"What are we looking for?" Kuikin asked.

"These," Elizeh said, grabbing a triangular piece of bark peeling loose from a trunk. The boat wobbled, she tugged, and it came free with a loud crack. Second and third pieces were less weathered, and she had to hack them loose with her ranger knife. "We'll use these to paddle."

Kuikin marked the sun just above the horizon, the long shadows cast by the cliffs, and the distant, dull roar of water. "Should we find a place on shore to camp for the night?"

"Not unless you want to wake up in a wedding dress," she said, a reference to the way the spiders wrapped up unwary travelers in silk.

"I've never looked good in dresses," Vertir said, whacking an aggressive monkey spider. Other spiders clambered out on the tips of the branches and squirted sticky balls of web at them. He batted a ball from the air. "Can you move us a little faster?"

Kuikin took up one of the paddles and vigorously muscled the water out of the way until they passed from under the trees. Once they were on the open lake, Vertir did the same, with less splashing and more grace. They made slow progress at first, but then the craft slipped into the current and shot forward. The sun sat like a boil on the horizon when they approached the gap.

Their speed seemed to double as they passed between the brown heights of the cliffs, and above the thundering from just ahead Elizeh shouted, "This is going to be a little rough!"

Kuikin gripped the flimsy wale and shut his eyes.

He felt a sudden weightlessness as the boat dropped away beneath him, the spray of water and then a hard shock against his legs as they hit, and his eyes snapped open, and waves poured in over the sides soaking him as they dropped again, slammed into something, tilted sideways, dropped, plunged through foam and spray, lodged hard against something, turned with the tow, slipped free, and then cascaded down a final staircase of cold, black water and *whump* came to rest in a current that, though as fast as the one before the gap, seemed blessedly languid.

Elizeh had grinned and whooped the whole time, driving them forward with her paddle. She pulled them downstream now.

"That was fun," said Vertir. "So is that the big danger?"

"Oh, no," said Elizeh. "That's the easy one. After this, it turns very rough. At least it's a fast trip."

Kuikin watched the water slosh in the bottom of the boat. It seemed to be getting deeper. "I think we're leaking."

VII

The river ran high, coursing against the rocky cliffs, scouring the steep slopes where the cliffs fell back, and drowning the few wide spots with stands of trees. Stars glittered in the sky when they finally found a narrow sandbar for their camp.

"Well," Kuikin said, climbing out of the boat, "it's flat enough so we won't roll into the stream."

Vertir stomped around, the sand sloshing under his feet. "It's a big wet sponge. If I had an animal, and it picked here to sleep, I'd kill it to keep it from ever breeding again."

"That's not funny." Elizeh glowered. "And trust me, it's the best we're going to find tonight."

She made the oblations required of her order, writing her prayers in the air while Kuikin and Vertir unloaded the boat and flipped it to drain.

"Who wants cold fish?" asked Vertir, holding up the netbag he had purchased that morning. It stank. "There's not enough wood here to start a fire."

"I'll set free the dead," Elizeh said solemnly, taking it from his hands.

"Fish dead, crazy you," Vertir said as she emptied the bag into the river with a blessing. But he didn't try to stop her.

Afterward they ate their meal cold, including uncooked flour mixed with river water. Elizeh unbraided her waist-length hair to let it dry, unfolded her blanket, and removed the knives one by one. "The boat's likely to tip over any time," she said. "Anything you absolutely need to have ought to be on you somewhere."

"I'll take care of the stores," Kuikin said.

Vertir hunched over, solid as a boulder in the night. A tap of two beads slipped into the silence. He was counting his wedding years, performing his own oblations. Skipping the memory of the one bad year, if Kuikin knew him.

"Why are you doing this?" Elizeh asked him.

Vertir's chin lifted. A piece of starlight shot across his eyes and burned out. "What do you mean?"

"You're from Shin, an ally of the Empire, but no part of it. Your wife is from Pyune across the sea. Why?"

Breath rushed out his nose. "I wonder the same thing sometimes. But I took an oath to serve. And this service has been demanded of me."

"Demanded because it is too much to ask. You are still a free man and not a slave. No one would think less of you had you turned back."

He forced a laugh. "Now you tell me, after it's too late."

Kuikin watched her silhouette as she carefully retied her braid. "What about you?" he asked.

"I took an oath also," she said. "Seven of them."

"But why?"

Silence but for the water, then, “Four of us planned to steal the treasures of Khorpis Kharn, at the bottom of this valley, where this river ends. We were going to be rich. Instead, everyone ended up dead but me. While I recovered—” She laughed. “Well, since I was already chaste and poverished, it didn’t tax me to take the other five vows and join the Sisterhood. Besides the righteous path appealed to me. I was sick to heart of killing things.” Her voice dropped to a whisper. “And now that path brings me back here. Perhaps I was never intended to escape the first time.”

“Perhaps the Great Balance of Souls owes you a debt and seeks to repay it,” Kuikin said.

“I never argue faith with the faithless, Kick.”

She only called him Kick when she was mad at him. “But—”

“I said I don’t want to talk about it.”

“I’m sorry, Elizeh—”

“My name’s Renn now. It changed. I’ve changed.”

He watched her, seeing nothing but a shadow among shadows, until Vertir said, “And you? Why are you here?”

Kuikin glanced at Vertir then back to Elizeh. “That’s a stupid question. I am where I am.”

He flopped down on his damp blankets and rolled over in them.

VIII

The walls of the canyon constricted their horizons to worn and pitted stone, straggling malformed vegetation, parched sky, and the passage from one churning, boulder-strewn rapids, across brief stretches of level water to the next violent drop.

By late afternoon of the second day, they were battered, bruised, and exhausted by the difficult portages around the worst of the waterfalls. Kuikin crouched in the middle of the boat, soaked and sick, when he heard an awful roar ahead. "Are those falls?" he shouted.

"Gorge," Elizeh answered from the bow. "No way around it but through. But it's the last bad passage left."

The boat rocketed through the overhanging cliffs, where the surge and rush of water reverberated at deafening volumes. The current whipped them toward one wall then the other, tossing them like an unbroken horse, leap to leap through a series of small, rough rapids. Somehow they stayed to the middle path, taking the water where it frothed whitest, until at last they emerged from the long chute. Elizeh used her paddle to fend them away from the massive rocks that littered that part of the river.

Kuikin clutched the sides of the boat so hard his hands ached, bracing against an impact. "Watch out!"

"Relax!" she shouted back, her voice tense as they shot through the gap between two boulders. "Clear is clear!"

Then the boat lifted into the air and dropped onto a third rock, just barely submerged. It landed with a wrenching crack, scraped sideways, and flipped, dumping them.

Chill water surged over Kuikin as he tumbled upside down, spilling into his nose, his throat. The current swept him away, up into air, around boulders, under, up, and then under again. The bag with their supplies, slung over his shoulder, snagged on something, the cord choking him, and though he slipped out of it somehow, the water bashed him with its mob of fists and he tumbled over and over, thrashing without surfacing. He felt dizzy, light-headed, sure he was about to drown, when something hard lashed the side of his face, then lashed him again. Elizeh's braid! He grabbed for it, for her, and felt her hand clamp onto his arm and yank him sputtering into the air.

She spilled him onto a ledge, where he lay coughing, gagging, drooling. Vertir's voice, downstream, "Are you all right?"

"We are," shouted Elizeh. "You?"

A pause. "I hurt my shoulder."

There was no comfortable shore to offer them respite, only a vertical wall of rock on one side and a steep slope on the other that was covered with nail-trees and some kind of poisonous vine that whipped its hooked tips at them when they came too close.

Holding tight to one another, Kuikin and Elizeh slipped off the rock and let the turbulent current take them away. He flowed over the rocks. He was noticing how the moss tickled his bare arms when his head kicked back, knocking against the stones, and then they were both clear, kicking hard to make it to the safety of Vertir's perch.

The muscle on Vertir's jaw bulged in suppressed pain and tension. He hunched over, gripping his left forearm away from his body. "Arm wedged between two rocks. But no bones sticking out through the skin, eh."

He grimaced with each word. "You all right?" Kuikin asked.

"No," he gasped. "Hurts like a dragon's bite."

"We lost a boat there in the gorge last time too," Elizeh said, looking back. "At least no one drowned this time."

"Don't tempt me," Vertir said.

Kuikin scanned the other direction, downstream. "Look, it's hung up on that curve." The boat floated upside down, wobbling in the eddies.

"We better recover it," Elizeh said, easing into the water.

"Can you float?" Kuikin asked Vertir.

"Maybe. Sure. I don't know. If I sink, don't try to bring me up again."

They slipped off the ledge and let the river carry them away again, swiftly still, but not as rough. Elizeh swam ahead, trying to reach the overturned boat as the current dragged it on. Vertir's nose and mouth were barely above the surface. Kuikin put a hand on Vertir's good arm, to pull him along.

"Gah!" Vertir screamed. "Don't!"

Kuikin let go, seeing that it hurt, but stayed close by.

They chased the boat along the swift rush-feathered stream, catching it where a narrow, muddy island split the river. Kuikin stood ready to help while Vertir sloshed onto the bank, still clutching his arm. Elizeh dragged the boat ashore. When she paused to rub her lower back, Kuikin noticed blood staining her thigh. "Are you hurt too?"

"Nnn," she muttered.

"I asked, are you hurt?"

"No," she said firmly. "I'm flying the red flag. I'm hailing the crimson brigand. I'm feeding the moon. *Understand?*"

A couple heartbeats. "Oh."

Vertir laughed at him, grimaced with the pain.

"The wale's busted," Elizeh said of the boat. "It sags like a swaybacked horse and I don't have anything I need to fix it. We still have one paddle but—Vertir!"

He had fallen to his knees. She came over. "We're going to need to bend your elbow here," she said, taking hold of his wounded arm, "and make a sling through your shirt."

He nodded, his nostrils flaring as he controlled his breathing, stifled the agony. When she moved his arm gently closer to his body, his face contorted.

"Are—" she said.

"Go on," he told her through his teeth.

"Kuikin! I need a swath of cloth, long."

Taking out his little knife, Kuikin cut into the hem of his shirt, tearing a strip loose lengthwise while she braced the bad arm. He handed it over to her, and she wrapped the arm against Vertir's body, immobilizing it.

"How's that?" she asked.

"It'll do," Vertir said, exhaling.

"I should have padded it first, but we lost all our blankets."

"I lost my bow, quiver, javelin too," Vertir said. "I had the bow, but that's what jammed in the rocks."

"And my ranger knife," she said, tipping the empty sheath. "But I still have some of the others."

Kuikin's hand shot to his neck, to where he'd had the bag. "Our supplies."

"What? That's all you had to—" She bit off her words.

"I kept a little back for us here." Vertir patted the pouch at his waist with his good arm. "Should we eat a bite now? Get our strength up and keep moving."

"Good idea," Kuikin said, taking the proffered dried meat, and tearing off a piece with his teeth.

Elizeh shook her head. "Eating meat violates my sixth vow."

"You take a vow against starving to death?" Vertir asked.

But Kuikin said, "That's true only if you killed it. The path allows for the consumption of meat in special circumstances where the beast died of natural causes, just as it permits you to wear the lizard-scale robes."

"Don't tell me what my faith allows, Kick," she said.

"You'll need your strength," he growled at her, holding up the strip of meat. "Trust me, this animal was struck by lightning and cooked in its own skin, reduced in a split second to the state you see it in now. I swear it. The divine will of the world clearly intended it for your sustenance, so eat it!"

She turned away from him to try to repair the boat.

IX

The boat limped along half under water, moving barely as fast as the current. Kuikin and Elizeh took turns with the paddle, but they could do little to hurry it.

By mid-morning the next day the clifts had fallen away revealing a great bowl of a valley, with strange trees that stretched a hundred feet and more into the sky. The air was warm, oppressive, vibrating with a grating hum. The mountains were no more than a vague darkness seen through distant haze.

"Why didn't the Dynast send anyone after the gaud chrysalis sooner?" Elizeh asked.

Vertir started to shrug, winced, stopped. "I hadn't even heard rumors of it until the day we set out to meet you."

"No one knew," Kuikin said. "No one even suspected, until the Bey's men arrived in Finis Opor and commenced first their inquiries, then their preparations. The Notary-General dispatched us immediately upon reading the report."

"How does he even know one's here then?" she asked. "It's been so long since a gaud last walked the earth. Why, hearing the rumors, would he believe them?"

Vertir looked at Kuikin. "The Bey has used sorcery in attempted rebellion before. Enough to take any report seriously."

"And," Kuikin said, "this explains other facts. One of the Bey's most powerful sorcerers disappeared a few years ago. Rumor had it that he was murdered for studying the doctrine of Transfiguration and for his ambition. Now we think that the rumor was planted, that instead his studies and his ambitions led him here, with the Bey's blessings, so that—"

Several dark shapes buzzed out of the sky, diving at their heads. Kuikin ducked, throwing his hands up to defend himself. "Bees!"

"Shhh!" hissed Elizeh, freezing her position. "Leave them alone and they won't bother you."

Vertir said, "Did anybody tell them that?"

The bees were saffron-and-charcoal blurs, bigger than fists, with glistening stingers the size of small knives. Their feet brushed the top of Kuikin's head, wings fanning his hair. Kuikin, who'd had bad experiences with stings, hesitated to trust Elizeh's advice. He draped one hand over the side of the boat, and tried to paddle them away.

A moment later the insects were gone. Elizeh shuddered and sighed. "We lost the second member of our party to one of the bees."

Kuikin was about to ask how it had happened when something brushed against his fingers. He looked into the water and saw a bunch of dark shapes, some as long as his hand, darting around the boat. His stomach rumbled. "It's a school of fish. I think I can catch one . . ."

Elizeh slammed the paddle into the water. "Those are leeches—make sure none get in the boat."

Kuikin yanked his hand out of the river and scanned the water filling the crippled craft. It was empty.

"Look," Vertir said.

A great gray wall of stone loomed dead ahead of them, still miles away but higher than the treetops, crossing the course of the river, running off toward the mountains in either direction.

"How does the river flow around that?" Vertir asked

"It doesn't," Elizeh said. "Those are the cliffs of Khorpis Kharn."

X

The falls rumbled like an avalanche down an endless mountainside, mist in the air like a cloud of dust. Elizeh steered their boat to the shore.

"But how can there be waterfalls at the bottom of a cliff?" Vertir asked.

"The river Xows into limestone caverns at the base," Elizeh said. "No one knows where it comes out again, or if it does."

Kuikin checked himself again for leeches as he climbed onto the river's bank. "Scrolls in the Dynast's archive say that the ancients who lived here, sent all sizes of things into the falls, checking the rivers on the other side of the mountain, and even the sea itself without ever finding them again."

"When was that?" Vertir grasped Elizeh's hand and she helped him ashore. His pain already seemed much diminished.

"In the days of the first gauds," Kuikin said.

"In the days," Elizeh said, "when sorcerors defied the natural winding of the path, awoke the world-dragon in its lair, and tugged its beard." She pointed above the falls. "What's that, Kuikin? We didn't know, when we saw it the last time."

A thin spine of stone protruded from the face of the cliff, spreading out into a flat top just below the rim of the city.

"Condemned men were lowered to that platform," he said. "If they dived clear of the rocks and swam free to the river's edge, they were permitted to live."

The three of them regarded the length of the drop, the breadth of the stones, the power of the current. "Did any ever make it?" she asked.

"Some of the scrolls say yes, some of them say no. They're all of dubious provenance."

Vertir was the first to turn away from the prisoner's perch. "We're not finished here yet. We should keep moving."

They carried the boat into the trees and hid it under the thick, leafy bushes. Two steps back and even they could not see where it was hidden. It was a futile gesture. They could not use it again. A shadow fell over them. The distant hum in the trees quieted. First Kuikin then the other two turned and stared at the mist-obscured cliff, the towering skirt of trees, the pale gleam of sunset on the distant city.

"Has anyone ever survived killing a gaud?" Elizeh asked.

"Some of the scrolls say yes," Kuikin said, "some say—"

Vertir interrupted: "No, no one ever did. Pence-the-martyr was turned into a shadow of black ash on the wall."

"That's what I've always heard too," Elizeh said. She waited a moment. "Kuikin, remember how when we left home, at the edge of the village, you said we'd stay together until we died?"

Vertir turned away, his hand resting on the hilt of his sword, permitting them a small space of privacy.

"Yes," Kuikin whispered. "And I know I left you when I went to study with the scribes. I'm sorry about that, El—Renn."

He would only think of her as Renn from now on. He couldn't change anything in the past, couldn't make those things better, but he could do that much.

"It's all right now," she said.

XI

The sky above them was still bright, so Vertir drew his sword and began hacking a way through the undergrowth to the wall.

"Doesn't that hurt?" Renn asked, but Kuikin knew better. Vertir controlled his pain by pushing against it.

"It's fine," Vertir said, grunting with each swing.

"My ranger knife would serve better," Renn said.

"Sure, if you hadn't lost it."

"Let me find something to beat back the branches." She reached for a long stick. When she touched it, it twitched, leapt up and ran away past Kuikin. He jumped.

"Persuade it to come back," Vertir said, slashing one-handed, sweating. "Maybe it can beat down the branches on its own."

The deeper they pressed on, the thicker the forest became. They could hear large shapes moving only five or ten feet away from them, scattering out of the way of Vertir's sword, yet they never glimpsed any creature. He hacked slower, but harder in the gloom, attempting to frighten them away, until his blade clanged, throwing sparks as the tip snapped off.

"Here's the cliff wall," he announced. He considered his broken sword then whacked another branch in frustration.

"Then the steps must be this way," Renn said. She bulled ahead, following the cliff a short way until they came to a broad, overgrown platform carved in the stone.

A narrow stairway zigzagged up the cliff face, becoming a faint line that disappeared in darkness before the summit.

"Shall we keep going?" Vertir asked.

Kuikin gauged the width of the stair and wasn't so sure, but Renn said, "It's too easy to fall. We should camp here, rest, and try it in the morning."

Vertir chopped away the brush, while Renn ripped things up by hand, and Kuikin tore down vines—petals from large fragant blossoms rained over his face—to create a tiny clearing.

Renn declined when Vertir shared the last of his stores. The dried meat turned to rawhide in Kuikin's mouth when Vertir asked Renn, "So where's your home, where the two of you grew up?"

"Kuikin's never told you?"

"He doesn't talk much about himself."

She shrugged. "It's a little village in the Pong Mountains about six days' journey from the river—"

"The Ankee River?"

"—right, the Ankee. Town so small it didn't have a prefect or even a notary. The year that Kuikin and I left, our mother—"

"Wait!" He laughed. "You're brother and sister?"

Kuikin choked, covered it with a cough. "More like cousins," he blurted as she mumbled, "Half-brother."

But Vertir was laughing too hard to hear them. "Here all along, I thought the two of you had been lovers. Kuikin usually grows this mopey and sullen around his former lovers."

Kuikin said nothing, denial the equivalent of confession. But he thought he could see Renn's cheeks flush as bright red as two coals in the night.

"It wasn't like that exactly," she said. "I mean, it was such a small village. And we were so isolated, so ignorant—"

Vertir's chuckles suddenly ceased.

"It's a long story," Kuikin said.

"So how did you and Kuikin both start working for the Notary-General?" she asked, abruptly trying to change the subject.

It was Vertir's turn to say nothing. That had been the year of the dark bead. Finally, he too said, "It's a long story."

A damp breeze stirred through the trees, brushing over them, rustling tendrils that tickled their skin.

"We should all just get some rest," Kuikin said.

"That's a good idea," Vertir said while Renn added, "We'll need it for the climb tomorrow."

They stretched out, close to one another, up against the base of the cliff and away from the unceasing purr and rustle that came from the trees. Kuikin's back pressed up against Renn. He tried not to think of the past. He had become quite good at it. He lay there for a long long time, silent, awake, not thinking.

"Kuikin," Renn growled, "keep your hands to yourself."

Resentment flushed through him—he wasn't that ignorant any more. He hated ignorance. He folded his hands under his arms and curled up in a ball. "My hands are to myself."

"I'm serious, get them off my leg—Kick!"

"I said my hands are to myself. And stop calling me Kick!"

"She said 'tick' you dungwit," Vertir cried. "'Tick!'"

Something crept on finger-sized feet over the back of his Kuikin's neck. He screamed and jumped up. "Ticks!"

A soupbowl-size bug tumbled from him; he booted it into the brush. He knocked another from his leg.

"One has its fangs in my thigh," Vertir said.

"Don't kill it," Renn said, flinging another into the dark. "Let it be reborn into something that doesn't bite!"

He pulled his knife and pried it loose while Kuikin spun around kicking at anything that moved. "How'd you not notice it?"

"It was," a shell cracked, "a very slight pain compared to others."

"Moon's up," Renn said. "Perhaps we should ascend."

XII

The steps switchbacked vertically up the wall, sometimes a foot wide, sometimes a foot and a half, obscured by the far-reaching branches of the trees, overgrown by vines, cracked by roots, slick with mist, worn, the sheer rock rising on one side, dropping off to the valley floor without handholds on the other.

Renn went first, since she had been this way before, with Vertir in the middle because of his injured shoulder. They made slow progress as Renn cleared one step after another.

Kuikin hated heights more than he hated speed: he inched along, finding one purchase for his fingers in the stone after the next, never glancing down. Not being able to see the ground below in the darkness only made it worse. "Can't you move a little faster?" Kuikin said, sweating, heart skipping, as the breeze jostled him.

"The moth rushes into the flame," she answered, and continued testing each foothold carefully before moving on.

They had reached the spot where the treetops were thickest, limbs crowding the steps. The branches broke when leaned on, snapped back when pushed out of the way, always hiding the path. The three of them pushed on through. Something shook the leaves, bent them aside, and for a split second, human-sized eyes peered at Kuikin, reflecting moonlight from the sky. Kuikin blinked.

"Here's the gap," Renn said quietly.

"What?" asked Kuikin. The eyes had disappeared. He thought he had imagined them, but was ready to ask Vertir and Renn.

"The gap in the stairs. Too wide to step across. You'll have to jump up. The landing is a couple feet higher." Her hand patted the stone and then she hopped, grunting as she pulled her self upright. "I'm holding my hand out—"

"Got it," Vertir said as he followed her. Then, "Kuikin—"

Kuikin nodded. "With that shoulder you can't catch me. Just move back. Give me some room."

Their shadows retreated higher up the stairs. He leaned over, tracing the gap along the wall with his fingers. After one false start, he gathered himself and leapt. His knee struck the stone, but he clutched at vines, pulling himself upright, panting.

"Tell me," he said to distract himself, trying to stop shaking enough to go on. "What we will find atop the staircase, in the city itself?"

"I don't know," Renn admitted. "This is as high as we made it. My," a long pause dropped here, "last companion fell off the cliff just back there. I returned to the ground to help him, but he was dead from the fall. The honey climbers captured me then."

"Should I just leap now?" Vertir said.

Her arm shot back, pinning him to the wall, and his right hand folded over hers, prepared to pry her fingers loose.

"Don't do that again," he said.

"Don't even say that in jest!"

"He doesn't mean it," Kuikin said.

She released her grip. "Not even in jest. We hurried last time and failed. I'll get us to the top this time. Be patient."

Kuikin had no patience, but neither did he have any choice except turning back and the prospect of looking down even to place his feet was too much to bear. Eyes lifted, he continuously remeasured their sluggish progress to the top, and when he could do that no longer he lowered his gaze merely to the next turn, and when that too became unbearable, he looked only to the next step, to the feet in front of his, and when that too became an ordeal, his breath fluttering in his chest, his fingertips dripping so much sweat he could no longer grip the stone, they turned a corner, took a few final steps, and the cliff disappeared as a wide platform spread before them, a starless slab beneath the slab of sky. They had reached the summit.

Renn and Vertir turned to look back at their ascent, but Kuikin hurried away from the edge. The forest grew up here as well, a dark blanket that covered the ruins. He thought he glimpsed pale stone here and there, but wasn't sure.

"I could defend this against all the soldiers of the Bey," Vertir was saying to Renn. "If only I had unbroken weapons and a left arm healed enough to parry with."

"Are those the Bey's soldiers over there?"

Kuikin whipped around at Renn's question and ran to the cliff. A fire glowed through the treetops below. "Dear gaud, we're just ahead of them. Quick, let's find the chrysalis and flee before they arrive."

Renn spun. "From down there, I thought I saw—"

Vertir started toward the ruins. "We'll split up—"

"No," Kuikin said. "Stay together. These old cities were laid out by geomancers. We'll find the temple at the conjunction of the dragon lines. The gaud will be there, needing to draw on that power himself."

"But how—"

"Where—"

"This way," he said, and took off, looking for any slope that led upward, scanning the distant horizon for the looming peaks of mountains and the intersections between them.

Through arches that pierced crumbling walls, around the pillared corners of palaces subsumed by jungle, up antique boulevards whose heavy paving stones still held clear a way forward, until they discovered in the heart of the city a vast dome rising through the canopy like a full moon. They searched the perimeter until they found an entrance, then went inside.

And nothing.

No light penetrated the nocturnal silence of the dome; no sound stirred within. They walked like blind beggars with their hands along the wall, feeling things crunch and break beneath their feet. The air had a dry, dusty, lifeless smell.

Vertir asked, "So what do we do—"

"SO WHAT?" echoed in the vast space around them.

Something rustled in the dome above them when the sound faded. "It'll be dawn soon," Kuikin whispered in each one's ear. "We have to wait."

They sat together with their backs against the wall.

XIII

Kuikin jerked awake, heart rolling like thunder, when Vertir jabbed him. He started to shout but his friend pressed a finger to his lips and pointed upward.

They must have fallen asleep. The sun was long risen, light pouring through the clerestory arches, illuminating the chapel. The famed riches of Khorpis Kharn were only devastation. The mosaics, even the plaster, had been torn from the walls. Some of the damage appeared recent, fresh gashes in long-defaced murals. Everything but the structure itself had been smashed. Kuikin scarcely noticed. Three stories up, in the dome's center, bathed in sunlight, hung a huge translucent chrysalis.

"Well, there it is," Vertir said. "Can we go now?"

Renn rose to her feet. "It hasn't hatched," she whispered.

Kuikin's heart pounded harder as he stood beside her. "All we have to do is knock it down. And kill it."

"How?" asked Vertir. "With what?" That stopped them all. As they pondered those questions, Vertir stood and paced, seeking an answer. "If we have to, we can scale the outside of the building somehow, use some kind of pole to reach through the clerestory to knock it loose."

The colors inside the chrysalis swirled. The thing twitched on the slender thread that suspended it aloft.

Kuikin hefted a chunk of stone. "Perhaps we can encourage its fall from here."

His first throw missed wildly and the missile crashed back to the floor of the temple, scattering the pieces of fallen mosaic that had crunched underfoot the night before. Vertir's throw came closer. His second throw caused him to grunt in suppressed pain. The rock glanced off the chrysalis with no effect.

"We need to head outside or find another route up there," Kuikin said.

Vertir stared hard at Renn. "Maybe if I had a good throwing knife, I might be able to do it some harm first."

"Ah," Renn said. She hesitated, then produced two knives from her sleeves. She frowned, then handed them over. "I'd have asked for a bow if I thought you had one."

His first throw bounced off the chrysalis and fell back among them, causing Kuikin to dive out of its way. His second throw stuck in the side of the sac.

The chrysalis vibrated. The knife wobbled and fell.

Vertir stepped back. "That's not going to work. We need to approach it more closely."

"No," Renn said. "Look!"

A blood-red drop bubbled up where the knife had stuck, swelling outward. Inside the chrysalis, colors swirled like a dust devil in the painted desert. The bubble burst and scarlet liquid rolled down the sac, fell forever through the air, and splashed on the floor near them like water breaking from a pregnant woman's womb.

The swirling stopped. A crack appeared in the chrysalis, split open, and a second gush of liquid poured out, followed by a steady drip, echoing *tap tap tap* as it fell.

"Maybe," Vertir said, "that wasn't such a good idea."

The split tore open, and a pair of double-wings unfolded out, then six legs gripped the bottom of its former cage and flipped upside down, hanging there as it fanned itself dry.

"So what will you do now?" whispered Renn.

Kuikin didn't know.

Vertir had already retrieved the pair of knives and held one ready to throw. "Maybe if we leave it alone, it won't bother us."

The gaud lifted its head towards them. An almost human face peered out exuberantly from behind the over-sized eyes and long, needle-like proboscis. "Oh," he rasped, "it's quite too late for that."

As the three of them backstepped toward the door, the gaud hissed and flagstones leapt up in a spray of dust and broken tile, flipping end over end, shedding chips of stone with every clunk, to build a waist-high wall around them.

"Sheep in the pen," the gaud panted, fanning his wings. His head angled toward the door. "It will only be a few moments."

Vertir went to leap over the stones, but one slammed down where he stood and he was only just able to dodge it. He tensed to leap again, but the stones reared up against him.

"The next one will crush you to bloody pulp," the gaud said.

Kuikin felt something poke around in his thoughts, like a knife stirring a bowl of soup. The hairs tingled all along the back of his neck and hackled on his arms. He looked at his companions, wondering if the fear showed as clearly in his face as it did in theirs.

The gaud inhaled sharply. "Yes, here, here."

A lean man with a narrow face and a long nose, dressed in filthy silver robes torn short at the sleeves and hem, staggered in through the door. It was the Bey's archsorcerer. Kuikin did not know him well, had only encountered him twice before. But he was a glutton for power and a gourmand of the profane.

He fell to his knees. "My gaud, you've forsaken me! You did not wait!"

"No, I felt your spark and it was enough to aid me," the gaud said, his voice grown stronger. "But our enemies outran you."

The archsorcerer looked across the room and saw them for the first time. He stared longest at Kuikin, as if trying to see past the beard. Then he turned and left.

Wings trembled, closed, and spread, the glistening wetness drying to brilliant shades of red and orange and yellow.

"Kuikin," whispered Renn.

A ball of broken tile formed and smashed into her back.

As she staggered, the gaud said, "Be silent or the next one shall stop your mouth."

Kuikin exchanged glances with the other two. A quick resort to force usually signaled weakness over strength.

Of course, weakness was a comparative term.

The gaud stared straight at him and made a clicking noise that might have been laughter.

The archsorcerer returned with the soldiers, berating them for cowardice as he drove them into the Temple. There were maybe half the original number, most bruised and bandaged.

Two of them held one of the honey climbers, stripped and bound. His jaw was set, but his eyes widened in dismay at the sight of the gaud. "Over there," said the archsorcerer, and they threw him forward onto his stomach and retreated.

The gaud dropped from the ceiling, flapped its wings twice, and landed on the prisoner. A brief struggle ended when the gaud thrust his straw into the man's neck and began sucking.

The flagstones trembled on their ends in pleasure as the gaud's tongue flicked at the corner of his diminished mouth. "Strip and search them. Bind them if they give you any trouble."

Kuikin shucked his clothes at once. Vertir followed a moment later, unknotting the wraps that bound his wounded arm, still cradling it close to his body after he pulled his shirt off. His left shoulder looked slightly concave, still wrong.

The soldiers poked their spears at Renn over the wall of flagstones before she started. They mocked her as the first layer came off. On her undergarments she had painted the words of the death prayer in indelible ink, a custom done only by those going off to die.

"If she's in that much of a hurry, we can help her along."

"No, no, make her wait," another said.

Men who had suffered were too eager to share their suffering with others, Kuikin thought. He breathed a sigh of relief when she removed those garments too.

While the soldiers insulted her again, one pointed his spear at Vertir's wrist. "Take off the bracelet."

"No."

The soldier slipped the point of the blade under the bracelet. "If you take off the bracelet, I won't hurt—"

Vertir grabbed that shaft one-handed and yanked the man forward as he kicked the flagstones over. A crunch of broken bone coincided with the crack of the shaft on the man's head.

"No compromises," he said, just loud enough for Renn and Kuikin.

Then the others surrounded him. He spun the shaft, deflecting their thrusts until the stones jumped back up and the spear flew out of his hand to clatter against the wall.

"He will be amusing," the gaud said. "Leave him."

The soldiers stepped back, closer to the exit than the gaud. Loathing and terror deformed their features as they clustered together.

The gaud rose, stretched its wings, and addressed the archsorcerer. "I can feel the longing in you."

Didn't need sorcery for that, thought Kuikin. Longing was written on the man's face as clear as a lease for rented property.

"Yes," he said. "You are what I wish to be!"

"The divine already resides within you," the gaud said. "Unleash it and you too can have power without limit, life without end."

Both were lies: Kuikin wondered whether he should point out the fate of Bahl-the-Gaud. That life certainly ended.

"Yes, yes," the archsorcerer said. "That is what I want, what I have prepared for. The holy age will soon return, when men shall be ruled by their betters. We'll build new monuments to outlast their meager lives."

"You must first lose your humanity to gain divinity."

The archsorcerer straightened, lifting his chin. His eyes glittered like gems. "I accept that. I accept Transfiguration."

The gaud's needle slipped out of the corpse and flexed toward the shabby archsorcerer. "Good. I will enjoy your company. I will need you, no doubt, even before you are ready. We have a world to re-create in our own image."

His large eyes bulging in concentration, the gaud folded his wings and tensed. His four top legs twitched.

The archsorcerer's lean face took on an aspect of rapture that rapidly transformed into an ecstasy of pain. He began to moan and writhe, tearing off his robe in agony. His arms atrophied before their eyes, shrinking back into his swelling body until only his fingers protruded from the stumps of his shoulders.

The soldiers shifted uneasily. A couple at the rear eased towards the arched doorway.

The archsorcerer toppled onto his stomach. He twisted, howling, "No, no, I take it back," but the words were garbled in his throat and the gaud only laughed in reply. Then ribs burst through the archsorcerer's skin, which healed behind them. His legs shriveled, suddenly melting together.

One of the soldiers wretched; another sagged against the wall, weeping. The gaud began to cackle now. "Yes, that's what it was like for me, too, but you'll forget it soon enough."

The air held the tang of lightning, setting Kuikin's teeth on edge. He bit down hard to hold the bile in his throat. Vertir's expression had gone blank, but his eyes darted from the soldiers' weapons to the gaud. Revulsion marred Renn's face. She averted her head, chin trembling.

No, she was pointing.

The flagstones wobbled unsteadily. The new gaud was still weak in his powers.

The agonizing screams of the transfigured man filled the temple. He squirmed across the floor. The fingers in his arm had become a set of tiny legs, the ribs another, and his feet a pair of hooks at the end of a long and narrow tail. His head still bore a human resemblance, a countenance like his own, but the mouth had widened and it seemed to be all teeth.

He looped around on himself, chasing his own tail, then leaped across the floor, mouth gnashing, in the direction of the soldiers. They broke and fled the chamber.

This creature, for he was no longer a man in any sense, reared up and, noticing the soldier Vertir had downed, cast itself upon him. The man was only unconscious, not dead, and he awoke as soon as the creature's teeth sank into his flesh. But his leg was broken and, unable to run, he screamed piteously while the creature dragged him off into a shadowed corner.

The gaud's laughter faded. "I'm hungry."

Needle-nose lifted, he sniffed them. He glanced away from Vertir as though he were dangerous, compared the size of Kuikin and Renn, then noticed a smear of blood on her bare thigh. The tip of the needle dilated.

"You were wearing the death prayer were you not?"

She said nothing, but her shoulders squared.

The scent of bad weather intensified. He beckoned her. The stones in front of her dropped, the one behind flipped forward, nipping at her heels. She stepped forward, ahead of it, reluctantly.

"My death, at least will be a true death," she said, "and my reincarnation a true one."

The gaud faced her, bending back on his two hind legs and beating his wings. "Don't quote your superstitions at me."

Over in the corner, the soldier's screams ceased.

She dragged her feet, quailing as she had before the Abbess, fidgeting with the end of her braid.

Kuikin tried to stall. "Enlighten us then!"

The gaud ignored him, hopping half the distance to Renn.

"If those who pass through death without death, who are reincarnated in a new form without first dying, do not cast themselves off the wheel of life to be consumed by the dragon's fire, then what happens to them when they die?"

The gaud turned his head to sneer. "We live forever. Come back in your next life and ask me about it."

Another flap of his wings hurled him toward Renn.

Vertir crouched to spring.

But she withdrew the hiltless blade of the poinard hidden in her braid and pinned it through the gaud's heart as he lighted.

She screamed and thrust forward.

The gaud squealed, tried to push her back with his four tiny, upper limbs, and then, as she lifted him off the ground, with all six. His wings beat at her in a shower of sunset-colored dust. The flagstone pen surrounding Kuikin and Vertir wobbled.

Renn held on, pushing him back all the way to the wall, twisting the blade and screaming, her voice merging with the shrill whine of the gaud, whose six legs embraced her, pulled her tight as his wings unfolded, vibrating so hard against the stone that they buzzed.

"No!" Kuikin shouted, meaning *yes!*

A blue fire rippled up the blade and into her arms. She yelped and fell backward, dead. The injured gaud slid down the wall, poniard protruding from his chest, and crumpled to the ground. A second, brighter flash of light and the wings stopped. Fire bolted out of the gaud into the ground; a burning smell pervaded the room. The flagstone wall toppled.

The creature in the shadows began an awful keening.

"Forever," gasped the gaud, "was so very brief."

Kuikin bolted forward, realizing as he did so that the gaud did not move, that Renn had spoken those words and not the gaud. She rolled over, face sheeted white beneath the jaundiced and vermillion dust, knees and elbows folded tight. She was alive! He froze where he stood.

Vertir scooped her up by the arm, dragging her stumbling to her feet, and hurried them all toward the door.

As the three rushed outside, the whole ridge began to shake, whipping sideways like the scaly tail of some giant beast. They staggered, trying to keep their feet. The ground swayed. A building somewhere off in the dead city tumbled, crashed. They ran past the corpses of the Bey's soldiers, pierced with darts from blowguns.

"Down the cliff?" Vertir asked.

Renn shook her head. "My hands—numb—can't feel."

"The leap?"

"No!" said Kuikin

"We'll take our chances in the trees then."

Kuikin followed after them, numb throughout his entire body. He couldn't believe that she still lived.

Knotted vines dropped down in front of them as the ground tremored again, more vigorously. The trees wobbled, vines quivering. Above them, honey climbers shouted, "Up you, up you!"

Kuikin looked up, saw them perched on branches rocking back and forth like the mast of a ship in a rough sea, and the vertigo immobilized him. He was safer on the ground.

"Hold on tight," Vertir told Renn, switching hands. He wrapped the vine around his forearm and gripped her with his left arm as the climbers pulled them up hand over hand.

Only a few feet from the ground, he grunted and Renn slipped out of his grasp. With his injured shoulder, he couldn't hold onto her. Kuikin rushed to her, hugging her tightly to him, squeezing a fistful of flesh.

"Just leave me," she said.

"Not this time."

He grasped the vine and held on in blind terror until hands gripped him and pulled him aboard a feeble platform of woven branches high above the ground. He crawled to the middle, clutching to it tightly as it swayed, his stomach reeling.

Voices around him shouted, fingers pointed.

From his perch, he could see through the branches to the edge of the city and the river below. A piece of the wall containing the condemned man's leap broke off from the cliff and plummeted into the water. Another section of cliff calved free, and, trailing pieces of buildings from the dead city, plunged into the pool, drowning the valley in a deluge of water.

One of the honey climbers turned to them. Kuikin thought he might have been the one from Finis Opor. He looked at the gill marks scarring the climber's torso and realized that here was an entire people who'd been offered Transfiguration, and had ultimately refused it

"Man," the climber said, tapping his chest, "in go to city."

"He dead," Renn said. "Dead clean. Dead true."

Some of the other climbers let out their breath at this, but the interrogator asked, "Big magic man, in go to city, long back."

"Dead, he dead," Renn said. "In go to dragon flame."

While he considered this, the ground rumbled again. He pointed the way out of the valley. "Nothing take you?"

"Nothing take we," Renn agreed. "Nothing, valley go."

He turned away, talking to men who went off toward the dead city. But apparently her answers satisfied him. A climber crossed over from another tree, carrying a section of giant comb on his back. A grail-sized chunk was broken off and handed to each of them. Vertir lifted his and sang:

"Honey is sweet when it's fresh from the comb,
but nothing is sweeter
Than a road leading home."

Crawling over to Renn, Kuikin lifted a section of the giant honeycomb to her lips. "I'm glad you're—" He faltered. "That was easier than I—"

A human-sized creature thrashed through the underbrush below them, keening like a lost soul. Even as they twisted their heads to look, it fell silent and disappeared.

Renn licked at the honey, raised her burn-scarred arm, and unfolded the fist into an open hand. "Murder has always been easy, Kuikin. It's the path of righteous peace that's hard."

"You had to—everyone strays from the path—"

"Don't say anything." She hung her head in shame.

The Swordsman Whose Name Was Not Death

ཀཀ

Ellen Kushner

Several years ago, a colleague showed me a copy of a 1980s Conan novel that was returned to the publisher by a passionate fan. Nowadays, that fan would probably write some remarks and post them on Amazon.com, but back then he scrawled angry responses throughout the book, x'ed out entire pages, and made his feelings abundantly clear in bold magic marker notes. What stays with me now is that he circled a sentence in which Conan stopped to think about his course of action. "Conan does not think," wrote this fan. "Conan acts!"

If you're a reader who thinks heroic fantasy is only about action, this story is probably not for you. Ellen Kushner's heroic fantasy stories blend action and thought into a combination that reads (in the words of Gene Wolfe) "as if Noel Coward had written a vehicle for Errol Flynn." Her novels Swordspoint *and* The Fall of the Kings *(the latter cowritten with Delia Sherman) owe as big a debt to the Regency romances of Georgette Heyer as they do to the adventure stories Fritz Leiber. The blend gives heroic fantasy a very different flavor, one that has been influential over the past fifteen years. "The Swordsman Whose Name Was Not Death" first appeared in our September 1991 issue.*

Ellen Kushner is the author of one other fantasy novel, Thomas the Rhymer. *She lives in the Boston area and hosts the acclaimed series "Sound and Spirit" for Public Radio International.*

After the fight, Richard was thirsty. He decided to leave the parrots alone for now. Parrots were supposed to be unlucky for swordsmen. In this case the curse seemed to have fallen on his opponent. Curious, he had asked the wounded man, "Did you slam into me on purpose?" People did sometimes, to provoke a fight with Richard St. Vier, the master swordsman who wouldn't take challenges from just anyone. But the wounded man only pressed his white lips together. The rest of him looked green. Some people just couldn't take the sight of their own blood.

Richard realized he'd seen him before, in a Riverside bar. He was a tough named Jim—or Tim—Something. Not much of a swordsman; the sort of man who made his way in the lawless Riverside district on bravado, and earned his living in the city doing cheapjack sword jobs for merchants aping the nobility in their hiring of swordsmen.

A man with a wreath of freesias hanging precariously over one ear came stumbling up. "Oh Tim," he said mournfully. "Oh Tim, I told you that fancy claret was too much for you." He caught hold of the wounded man's arm, began hauling him to his feet. As a matched set, Richard recognized them: they'd been the ritual guards in the wedding procession he'd seen passing through the market square earlier that afternoon.

"Sorry," the flower-decked drunk said to St. Vier. "Tim didn't mean to give you trouble, you understand?" Tim groaned. "He's not used to claret, see."

"Don't worry about it," Richard said charitably. No wonder Tim's swordplay had been less than linear.

Over their heads the caged parrots started squawking again. The parrot lady climbed down from the box where she'd escaped to get a better view of the fight. With St. Vier there to back her up, she shook her apron at the two ruffians to shoo them as if they were chickens escaped from the yard. The children who'd surrounded them, first to see if the quiet man was going to buy a parrot so they could see one taken down, and then to watch the fight, laughed and shrieked and made chicken noises after the disappearing toughs.

But people made way for Richard St. Vier as he headed in the direction of a stall selling drinks. The parrot lady collared one of the street kids, saying, "See that? You can tell your grandchildren you saw St. Vier fight right here." Oh, honestly, Richard thought, it hadn't been much of a fight; more like bumping into someone on the street.

He leaned on the wooden counter, trying to decide what he wanted.

"Hey," said a young voice at his elbow. "I'll buy you a drink."

He thought it was a woman, from the voice. Women sometimes tried to pick him up after fights. But he glanced down and saw a pug-faced boy looking at him through slitted eyes, the way kids do when they're trying to look older than they are. This one wasn't very old. "That was real good, the way you did that," the boy said. "I mean the quick double feint and all."

"Thank you," the swordsman answered courteously. His mother had raised him with good manners, and some old habits cling, even in the big city. Sometimes he could almost hear her say, *Just because you can kill people whenever you want to doesn't mean you have a license to be rude to anyone.* He let the boy buy them both some fancy drink made with raspberries. They drank silently, the boy peering over the rim of his cup. It was good; Richard ordered them both another.

"Yeah," the kid said. "I think you're the best there is, you know?"

"Thanks," said the swordsman. He put some coins on the counter.

"Yeah." The kid self-consciously fingered the sword at his own side. "I fight too. I had this idea, see—if you needed a servant or something."

"I don't," the swordsman said.

"Well, you know," the boy went on anyway. "I could, like, make up the fire in the morning. Carry water. Cook you stuff. Maybe when you practice, I could be—if you need somebody to help you out a little—"

"No," said St. Vier. "Thank you. There are plenty of schools for you to learn in."

"Yeah, but they're not . . ."

"I know. But that's the way it is."

He walked away from the bar, not wanting to hear any more argument. Behind him the kid started to follow, then fell back.

Across the square he met his friend Alec. "You've been in a fight," Alec said. "I missed it," he added, faintly accusing.

"Someone slammed into me by the parrot cages. It was funny." Richard smiled now at the memory. "I didn't see him coming, and for a moment I thought it was an earthquake! Swords were out before he could apologize—if he meant to apologize. He was drunk."

"You didn't kill him," Alec said, as if he'd heard the story already.

"Not in this part of town. That doesn't go down too well with the Watch here."

"I hope you weren't thinking of getting a parrot again."

Richard grinned, falling into step beside his tall friend. It was a familiar argument. "They're so decorative, Alec. And you could teach it to talk."

"Let some bird steal all my best lines? Anyhow, they eat worms. *I'm* not getting up to catch worms."

"They eat bread and fruit. I asked this time."

"Too expensive."

They were passing through the nice section of the city, headed down to the wharves. On the other side of the river was the district called Riverside, where the swordsman lived with sharpsters and criminals, beyond reach of the law. It would not have been a safe place for a man like Alec, who barely knew one end of a knife from another; but the swordsman St. Vier had made it clear what would happen to anyone who touched his friend. Riverside tolerated eccentrics. The tall scholar, with his student slouch and aristocratic accent, was becoming a known quantity along with the master swordsman.

"If you're feeling like throwing your money around," Alec persisted, "why don't you get us a servant? You need someone to polish your boots."

"I take good care of my boots," Richard said, stung in an area of competence. "*You're* the one who needs it."

"Yes," Alec happily agreed. "I do. Someone to go to the market for us, and keep visitors away, and start the fire in winter, and bring us breakfast in bed. . . ."

"Decadent," St. Vier said. "You can go to the market yourself. And I keep 'visitors' away just fine. I don't understand why you think it would be fun to have some stranger living with us. If you wanted that sort of life, you should have—" He stopped before he could say the unforgivable. But Alec, in one of his sudden shifts of attitude, which veered liked the wind over a small pond, finished cheerfully for him, "I should have stayed on the Hill with my rich relatives. But they never kill people—not out in the open where we can all enjoy it, anyway. You're so much more entertaining. . . ."

Richard's lips quirked downward, unsuccessfully hiding a smile. "Loved only for my sword," he said.

Alec said carefully, "If I were the sort of person who makes crude jokes, you would be very embarrassed now."

Richard, who was never embarrassed, said, "What a good thing you're not. What do you want for dinner?"

****

They went to Rosalie's, where they ate stew in the cool underground tavern and talked business with their friends. It was the usual hodgepodge of fact and rumor: A new swordsman had appeared across town claiming to be a foreign champion, but someone's cousin in service had recognized him as Lord Averil's old valet, with fencing lessons and a dyed mustache . . . Hugo Seville had finally gotten so low as to take a job offing some noble's wife . . . or maybe he'd only been offered it, or someone wished he had.

Nobles with jobs for St. Vier sent their messages to Rosalie's. But today there was nothing. "Just some nervous jerk looking for an heiress."

"Aren't we all?"

"Sorry, Reg, this one's taken; run off with some swordsman."

"Anyone we know?"

"Naw . . . fairy-tale swordsman—they say all girls have run off with one, when it's really their father's clerk."

Big Missy, who worked the mattress trade at Glinley's, put her arm around Richard. "I could run off with a swordsman." Seated, he came up only to her bosom, which he leaned back into, smiling across to Alec, eyebrows raised a little provocatively.

Alec took the bait: "Careful," the tall scholar told her; "he bites."

"Oh?" Missy leered becomingly at him. "Don't *you,* pretty baby?"

Alec tried to hide a flush of pure delight. No one had ever called him "pretty baby" before, especially not women other people paid to get into.

"Of course I do," he said with all the brittle superciliousness he was master of. "Hard."

Missy released St. Vier, advancing on his tall young friend. "Oh *good* . . ." she breathed huskily. "I like 'em rough." Her huge arms pointed like weather vanes into the rising wind. “Come to me, lover.”

The old-time crowd at Rosalie’s was ecstatic. “Missy, don’t leave me for that bag of bones!” “So long, then, Alec; let us know how it comes out!” “Try it, boy; you just might like it!”

Alec looked like he wanted to sink into the floor. He held his ground, but his hauteur, already badly applied, was slipping treacherously.

At the last minute, Richard took pity on him. “I saw a wedding today,” he said to the room at large.

“Oh yeah,” said Lucie; “we heard you killed one of the guards. Finally made them earn their pay, huh?”

“Thought you didn’t *do* weddings, Master St. Vier.” Sam Bonner looked around for approval of his wit. Everyone knew that St. Vier disdained guard work.

“I don’t,” Richard said. “This was after. And I didn’t kill him. Tim somebody.”

“No lie! Tim Porker? Half-grown mustache, big ears? Said he hurt himself falling down some stairs. Dirty liar.”

“No weddings for Richard,” Alec said. He’d regained his aplomb, but was still eyeing Missy warily from across the room. “He is morally opposed to the buying and selling of heiresses.”

“No, I’m not. It’s just not interesting work, being a wedding guard. It doesn’t mean anything anymore, just rich people showing they can afford swordsmen to make their procession look pretty. It’s no—”

“Challenge,” Alec finished for him. “You know, we could set that to music, you say it so often, and hawk it on the street as a ballad. What a good thing for the rich that other swordsmen aren’t too proud to take their money, or we’d never see an heiress safely bedded down. What’s the reward offered for the runaway? Is there one? Or is she damaged goods already?”

"There's a reward for information. But you have to go Uptown to get it."

"I'm not above going Uptown," said Lucie haughtily; "I've been there before. But I don't know as I'd turn in a girl that's run away for love . . ."

"Ohh," bawled Rosalie across the tavern; "is that what you call it?"

"Speaking of money," Alec said, rattling the dicebox, "is anyone interested in a small bet on whether I can roll multiples of three three times running?"

Richard got up to go. When Alec had drunk enough to become interested in mathematical odds, the evening's entertainment was over for him. St. Vier was not a gambling man.

The Riverside streets were dark, but St. Vier knew his way between the close-set houses, past the place where the broken gutter overflowed, around the potholes of pried-up cobbles, through the back alleys and home. His own lodgings were in a cul-de-sac off the main street; part of an old townhouse, a discarded veteran of grander days. Richard lived on the second story, in what had once been the music rooms.

On the ground floor, Marie's rooms were dark. He stopped before the front door; in the recessed entryway, there was a flash of white. Cautiously, St. Vier drew his sword and advanced.

A small woman practically flung herself onto his blade. "Oh help!" she cried shrilly. "You must help me!"

"Back off," said St. Vier. It was too dark to see much but her shape. She was wearing a heavy cloak, and something about her was very young. "What's the matter?"

"I am desperate," she gasped. "I am in terrible danger. Only you can help me! My enemies are everywhere. You must hide me."

"You're drunk," said Richard, although her accent wasn't Riverside. "Go away before you get hurt."

The woman fell back against the door. "No, please. It means my life."

"You had better go home," Richard said. To speed her on her way, he said, "Do you need me to escort you somewhere? Or shall I hire you a torch?"

"No!" It sounded more annoyed than desperate, but quickly turned back to pleading: "I dare not go home. Please listen to me. I am—a Lady of Quality. My parents want to marry me to a man I hate—an old miser with bad breath and groping hands."

"That's too bad," Richard said politely, amused in spite of the inconvenience. "What do you want me to do about it? Do you want him killed?"

"Oh! Oh. No. Thank you. That is, I just need a place to stay. Until they stop looking for me."

Richard said, "Did you know there's a reward out for you?"

"There *is?*" she squeaked. "But—oh. How gratifying. How . . . like them."

"Come upstairs." St. Vier held the door open. "Mind the third step; it's broken. When Marie gets back, you can stay with her. She's a, she takes in customers, but I think propriety says you're better off with her than with me."

"But I'd *rather* stay with you, sir!"

In the pitch-black of the stairs, Richard halted. The girl almost stumbled into him. "No," St. Vier said. "If you're going to start that, you're not coming any farther."

"I didn't—" she squeaked, and began again: "That's not what I meant at all. Honestly."

Upstairs, he pushed open the door and lit a few candles. "Oh!" the girl gasped. "Is this—is this where you—"

"I practice in this room," he said. "The walls are wrecked. You can sit on that chaise, if you want—it's not as rickety as it looks." But the girl went over to the wall, touching the pock-marks where his practice sword had chipped holes in the old plaster. Her fingertips were gentle, almost reverent.

It was an old room, with traces of its former grandeur clinging about the edges in the form of gilded laurel-leaf molding and occasional pieces of cherub. The person who had last seen fresh paint there had long since turned to dust. The only efforts that its present occupants had made to decorate it were an expensive tapestry hung over the fireplace, and a couple of very detailed silver candlesticks, a few leather-bound books, and an enamel vase, scattered about the room in no discernible order.

"I'd offer you the bed," said Richard, "but it would annoy Alec. Just make yourself comfortable in here."

With the pleasantly light feeling of well-earned tiredness, the swordsman drifted into the room that held his big carven bed and his chests for clothes and swords, undoing the accoutrements of his trade: unbuckling the straps of his sword belt, slipping the knife sheath out of his vest. He paced the room, laying them down, unlacing and unpeeling his clothes, and got into bed. He was just falling asleep when he heard Alec's voice in the other room:

"Richard! You've found us a servant after all—how enterprising of you!"

"No—" he started to explain, and then thought he'd better get up to do it.

The girl was hunched up at the back of the chaise lounge, looking awed and defenseless, her cloak still wrapped tight around her. Alec loomed over her, his usual untoward clutter of unruly limbs. Sometimes drinking made him graceful, but not tonight.

"Well," the girl was offering hopefully, "I can cook. Make up the fire. Carry water."

Richard thought, That's the second time I've heard that today. He started to say, "We couldn't ask a Lady of Quality—"

"Can you do boots?" Alec asked with interest.

"No," Richard stated firmly before she could say yes. "No servants."

"Well," Alec asked peevishly, "then what's she doing here? Not the obvious, I hope."

"Alec. Since when am I obvious?"

"Oh, never mind." Alec turned clumsily on his heel. "I'm going to bed. Have fun. See that there's hot shaving water in the morning."

Richard shrugged apologetically at the girl, who was staring after them in fascination. It was a shrug meaning, *Don't pay any attention to him;* but he couldn't help wondering if there would be hot water to shave with. Meanwhile, he meant to pay attention to Alec himself.

****

Alec woke up unable to tell where his limbs left off and Richard's began. He heard Richard say, "This is embarrassing. Don't move, Alec, all right?"

A third person was in the room with them, standing over the bed with a drawn sword. "How did you get in here?" Richard asked.

The pug-faced boy said, "It was easy. Don't you recognize me? My enemies are everywhere. I think I should, you know, get some kind of prize for that, don't you? I mean, I tricked you, didn't I?"

St. Vier eased himself onto his elbows. "Which are you, an heiress disguised as a snotty brat, or a brat disguised as an heiress?"

"Or," Alec couldn't resist adding, "a boy disguised as a girl disguised as a boy?"

"It doesn't matter," St. Vier said. "Your grip is too tight."

"Oh—sorry." Still keeping the sword's point on target, the kid eased his grip. "Sorry—I'll work on it. I knew I'd never get in like this. And girls are safe with you; everyone knows you don't like girls."

"Oh no," Richard protested, surprised. "I like girls very much."

"Richard," drawled Alec, whose left leg was beginning to cramp, "you're breaking my heart."

"But you like *him* better."

"Well, yes, I do."

"Jealous?" Alec snarled sweetly. "Please die and go away. I'm going to have the world's worst hangover if I don't get back to sleep soon."

Richard said, "I don't teach. I can't explain how I do what I do."

"Please," said the boy with the sword. "Can't you just take a look at me? Tell me if I'm any good. If you say I'm good, I'll know."

"What if I say you're not?"

"I'm good," the kid said stiffly. "I've got to be."

Richard slid out of bed, in one fluid motion regathering his limbs to himself. Alec admired that—like watching a chess expert solve a check in one simple move. Richard was naked, polished as a sculpture in the moonlight. In his hand was the sword that had been there from the start.

"Defend yourself," St. Vier said, and the boy fell back in cautious *garde.*

"If you kill him," said Alec, hands comfortably behind his head, "try not to make it one of the messy ones."

"I'm *not*—going to *kill*—him." With what was, for him, atypical flashiness, Richard punctuated each word with a blow of steel on steel. At his words the boy rallied, and returned the strokes. "Again," snapped the swordsman, still attacking. There was no kindness in his voice. "We're going to repeat the whole sequence, if you can remember it. Parry all my thrusts this time."

Sometimes the boy caught the quick-darting strokes, and sometimes his eye or his memory failed, and the blade stopped an inch from his heart, death suspended by the swordsman's will.

"New sequence," Richard rapped out. "Learn it."

They repeated the moves. Alec thought the boy was getting better, more assured. Then the swordsman struck hard on the boy's blade, and the sword flew out of his pupil's hand, clanging on the floor, rolled into a corner. "I told you your grip was too tight. Go get it."

The boy retrieved his sword, and the lesson resumed. Alex began to be bored by the endless repetition. "Your arm's getting tired," St. Vier observed. "Don't you practice with weights?"

"Don't have—any weights."

"Get some. No, don't stop. In a real fight, you can't stop."

"A real fight—wouldn't go on this long."

"How do you know? Been in any?"

"Yes. One—*Two.*"

"You won both," Richard said coldly, his arm never resting, his feet never still. "Makes you think you're a hero of the field. *Pay attention.*" He rapped sharply on the blade. "Keep going." The boy countered with a fancy double riposte, changing the line of attack with the lightest pressure of his fingers. Richard St. Vier deflected the other's point, and brought his own clean past the boy's defenses.

The boy cried out at the light kiss of steel. But the swordsman did not stop the movements of the play. "It's a nick," he said. "Never mind the blood."

"Oh. But—"

"You wanted a lesson. Take it. All right, fine, you're scared now. You can't let it make a difference."

But it did make a difference. The boy's defense turned fierce, began to take on the air of desperate attack. Richard let it. They were fighting silently now, and really fighting, although the swordsman kept himself always from doing real damage. He began to play with the boy, leaving tiny openings just long enough to see if he would take advantage of them. The boy took about half—either his eye missed the others, or his body was too slow to act on them. Whatever he did, Richard parried his attacks, and kept him on the defensive.

"Now—" the swordsman said harshly—"Do you want to kill me, or just take me out?"

"I—don't know—"

"For death"—Richard's blade flew in—"straight to the heart. Always the heart."

The boy froze. His death was cold against his burning skin. Richard St. Vier dropped the point, raised it to resume the fight. The boy was sweating, panting, from fear as much as exertion. "A good touch—can be anywhere. As light as you like—or as deep."

The pug-nosed boy stood still. His nose was running. He still held his sword, while blood welled onto his skin and clothing from five different places.

"You're good," Richard St. Vier said, "but you can be better. Now get out of here."

"Richard, he's bleeding," Alec said quietly.

"I know he's bleeding. People do when they fight."

"It's night," Alec said, "in Riverside. People are out. You said you didn't want to kill him."

"Hand me that sheet." Sweat was cooling on Richard's body; he wrapped the linen around himself.

"There's brandy," Alec said. "I'll get it."

"I'm sorry I'm bleeding on your floor," the boy said. He wiped his nose with his sleeve. "I'm crying from shock, that's all. Not really crying."

He did not examine his own wounds. Alec did it for him, dabbing them with brandy. "You're remarkable," he told the boy. "I've been trying to get Richard to lose his temper forever." He handed the flask to St. Vier. "You can drink the rest."

Alec undid what the sword had left of the boy's jacket, and began pulling out the shirt. "It's a girl," he said abruptly, unsuspecting midwife to unnatural birth.

The girl said something rude. She'd stopped crying.

"So are you," Alec retorted. His hand darted into her breast pocket, pulled out the small book that had rested there, its soft leather cover warm and sweaty. He flipped it open, snapped it shut.

"Don't you know how to read?" the girl asked nastily.

"I don't read this kind of trash. *The Swordsman Whose Name Was Not Death.* My sister had it; they all do. It's about some Noble girl who comes home from a ball and finds a swordsman waiting in her room for her. He doesn't kill her; he fucks her instead. She loves it. The End."

"No—" she said, her face flushed—"You've got it wrong. You're stupid. You don't know anything about it."

"Hey," said Alec, "you're cute with your nose running, sweetheart—you know that?"

"You're stupid!" she said again fiercely. "*Stupid bastard.*" Harsh and precise, as though the words were new in her mouth. "What do you know about anything?"

"I know more than you think. I may not have your exceptional skill with steel, but I know about your other tricks. I know what works for you."

"Oh," she flared, "so it's come down to *that.*" Furious, she was starting to cry again, against her will, furious about that, too. "The sword doesn't matter to you; the book doesn't matter—*that's* all you can understand. You don't know anything—anything at all!"

"Oh, don't I?" Alec breathed. His eyes were bright, a spot of color high on each cheek. "You think I don't know all about it? With my sister, it was horses—both real and imaginary." He mastered himself enough to assume his usual sneer, passionless and obnoxious. "Mares in the stable, golden stallions in the orchard. She told me their names. I used to eat the apples she picked for them, to make it seem more real. I know about it," he said bitterly. "My sister's magic horses were powerful; she rode them across sea and land; she loved them and gave them names. But in the end they failed her, didn't they? In the end they took her nowhere, brought her nothing at all."

Richard sat on the edge of the bed, brandy forgotten in his hand. Alec never spoke of his family. Richard didn't know he had a sister. He listened.

"My sister was married—to a man chosen for her, a man she didn't like, a man she was afraid of. Those goddamned horses waited for her in the orchard, waited all night for her to come to them. They would have borne her anywhere, for love of her—but she never came . . . and then it was her wedding day." Alec lifted the book high, slammed it against the far wall. "I know all about it."

The girl was looking at Alec, not at her broken book. "And where were you?" she said. "Where were you when this forced marriage took place—waiting in the orchard with them? Oh, I know, too—You took them and you escaped." Holding herself stiffly against her cuts, she bent over, picked up the book, smoothed it back into shape. "You don't know. You don't know at all. And you don't want to. Either of you."

"Alec," Richard said, "come to bed."

"Thank you for the lesson," she said to the swordsman. "I'll remember."

"It wouldn't have made a difference," he told her. "You'll have to find someone else. That's the way it is. Be careful, though."

"Thank you," she said again. "I will be careful, now that there's something to be careful for. You meant what you said, didn't you?"

"Yes," Richard said. "I don't usually get that angry. I meant it."

"Good." She turned in the doorway, asked in the same flat, cold tone, "What's your sister's name?"

Alec was still where he'd been when he threw the book, standing still and pale. Richard knew that his reaction, when it hit, would be violent.

"I said, what's her name?"

Alec told her.

"Good. I'm going to find her. I'll give her this"—the book, now fingerprinted with dried blood—"and your love."

She stopped again, opened the book, and read: "'I was a girl until tonight. I am a woman now.' That's how it ends. But you never read it, so you'll never know what comes in between." She smiled a steel-biting smile. "I have, and I do. I'll be all right out there, won't I?"

"Come to bed, Alec," Richard said again; "you're shaking."

The Island in the Lake

ཧྲ྄ཋ

Phyllis Eisenstein

The bard Alaric was introduced to us in "Born to Exile," Phyllis Eisenstein's first published story, back in 1971. Since then, he has been the subject of many a tale, most of which have been published in book form as Born to Exile *and* In the Red Lord's Reach. *Here we bring you his latest adventure, a tale of witches and magic and a lake of poison . . .*

Phyllis Eisenstein lives in Chicago with her husband, Alex. She teaches writing at Columbia College Chicago. Her other books include The Book of Elementals, In the Hands of Glory, *and* Shadow of Earth. *This story ran in our December 1998 issue.*

Long ago, in the morning of time, the people lived in a warm and green place, where the sun had cared for them since first they opened their eyes. And life was sweet in that place, in the care of that good and generous sun. But the people were wanderers in their hearts, and at last they turned their backs on that green place, and on that good sun, and set out into the Great Night to find another home.

Their journey was long, for the darkness was vast, and homelands were as tiny and lost in it as flowers on the grassy plain. But the Pole Star had looked upon them in that darkness, and finding them worthy, he claimed them for his own, and guided them safe to this sun and this place. Yet when they came to their new home, it was not a land such as they had known before. No, it was a land strange and beautiful, a land where magic grew in every meadow, and flowed in every river, and breathed in the very wind. And foolishly, they destroyed that magic, and made the land over in the image of their old home, which they had left so far behind in the Great Night. And they were happy in their new home, not understanding what they had done.

But the Pole Star, who loved them in spite of their folly, preserved that magic in a few hidden places, and laid a net of his own power over land and sea, that the magic might be protected and perpetuated, forever living. And the Pole Star gave the knowledge of that magic to those who chose to dwell in his own favored domain, to hold and to use to ease their hardships. For they are wanderers, as the people were once wanderers every one, and the Pole Star has claimed them before all others. And the sign of that gift is the promise of the sun—that no matter how great the night grows, there will always be a dawn.

—Song of the World's Beginning (among the People of the North)

Alaric the minstrel paused at the crest of the hill. To his left and right, a line of hills stretched as far as the eye could see, but before him, to the west, the land sloped downward gently to a broad, flat plain. Upon that plain lay an irregular grid of ocher fields, their grain all reaped, only the yellow stubble of barley, wheat, and oats left to dry in the last warm days of the year. The two dozen dwellings of the peasants who worked those fields were clustered together into a village near the center of that grid; Alaric could just make out their stone walls and thatched roofs, and the stone fences of the animal pens that flanked them. Farther on, much too far from the village to be a comfortable walk for fetching water, was the lake, shining like burnished silver under the autumn sun. The Lake of Death.

The day had been hot, even so late in the year, and Alaric was stripped to the waist, his face shaded by the wide-brimmed hat he had plaited from the sparse wayside grass. Slung over one shoulder was his knapsack, with only a cloak and a shirt and some scraps of bread inside; over the other was his lute, the minstrel's boon companion. The strange and magical north lay far behind him—the great glacial waste, the lodestone mountains, the witchcraft of a woman who read men's souls and of her elixir that healed the dying and could even raise the dead. Lately, he had moved through less exotic lands, through arid hills cloaked in scrub, their infrequent streams shallow and meandering over pebbly beds, their scattered inhabitants scrabbling to draw a living from the parched soil. Yet in those lands he had heard again and again of a bountiful plain beside a mirror-bright lake, a place where a strong lord ruled and enemies had never conquered. A place where the people used water from that lake as their weapon—water that killed what it touched.

The first time he heard the tale, Alaric knew that a minstrel whose stock in trade was legend and wonders would be a fool to pass it by.

He could have reached it earlier in the year. He could have used his witch's power to leap from horizon to horizon, from village to village, tracking the place down in a matter of days. But he had walked instead, as an ordinary man would walk, because this was the south, where the cry of *witch* made folk strike out at what they feared. And he had walked, too, because he was in no great hurry to see what lay beyond the next hill as long as there were listeners for his songs before it. Barely nineteen summers old, he had lost everything in his life, or abandoned it, and now nothing called him to one place over another. Nothing but curiosity.

The track he followed to the hilltop had been broad and rutted, but overgrown, as if little used in recent times. As it descended among the fields, though, it became a real road, cleared of weeds and graded smooth. It led directly to the village and on past, to the lake shore, where it became a stone causeway linking that shore with an island in the very center of the water. The island was a small one, and occupied entirely by a single building, a high-walled fortress with pennons flying from its many turrets—the fortress of the lord of the Lake of Death.

Alaric had not even reached the village when he saw two stocky, middle-aged men and a boy of nine or ten walking toward him. They were dark-haired and sun-browned, dressed in sleeveless gray tunics and breeches, and they strode fearlessly toward the stranger. Before they were near enough to ask his business, he halted, doffed his plaited hat, and bowed low. The lute slid from his shoulder, and he caught it with one curled arm and strummed a chord as he held it against his bare chest.

"Greetings, good sirs!" he called. "Alaric the minstrel, at your service with songs for every mood and every season!"

They halted a few steps away, and the men smiled, but the boy just stared at the lute, wide-eyed, as if it were some unknown animal.

"A long time since a minstrel came this way," said the shorter of the men; he had the guttural accent Alaric had become accustomed to in these western lands. He laid an arm across the boy's shoulders. "Not since before my son was born."

Alaric answered the man's smile with his own. "So much the better for me. Thirsty folk drink deep and are usually kind to the water-bearer."

The man laughed then. "Well, I suppose there will be quite a few thirsty folk, when they discover that water has arrived. I hope your water is sweet, my friend."

"Always," said Alaric.

"We have both kinds of water here," said the boy. " Sweet from the springs and bitter in the lake."

His father laughed again, and the other man joined him. "The child is a little young to understand figures of speech. But he tells the truth. And you should be warned—don't try to drink the bitter water of our lake. It would ruin your voice, and the rest of you, forever."

"I've heard something like that," said Alaric.

"Good," said the man. "I wouldn't want to think that the tale has died in recent years. For it's as true as it ever was. Anyone who touches that water, who so much as dips a hand in it, hardly has time to regret the act."

"And yet they say you toss it at your enemies. Can you avoid touching it yourselves when you do that?"

"We have pumps," said the boy, "and special clothing."

His father shook his shoulder gently, as if to silence him. "We have been here a long time, minstrel," he said. "We know how to live with the water in the Lake of Death."

Alaric glanced at the lake, at the island in its center. "I see that."

The man nodded. "My Lord Gazian lives there. Come now, minstrel. I am the headman of this village, and Taskol is my name. And these are my son Yosat and my brother Adeen. Come to our home and sing for us, and we'll reward you according to your merits."

Alaric grinned. "Then I look forward to a fine reward. But should I not pay my respects to Lord Gazian first of all?" He gestured toward the fortress.

"Oh, he's a busy man. He wouldn't have time to hear a minstrel until much later in the day. You can sing for the village this afternoon and for him this evening." And when Alaric still hesitated, he added, "I think you should prove yourself to lesser folk before being allowed to entertain such a great man, don't you?"

Alaric strummed a chord on his lute, and then another. "Are you perhaps afraid he'll keep me to himself and not let you listen if I go to his castle first?"

Taskol shrugged. "He is a man who likes the best of things. And he deserves them, of course, for he keeps us safe. But as headman, I must look out for my villagers, in my own small way. Surely you understand."

"I don't wish to offend such a great man," said Alaric.

"I will escort you to him myself this evening," said the headman.

Alaric looked at him for a long moment. There had been trouble once or twice in his life over such matters of courtesy. Not so long ago, men-at-arms had been sent to terrorize a peasant family that had kept Alaric from their lord for a single night. But looking at the village headman, at his son and his brother, Alaric saw no uneasiness, no sign of fear of the man who lived in the middle of the Lake of Death. "I would like to rest my legs a little before crossing that causeway," he said at last.

"Indeed you shall," said Taskol. "I wager you've walked a fair distance today."

Alaric nodded.

"And some ale would not go amiss, would it?"

"Indeed it would not."

The headman's hut was the largest of the village, and the only one with a door of wood rather than hard-tanned leather, though the wood was old and weathered. Inside, there was hardly any wood at all. Where settees and chairs might have stood in another household, this one offered stone stools and a stone bench, roughly shaped and thickly cushioned with straw mats. Even the bed in the corner had not the simplest wooden frame to raise it above the hard-packed earthen floor; it was a mere straw pallet, though a thick one, draped with a woolen blanket. Of all the furniture, only the tabletop was made of wood, as weathered as the door, and resting on stone pillars instead of legs. And in the fireplace, dried dung smoldered beneath the big cookpot. There was plenty of straw and stone and dung around the Lake of Death, Alaric realized, but not a single tree.

Taskol's wife brought ale, and when the minstrel had quenched his thirst, he sat outdoors on another straw-cushioned stone bench and entertained the village with songs of the ice-choked Northern Sea and the deer-riding nomads who hunted on its shores. Nearly a hundred listeners crowded the space beside the headman's home, standing, sitting on the stone wall that penned his sheep and cows, squatting on the dusty ground—the whole of the village, Alaric guessed, from the eldest graybeard to the smallest babe in arms. He made them laugh first, with the tale of the herder boy who discovered that his deer could speak and was disbelieved until he revealed some of the embarrassing human secrets that the deer knew; and then he made them gasp at the tale of the nomad who tried to save his people from starvation by hunting the huge and terrible Grandfather of All Bears. Afterward, when the crowd had dispersed with many an appreciative word, Taskol served him fresh bread and new butter and admitted that his skill was great enough for the lord of the Lake of Death.

"But remind him, please, that we of the village like music, too," he said. "So that he does not keep you entirely to himself."

Alaric savored the crusty, still-warm bread. "I will do what I can," he said between bites.

"I suppose I must deliver you to him, then. If you are ready . . ."

"Is there bread like this on the island?" asked the minstrel.

"There is the best of everything on the island," the headman replied.

Alaric downed a last draft of ale to clear the butter from his throat, then drew the dark shirt from his knapsack and slipped it on. "I am ready."

The lake shore was a broad, barren margin marked at the water's very edge with a thick pale crust, like hardened foam. The causeway, made of fine, squared blocks of stone so white it dazzled the eye, began well before this crust and rose smoothly till, where it entered the water, it stood a man-height high above the surface. Broad enough to accommodate two wagons abreast, it ran arrow-straight to the island, broken by two gaps, each spanned by a heavy, iron-banded drawbridge. At the very gate of the fortress was a third bridge, guarded by a spearman in bossed leather armor. Taskol identified Alaric to the man, and the two were admitted.

Inside the gate was a courtyard large enough to hold half the houses in the village.

"This is a strong citadel," Alaric said, looking up at the high, crenelated walls. Only a handful of armed men stood at the crenelations, scanning the world beyond the lake. At any other castle, there would be dozens. "It's given you safety for quite a long time, I would think."

"For my lifetime, and my grandfather's, and more," said Taskol. "No one living remembers the last time we had to lock ourselves inside these walls for a siege. Of course, the lake is our true defender."

"I would hate to fall off that causeway."

Taskol nodded. "So would I."

"Has anyone?"

"Not lately."

Alaric glanced over his shoulder. Beyond the gate, the lake lapped gently at the pure white sides of the raised stone road. "What would happen if someone did?"

"No one could save him. Within a few heartbeats, the flesh would begin to shred from his bones, and then the bones themselves would begin to dissolve. It's an ugly sight."

Alaric shuddered. "You've seen it?"

"When I was a child, we chased a fox off the causeway. It floated, for a short time, while the water worked on it." He shook his head. "Poor hapless fox. Normally, animals stay away from the lake. They know what it holds."

Looking up at the walls again, the minstrel said, "How strange to live surrounded by . . . that." Then he smiled a slow smile. "I'll make a song of it, if I can."

Taskol smiled back. "I think that would not displease my lord." He pointed to the doorway of the keep, at the far end of the courtyard. "I imagine he awaits his dinner just now. If I introduce you, he might invite me to stay for the meal."

"By all means, then, introduce me."

The great hall of the keep was not so large as some Alaric had visited, but it was one of the most luxurious, at least at first glance. High, narrow windows admitted the afternoon sunlight, showing the walls hung with tapestries, the stone floor scattered with carpets and furniture of velvet and fine-carved wood. Only on closer inspection, as he walked the length of the chamber, did he see that the carpets were worn almost to their backings in many places, the tapestries were moth-eaten, the velvets thin-napped and shiny, and the fine woods dry and cracked. The riches of the citadel were of an earlier generation, and had not been renewed. He realized that more than a few seasons must have passed since that overgrown road had known much traffic.

Yet there was newer wealth here, even so. The trestle table at the far end of the room, ancient as it appeared, was heavy laden with fresh bread, meats, and vegetables, with butter, cheese, and ale. And the two men who sat behind it were dressed well enough, in supple leather, light wool, and golden chains. They looked like brothers, both dark and strong-jawed, though one was much older than the other.

Taskol bent the knee before them, and Alaric imitated him.

"My lord," said Taskol, "I beg to present Alaric the minstrel, lately come into our land to offer his songs for our pleasure."

The older of the two men pushed his chair back and rose to his feet. "It has been long and long since a minstrel came to this land. You are welcome, sir." But he said the words gravely, without any smile. He was a tall man, and broad with muscle, though his hair was touched with gray and there were deep lines carved about his mouth and across his forehead, and dark pouches beneath his eyes. "As you see, we are dining. Join us, minstrel, and afterward show us your wares. We would welcome something new." He sat down again. Then he added,

"Stay, too, Taskol. You threshed the grain that made this bread."

Taskol bowed. "I thank you, my lord."

He and the minstrel took places on a bench at one end of the table, and they ate well of the viands spread before them. From time to time, other leather-clad men entered the hall, made their obeisances, and sat to the meal, but none of them stayed long, and none of them wore gold. Alaric recognized one as the guard of the gate.

Two young serving women cleared the table and set out more ale to signal the end of dinner. They eyed Alaric curiously but said nothing, only hurried off when they were done, to a door that stood at a corner of the hall, between two tapestries. They did not close themselves away behind it, though, but stayed in the open doorway, looking at him, and other men and women crowded there with them, half a dozen or more. The castle servants, Alaric thought, waiting for whatever novelty the stranger was about to provide.

Lord Gazian waved at him to proceed. Pushing his bench away from the table, Alaric settled the lute on his lap. There was a song he had been working on for quite some time, and he thought it was ready for singing now—a tale of darkness for half the year and light for the rest, of blossoms growing from the very ice at the pole of the world and spawned by seeds fallen from above the sky, from whose leaves a curing elixir could be made. In the song, a young man fought storms and monsters and the Northern Sea itself to reach those blossoms, for his beloved lay ill, and not even the wisest healer knew another way to keep her from death. When he had won through and saved her, and they had celebrated their wedding in the final verse, the listeners at the doorway clapped their hands and chattered among themselves until their lord cast a single dark glance in their direction.

"A well-sung song," he said, "but I like not the subject matter. Sing of something real, minstrel."

Alaric almost said that the elixir was real enough, though the monsters were inventions, but he caught himself and bowed his head. He had no proof, just his word, and he had learned over the years that it was rarely healthy to contradict a nobleman, even with proof. He sang another song, a comic one of squabbling neighbors and stolen sheep, and of a man who was fooled into counting his sheep three times and reckoning a different number at each. Before he was done, the folk at the doorway were laughing, and even Lord Gazian himself had smiled a little.

"You have much skill," he said. "And your songs are . . . interesting. You could make your fortune in some large and powerful household, but instead you've come here to these remote and sparsely peopled lands." He sat forward, leaning his elbows on the table, the cup of ale between his hands. "What brings you to us, minstrel?"

Alaric bowed again. "Nothing, my lord, but a boundless desire to see the world and add to my stock of songs. Those songs are my fortune, and an easier one to carry than any gold."

The younger man spoke for the first time. "You are brave to come here, sir minstrel. Unless Taskol has not told you of the lake . . ." He looked narrowly at the headman.

"I had already heard, in far-distant places, and he told me as well," said the minstrel. "But I think I am less brave than the folk who live here. I would not wish to try this lake during a storm, when the deadly waves splash high."

"These stout walls protect us," said Lord Gazian. "And we take care. It has been many a year since one of our own was claimed by the lake."

"Still, I see high courage in living here. You and your people have all my admiration."

"Enough admiration," said the younger man. "Sing another song."

Gazian looked at his companion for a moment, and Alaric saw a flicker of anger pass between them before the lord of the castle turned back and said, "Go ahead, another song."

Another song led to another, and at last the sunlight in the high windows reddened and faded, and tripod oil lamps were lit to take its place. Finally, Alaric pleaded weariness after a long day of walking and said that he would sing again the next day, if desired.

Lord Gazian nodded and rose abruptly from his place at the table. "You have our thanks, minstrel, for this afternoon's entertainment. My brother will see that you are made comfortable for the night." He nodded to the younger man and, without waiting for any acknowledgement, crossed the room to a tapestry-fringed archway in the farther wall. Stairs were visible beyond the arch, and in a moment, he had climbed out of sight.

The younger man rose, when his brother had gone, and he came around the table to stand above the minstrel. "You sing well, young minstrel. What was your name?"

"Alaric, my lord."

The man's mouth tightened for a moment. "I am not known as *lord*," he said. Then he made a peremptory gesture toward the doorway that was still crowded with servants, and the two young women came scurrying. "Make him a pallet in the kitchen," he said, and turned away. With a swift stride, he went out to the courtyard.

Alaric glanced at Taskol. "Have I insulted him?" he asked.

Taskol shrugged. "Master Demirchi is the heir. But while his brother lives, there is only one lord here—we haven't room for more in our little land. I'm sorry, minstrel; I should have thought to warn you. We call him *sir*."

"I will do that, then, and hope he forgives a stranger. Though I've never before met a man who didn't like being addressed above his station. What would he have done if I had called him *majesty*?"

Taskol laughed and shook his head and led the way to the kitchen, while the serving women trailed behind.

The kitchen was a small room, dominated by a great fireplace and crowded with worn trestle tables and deeply grooved butchers' blocks, with cauldrons and platters and roasting spits. It was also a warm room, but now that darkness had fallen and cool night air had begun to slide through the high windows of the keep, that warmth was pleasant enough. The kitchen servants made Alaric a pallet near the embers of the hearthfire, and they left a few choice tidbits from dinner on a table nearby, in case he woke hungry in the middle of the night. Taskol packed a few of those tidbits into a sack, to take home to his family, before he bade Alaric good night. Then he and the servants put out the lamps and left the minstrel to sleep his first sleep surrounded by the Lake of Death.

Alaric lay on his back for a time, staring up at the kitchen's single window, far above his reach. He could see a few stars there, for the red glow of the embers was not enough to drown them out. The window was much too high, he told himself, to be touched by the waves, even in the wildest storm. And there was no storm tonight, just a gentle autumn breeze. Still, he thought that if this were *his* castle, he would shutter the windows, just to be sure. Finally, he got up and took his pallet out to the empty hall and set it where there was a wall between himself and that kitchen window, and all the other windows were far away. One lamp still lit the room, leaving heavy shadows in all the corners, but Alaric had no fear of shadows. He fell asleep, an arm crooked protectively about his lute, both of them wrapped against the gentle autumn breeze in his well-worn cloak.

When he woke to a touch on his shoulder, the lamp no longer burned, and dawn twilight showed through the windows. He knuckled sleep from his eyes and blinked up at the man who leaned over him. It was Lord Gazian, wearing a dressing gown of fine, pale wool that gave his body a ghostly cast in the dimness.

"My lord?" said Alaric.

"Will you come upstairs, minstrel? There is someone who would hear you sing."

Odd though the time was, Alaric rose, knowing that no good could come of reluctance. Carrying his lute close against his body, he followed the master of the lake through the arch and up the narrow, winding stairway beyond. At the third landing, they turned off the stair and walked along a curving corridor that was marked every ten paces by a narrow window. Through each window, Alaric could see the lake below, the water reflecting the soft, gray-pink color of the eastern sky. They had passed four windows, making nearly a half-circle, before Lord Gazian halted at a door on the inner wall. He eased it open.

The room was small, though richly hung with tapestries, and crowded by a bed, a chair, and some low chests. A bedside table held a small oil lamp, a tray of tiny pastries, and a cup. And the bed itself, wide enough for three men, held a boy of no more than seven summers, propped up on bolsters and covered with a light blanket. Even in the candlelight, Alaric could see that the boy was ill—his face was pale, with a sheen of moisture, and his dark eyes were sunk deep above his hollow cheeks. He said nothing when the lord of the castle and Alaric entered, though his gaze followed them to the side of his bed.

Lord Gazian sat down on the edge of the mattress and gently stroked the damp dark hair away from the child's forehead. "I've brought the minstrel for you." He nodded at Alaric.

"Thank you, Father," said the boy in a small, soft voice. He looked at Alaric. "I'm sorry to get you up so early. It is early, isn't it?"

"A little," said Alaric. "But I don't mind."

"Sometimes he doesn't sleep well," said his father, resting one large hand on the boy's shoulder. "And last night the servants told him about you, and he hardly slept at all for asking when you would come upstairs."

"My nurse sings to me," said the boy. "But they told me you sing much better."

"I am flattered," said the minstrel. "Do you like songs about magic?"

"Oh, yes."

"About knights and dragons and fair maidens?"

The boy's eyes widened. "Is that what you sing about?"

"Sometimes. For special listeners."

"Please," breathed the boy.

"Very well." Alaric sat down on the foot of the bed and balanced his lute on his knee. "This is the tale of a boy who grew up to fight dragons." And he launched into an old favorite in more familiar lands—the song of the youth who found an enchanted sword in a hollow tree, a sword that itself became his teacher. By the time he finished, with the young man slaying his monster and winning the hand of a king's daughter, and the kingdom as well, the boy's mouth hung open in wonder, and there was a bit of color in his cheeks.

"Oh, another, please, minstrel," he begged.

Alaric looked at Lord Gazian, who nodded.

In the end, he sang of magical adventures until the boy's nurse came with his morning meal.

"You mustn't stop in the middle!" the boy cried. The color in his cheeks was hectic now, and his eyes were very bright.

"The child must eat," said the nurse, as she set the tray on the bed. She was a stout woman, old enough to be Alaric's grandmother, and the expression on her face was stern. She pointed to the tray of pastries, all untouched. "He's eaten nothing since yesterday noon, not even one dainty, and you have excited him on an empty stomach, as well as keeping him from sleep."

"I didn't want to sleep," said the boy.

She propped him up farther on his bolsters. "You must sleep. And you must eat. How can you ever get well if you don't sleep and eat, I ask?" She lifted a cover from a bowl of porridge and dipped up a spoonful for him.

He turned his head away from it.

"Eat a little, my son," said his father. He glanced at Alaric. "I'm sure the minstrel would say the same."

"Indeed," said Alaric. "I'll be eating this very porridge downstairs shortly, and it smells excellent."

The boy frowned, but then he nibbled at the edge of the spoon and finally swallowed the whole amount.

"A little more," said the nurse, with another spoonful.

The boy looked up at Alaric. "What is your name, minstrel?"

"Alaric."

"Mine is Ospir."

Alaric bowed. "Greetings, Ospir."

"Will you come back later?"

"If your father wishes it. The decision lies with him."

"Father?"

Lord Gazian caught the boy's small hand for a moment. "If you will promise to eat your porridge, and to try to sleep, I'll bring the minstrel back later."

The boy sighed. "Very well, Father."

"Good child," said the lord of the castle, and he stood up. "Till later." And he gestured Alaric toward the door.

They were halfway down the stairs before Alaric asked, "My lord, what ails the boy?"

Lord Gazian kept walking. "No one knows, minstrel. He has been sickly for most of his life. He is a good boy, though, and a patient one." When they reached the foot of the steps, with the archway to the great hall before them, he stopped and turned back to Alaric. "Thank you, minstrel, for being kind to him."

"My lord, I am here to serve you. It would be poor service indeed to be unkind to your son."

The lord of the castle nodded and stepped through the arch.

They broke their fast with more than porridge—with eggs and bread spread thick with butter, with slices of fat mutton and grilled fowl, and with a drink made of soured milk that Alaric found not as attractive as plain, clear water. But water there was in plenty—from a spring, servants explained, that rose from deep within the island and never failed.

"How strange," Alaric said, "that pure water should flow in the midst of the Lake of Death."

"This land is full of such springs," said Master Demirchi. "There would be no fields without them." Unlike his liege and brother, he was fully dressed for the day, in leather and soft, thin wool. "And without the fields, we would all be elsewhere." He picked at his plate of mutton and eggs. "But I think a few people would come here anyway, just to carry off some of our deadly waters for a weapon. We are especially rich in that weapon, are we not, my brother?"

Lord Gazian cast him a sour glance. "Don't ask again," he said.

Demirchi nodded toward Alaric. "The minstrel has traveled the world. Speak to him about it."

"I don't wish to speak about it. I've made my decision."

Demirchi peered with slitted eyes at Alaric. "How much gold do you think an outsider would pay for a few sealed containers of water from the Lake of Death?"

Alaric looked from one man to the other. "I don't know, sir. Perhaps it is too dangerous to transport elsewhere."

"Nonsense," said Demirchi. "We know how to deal with it."

"We have no need of outsiders' gold," said Lord Gazian.

With two fingers, Demirchi lifted the gold chain that hung at his throat. "This may be enough for you, but it won't buy new carpets for this room, or furniture, or weapons. I want a new sword; must I trade my only chain for it when a cask of water would suffice?"

Gazian set the flats of both hands on the table. "I will not sell death, and that's an end to it. When you rule here, *if* you rule, you may decide otherwise. Till then, we will leave off speaking of it."

"My brother, you are not thinking to our advantage."

Gazian looked at him for a long moment, and then he said, “I know you have many responsibilities to attend to today. I would not keep you from them.”

Demirchi made a disgusted noise and then stood up and strode from the room.

The lord of the castle and the visiting minstrel were both quiet for a time, eating. Shortly after Demirchi left, a couple of other men came in and sat down to partake of the meal, and seeing the frown that lingered on their lord’s face, they said little and excused themselves quickly. Alone with Gazian again, Alaric was unsure of what to do. At last, he said, “Shall I sing for you, my lord?”

Gazian looked up from the remnants of his meal. There was tiredness in his eyes, in the slope of his shoulders. “You must be weary, minstrel, from waking so early. There is an empty chamber upstairs, just beyond my son’s room. Perhaps you would like to take your pallet up there and sleep a bit more. Tell one of the servants I said to help you with it. You can sing again later.”

“You are kind, my lord.”

He shook his head. “I think not, but I thank you for being so willing this morning. Go on. Rest.”

“As you will,” said Alaric.

Rather than disturb the servants, who all seemed busy enough, Alaric took the pallet upstairs himself. Half a dozen steps past young Ospir’s door was another; he pushed it open.

At first he thought he must be in the wrong chamber, for this one was not at all empty. Illuminated by a single narrow window, it was fully three times the size of the boy’s bedchamber, and richly furnished. The floor was almost entirely covered by a single large carpet, and the walls were hung partly with tapestries and partly with thick velvet curtains. A velvet settee stood in the center of the carpet, with a pair of finely carved tables flanking it and a needlework footstool before it. On one wall was a fireplace of white stone, and against the other was a wide bed made up with fine pillows and quilts.

Alaric backed out the door, to see if he had missed the room he was supposed to find. But this one was indeed beside the boy's, and the corridor ended in a blank wall after it.

Inside again, he laid his pallet on the floor beside the settee and made a circuit of the room. The fireplace contained no trace of wood or dung or ash, just a naked grate. The carpet, the tapestries, the settee and tables were worn much as the furnishings of the great hall were worn, but all were covered with a thin layer of dust. The bed was dusty, too, and stale-smelling, as if the bedclothes had not been aired in a long time.

There was a chest at the foot of the bed, half covered by the quilt, with no lock to keep a curious minstrel out. Alaric turned the quilt back and lifted the wooden lid. Immediately, the sweet scents of cedar and lavender wafted up at him, the one lining the chest, the other sprinkled over the contents as dried blossoms. A woman's clothing was packed inside—linen and lace and embroidery, all heavily creased from lying long undisturbed. Alaric closed the lid again, and draped the quilt back over it. Whoever's clothes they were, he thought, she had not worn them in quite some time.

He moved his pallet nearer the window and looked out for a moment. It was a beautiful view, if one ignored its deadliness—the lake shining like polished metal, the fields spread out in a golden array, the sky clear and cloudless above the line of hills on the horizon. He imagined her, whoever she was, sitting on the windowsill and gazing out, perhaps with embroidery in her hands. And then he realized he was thinking of other castles, other hands, other embroidery left far behind, and he turned his mind away from them. No one had sat on this windowsill lately, for it was as dusty as everything else in the room. He lay down on the pallet and closed his eyes. He was tired, as Lord Gazian had known, and he fell asleep quickly.

A rough hand on his arm brought him out of jumbled dreams of the past. For a moment he thought Lord Gazian must be shaking him, and then he looked up and recognized Ospir's nurse.

"What are you doing here, minstrel?" she demanded.

Yawning, he stretched his arms out above his head. "Lord Gazian told me to sleep here."

"Did he?" She loomed over him, hands on her hips, suspicion on her face and in her voice. Then, less sharply, she said, "Well, I suppose if you had come here without permission, you would have closed the door. But to send you to *her* room." She clucked her tongue.

"Whose room is it?" asked Alaric.

"His lady's, of course. What other room would be so near the boy's?"

"Yours."

"Not a room like this," she said indignantly. "Mine is on the other side, and befitting my station. This is a finer chamber than even Lord Gazian's own."

"But Lord Gazian's lady doesn't live in this chamber," said Alaric.

The corners of the nurse's mouth turned down. "She died giving my lord an heir." And she nodded toward the wall behind which Ospir lay.

"And Lord Gazian never took another wife?"

She shook her head. "None could compare to *her*. He loved her, minstrel." She laid a hand on the back of the settee and stroked the worn velvet. "Many was the time they sat here together, and I brought them dinner, just the two of them here in this room. It seems so long ago. I air the room sometimes, just for the memory of her. Poor lady."

Alaric sighed, thinking how often love led to unhappiness in the real world. Far more often than in song. "A sad tale," he said.

She looked at him sharply. "One you could put to music, I suppose, just one tale among many. I heard about your tales from the other servants. Fancies and lies, most of them, it seems."

"Some. Others have a bit of truth to them."

"A small bit, I'd think. But the boy likes them—I'll say that for you."

"That pleases me," said the minstrel. He glanced out the window, saw that the sun was high; he had slept most of the morning away. "Is he awake now?"

She had already turned toward the door, but she paused at his question. "Yes. Why do you ask?"

"I thought I would visit him before going downstairs, if he were awake."

"His uncle is with him."

"Master Demirchi?"

"He has only the one uncle."

Alaric pushed his covering cloak aside and got to his feet. "I was told yesterday that Demirchi was the heir. But you just said it was the boy. Surely this land isn't large enough for two."

The nurse lowered her voice. "No one expects the boy to live out the winter. He has never been well, not since his babyhood, and two years ago my lord decided that another heir must be named."

"Poor child," murmured Alaric.

"He is a good boy," said the nurse.

"Will Master Demirchi stay long with him now?"

"He never stays very long."

"Then I will wait."

His lute under one arm, he followed the nurse to the door of Ospir's room and stood outside as the woman slipped in. He caught a glimpse of Demirchi sitting on the bed, holding the boy's hand, and then the nurse closed the door again. Shortly, Demirchi came out.

"He is eager for your songs, minstrel," he said, "but I beg you not to tire him. He has little strength these days."

Alaric bowed. "It must be hard to lie in bed for so much time, sir. I only desire to make it a bit easier for him."

Demirchi nodded. "We will see you later in the great hall?"

"Of course, sir. I am here to sing for all who will listen."

"At dinner, then." He walked off down the corridor.

Inside the room, Ospir greeted Alaric in his small, soft voice. "Thank you for coming back so soon."

"I had some porridge and took a nap, which I hope you did as well, and now I am ready for a little more music."

"He ate and slept," said the nurse. "He has been a good child this morning."

"And my uncle came to visit," said Ospir. "I wish he had stayed longer. He always makes me laugh. But you are here, and that makes up for his going."

Alaric sat down on the edge of the bed. "Well, I will try to make you laugh, too, if your nurse does not mind."

The woman waved a hand, as if in permission, and Alaric began a long, complicated song about a wolf who tried to trick eight sheep into leaving their fold to run away with him. By the time he was done, the boy was laughing, and the nurse was as well. But in the midst of his laughter, Ospir began to cough, a deep, hollow cough; and when he could not stop, his nurse had to help him sit up, and she rubbed his thin chest until at last the spasms passed. By that time he was half-fainting, and as he fell back on the pillow, a trickle of blood started from a corner of his mouth. The nurse swabbed his sweaty forehead and wiped the blood away with a damp cloth.

"I think you should go now, minstrel."

"No," gasped the boy, his voice smaller than ever. "Please." He closed his eyes, and he was so pale, and his breathing became so shallow, that Alaric thought he must be dying that very moment.

"Shouldn't we call his father?" he asked the nurse.

Then Ospir's eyes opened, and the look in them was beseeching. "I'll be all right," he whispered. "Please sing."

The nurse nodded to Alaric. "Something more serious."

And so Alaric returned to songs of knights and fair maidens, of sorcerers and monsters, and of lands beyond the horizon. He sang softly, though, and after a time he left a song unfinished, because he knew the boy slept.

The nurse walked with him into the corridor and closed the door gently between them and the child.

"I'm sorry," said Alaric. "I didn't know."

The nurse shook her head. "He has had congestion of the lungs before, but never so bad. They die sometimes, after the blood comes. And he is very weak, poor child." She looked down at her hands, which were clenched in the voluminous fabric of her skirt. "I shall call his father now."

Alaric trailed after her to the great hall, where Lord Gazian sat talking with two men in bossed armor. When informed of his son's condition, he directed the two to find his brother, and then he went upstairs. Master Demirchi came in from the courtyard a short time later and went up, too. Neither man asked Alaric to come along.

He went to the kitchen for a time, and listened to the talk among the servants. None was surprised that the child was so gravely ill; they had been expecting his death for two years already. They speculated on how long the mourning period would be, and then they asked Alaric to sing, because there might not be much singing allowed when the household was in mourning. Finally, Alaric went upstairs, though unbidden, to see what he could see.

The door to the boy's chamber stood ajar, and inside both Gazian and Demirchi sat on the bed, on opposite sides, and the nurse hovered near. That left little space for another visitor, so he did not attempt to enter. He could see, though, that the boy was awake, with one hand held by his father and the other by his uncle. None of them seemed to notice Alaric standing in the corridor.

Silently, he slipped on down the passageway to Ospir's mother's chamber. Entering, he shut the door quietly but firmly, and then he bolted it. He laid his lute on the settee.

The strange and magical north lay far behind him, and in it the elixir so powerful that it brought the dead back to life. He had never intended to return there, never intended to revisit Kata the witch, who brewed that elixir, but now he knew that he must.

A heartbeat later, he stood on a mountainside above the northern valley that was now her home. The air about him was suddenly crisp with the northern autumn, and he shivered a little as he scanned the valley floor. He looked past the harvested fields and the peasant dwellings, past the great fortress that guarded all and the people who walked its battlements and strolled in and out through its gate. He looked, finally, to the shore of the river that had created the valley, and there he saw the tent, figured all over with the symbol of the sacred Pole Star, that belonged to Kata. A moment later, he was thrusting aside its entrance flap and stepping into her firelit domain.

She sat cross-legged by the fire, a grinding stone upon her lap, a pestle in her hand, the bags and bundles that held her possessions piled all around her. Her thick, dark braids brushed her knees as she bent over her work, the smooth muscles of her slender arms flexed beneath their load of leather bracelets. When she looked up, and her eyes met his, there was not the slightest trace of surprise in her face.

"Greetings, my Alaric," she said in the soft, lilting accent of the north. "You return to us."

He shook his head. "No. I only come to ask a favor."

She smiled a little. "If you wish a favor, you must give one in return."

He sat down beside her. "This is not for myself. It is for a child."

One of her eyebrows rose. "Whose child?"

"Not mine. The child of my host, far to the south. He is sick, perhaps near death, and I would help him."

"Ah, soft-hearted Alaric. Has your softness not found you enough trouble in your life? Had you stayed in the north, you would have become hard, as we are hard."

"I am what I am, lady. Will you give me the elixir?"

She brushed fine dark powder from her stone into a square of muslin, twisted the cloth into a sack, and tied its mouth with a strip of sinew. "These are the leaves you helped us bring back from the Great Waste. Shall I withhold from you your share of what I make of them? It would be ungrateful of me."

"You are fair, lady. You have always been fair to me."

"How old is the child?"

"Seven, I believe, and small for his age."

She dipped into a bag and pulled out a ceramic flask the size of her fist and sealed with wax. She also found a spoon made of horn. "Give him two spoonfuls diluted in a cup of wine each day till the elixir is gone. If it can help him at all, that will be enough."

Alaric took the flask and the spoon. "Thank you, lady. Now, what favor can I offer you in return?"

She caught his wrist. "Only one, my Alaric."

He shook his head. "I can't stay."

"You will never find what you seek."

"I have given up seeking, lady."

She looked long into his eyes. "No," she said at last. "Don't fool yourself, minstrel. You will never give up. Songs and travel will never be enough for you. One day, I think, you will go back to your past, you will not be able to resist it any longer. I hope it does not disappoint you too badly."

"I have nothing to go back to," said Alaric, and the words were thick in his throat.

"Those are only words, my minstrel." She let go of his wrist. "Is there a woman in this place you've come from? The mother of the child, perhaps?"

"No. No woman."

She smiled again and stroked his cheek with one finger. "I find that hard to believe, pretty boy."

He smiled back. “I’ve only been there two days.”

“Then there is still plenty of time. Tell me about this place,” she said. “Tell me about all your wanderings since you left us.”

He looked down at the flask and the spoon. “Lady, I cannot. The child might die while I entertained you. You must understand . . .”

She nodded slowly. “I do understand. And you must also understand that you will always be welcome among us. Always.”

“Farewell,” he whispered.

An instant later he was back in the chamber next to Ospir’s.

Lord Gazian, Demirchi, and the nurse were still in the tiny bedroom, and Ospir was still breathing, though laboriously, when Alaric slipped in. Demirchi was the first to look up at him. “Not now, minstrel,” he murmured.

“I have an elixir which I picked up in my travels,” Alaric said, showing the flask. “It has proven itself in the past in any number of grave illnesses, and I believe that it might help the boy.”

Demirchi glanced at the flask. “Are you a healer as well as a minstrel, Master Alaric?”

“I’ve used it myself more than once. I know its power.”

Demirchi shook his head sharply. “We want no unknown elixirs for the boy.”

Lord Gazian looked up then. “You’ve taken it?” he said.

“Yes, my lord,” said Alaric.

“Had you a fever?”

“A high one, my lord.”

“And so has my son. Bring your elixir here.”

Alaric squeezed by Demirchi and the nurse to stand beside the lord of the castle.

“Give it to me,” said Gazian.

Alaric handed over the flask. “Two spoonfuls should be given each day in a cup of wine,” he said. He held the horn spoon up. “This is the measure.”

Gazian perforated the wax seal with his sheath knife and sniffed of the elixir. "It has a pungent smell," he said. "Harsh. Like cloves. Is it bitter?"

"Not in wine, my lord," said Alaric.

"Fetch some wine," Gazian said to Demirchi.

"Brother, what do we know of this stuff?" said Demirchi. "It might be poisonous."

"I will taste it if you wish," said Alaric.

"The wine, brother," said Gazian.

"Let me get it, my lord," the nurse said suddenly, and before anyone could object, she hurried from the room.

In a voice barely audible, Ospir murmured, "I will take it, Father."

"Good boy," said Gazian, caressing his son's cheek.

The nurse returned shortly with a carafe and a cup. Alaric measured the elixir and mixed it with the wine, and then he spooned out a mouthful and swallowed it in full sight of the others.

"What proof is this?" said Demirchi. "One spoonful of dilute poison might be harmless to a grown man, and a cup of it deadly to a weakened child."

Lord Gazian looked at his son. "We have nothing better to try," he said. "Come, my child, drink." And he held the cup to Ospir's lips.

It took some time to finish the cup, for the wine was strong for such a young child, and the elixir, Alaric knew, made it taste odd, but at last he drank it all. Then he closed his eyes and whispered, "May the minstrel sing for me?"

Gazian nodded to Alaric.

The minstrel chose a lullaby of many soft, sweet verses, and by the time he was finished, Ospir was sleeping.

Lord Gazian gestured for all but the nurse to leave, and out in the corridor, he said, "If your elixir helps him, you will be well-rewarded, minstrel."

"If it helps him, that will be reward enough, my lord," said Alaric.

Gazian took his arm. "Come down to the hall and sing for us now. I have need of diversion."

The remainder of the afternoon was a restless one. For a time, Alaric sang, and the lord of the castle and his brother listened. And for a time, other men joined them and the group played at a game with colored stones on an octagonal board. Master Demirchi got up often and went to the foot of the stairway, but Gazian always called him back, saying that word would be sent if there were anything to know. The household dined, though Lord Gazian ate little, and then Alaric sang again. Night fell, and at last the master of the Lake of Death dispatched a servant to his son's room, but the servant could only report that the boy was sleeping still.

Lord Gazian looked at his brother. "Perhaps you should see to the mourning ceremonies, in case they become necessary." He rose heavily from his chair. "I will be on the postern balcony, not to be disturbed . . . unless there is some word from above."

Demirchi inclined his head. "As you wish."

"Come, minstrel. I would listen to more music, if you can."

"I can, my lord."

Alaric followed him up the stairs, to the second landing this time, through a doorway, and down a broad, shallow flight of steps. At the bottom was a door heavier than any he had seen elsewhere in the castle, oak almost solid with iron banding, and fastened shut by two great horizontal beams. Gazian unbarred it with one hand, the beams swinging easily on well-oiled pivots, and pulled it open. Beyond lay a balcony open to the night sky.

There were no lamps on the balcony, but the moon rode low on the horizon, casting its silver gleam upon a space three paces deep and a dozen wide, with a hip-high wall guarding its rim. Lord Gazian went to that wall and leaned upon it with both forearms, and when Alaric joined him there, he saw that the surface of the water lay only a couple of man-heights below. The waves were calm beneath the moon, but a pale mist was rising from them, swirling in the gentle breeze. Alaric stepped back from the wall.

"No need to be afraid, minstrel," said Lord Gazian. "The waves never come this high."

"The mist," said Alaric.

Gazian shook his head. "Harmless." He looked out over the water. "Though they say the ghosts of everyone who ever died in this land are in that mist. They say the lake holds them prisoner, and they wander over its surface every night, trying to escape. I've seen them myself, whatever they are—vague figures in the distance, writhing. Sometimes I've even heard them moan. Or perhaps it was just the wind."

Alaric looked where he was looking and saw only mist, thicker here and thinner there.

"I wonder, sometimes," Gazian said, "if my lady wife is among them. And I wonder if she will be happy if our son joins her."

Alaric said nothing.

Gazian glanced at him over one shoulder. "He sleeps long. Is it the sleep that comes before death?"

"The elixir always brings sleep," said Alaric.

"It may be too late for your elixir, minstrel."

"I hope not."

He sighed. "I have not much hope left in me. Once, I had hoped to see him grow up strong to care for my people after me. I can no longer remember when anyone still thought that was possible." His head sank down between his arms. "Sing, Master Alaric. Sing of hope."

And Alaric sang, as the moon glimmered on the deadly waters and the mist writhed and twisted above them. He sang of quests successful and of love affirmed. And as the moon rose ever higher, he thought, once or twice, that he too could see vague figures in the mist, as if his music had raised them. Later, Lord Gazian dismissed him, with permission to use his lady's old bedchamber once more.

In the morning, before breaking fast, Alaric tapped at Ospir's door to make sure the nurse administered another dose of elixir. She woke the boy to do so, but he went to sleep almost immediately afterward. For the brief moments his eyes were open, he did not seem to recognize either her or the minstrel.

In the great hall, all the day was as restless as the previous afternoon had been. Halfway through, Lord Gazian sent his brother out on some errand to keep him from going to the stairway so often. He himself saw to all the myriad details of life in the castle, but offhandedly. He spurned the game of colored stones and dismissed the men who would play it with him. And he hardly listened when Alaric sang, pacing instead, back and forth across the hall, even going out to the courtyard and up onto the battlements. He stayed on the battlements for quite some time, looking out toward the village of his peasants. He was there when a servant came running through the great hall with word that Ospir was awake, hungry and thirsty, and asking for the minstrel.

Gazian raced up the stairway. Alaric and a servant with a tray of broth and bread followed at a more demure pace.

They found the boy sitting up, supported by his bolsters, his nurse's arm, and his father's strong hands. The nurse gestured peremptorily for the tray and, choosing the cup of broth, held it to the boy's lips. He drank greedily.

"Not so fast, my darling," she said. "Small sips at first." She moved the cup away from his mouth.

"But I am so thirsty," he said.

"Drink again in a moment."

He saw Alaric standing in the doorway. "Sing for me, please minstrel. I dreamed you sang for me."

"As you wish, young master," Alaric replied. And as the boy drank more broth and even ate a little bread, Alaric sang of knights and fair maidens and fire-breathing monsters.

Over the next few days, as he continued to drink the elixir, the boy improved dramatically. His fever vanished, his paleness was replaced by healthy color, his eyes brightened, his cheeks lost their sunken look. By the time the flask was empty, he could even stand up, though his legs were weak and shaky after so much time in bed. But his small, soft voice was stronger, and his laugh was clear and unmarred by any coughing. Three days later, he insisted upon going downstairs to the great hall, so that he could dine with his father and uncle; he even walked part of the way.

Seeing him sitting so straight upon his cushioned bench, the servants and the men in bossed leather made much of him, and he answered them like a little lord, graciously, his face glowing with the attention. But his nurse would not let him stay long, for fear of overtiring him, and as soon as the meal was done, his father carried him back upstairs, laughing with him, laughing loud and long. That night, Alaric sang him to sleep, as had become his habit.

"How can I reward you, minstrel?" Lord Gazian asked for the dozenth time as he and his brother and Alaric sat by lamplight in the great hall.

Alaric just shook his head and strummed his lute. He had already politely refused Gazian's own gold chain as being a gift that would only be stolen from him somewhere along the road. He understood how rare such wealth was near the Lake of Death and he, who could steal all the gold he wished, did not want to carry off any of their poor treasures. "I have everything I want—good food, a soft place to sleep, music, and listeners who like what I offer."

"But you wander the world, never knowing where your next meal will come from, never knowing even whether you will sleep with a roof over your head."

"Minstrels are born wanderers, my lord. We don't mind sleeping in the open or hunting game for our suppers."

"A homeless life. Not one most men would choose."

Alaric shrugged. "In truth, I have a thousand homes, for wherever folk are good hosts, there I feel welcome. As here."

"Do you indeed feel welcome here, Master Alaric?"

"I do."

Lord Gazian leaned forward. "Then stay with us. Make your life here. The boy would like that, I know, and I would as well."

"This is a kind offer, my lord."

"And there would be no need to sing every night, only when you wished it. You would be as a member of my own family, like a second younger brother."

Alaric glanced at Demirchi, who was lounging back in his chair, playing with his gold chain. "That is too high for me," said the minstrel. "You have a brother already."

"Call it what you will," said Gazian. "This is my desire."

Alaric drew another chord from the lute. "You overwhelm me, my lord."

"Will you do it?"

"I must think. This is a great decision. I have a certain sort of life, and giving it up would be hard."

"This is a wealthy land," said Gazian, "and a safe one, as you know."

"Wealthy?" muttered Demirchi. He looked at Alaric from beneath lowered eyelids. "Surely our young minstrel has seen wealthier. He's traveled the world and seen castles full of gold, haven't you, lad?"

"Occasionally," said Alaric.

"Our wealth is our grain and livestock," said Gazian. "That is the only wealth that matters. The rest is mere display."

"And will you still be saying that when we are all sitting on the floor because our chairs are broken?" asked Demirchi.

"You exaggerate, my brother."

Demirchi snorted. "The peasants already sit on stone. And you won't even sell a little of our surplus grain to buy us wood."

Gazian looked at him. "The lord who sells his grain is a fool. I've told you I will not flirt with famine."

"There hasn't been a famine since our great-grandfather's day."

"And you can promise me there never will be, is that it?"

"Brother—"

"Enough. I won't hear you try to win the minstrel to your side with these tired old arguments. If you want wood, go trade your own gold chain for a fine chair at some great town. I won't stop you."

Demirchi made no reply to that, only frowned at his brother and fingered the chain.

Alaric looked from one of them to the other. "I am sorry to be the cause of such a quarrel, my masters," he said softly.

Demirchi straightened in his chair. "It is an old quarrel, minstrel," he said, and then his frown twisted into a sardonic smile. "One I never win. But that does not make me give up. Perhaps when we, too, are sitting on stone benches, my brother will finally think again about our wealth." He rose to his feet. "Now I shall bid you good night, brother, and you, Master Alaric. I hope you *will* stay with us, minstrel, for every time he sees you, my brother will remember that there is a world beyond this lake." He bowed slightly and left by way of the stairway to the upper floors.

Lord Gazian looked at his own gold chain for a moment after his brother had gone. Then he raised his eyes to Alaric's. "Are we too poor for you, minstrel?"

Alaric smiled. "I have sung at great houses and small, to listeners clothed in velvet and listeners clothed in rags. There was not much difference in their enjoyment. Just in the food they offered. And your food is excellent, my lord."

Gazian nodded. "And our enjoyment is high. It always would be. Think hard on your decision, Alaric."

"I will, my lord. I promise."

"Now . . . perhaps one last song before we sleep?"

"Of course, my lord."

And he sang of a long dark journey to a distant land where a sip of the water could make one immortal, as long as one never left. The youth who made the journey stayed many centuries and was happy, but he went out at last, homesick for the place of his birth, and crumbled to dust as soon as he passed the land's enchanted border.

When the song was done, Gazian said, "Is that what you think of my offer? That someday you would regret staying?"

Alaric shook his head. "It is only a song, my lord."

"The boy wants you to stay. And he needs you. He is not completely well yet. What if he falls ill again? Only you know where to find the elixir. He has been ill so much of his life!"

Alaric slid his hand along the strings of his lute, eliciting only the faintest murmur of sound. Then he said, "I could draw you a map. But it is a long, hard journey. And no promise that at the end the maker of the elixir would give any to a stranger."

"So much the more do we need you."

"I need time to think, my lord."

Gazian leaned toward him and gripped his arm. "You will be a brother to me. I swear it."

Alaric smiled. "It is not a repellent offer, my lord. But I need a little time."

"Of course," said Gazian, letting go of him. "I look forward to your answer, whenever you are ready with it."

Alaric bowed to him, bade him good-night, and went upstairs.

He lay awake for a while, considering the offer. It was not the best he had ever had, nor the worst. It had certain attractions, not the least the quality of the food. But he had eaten good food elsewhere. And he had met kind people elsewhere. And he had never stayed. He had not decided what to tell Lord Gazian by the time he fell asleep.

He awoke to the sound of someone entering the room and to light, though not the light of morning. It was a small oil lamp, and Master Demirchi held it high. Outside the chamber window, the sky was still black as midnight.

"Minstrel?" said Demirchi.

Alaric sat up on his pallet. "Yes?"

"My lord and brother wishes to see you on the postern balcony."

"Is it Ospir?"

"No. Will you come?"

Alaric pushed his cloak aside and reached for his lute. "Of course."

Demirchi led the way down the stair and out the great iron-banded door. A low half-moon illuminated the lake and the stone balcony. The lake was misty, the balcony was empty.

"He'll be here shortly," said Demirchi. "You were quicker to wake and gather yourself together than we presumed."

"Very well," said Alaric, and he played a chord on the lute.

Demirchi went to the stone railing and looked out over the lake. "You wouldn't think that something so beautiful could be so deadly," he said.

"No," said Alaric. The mist swirled, so heavy in some places that the surface of the water was hidden. Peering at it, Alaric now had no trouble imagining shapes in the wind-stirred whiteness—buildings, trees, even human figures moving upon the water. "My lord Gazian says there are ghosts on the lake. In the mist."

"Oh, yes. I see them often. But they never come near the castle."

Alaric stepped closer to the railing. "Do the people of the village also see them?"

"I don't know," said Demirchi. "I've never asked. Ah, look at that one there. A woman with her arms stretched out to us."

Alaric followed the line of his pointing finger. "Where?"

"Farther to the right."

Alaric squinted into the mist. "I don't quite—"

At that moment, he felt a tremendous blow on the back of his head, an impact so sudden and sharp that it pushed him beyond pain and into a moonless, starless, insensate dark. But he was there, it seemed, for only an instant, wrapped in the thick black velvet of nothing; and then, abruptly, he was enveloped in water, and his mouth and nose were filled with the thick bitterness of brine. He swallowed the vile stuff, breathed it in, choked, and flailed his arms and legs in panic. His struggles brought him to the surface, coughing and gasping. Through burning eyes he saw Lord Gazian's castle looming above him, the postern balcony jutting out over the deadly water. He fought the terror that told him his skin was stripping away from his bones, running like wax melting from a candle. With horrible clarity, he knew where he was and where he wanted to be. In his own special way, he leaped.

And tumbled into the cold, fresh water of the river beside Kata's tent.

In a moment, he was pulling himself up its grassy bank, stopping half in and half out of the water, vomiting and coughing and drawing great ragged breaths of air. Then he rolled back into the river to rinse himself again. By the time he finally crawled out of the water, Kata was waiting for him, a burning brand held high in one hand.

"What is all this commotion?" she said.

He tried to strip off his clothes, thinking that they might still bear some trace of the deadly water, and when she moved to help him, he thrust her away, fearful of harming her with its touch. "It will kill you," he told her. " Maybe it has killed me already." The wet shirt came off at last.

"What are you talking about? Are you wounded?" She held the torch close and peered at him.

"I fell into the Lake of Death. The water will eat the flesh from your bones in a few heartbeats. They spray it at their enemies." He had his trews off now and was shivering in the northern breeze. He clutched himself with crossed arms.

Kata gripped his shoulder hard, and when he tried to pull away, she slapped his face and gripped him again. "This flesh looks well enough to me."

He looked at his shaking hands, his arms, his chest.

"Not a mark on you," she said. "Now come sit by the fire."

Inside her warm tent, Alaric's shivering subsided. Kata thrust the brand into the fire, stirring it to a bright blaze, and inspected him again, more closely. Again she found no signs of damage.

"There are substances which can dissolve flesh," she said, running her hands firmly over his arms and torso, "but they make it slippery first, and your flesh is not. Tell me, does this Lake of Death have a scent? Pungent? Sharp? Making the eyes stream?"

Alaric shook his head.

"And what is the taste of it?"

"Salty and bitter."

"Open your mouth." She lit a splint and held it near his face. "Your tongue is normal, and the inside of your mouth. Is your throat painful?"

"No. But it made my eyes burn."

"Any brine would do that. Is your vision harmed?"

"I don't think so. And the burning is less now."

Kata dropped the splint into the fire. "This deadly lake water would seem not so deadly then."

"But it is. It must be. They all said so."

Kata looked at him sharply. "Is this my Alaric speaking?"

He hesitated, remembering Taskol's cautions, Demirchi's desire to sell the water as a weapon. "It has kept their enemies away for generations."

Kata nodded, then she dipped into one of her bags and pulled out a long-handled bronze ladle. "Bring me a sample of this water, Alaric. I would examine it closely."

Alaric took the ladle, but he said, "This will not reach the water, lady, not from any safe place."

"Then we will give it a longer handle." Under the bundles on one side of her tent she found a spare support pole, as long as Alaric was tall. "Will this suffice?"

Outside, they bound the pole to the ladle with strong sinew.

"You must promise me to be very careful, lady," Alaric said, the pole set on his shoulder like a pike, the bowl of the ladle resting in his hand.

"Of course."

Naked, he traveled to the lake shore near the place where the causeway began. The mist was thick there, and the shore deserted, as he expected. He flitted to a spot a dozen paces along the stone road, and lying flat on his stomach, stretching his arm downward to its limit, he was able to scoop up a small amount of water. He climbed to his feet carefully, waited a few moments for the ladle to stop dripping, and returned to the north.

Kata held a ceramic bowl while he poured the contents of the ladle into it. Then they went inside her tent.

"No, there is no odd scent," she said, after sniffing at the liquid. "Nor the oiliness that would mark some of the more powerful flesh-dissolvers." She found a thin strip of leather and dangled one end into the bowl. She moved it around, stirring the water. "A few heartbeats, you say."

"That's what they told me."

She pulled the strip out and peered at it closely. Then she dunked it again, for a longer time, and pulled it out. "I see nothing."

"I don't know that this is a fair test," said Alaric.

"Leather is skin, is it not?"

"Cured skin. Perhaps that makes it proof against the deadliness, I was told the people have ways of carrying it, even of pumping it."

"No doubt," said Kata, and she thrust her finger into the bowl.

"No!" said Alaric.

"My Alaric, this is a brine, nothing more." She stirred it with her finger. "Look." She raised her unharmed finger from the bowl. And then she licked it and nodded. "A strong brine and a bitter one. Saltier by far than the Northern Sea, and with more salts than just the one we put on our food. But a pleasant enough bath, I think, if you hadn't feared it would kill you. That was a clumsy thing, my Alaric, falling into a lake you so feared."

"I didn't fall," he said. "I was pushed. By someone who believed the water would kill me. I know he believed it."

"Ah." She set the bowl down by the fire. "Well, I suppose they must, and their enemies, too. What strange beliefs there are in the south, with no proof behind them!"

He sighed. "Well, the water will prove deadly enough to something. I had my lute when I went in. And I didn't think to bring it north with me. So it floats . . . somewhere in the lake."

"And it won't survive the wetting."

"No. I shall have to find another."

"You've done that before."

"Yes. Yes." He stared into the fire, but his inner eye saw the Lake of Death instead. He thought back over the time he had been in Lord Gazian's castle. He thought about Gazian himself, and Ospir and Demirchi. Especially Demirchi. And he wondered if Demirchi had paused on the stairs to listen to his last song, and to the conversation that followed it. Or perhaps he had not needed to hear them. Perhaps his decision had been made while he played with his gold chain. "I must go back," he said at last.

"To a place where they tried to kill you?"

"I must."

"For revenge, my Alaric? That is not like you."

"No. To protect someone."

They dried his clothes over Kata's fire, and a moment after he put them on, he was back in his temporary bedchamber in Lord Gazian's castle. Dawn had not yet come.

He slipped into Ospir's room. The boy was sleeping soundly, and the nurse was dozing in the chair at the foot of the bed. Gently, Alaric touched her shoulder, and when she opened her eyes, he made a sign for her to follow him.

In the corridor, the door closed between themselves and Ospir, he said, "Why were you so eager to fetch the wine the first night we gave the boy the elixir?"

She frowned. "I, Master Alaric? I only wanted to bring it so that the boy could drink."

"Lord Gazian had ordered his brother to fetch it."

"But he was delaying, Master Alaric."

"He would have gone in another moment, you know that. Or my lord would have given you the order. But you didn't wait."

"Master Alaric—"

"With all that talk of poison, were you afraid of what Master Demirchi might fetch?"

Her eyes became wary. "I would never say anything like that!"

"But I think you must know that Master Demirchi did not want the boy to live. Does not want the boy to live."

The woman hesitated. "He was happy to be the heir, everyone knows that."

"But the boy is no longer ill. Demirchi will not be the heir."

"Master Alaric—"

He gripped her shoulder hard. Tell me the truth, woman. Don't you think Demirchi knows that you suspect him? Or do you try to ingratiate yourself with him by your silence?"

She shook her head. "I don't know what you mean."

"And you left the two of them together many a time, didn't you, so that Demirchi could put his evil powders in the boy's cup, his bowl, his pastries?"

"The boy loves him, and he loves the boy. What is this talk of evil powders?"

"Or perhaps you put them there yourself."

"I? No!"

"Shall I tell Lord Gazian why his son has been so sick for so many years?"

"You would not accuse me!"

"I would tell the truth. And because I saved the boy's life, he would believe me."

Tears started in the woman's eyes. "Oh, Master Alaric, don't accuse me. What could I do? I am only a servant, and he is my lord's brother. He could throw me into the lake! I never wished the boy ill. I love him dearly."

"But not as much as your own life."

The tears overflowed down her cheeks. "No, not as much." She covered one side of her face with her hand. "You are an outsider. You don't know. It is a terrible death."

"I do know," he said softly. "He killed me that way."

Her mouth dropped open.

"Yes," said Alaric. "I am dead. And I am part of the mist on the lake now. But I know how to enter the castle. Go tell Master Demirchi that I wish to see him on the postern balcony. Now."

She shook her head. "He sleeps. I cannot disturb him."

"Yes, you can," said Alaric and, letting go of her abruptly, he vanished.

The balcony was deserted when, in the next heartbeat, he appeared there. The iron-banded door was closed and barred from the inside—he checked it to be sure, flitting in and out in an instant. He sat down, then, on the hip-high wall, one knee drawn up, his crossed arms resting on it. He waited. Shortly, he heard the sound of the bars being drawn. The door swung inward, revealing Demirchi.

"Come out, Master Demirchi," he said, smiling.

Demirchi stood where he was.

"Now I know without any doubt that there are ghosts in the mist," said Alaric. "They thank you for sending me to them, for they liked my singing and wanted the singer among them forever."

"No," said Demirchi.

"Yes," said Alaric. "The flesh stripped off my bones quite cleanly, and then even my bones dissolved. And my lute, too, poor thing. But I shall seek its ghost shortly, and we will make ghostly music on the lake. You will hear it at night, Demirchi, and remember what you did."

Demirchi gripped the edge of the door. "Go away," he said hoarsely.

"Oh, I will never go away now. You have made certain of that. I will visit you often, mostly at night, but perhaps in the daytime, too. And perhaps I will bring my ghost friends with me. And together, tomorrow or the next day or the next, we will tell Lord Gazian how you killed me, and how you tried to kill his son. I imagine such ghost testimony would be believed, don't you?"

"You can't come inside," said Demirchi. "The ghosts must stay on the lake!"

"But you know I've already been inside. You can't keep me out. Unless . . ."

"Unless what?"

"Unless you and I can make a bargain."

"What sort of bargain?"

Alaric drew his other leg up and sat tailor-fashion on the wall. "You must swear that you will never try to harm the boy again. That's simple, isn't it? Your promise in return for mine not to bother you and not to tell Lord Gazian."

Demirchi took one small step forward, still clinging to the door. "How do I know you will keep your promise?"

"You have only my word. And I will have only yours. Is that not enough? I won't be far, of course. I'll know if you forswear yourself. And don't think you can evade me by persuading someone else to do the deed. I'll know where the responsibility lies. Ghosts always know things like that. You would be amazed at what the ghosts of this lake know."

Demirchi took another step forward. "You don't look like a ghost."

Alaric shrugged. "I suppose that's because I'm new. Perhaps later I'll fade into the mist. Or perhaps the other ghosts will learn from me how to become . . . more substantial."

Abruptly, Demirchi leaped, arms outstretched. But Alaric was too quick this time, and vanished, reappearing at the far end of the balcony.

Demirchi's thighs struck the stone railing, and his momentum, unchecked by his intended target, carried him over the edge. He screamed once before he splashed into the water. But after the splash not a sound came from him, not a cough or a gasp or the slightest audible hint of limbs flailing in water.

Alaric leaned over the railing and saw him by moonlight, floating half submerged, face upward, motionless. Even if he had been struggling, there was no way he could climb back to the overhanging balcony, and the shore was a long swim away, especially for someone who had feared the water so much that he surely had never learned to swim. Resigning himself to being wet again, Alaric used his witch's power to reach Demirchi. Treading water, he gripped the man's arms, and in another moment, they were both back on the balcony.

Demirchi sagged limply in Alaric's grasp, and Alaric eased him to the stone floor. "Wake up, Master Demirchi!" he said sharply, kneeling over him and slapping his face. But Demirchi did not wake, and at last Alaric put a hand on the great vein of his neck and then bent to press an ear against his chest. He found no heartbeat.

"Is he dead?" came a small, soft voice from nearby.

Alaric looked up and saw Ospir in the doorway, clutching the curved handle of the great iron and oaken door with both hands. "How long have you been standing there?"

Ospir edged forward slightly. "I heard what you said to my nurse. I listened at the bottom of the door, where it doesn't quite meet the floor. And then I followed him and stood at the next landing." He peered down at Demirchi. "He *is* dead, isn't he? He was in the water. But he looks all right. I've heard the water makes you look horrible."

"Yes, he's dead. But the water didn't kill him, Ospir. His fear of it did. Would you like to know a secret?"

The boy nodded.

"The water is harmless. It tastes bad, but touching it won't hurt you."

"That isn't what Father says."

"No. It isn't." Alaric climbed slowly to his feet. Water dripped down his arms, his back, his legs, joining the puddle in which Demirchi lay. The boy clung to the door, two paces from that puddle, and did not try to move closer. Alaric wanted to reach out to him, to caress that small dark head, to give him comfort at the sight of death. But he did not. "Well, you must believe your father," he said finally. "He is a good man. Not like your uncle."

The boy looked up at him. "You said he tried to kill me."

"Yes. He made you very sick. But he won't be able to do that anymore, and you'll be well from now on."

"He did bring me things. Sweets. Were they bad for me?"

"His were. But you'll have others now, and they won't hurt you."

The boy heaved a great sigh. "I did like him. I did. Why did he want to kill me?"

"Because he wanted to be lord of this land after your father. And that is your right, as long as you are alive."

"I liked him very much." For a moment, Ospir's voice was as tiny as at the depth of his illness. "Was that wrong, Master Alaric?"

"No, Ospir, it's not wrong to like people."

"I like you."

"And I, you."

Ospir stretched one hand out toward Alaric, then pulled it back without touching him. "You're really a ghost, aren't you?"

"What do you think?"

"You appeared and disappeared. Only a ghost can do that. Or one of the magic people from your songs."

Alaric looked down at Demirchi's body for a moment, and then he nodded. "Yes, I am a ghost. And now I must leave the castle, because dawn will come soon."

"Oh, don't go!"

"I must. But if you look out on the lake at night, and you see the mist swirling above the water, you'll be seeing me. Never doubt that, Ospir. You'll always be seeing me. And I will never let any of the other ghosts harm you. Not even his." He smiled at the boy one last time. "Farewell, future lord of the Lake of Death."

"Oh, won't you sing just one more song?"

Alaric shook his head. "Ask your nurse to sing."

"She's crying."

"Then tell her for me that she should sing instead." And he vanished.

But he did not go far, just to the shore of the lake, just beyond the wavering mist. From there, the castle was ghostly, wreathed in wispy whiteness, the postern balcony invisible. Walking at the verge, beside the crust of salts, he began to circle the lake. He had not gotten more than a quarter of the way around when he saw ghosts in the mist. Not vague, distant figures that might as easily have been imaginary as real, but solid bodies of flesh and bone, dressed in thin white wool, moving across the surface of the water not a score of paces from the shore. There were four of them, and all were shorter than he.

"I see you," he said. "You might as well come here."

After some hesitation, one of the bodies began to move toward him, and one by one the others followed. Their feet seemed to slide over the water's surface, and when they were closer, he realized that they walked on that surface on wide wooden boards that were strapped to their feet like huge sandals, like the webbed frameworks that the people of the north used for walking on top of snow. When they grounded at the verge, he recognized Yosat, Taskol's son, and three of the other village boys who had listened to him sing beside the headman's home.

"So you are the ghosts of the lake," he said, watching them unfasten the boards from their feet. "Do your parents know what games you play at night?"

"Our fathers gave us these foot-rafts," said Yosat.

"Aren't you afraid of the water? The deadly water."

The boys looked at one another and shuffled uneasily.

"So you all know," said Alaric. "It's only the people of the island who don't know. And outsiders."

"You won't tell anyone, will you?" said Yosat, his voice anxious.

"I? Oh, I won't be able to tell anyone. I'm a ghost, too, killed this very night by the terrible water. You'll hear about me tomorrow, I'd guess. And if, someday, some minstrel happens to sing of this place, why, folk will marvel at water that strips the flesh from a man's bones and then dissolves those bones to nothing. It's a very good tale. I wouldn't change it for anything." He reached out to grip the boy's shoulder. "I would ask you to tell your father farewell for me, but I think perhaps you would do better not to let him know we saw each other."

Yosat nodded. "Thank you, minstrel."

"But there is one thing I will ask—a favor from you in return for that favor from me."

"Anything." And the others murmured their agreement.

"There's a boy on that island. He was sick for a long time, but he's well now. Visit him. Play with him. He needs friends." He smiled. "Perhaps someday you might even show him how to play ghost." Then he turned and, with a wave of his hand, walked into the night.

When he could no longer see them, looking back over his shoulder—when their pale, moonlit shapes had been swallowed up by darkness and distance—he vanished in search of daylight, a fire to dry his clothes by, and a new lute.

Darkrose and Diamond

ꕥ

Ursula K. Le Guin

*Ursula Le Guin's "Earthsea" novels–*A Wizard of Earthsea, The Tombs of Atuan, The Farthest Shore*—rank among the most popular high fantasy novels of all time. The books were originally written in the late-1960s and early-1970s, but in recent years, Ms. Le Guin found she had more to say about the world of Earthsea and the wizard Ged, and she returned to it, first with the novel* Tehanu *and then with several shorter stories, including the lovely fantasy that follows.*

Ms. Le Guin's far-ranging body of work includes poetry, children's books, translations, essays, anthologies, and of course science fiction novels like the classic The Left Hand of Darkness *and* The Dispossessed. *Her essays on fantasy, particularly "From Elfland to Poughkeepsie," are essential reading for anyone with an interest in studying heroic and high fantasy. Her recent honors include the Pen/Malamud Award and the Grand Master Award presented by the Science Fiction and Fantasy Writers of America. She lives in Portland, Oregon.*

A Boat-Song from West Havnor

Where my love is going
There will I go.
Where his boat is rowing
I will row.

We will laugh together,
Together we will cry.
If he lives I will live,
If he dies I die.

Where my love is going
There will I go.
Where his boat is rowing
I will row.

I

In the west of Havnor, among hills forested with oak and chestnut, is the town of Glade. A while ago, the rich man of that town was a merchant called Golden. Golden owned the mill that cut the oak boards for the ships they built in Havnor South Port and Havnor Great Port; he owned the biggest chestnut groves; he owned the carts and hired the carters that carried the timber and the chestnuts over the hills to be sold. He did very well from trees, and when his son was born, the mother said, "We could call him Chestnut, or Oak, maybe?" But the father said, "Diamond," diamond being in his estimation the one thing more precious than gold.

So little Diamond grew up in the finest house in Glade, a fat, bright-eyed baby, a ruddy, cheerful boy. He had a sweet singing voice, a true ear, and a love of music, so that his mother, Tuly, called him Songsparrow and Skylark, among other loving names, for she never really did like "Diamond." He trilled and carolled about the house; he knew any tune as soon as he heard it, and invented tunes when he heard none. His mother had the wisewoman Tangle teach him *The Creation of Éa* and *The Deed of the Young King*, and at Sunreturn when he was eleven years old he sang the Winter Carol for the Lord of the Western Land, who was visiting his domain in the hills above Glade. The Lord and his Lady praised the boy's singing and gave him a tiny gold box with a diamond set in the lid, which seemed a kind and pretty gift to Diamond and his mother. But Golden was a bit impatient with the singing and the trinkets. "There are more important things for you to do, son," he said. "And greater prizes to be earned."

Diamond thought his father meant the business—the loggers, the sawyers, the sawmill, the chestnut groves, the pickers, the carters, the carts—all that work and talk and planning, complicated, adult matters. He never felt that it had much to do with him, so how was he to have as much to do with it as his father expected? Maybe he'd find out when he grew up.

But in fact Golden wasn't thinking only about the business. He had observed something about his son that had made him not exactly set his eyes higher than the business, but glance above it from time to time, and then shut his eyes.

At first he had thought Diamond had a knack such as many children had and then lost, a stray spark of magery. When he was a little boy, Golden himself had been able to make his own shadow shine and sparkle. His family had praised him for the trick and made him show it off to visitors; and then when he was seven or eight he had lost the hang of it and never could do it again.

When he saw Diamond come down the stairs without touching the stairs, he thought his eyes had deceived him; but a few days later, he saw the child float up the stairs, just a finger gliding along the oaken banister-rail. "Can you do that coming down?" Golden asked, and Diamond said, "Oh, yes, like this," and sailed back down smooth as a cloud on the south wind.

"How did you learn to do that?"

"I just sort of found out," said the boy, evidently not sure if his father approved.

Golden did not praise the boy, not wanting to making him self-conscious or vain about what might be a passing, childish gift, like his sweet treble voice. There was too much fuss already made over that.

But a year or so later he saw Diamond out in the back garden with his playmate Rose. The children were squatting on their haunches, heads close together, laughing. Something intense or uncanny about them made him pause at the window on the stairs landing and watch them. A thing between them was leaping up and down, a frog? a toad? a big cricket? He went out into the garden and came up near them, moving so quietly, though he was a big man, that they in their absorption did not hear him. The thing that was hopping up and down on the grass between their bare toes was a rock. When Diamond raised his hand the rock jumped up in the air, and when he shook his hand a little the rock hovered in the air, and when he flipped his fingers downward it fell to earth.

"Now you," Diamond said to Rose, and she started to do what he had done, but the rock only twitched a little. "Oh," she whispered, "there's your dad."

"That's very clever," Golden said.

"Di thought it up," Rose said.

Golden did not like the child. She was both outspoken and defensive, both rash and timid. She was a girl, and a year younger than Diamond, and a witch's daughter. He wished his son would play with boys his own age, his own sort, from the respectable families of Glade. Tuly insisted on calling the witch "the wisewoman," but a witch was a witch and her daughter was no fit companion for Diamond. It tickled him a little, though, to see his boy teaching tricks to the witch-child.

"What else can you do, Diamond?" he asked.

"Play the flute," Diamond said promptly, and took out of his pocket the little fife his mother had given him for his twelfth birthday. He put it to his lips, his fingers danced, and he played a sweet, familiar tune from the western coast, "Where My Love Is Going."

"Very nice," said the father. "But anybody can play the fife, you know."

Diamond glanced at Rose. The girl turned her head away, looking down.

"I learned it really quickly," Diamond said.

Golden grunted, unimpressed.

"It can do it by itself," Diamond said, and held out the fife away from his lips. His fingers danced on the stops, and the fife played a short jig. It hit several false notes and squealed on the last high note. "I haven't got it right yet," Diamond said, vexed and embarrassed.

"Pretty good, pretty good," his father said. "Keep practicing." And he went on. He was not sure what he ought to have said. He did not want to encourage the boy to spend any more time on music, or with this girl; he spent too much already, and neither of them would help him get anywhere in life. But this gift, this undeniable gift—the rock hovering, the unblown fife—Well, it would be wrong to make too much of it, but probably it should not be discouraged.

In Golden's understanding, money was power, but not the only power. There were two others, one equal, one greater. There was birth. When the Lord of the Western Land came to his domain near Glade, Golden was glad to show him fealty. The Lord was born to govern and to keep the peace, as Golden was born to deal with commerce and wealth, each in his place; and each, noble or common, if he served well and honestly, deserved honor and respect. But there were also lesser lords whom Golden could buy and sell, lend to or let beg, men born noble who deserved neither fealty nor honor. Power of birth and power of money were contingent, and must be earned lest they be lost.

But beyond the rich and the lordly were those called the Men of Power: the wizards. Their power, though little exercised, was absolute. In their hands lay the fate of the long-kingless kingdom of the Archipelago.

If Diamond had been born to that kind of power, if that was his gift, then all Golden's dreams and plans of training him in the business, and having him help in expanding the carting route to a regular trade with South Port, and buying up the chestnut forests above Reche—all such plans dwindled into trifles. Might Diamond go (as his mother's uncle had gone) to the School of Wizards on Roke Island? Might he (as that uncle had done) gain glory for his family and dominion over lord and commoner, becoming a Mage in the Court of the Lords Regent in the Great Port of Havnor? Golden all but floated up the stairs himself, borne on such visions.

But he said nothing to the boy and nothing to the boy's mother. He was a consciously close-mouthed man, distrustful of visions until they could be made acts; and she, though a dutiful, loving wife and mother and housekeeper, already made too much of Diamond's talents and accomplishments. Also, like all women, she was inclined to babble and gossip, and indiscriminate in her friendships. The girl Rose hung about with Diamond because Tuly encouraged Rose's mother the witch to visit, consulting her every time Diamond had a hangnail, and telling her more than she or anyone ought to know about Golden's household. His business was none of the witch's business. On the other hand, Tangle might be able to tell him if his son in fact showed promise, had a talent for magery . . . but he flinched away from the thought of asking her, asking a witch's opinion on anything, least of all a judgment on his son.

He resolved to wait and watch. Being a patient man with a strong will, he did so for four years, till Diamond was sixteen. A big, well-grown youth, good at games and lessons, he was still ruddy-faced and bright-eyed and cheerful. He had taken it hard when his voice changed, the sweet treble going all untuned and hoarse. Golden had hoped that that was the end of his singing, but the boy went on wandering about with itinerant musicians, ballad-singers and such, learning all their trash. That was no life for a merchant's son who was to inherit and manage his father's properties and mills and business, and

Golden told him so. "Singing time is over, son," he said. "You must think about being a man."

Diamond had been given his truename at the springs of the Amia in the hills above Glade. The wizard Hemlock, who had known his great-uncle the Mage, came up from South Port to name him. And Hemlock was invited to his nameday party the year after, a big party, beer and food for all, and new clothes, a shirt or skirt or shift for every child, which was an old custom in the West of Havnor, and dancing on the village green in the warm autumn evening. Diamond had many friends, all the boys his age in town and all the girls too. The young people danced, and some of them had a bit too much beer, but nobody misbehaved very badly, and it was a merry and memorable night. The next morning Golden told his son again that he must think about being a man.

"I have thought some about it," said the boy, in his husky voice.

"And?"

"Well, I," said Diamond, and stuck.

"I'd always counted on your going into the family business," Golden said. His tone was neutral, and Diamond said nothing. "Have you had any ideas of what you want to do?"

"Sometimes."

"Did you talk at all to Master Hemlock?"

Diamond hesitated and said, "No." He looked a question at his father.

"I talked to him last night," Golden said. "He said to me that there are certain natural gifts which it's not only difficult but actually wrong, harmful, to suppress."

The light had come back into Diamond's dark eyes.

"The Master said that such gifts or capacities, untrained, are not only wasted, but may be dangerous. The art must be learned, and practiced, he said."

Diamond's face shone.

"But, he said, it must be learned and practiced for its own sake."

Diamond nodded eagerly.

"If it's a real gift, an unusual capacity, that's even more true. A witch with her love potions can't do much harm, but even a village sorcerer, he said, must take care, for if the art is used for base ends, it becomes weak and noxious. . . . Of course, even a sorcerer gets paid. And wizards, as you know, live with lords, and have what they wish."

Diamond was listening intently, frowning a little.

"So, to be blunt about it, if you have this gift, Diamond, it's of no use, directly, to our business. It has to be cultivated on its own terms, and kept under control—learned and mastered. Only then, he said, can your teachers begin to tell you what to do with it, what good it will do you. Or others," he added conscientiously.

There was a long pause.

"I told him," Golden said, "that I had seen you, with a turn of your hand and a single word, change a wooden carving of a bird into a bird that flew up and sang. I've seen you make a light glow in thin air. You didn't know I was watching. I've watched and said nothing for a long time. I didn't want to make too much of mere childish play. But I believe you have a gift, perhaps a great gift. When I told Master Hemlock what I'd seen you do, he agreed with me. He said that you may go study with him in South Port for a year, or perhaps longer."

"Study with Master Hemlock?" said Diamond, his voice up half an octave.

"If you wish."

"I, I, I never thought about it. Can I think about it? For a while—a day?"

"Of course," Golden said, pleased with his son's caution. He had thought Diamond might leap at the offer, which would have been natural, perhaps, but painful to the father, the owl who had—perhaps—hatched out an eagle.

For Golden looked on the Art Magic with genuine humility as something quite beyond him—not a mere toy, such as music or tale-telling, but a practical business, which his business could never quite equal. And he was, though he wouldn't have put it that way, afraid of wizards. A bit contemptuous of sorcerers, with their sleights and illusions and gibble-gabble, but afraid of wizards.

"Does Mother know?" Diamond asked.

"She will when the time comes. But she has no part to play in your decision, Diamond. Women know nothing of these matters and have nothing to do with them. You must make your choice alone, as a man. Do you understand that?" Golden was earnest, seeing his chance to begin to wean the lad from his mother. She as a woman would cling, but he as a man must learn to let go. And Diamond nodded sturdily enough to satisfy his father, though he had a thoughtful look.

"Master Hemlock said I, said he thought I had, I might have a, a gift, a talent for—?"

Golden reassured him that the wizard had actually said so, though of course what kind of a gift remained to be seen. The boy's modesty was a great relief to him. He had half-consciously dreaded that Diamond would triumph over him, asserting his power right away—that mysterious, dangerous, incalculable power against which Golden's wealth and mastery and dignity shrank to impotence.

"Thank you, Father," the boy said. Golden embraced him and left, well pleased with him.

II

Their meeting place was in the sallows, the willow thickets down by the Amia as it ran below the smithy. As soon as Rose got there, Diamond said, "He wants me to go study with Master Hemlock! What am I going to do?"

"Study with the wizard?"

"He thinks I have this huge great talent. For magic."

"Who does?"

"Father does. He saw some of the stuff we were practicing. But he says Hemlock says I should come study with him because it might be dangerous not to. Oh," and Diamond beat his head with his hands.

"But you do have a talent."

He groaned and scoured his scalp with his knuckles. He was sitting on the dirt in their old play-place, a kind of bower deep in the willows, where they could hear the stream running over the stones nearby and the clang-clang of the smithy further off. The girl sat down facing him.

"Look at all the stuff you can do," she said. "You couldn't do any of it if you didn't have a gift."

"A little gift," Diamond said indistinctly. "Enough for tricks."

"How do you know that?"

Rose was very dark-skinned, with a cloud of crinkled hair, a thin mouth, an intent, serious face. Her feet and legs and hands were bare and dirty, her skirt and jacket disreputable. Her dirty toes and fingers were delicate and elegant, and a necklace of amethysts gleamed under the torn, buttonless jacket. Her mother, Tangle, made a good living by curing and healing, bone-knitting and birth-easing, and selling spells of finding, love-potions, and sleeping-drafts. She could afford to dress herself and her daughter in new clothes, buy shoes, and keep clean, but it didn't occur to her to do so. Nor was housekeeping one of her interests. She and Rose lived mostly on boiled chicken and fried eggs, as she was often paid in poultry. The yard of their two-room house was a wilderness of cats and hens. She liked cats, toads, and jewels. The amethyst necklace had been payment for the safe delivery of a son to Golden's head forester. Tangle herself wore armfuls of bracelets and bangles that flashed and crashed when she flicked out an impatient spell. At times she wore a kitten on her shoulder. She was not an attentive mother. Rose had demanded, at seven years old, "Why did you have me if you didn't want me?"

"How can you deliver babies properly if you haven't had one?" said her mother.

"So I was practice," Rose snarled.

"Everything is practice," Tangle said. She was never ill-natured. She seldom thought to do anything much for her daughter, but never hurt her, never scolded her, and gave her whatever she asked for, dinner, a toad of her own, the amethyst necklace, lessons in witchcraft. She would have provided new clothes if Rose had asked for them, but she never did. Rose had looked after herself from an early age; and this was one of the reasons Diamond loved her. With her, he knew what freedom was. Without her, he could attain it only when he was hearing and singing and playing music.

"I do have a gift," he said now, rubbing his temples and pulling his hair.

"Stop destroying your head," Rose told him.

"I know Tarry thinks I do."

"Of course you do! What does it matter what Tarry thinks? You already play the harp about nine times better than he ever did."

This was another of the reasons Diamond loved her.

"Are there any wizard musicians?" he asked, looking up.

She pondered. "I don't know."

"I don't either. Morred and Elfarran sang to each other, and he was a mage. I think there's a Master Chanter on Roke, that teaches the lays and the histories. But I never heard of a wizard being a musician."

"I don't see why one couldn't be." She never saw why something could not be. Another reason he loved her.

"It always seemed to me they're sort of alike," he said, "magic and music. Spells and tunes. For one thing, you have to get them just exactly right."

"Practice," Rose said, rather sourly. "I know." She flicked a pebble at Diamond. It turned into a butterfly in midair. He flicked a butterfly back at her, and the two flitted and flickered a moment before they fell back to earth as pebbles. Diamond and Rose had worked out several such variations on the old stone-hopping trick.

"You ought to go, Di," she said. "Just to find out."

"I know."

"What if you got to be a wizard! Oh! Think of the stuff you could teach me! Shapechanging—We could be anything. Horses! Bears!"

"Moles," Diamond said. "Honestly, I feel like hiding underground. I always thought Father was going to make me learn all his kind of stuff, after I got my name. But all this year he's kept sort of holding off. I guess he had this in mind all along. But what if I go down there and I'm not any better at being a wizard than I am at bookkeeping? Why can't I do what I know I can do?"

"Well, why can't you do it all? The magic and the music, anyhow? You can always hire a bookkeeper."

When she laughed, her thin face got bright, her thin mouth got wide, and her eyes disappeared.

"Oh, Darkrose," Diamond said, "I love you."

"Of course you do. You'd better. I'll witch you if you don't."

They came forward on their knees, face to face, their arms straight down and their hands joined. They kissed each other all over their faces. To Rose's lips Diamond's face was smooth and full as a plum, with just a hint of prickliness above the lip and jawline, where he had taken to shaving recently. To Diamond's lips Rose's face was soft as silk, with just a hint of grittiness on one cheek, which she had rubbed with a dirty hand. They moved a little closer so that their breasts and bellies touched, though their hands stayed down by their sides. They went on kissing.

"Darkrose," he breathed in her ear, his secret name for her.

She said nothing, but breathed very warm in his ear, and he moaned. His hands clenched hers. He drew back a little. She drew back.

They sat back on their ankles.

"Oh Di," she said, "it will be awful when you go."

"I won't go," he said. "Anywhere. Ever."

III

But of course he went down to Havnor South Port, in one of his father's carts driven by one of his father's carters, along with Master Hemlock. As a rule, people do what wizards advise them to do. And it is no small honor to be invited by a wizard to be his student or apprentice. Hemlock, who had won his staff on Roke, was used to having boys come to him begging to be tested and, if they had the gift for it, taught. He was a little curious about this boy whose cheerful good manners hid some reluctance or self-doubt. It was the father's idea, not the boy's, that he was gifted. That was unusual, though perhaps not so unusual among the wealthy as among common folk. At any rate he came with a very good prenticing fee paid beforehand in gold and ivory. If he had the makings of a wizard Hemlock would train him, and if he had, as Hemlock suspected, a mere childish flair, then he'd be sent home with what remained of his fee. Hemlock was an honest, upright, humorless, scholarly wizard with little interest in feelings or ideas. His gift was for names. "The art begins and ends in naming," he said, which indeed is true, although there may be a good deal between the beginning and the end.

So Diamond, instead of learning spells and illusions and transformations and all such gaudy tricks, as Hemlock called them, sat in a narrow room at the back of the wizard's narrow house on a narrow back street of the old city, memorizing long, long lists of words, words of power in the Language of the

Making. Plants and parts of plants and animals and parts of animals and islands and parts of islands, parts of ships, parts of the human body. The words never made sense, never made sentences, only lists. Long, long lists.

His mind wandered. "Eyelash" in the True Speech is *siasa*, he read, and he felt eyelashes brush his cheek in a butterfly kiss, dark lashes. He looked up startled and did not know what had touched him. Later when he tried to repeat the word, he stood dumb.

"Memory, memory," Hemlock said. "Talent's no good without memory!" He was not harsh, but he was unyielding. Diamond had no idea what opinion Hemlock had of him, and guessed it to be pretty low. The wizard sometimes had him come with him to his work, mostly laying spells of safety on ships and houses, purifying wells, and sitting on the councils of the city, seldom speaking but always listening. Another wizard, not Roke-trained but with the healer's gift, looked after the sick and dying of South Port. Hemlock was glad to let him do so. His own pleasure was in studying and, as far as Diamond could see, doing no magic at all. "Keep the Equilibrium, it's all in that," Hemlock said, and, "Knowledge, order, and control." Those words he said so often that they made a tune in Diamond's head and sang themselves over and over: knowledge, or-der, and contro———l . . .

When Diamond put the lists of names to tunes he made up, he learned them much faster; but then the tune would come as part of the name, and he would sing out so clearly—for his voice had re-established itself as a strong, dark tenor—that Hemlock winced. Hemlock's was a very silent house.

Mostly the pupil was supposed to be with the Master, or studying the lists of names in the room where the lorebooks and wordbooks were, or asleep. Hemlock was a stickler for early abed and early afoot. But now and then Diamond had an hour or two free. He always went down to the docks and sat on a pierside or a waterstair and thought about Darkrose. As soon as he was out of the house and away from Master Hemlock, he began to think about Darkrose, and went on thinking about her and very little else. It surprised him a little. He thought he ought to be homesick, to think about his mother. He did think about his mother quite often, and often was homesick, lying on his cot in his bare and narrow little room after a scanty supper of cold pea-porridge—for this wizard, at least, did not live in such luxury as Golden had imagined. Diamond never thought about Darkrose, nights. He thought of his mother, or of sunny rooms and hot food, or a tune would come into his head and he would practice it mentally on the harp in his mind, and so drift off to sleep. Darkrose would come to his mind only when he was down at the docks, staring out at the water of the harbor, the piers, the fishing boats, only when he was outdoors and away from Hemlock and his house.

So he cherished his free hours as if they were actual meetings with her. He had always loved her, but had not understood that he loved her beyond anyone and anything. When he was with her, even when he was down on the docks thinking of her, he was alive. He never felt entirely alive in Master Hemlock's house and presence. He felt a little dead. Not dead, but a little dead.

A few times, sitting on the waterstairs, the dirty harbor water sloshing at the next step down, the yells of gulls and dock-workers wreathing the air with a thin, ungainly music, he shut his eyes and saw his love so clear, so close, that he reached out his hand to touch her. If he reached out his hand in his mind only, as when he played the mental harp, then indeed he touched her. He felt her hand in his, and her cheek, warm-cool, silken-gritty, lay against his mouth. In his mind he spoke to her, and in his mind she answered, her voice, her husky voice saying his name, "Diamond . . ."

But as he went back up the streets of South Port he lost her. He swore to keep her with him, to think of her, to think of her that night, but she faded away. By the time he opened the door of Master Hemlock's house he was reciting lists of names, or wondering what would be for dinner, for he was hungry most of the time. Not till he could take an hour and run back down to the docks could he think of her.

So he came to feel that those hours were true meetings with her, and he lived for them, without knowing what he lived for until his feet were on the cobbles, and his eyes on the harbor and the far line of the sea. Then he remembered what was worth remembering.

The winter passed by, and the cold early spring, and with the warm late spring came a letter from his mother, brought by a carter. Diamond read it and took it to Master Hemlock, saying, "My mother wonders if I might spend a month at home this summer."

"Probably not," the wizard said, and then, appearing to notice Diamond, put down his pen and said, "Young man, I must ask you if you wish to continue studying with me."

Diamond had no idea what to say. The idea of its being up to him had not occurred to him. "Do you think I ought to?" he asked at last.

"Probably not," the wizard said.

Diamond expected to feel relieved, released, but found he felt rejected, ashamed.

"I'm sorry," he said, with enough dignity that Hemlock glanced up at him.

"You could go to Roke," the wizard said.

"To Roke?"

The boy's drop-jawed stare irritated Hemlock, though he knew it shouldn't. Wizards are used to overweening confidence in the young of their kind. They expect modesty to come later, if at all. "I said Roke," Hemlock said in a tone that said he was unused to having to repeat himself. And then, because this boy, this soft-headed, spoiled, moony boy had endeared himself to Hemlock by his uncomplaining patience, he took pity on him and said, "You should either go to Roke or find a wizard to teach you what you need. Of course you need what I can teach you. You need the names. The art begins and ends in naming. But that's not your gift. You have a poor memory for words. You must train it diligently. However, it's clear that you do have capacities, and that they need cultivation and discipline, which another man can give you better than I can." So does modesty breed modesty, sometimes, even in unlikely places. "If you were to go to Roke, I'd send a letter with you drawing you to the particular attention of the Master Summoner."

"Ah," said Diamond, floored. The Summoner's art is perhaps the most arcane and dangerous of all the arts of magic.

"Perhaps I am wrong," said Hemlock in his dry, flat voice. "Your gift may be for Pattern. Or perhaps it's an ordinary gift for shaping and transformation. I'm not certain."

"But you are—I do actually—"

"Oh yes. You are uncommonly slow, young man, to recognize your own capacities." It was spoken harshly, and Diamond stiffened up a bit.

"I thought my gift was for music," he said.

Hemlock dismissed that with a flick of his hand. "I am talking of the True Art," he said. "Now I will be frank with you. I advise you to write your parents—I shall write them too—informing them of your decision to go to the School on Roke, if that is what you decide; or to the Great Port, if the Mage Restive will take you on, as I think he will, with my recommendation. But I advise against visiting home. The entanglement of family, friends, and so on is precisely what you need to be free of. Now, and henceforth."

"Do wizards have no family?"

Hemlock was glad to see a bit of fire in the boy. "They are one another's family," he said.

"And no friends?"

"They may be friends. Did I say it was an easy life?" A pause. Hemlock looked directly at Diamond. "There was a girl," he said.

Diamond met his gaze for a moment, looked down, and said nothing.

"Your father told me. A witch's daughter, a childhood playmate. He believed that you had taught her spells."

"She taught me."

Hemlock nodded. "That is quite understandable, among children. And quite impossible now. Do you understand that?"

"No," Diamond said.

"Sit down," said Hemlock. After a moment Diamond took the stiff, high-backed chair facing him.

"I can protect you here, and have done so. On Roke, of course, you'll be perfectly safe. The very walls, there . . . But if you go home, you must be willing to protect yourself. It's a difficult thing for a young man, very difficult—a test of a will that has not yet been steeled, a mind that has not yet seen its true goal. I very strongly advise that you not take that risk. Write your parents, and go to the Great Port, or to Roke. Half your year's fee, which I'll return to you, will see to your first expenses."

Diamond sat upright and still. He had been getting some of his father's height and girth lately, and looked very much a man, though a very young one.

"What did you mean, Master Hemlock, in saying that you had protected me here?"

"Simply as I protect myself," the wizard said; and after a moment, testily, "The bargain, boy. The power we give for our power. The lesser state of being we forego. Surely you know that every true man of power is celibate."

There was a pause, and Diamond said, "So you saw to it . . . that I . . ."

"Of course. It was my responsibility as your teacher."

Diamond nodded. He said, "Thank you." Presently he stood up. "Excuse me, Master," he said. "I have to think."

"Where are you going?"

"Down to the waterfront."

"Better stay here."

"I can't think, here."

Hemlock might have known then what he was up against; but having told the boy he would not be his master any longer, he could not in conscience command him. "You have a true gift, Essiri," he said, using the name he had given the boy in the springs of the Amia, a word that in the Old Speech means Willow. "I don't entirely understand it. I think you don't understand it at all. Take care! To misuse a gift, or to refuse to use it, may cause great loss, great harm."

Diamond nodded, suffering, contrite, unrebellious, unmovable.

"Go on," the wizard said, and he went.

Later he knew he should never have let the boy leave the house. He had underestimated Diamond's willpower, or the strength of the spell the girl had laid on him. Their conversation was in the morning; Hemlock went back to the ancient cantrip he was annotating; it was not till supper time that he thought about his pupil, and not until he had eaten supper alone that he admitted that Diamond had run away.

Hemlock was loth to practice any of the lesser arts of magic. He did not put out a finding spell, as any sorcerer might have done. Nor did he call to Diamond in any way. He was angry; perhaps he was hurt. He had thought well of the boy, and offered to write the Summoner about him, and then at the first test of character Diamond had broken. "Glass," the wizard muttered. At least this weakness proved he was not dangerous. Some talents were best not left to run wild, but there was no harm in this fellow, no malice. No ambition. "No spine," said Hemlock to the silence of the house. "Let him crawl home to his mother."

Still it rankled him that Diamond had let him down flat, without a word of thanks or apology. So much for good manners, he thought.

IV

As she blew out the lamp and got into bed, the witch's daughter heard an owl calling, the little, liquid hu-hu-hu-hu that made people call them laughing owls. She heard it with a mournful heart. That had been their signal, summer nights, when they sneaked out to meet in the willow grove, down on the banks of the Amia, when everybody else was sleeping. She would not think of him at night. Back in the winter she had sent to him night after night. She had learned her mother's spell of sending, and knew that it was a true spell. She had sent him her touch, her voice saying his name, again and again. She had met a wall of air and silence. She touched nothing. He would not hear.

Once or twice, all of a sudden, in the daytime, there had been a moment when she had known him close in mind and could touch him if she reached out. But at night she knew only his blank absence, his refusal of her. She had stopped trying to reach him, months ago, but her heart was still very sore.

"Hu-hu-hu," said the owl, under her window, and then it said, "Darkrose!" Startled from her misery, she leaped out of bed and opened the shutters.

"Come on out," whispered Diamond, a shadow in the starlight.

"Mother's not home. Come in!" She met him at the door.

They held each other tight, hard, silent for a long time. To Diamond it was as if he held his future, his own life, his whole life, in his arms.

At last she moved, and kissed his cheek, and whispered, "I missed you, I missed you, I missed you. How long can you stay?"

"As long as I like."

She kept his hand and led him in. He was always a little reluctant to enter the witch's house, a pungent, disorderly place thick with the mysteries of women and witchcraft, very different from his own clean comfortable home, even more different from the cold austerity of the wizard's house. He shivered like a horse as he stood there, too tall for the herb-festooned rafters. He was very highly strung, and worn out, having walked forty miles in sixteen hours without food.

"Where's your mother?" he asked in a whisper.

"Sitting with old Ferny. She died this afternoon, Mother will be there all night. But how did you get here?"

"Walked."

"The wizard let you visit home?"

"I ran away."

"Ran away! Why?"

"To keep you."

He looked at her, that vivid, fierce, dark face in its rough cloud of hair. She wore only her shift, and he saw the infinitely delicate, tender rise of her breasts. He drew her to him again, but though she hugged him she drew away again, frowning.

"Keep me?" she repeated. "You didn't seem to worry about losing me all winter. What made you come back now?"

"He wanted me to go to Roke."

"To Roke?" She stared. "To Roke, Di? Then you really do have the gift—you could be a sorcerer?"

To find her on Hemlock's side was a blow.

"Sorcerers are nothing to him. He means I could be a wizard. Do magery. Not just witchcraft."

"Oh I see," Rose said after a moment. "But I don't see why you ran away."

They had let go of each other's hands.

"Don't you understand?" he said, exasperated with her for not understanding, because he had not understood. "A wizard can't have anything to do with women. With witches. With all that."

"Oh, I know. It's beneath them."

"It's not just beneath them—"

"Oh, but it is. I'll bet you had to unlearn every spell I taught you. Didn't you?"

"It isn't the same kind of thing."

"No. It isn't the High Art. It isn't the True Speech. A wizard mustn't soil his lips with common words. 'Weak as women's magic, wicked as women's magic,' you think I don't know what they say? So, why did you come back here?"

"To see you!"

"What for?"

"What do you think?"

"You never sent to me, you never let me send to you, all the time you were gone. I was just supposed to wait until you got tired of playing wizard. Well, I got tired of waiting." Her voice was nearly inaudible, a rough whisper.

"Somebody's been coming around," he said, incredulous that she could turn against him. "Who's been after you?"

"None of your business if there is! You go off, you turn your back on me. Wizards can't have anything to do with what I do, what my mother does. Well, I don't want anything to do with what you do, either, ever. So go!"

Starving hungry, frustrated, misunderstood, Diamond reached out to hold her again, to make her body understand his body, repeating that first, deep embrace that had held all the years of their lives in it. He found himself standing two feet back, his hands stinging and his ears ringing and his eyes dazzled. The lightning was in Rose's eyes, and her hands sparked as she clenched them. "Never do that again," she whispered.

"Never fear," Diamond said, turned on his heel, and strode out. A string of dried sage caught on his head and trailed after him.

V

He spent the night in their old place in the sallows. Maybe he hoped she would come, but she did not come, and he soon slept in sheer weariness. He woke in the first, cold light. He sat up and thought. He looked at life in that cold light. It was a different matter from what he had believed it. He went down to the stream in which he had been named. He drank, washed his hands and face, made himself look as decent as he could, and went up through the town to the fine house at the high end, his father's house.

After the first outcries and embraces, the servants and his mother sat him right down to breakfast. So it was with warm food in his belly and a certain chill courage in his heart that he faced his father, who had been out before breakfast seeing off a string of timber-carts to the Great Port.

"Well, son!" They touched cheeks. "So Master Hemlock gave you a vacation?"

"No, sir. I left."

Golden stared, then filled his plate and sat down. "Left," he said.

"Yes, sir. I decided that I don't want to be a wizard."

"Hmf," said Golden, chewing. "Left of your own accord? Entirely? With the Master's permission?"

"Of my own accord entirely, without his permission."

Golden chewed very slowly, his eyes on the table. Diamond had seen his father look like this when a forester reported an infestation in the chestnut groves, and when he found a mule-dealer had cheated him.

"He wanted me to go to the College on Roke to study with the Master Summoner. He was going to send me there. I decided not to go."

After a while Golden asked, still looking at the table, "Why?"

"It isn't the life I want."

Another pause. Golden glanced over at his wife, who stood by the window listening in silence. Then he looked at his son. Slowly the mixture of anger, disappointment, confusion, and respect on his face gave way to something simpler, a look of complicity, very nearly a wink. "I see," he said. "And what did you decide you want?"

A pause. "This," Diamond said. His voice was level. He looked neither at his father nor his mother.

"Hah!" said Golden. "Well! I will say I'm glad of it, son." He ate a small porkpie in one mouthful. "Being a wizard, going to Roke, all that, it never seemed real, not exactly. And with you off there, I didn't know what all this was for, to tell you the truth. All my business. If you're here, it adds up, you see. It adds up. Well! But listen here, did you just run off from the wizard? Did he know you were going?"

"No. I'll write him," Diamond said, in his new, level voice.

"He won't be angry? They say wizards have short tempers. Full of pride."

"He's angry," Diamond said, "but he won't do anything."

So it proved. Indeed, to Golden's amazement, Master Hemlock sent back a scrupulous two-fifths of the prenticing fee. With the packet, which was delivered by one of Golden's carters who had taken a load of spars down to South Port, was a note for Diamond. It said, "True art requires a single heart." The direction on the outside was the Hardic rune for willow. The note was signed with Hemlock's rune, which had two meanings: the hemlock tree, and suffering.

Diamond sat in his own sunny room upstairs, on his comfortable bed, hearing his mother singing as she went about the house. He held the wizard's letter and reread the message and the two runes many times. The cold and sluggish mind that had been born in him that morning down in the sallows accepted the lesson. No magic. Never again. He had never given his heart to it. It had been a game to him, a game to play with Darkrose. Even the names of the True Speech that he had learned in the wizard's house, though he knew the beauty and the power that lay in them, he could let go, let slip, forget. That was not his language.

He could speak his language only with her. And he had lost her, let her go. The double heart has no true speech. From now on he could talk only the language of duty: the getting and the spending, the outlay and the income, the profit and the loss.

And beyond that, nothing. There had been illusions, little spells, pebbles that turned to butterflies, wooden birds that flew on living wings for a minute or two. There had never been a choice, really. There was only one way for him to go.

VI

Golden was immensely happy and quite unconscious of it. “Old man’s got his jewel back,” said the carter to the forester. “Sweet as new butter, he is.” Golden, unaware of being sweet, thought only how sweet life was. He had bought the Reche grove, at a very stiff price to be sure, but at least old Lowbough of Easthill hadn’t got it, and now he and Diamond could develop it as it ought to be developed. In among the chestnuts there were a lot of pines, which could be felled and sold for masts and spars and small lumber, and replanted with chestnut seedlings. It would in time be a pure stand like the Big Grove, the heart of his chestnut kingdom. In time, of course. Oak and chestnut don’t shoot up overnight like alder and willow. But there was time. There was time, now. The boy was barely seventeen, and he himself just forty-five. In his prime. He had been feeling old, but that was nonsense. He was in his prime. The oldest trees, past bearing, ought to come out with the pines. Some good wood for furniture could be salvaged from them.

“Well, well, well,” he said to his wife, frequently, “all rosy again, eh? Got the apple of your eye back home, eh? No more moping, eh?”

And Tuly smiled and stroked his hand.

Once instead of smiling and agreeing, she said, “It’s lovely to have him back, but” and Golden stopped hearing. Mothers were born to worry about their children, and women were born never to be content. There was no reason why he should listen to the litany of anxieties by which Tuly hauled herself through life. Of course she thought a merchant's life wasn't good enough for the boy. She'd have thought being King in Havnor wasn't good enough for him.

"When he gets himself a girl," Golden said, in answer to whatever it was she had been saying, "he'll be all squared away. Living with the wizards, you know, the way they are, it set him back a bit. Don't worry about Diamond. He'll know what he wants when he sees it!"

"I hope so," said Tuly.

"At least he's not seeing the witch's girl," said Golden. "That's done with." Later on it occurred to him that neither was his wife seeing the witch anymore. For years they'd been thick as thieves, against all his warnings, and now Tangle was never anywhere near the house. Women's friendships never lasted. He teased her about it. Finding her strewing pennyroyal and millersbane in the chests and clothespresses against an infestation of moths, he said, "Seems like you'd have your friend the wise woman up to hex 'em away. Or aren't you friends anymore?"

"No," his wife said in her soft, level voice, "we aren't."

"And a good thing too!" Golden said roundly. "What's become of that daughter of hers, then? Went off with a juggler, I heard?"

"A musician," Tuly said. "Last summer."

VII

"A nameday party," said Golden. "Time for a bit of play, a bit of music and dancing, boy. Nineteen years old. Celebrate it!"

"I'll be going to Easthill with Sul's mules."

"No, no, no. Sul can handle it. Stay home and have your party. You've been working hard. We'll hire a band. Who's the best in the country? Tarry and his lot?"

"Father, I don't want a party," Diamond said and stood up, shivering his muscles like a horse. He was bigger than Golden now, and when he moved abruptly it was startling. "I'll go to Easthill," he said, and left the room.

"What's that all about?" Golden said to his wife, a rhetorical question. She looked at him and said nothing, a non-rhetorical answer.

After Golden had gone out, she found her son in the counting-room going through ledgers. She looked at the pages. Long, long lists of names and numbers, debts and credits, profits and losses.

"Di," she said, and he looked up. His face was still round and a bit peachy, though the bones were heavier and the eyes were melancholy.

"I didn't mean to hurt Father's feelings," he said.

"If he wants a party, he'll have it," she said. Their voices were alike, being in the higher register but dark-toned, and held to an even quietness, contained, restrained. She perched on a stool beside his at the high desk.

"I can't," he said, and stopped, and went on, "I really don't want to have any dancing."

"He's matchmaking," Tuly said, dry, fond.

"I don't care about that."

"I know you don't."

"The problem is . . ."

"The problem is the music," his mother said at last.

He nodded.

"My son, there is no reason," she said, suddenly passionate, "there is no reason why you should give up everything you love!"

He took her hand and kissed it as they sat side by side.

"Things don't mix," he said. "They ought to, but they don't. I found that out. When I left the wizard, I thought I could be everything. You know—do magic, play music, be Father's son, love Rose . . . . It doesn't work that way. Things don't mix."

"They do, they do," Tuly said. "Everything is hooked together, tangled up!"

"Maybe things are, for women. But I . . . I can't be double-hearted."

"Doublehearted? You? You gave up wizardry because you knew that if you didn't, you'd betray it."

He took the word with a visible shock, but did not deny it.

"But why did you give up music?"

"I have to have a single heart. I can't play the harp while I'm bargaining with a mule-breeder. I can't sing ballads while I'm figuring what we have to pay the pickers to keep 'em from hiring out to Lowbough!" His voice shook a little now, a vibrato, and his eyes were not sad, but angry.

"So you put a spell on yourself," she said, "just as that wizard put one on you. A spell to keep you safe. To keep you with the mule-breeders, and the nut-pickers, and these." She struck the ledger full of lists of names and figures, a flicking, dismissive tap. "A spell of silence," she said.

After a long time the young man said, "What else can I do?"

"I don't know, my dear. I do want you to be safe. I do love to see your father happy and proud of you. But I can't bear to see you unhappy, without pride! I don't know. Maybe you're right. Maybe for a man it's only one thing ever. But I miss hearing you sing."

She was in tears. They hugged, and she stroked his thick, shining hair and apologized for being cruel, and he hugged her again and said she was the kindest mother in the world, and so she went off. But as she left she turned back a moment and said, "Let him have the party, Di. Let yourself have it."

"I will," he said, to comfort her.

VIII

Golden ordered the beer and food and fireworks, but Diamond saw to hiring the musicians.

"Of course I'll bring my band," Tarry said. "Fat chance I'd miss it! You'll have every tootler in the west of the world here for one of your dad's parties."

"You can tell 'em you're the band that's getting paid."

"Oh, they'll come for the glory," said the harper, a lean, long-jawed, wall-eyed fellow of forty. "Maybe you'll have a go with us yourself, then? You had a hand for it, before you took to making money. And the voice not bad, if you'd worked on it."

"I doubt it," Diamond said.

"That girl you liked, witch's Rose, she's runing about with Labby, I hear. No doubt they'll come by."

"I'll see you then," said Diamond, looking big and handsome and indifferent, and walked off.

"Too high and mighty these days to stop and talk," said Tarry, "though I taught him all he knows of harping. But what's that to a rich man?"

IX

Tarry's malice had left his nerves raw, and the thought of the party weighed on him till he lost his appetite. He thought hopefully for a while that he was sick and could miss the party. But the day came, and he was there. Not so evidently, so eminently, so flamboyantly there as his father, but present, smiling, dancing. All his childhood friends were there too, half of them married by now to the other half, it seemed, but there was still plenty of flirting going on, and several pretty girls were always near him. He drank a good deal of Gadge Brewer's excellent beer, and found he could endure the music if he was dancing to it and talking and laughing while he danced. So he danced with all the pretty girls in turn, and then again with whichever one turned up again, which all of them did.

It was Golden's grandest party yet, with a dancing floor built on the town green down the way from Golden's house, and a tent for the old folks to eat and drink and gossip in, and new clothes for the children, and jugglers and puppeteers, some of them hired and some of them coming by to pick up whatever they could in the way of coppers and free beer. Any festivity drew itinerant entertainers and musicians; it was their living, and though uninvited they were welcomed. A tale-singer with a droning voice and a droning bagpipe was singing *The Deed of the Dragonlord* to a group of people under the big oak on the hilltop. When Tarry's band of harp, fife, viol, and drum took time off for a breather and a swig, a new group hopped up onto the dance floor. "Hey, there's Labby's band!" cried the pretty girl nearest Diamond. "Come on, they're the best!"

Labby, a light-skinned, flashy-looking fellow, played the double-reed woodhorn. With him were a violist, a tabor-player, and Rose, who played fife. Their first tune was a stampy, fast and brilliant, too fast for some of the dancers. Diamond and his partner stayed in, and people cheered and clapped them when they finished the dance, sweating and panting. "Beer!" Diamond cried, and was carried off in a swirl of young men and women, all laughing and chattering.

He heard behind him the next tune start up, the viol alone, strong and sad as a tenor voice: "Where My Love Is Going."

He drank a mug of beer down in one draft, and the girls with him watched the muscles in his strong throat as he swallowed, and they laughed and chattered, and he shivered all over like a cart horse stung by flies. He said, "Oh! I can't—!" He bolted off into the dusk beyond the lanterns hanging around the brewer's booth. "Where's he going?" said one, and another, "He'll be back," and they laughed and chattered.

The tune ended. "Darkrose," he said, behind her in the dark. She turned her head and looked at him. Their heads were on a level, she sitting crosslegged up on the dance platform, he kneeling on the grass.

"Come to the sallows," he said.

She said nothing. Labby, glancing at her, set his woodhorn to his lips. The drummer struck a triple beat on his tabor, and they were off into a sailor's jig.

When she looked around again Diamond was gone.

Tarry came back with his band in an hour or so, ungrateful for the respite and much the worse for beer. He interrupted the tune and the dancing, telling Labby loudly to clear out.

"Ah, pick your nose, harp-picker," Labby said, and Tarry took offense, and people took sides, and while the dispute was at its brief height, Rose put her fife in her pocket and slipped away.

Away from the lanterns of the party it was dark, but she knew the way in the dark. He was there. The willows had grown, these two years. There was only a little space to sit among the green shoots and the long, falling leaves.

The music started up, distant, blurred by wind and the murmur of the river running.

"What did you want, Diamond?"

"To talk."

They were only voices and shadows to each other.

"So," she said.

"I wanted to ask you to go away with me," he said.

"When?"

"Then. When we quarreled. I said it all wrong. I thought . . ." A long pause. "I thought I could go on running away. With you. And play music. Make a living. Together. I meant to say that."

"You didn't say it."

"I know. I said everything wrong. I did everything wrong. I betrayed everything. The magic. And the music. And you."

"I'm all right," she said.

"Are you?"

"I'm not really good on the fife, but I'm good enough. What you didn't teach me, I can fill in with a spell, if I have to. And the band, they're all right. Labby isn't as bad as he looks. Nobody fools with me. We make a pretty good living. Winters,

I go stay with Mother and help her out. So I'm all right. What about you, Di?"

"All wrong."

She started to say something, and did not say it.

"I guess we were children," he said. "Now . . ."

"What's changed?"

"I made the wrong choice."

"Once?" she said. "Or twice?"

"Twice."

"Third time's the charm."

Neither spoke for a while. She could just make out the bulk of him in the leafy shadows. "You're bigger than you were," she said. "Can you still make a light, Di? I want to see you."

He shook his head.

"That was the one thing you could do that I never could. And you never could teach me."

"I didn't know what I was doing," he said. "Sometimes it worked, sometimes it didn't."

"And the wizard in South Port didn't teach you how to make it work?"

"He only taught me names."

"Why can't you do it now?"

"I gave it up, Darkrose. I had to either do it and nothing else, or not do it. You have to have a single heart."

"I don't see why," she said. "My mother can cure a fever and ease a childbirth and find a lost ring, maybe that's nothing compared to what the wizards and the dragonlords can do, but it's not nothing, all the same. And she didn't give up anything for it. Having me didn't stop her. She had me so that she could *learn* how to do it! Just because I learned how to play music from you, did I have to give up saying spells? I can bring a fever down now too. Why should you have to stop doing one thing so you can do the other?"

"My father," he began, and stopped, and gave a kind of laugh. "They don't go together," he said. "The money and the music."

"The father and the witchgirl," said Darkrose.

Again there was silence between them. The leaves of the willows stirred.

"Would you come back to me?" he said. "Would you go with me, live with me, marry me, Darkrose?"

"Not in your father's house, Di."

"Anywhere. Run away."

"But you can't have me without the music."

"Or the music without you."

"I would," she said.

"Does Labby want a harper?"

She hesitated; she laughed. "If he wants a fife-player," she said.

"I haven't practiced ever since I left, Darkrose," he said. "But the music was always in my head, and you . . ." She reached out her hands to him. They knelt facing, the willow-leaves moving across their hair. They kissed each other, timidly at first.

X

In the years after Diamond left home, Golden made more money than he had ever done before. All his deals were profitable. It was as if good fortune stuck to him and he could not shake it off. He grew immensely wealthy. He did not forgive his son. It would have made a happy ending, but he would not have it. To leave so, without a word, on his nameday night, to go off with the witchgirl, leaving all the honest work undone, to be a vagrant musician, a harper twanging and singing and grinning for pennies—there was nothing but shame and pain and anger in it for Golden. So he had his tragedy.

Tuly shared it with him for a long time, since she could see her son only by lying to her husband, which she found hard to do. She wept to think of Diamond hungry, sleeping hard. Cold nights of autumn were a misery to her. But as time went on and she heard him spoken of as Diamond the sweet singer of the West of Havnor, Diamond who had harped and sung to the great lords in the Tower of the Sword, her heart grew lighter. And once, when Golden was down at South Port, she and Tangle took a donkey cart and drove over to Easthill, where they heard Diamond sing the *Lay of the Lost Queen*, while Rose sat with them, and Little Tuly sat on Tuly's knee. And if not a happy ending, that was a true joy, which may be enough to ask for, after all.

King Rainjoy's Tears

ഈ

Chris Willrich

Fritz Leiber's influence is obvious in Chris Willrich's tales of Persimmon Gaunt and Imago Bone, but you might also detect a strong helping of Lord Dunsany here. These tales of the Thief with Two Deaths, of which this one's the second, strike a rare combination of adventure and metaphor, wrapped in prose as lush as any to be found these days.

Chris Willrich hails from the Puget Sound environs and attended the University of Washington. He managed a one-person library in Seattle before moving to California and earning a Masters Degree in Library Science from San Jose State University. Nowadays he works in the Stanford University Library. "King Rainjoy's Tears" appeared in our July 2002 issue.

A king of Swanisle delights in rue
And his name's a smirking groan.
Laughgloom, Bloodgrin, Stormproud we knew
Before Rainjoy took the throne.
—Rainjoy's Curse

I

It was sunset in Serpenttooth when Persimmon Gaunt hunted the man who put oceans in bottles.

The town crouched upon an islet off Swanisle's west coast, and scarlet light lashed it from that distant (but not unreachable) place where the sunset boiled the sea. The light produced a striking effect, for the people of Serpenttooth were the desperate and outcast, and they built with what they found, and what they found were the bones of sea serpents. And at day's end it seemed the gigantic, disassembled beasts struggled again toward life, for a pale, bloody sheen coated the town's archways, balustrades, and rooftops. Come evening the illusion ceased, and the bones gave stark reflection to the moon.

But the abductor meant to be gone before moonrise.

From the main town she ascended a cliffside pathway of teeth sharp as arrowheads, large as stepping-stones. The teeth ended at a vast, collapsed skull, reinforced with earth, wood, and thatch, bedecked with potted plants. There was a door, a squarish fragment of cranium on hinges, with a jagged eyeslit testifying to some ancient trauma.

Shivering in the briny sea-wind, Gaunt looked over her shoulder at the ruddy sunset rooftops. She did not see the hoped-for figure of a friend, leaping among the gables. "Your last chance to help, Imago," she murmured. She sighed, turned, and knocked.

Blue eyes, dimly glowing, peered through the eyeslit. "Eh?" wheezed a harsh voice. Gaunt imagined in it the complaints of seagulls, the slap of breakers.

"Persimmon Gaunt," she answered. "A poet."

"A bard?" The voice snorted. "The king exiled those witch-women, ten years gone."

"I am not a bard! My tools are stylus and wax, paper and quill, not voice and memory. I have the distinction of being banished by the bards, before the king banished them."

Gaunt could be charming, particularly in such a setting: her specialty in verse was morbidity, the frail railing of life against merciless time. Serpenttooth suited her. More, she suited Serpenttooth, her fluttering auburn hair a wild contrast to her pale, angular face, the right cheek tattooed with a rose ensnared by a spiderweb.

But these charms failed. "What do you want, *poet*?"

"I am looking for the maker."

"Maker of *what*?"

"Of this."

She lifted a small, corked bottle. Within nestled an intricate, miniature sailing ship fashioned of bone. Its white sails curved in an imaginary wind; its banners were frozen in the midst of rippling. Yet the ship was not the extraordinary thing. There was water below it, not bone or glass, and the water moved: not the twitching of droplets but the roiling of a shrunken corner of the sea. It danced and flickered, and the ship heaved to and fro, riding the tiny surge.

Gaunt waved the bottle in various directions, but the ship cared nothing for gravity, forever hugging its tiny sea.

"Exquisite," Gaunt murmured, and not for the first time.

"A trinket," sniffed the other.

"Trinket? For four years these 'trinkets' have been the stuff of legend along the coast! And yet their fame does not travel further. Most who own such bottles—sailors, fishermen, pirates, and all their wives, lovers, and children—will not sell at any price. It's said these folk have all lost something dear to the sea."

"Nothing to do with me."

"There is more." Gaunt unstoppered the bottle. "Listen. Hear the sound of the sea. Hear the deep loneliness, and the deep romance. To know it is to know mischievous waves, and alluring shores. To brush raw fingertips against riches and fame. To wrap scarred arms around hunger and harm. To know the warm fantasy of a home long abandoned, and the cold acceptance of a five fathom grave."

And there was a susurrant murmur from the bottle which held all these things, and more which Gaunt, too chill already, would not say. There came a long answering sigh from behind the door. It blended with the murmur, and Gaunt could not distinguish them.

Weakly, the voice said, "Nothing to do with me. Go."

"I cannot. When an . . . associate of mine procured this item, he found the private memoirs of the owner. We know who you are, Master Salt."

A pause. "You are base thieves."

Gaunt smiled. "Imago would insist he is a *refined* thief, I'm sure. And our victim was a dying lord who had no further use for the bottle."

"What do you want?"

"I bring you greetings," Gaunt said, "from your own maker."

There was silence. The door opened on creaking hinges. A figure stepped aside, and Gaunt entered.

The room resembled a captain's cabin, though it filled a sea serpent's skull, not a vessel's stern. Two oval, bone-framed windows overlooked the ruddy sunset sea. Underneath, shutters covered twin ventilation passages to the skull's nostrils. Nearby, a spyglass rested atop a bookcase of nautical texts. But the other dozen bookcases cradled dozens of ships-in-bottles, each bearing its own churning, miniature sea. Half-constructed vessels listed upon a vast table, pieces scattered like wreckage.

Gaunt plunked her bottle upon the table, ship sailing forever ceilingward.

Master Salt bent over it. "The Darkfast Dreamweaver. Fitting. Named for a great philosopher-thief of Ebontide." A smile sliced his face.

He was built like a sea barrel, yet possessed delicately shimmering blue skin. His bald head resembled a robin's egg gleaming with dew. "Her crew captured the hatchling of a Serpent of the Sunset. Quite a story. But they overfed the child, to keep it from thrashing. It outgrew its bonds, fed well indeed."

He nodded at the shelves. "Lost ships, all of them. I see their profiles in my dreams. Hear their names on the morning wind."

"They are astonishing. The king will be enthralled."

"Him," muttered Salt. "He neglected me, my sisters. Left us eight years in our tower, because we dared remind him he had a soul. We resolved to seek our own lives."

Gaunt said, "Now your exile is ended."

"Not exile. Escape."

"Surely you cannot abandon him," Gaunt persisted, "being what you are."

"If you know what I am, poet, you should fear me. Inhuman myself, I read the sorrow behind human eyes."

His gaze locked hers. Gaunt shivered as though a westerly wind scoured her face, but could not look away.

Salt squinted, then smirked. "You say *I* abandon? I see what you've left behind. You forsook the bards for the written word. And now you even neglect your art . . . for the love of a thief."

Master Salt's eyes changed. One moment they glowed a pale blue; then they resembled blue-sheened, mirrored glass. Yet the person reflected in them was not Gaunt, nor was the moment this one. Instead she beheld a scene from an hour ago.

A man leapt to and fro upon buildings of bone. There was a strange style to his movements. Though he chose his destinations in a boyish rush, his rooftop dance obeyed a strict economy, as though an old man carefully doled out a youth's energy. When he paused, Gaunt could see the two scars of his lean, ferretlike face, one made by steel, one by fire. He gazed out from Master Salt's eyes as if searching for her. Then he leapt to a new height.

"The thief Imago Bone, your lover and sometimes your mentor, prancing about on bone rooftops. Suppose he couldn't resist." Salt blinked his eyes back to their former, glowing state. "But you knew he might be gone for hours. Impatient, you continued alone."

Gaunt's breathing quickened. She found she could not evade Master Salt, nor lie. "Yes. For all Bone's skill . . ."

" . . . he is a boy," Master Salt said. "Yes, I see. I can taste sorrows, poet. Imago Bone's life is an accident, is it not? Bizarre magics stretched his adolescence nearly a century. Only now is he aging normally. He is a great thief; but he is a child in many ways. You fear for him. You are as often his guardian as his student. An unlikely pair, following foolish quests."

"They are not foolish." Gaunt shivered, staring into the shimmering blue eyes. "Not all . . ."

"Quests are excuses, poet. You must live as you wish. As I have done. You do not need bards, or Imago Bone, or King Rainjoy to justify your wanderlust."

Gaunt imagined she felt the tug of the trade winds. Or perhaps it was the clatter of a horse beneath her, the taste of bowspray from a river canoe, the scent of a thousand fragile mountain wildflowers.

"A true wanderer," Salt said, "needs no nation, no captain, no hope of gold to answer the siren lure."

And Gaunt wondered, why had she tried to refashion Bone and herself as heroes, when they could simply travel, drink in the world?

But no, this quest was *not* foolish. She must resist Salt's words. "There—will be war," she stammered, "unless Rainjoy can learn compassion . . . . And he never can, without you."

"I see also," Salt said unmoved, "why you help him."

Gaunt lowered her eyes.

"Abandon that guilt, poet. Abandon all that imprisons you! Leave this quest; join Bone as a thief if it suits you, or shirk him as well—either way, seize your freedom, and do not abuse mine." Salt lifted his hand to Gaunt's mouth. "I did not ask to become a *someone*, any more than humans do. Yet here I am, and I will set my own course. I will hear the sea, and trap its cries."

Now Master Salt scraped a thumbnail against the tip of an index finger, and a blue droplet fell against Gaunt's lips. As the salty tang kissed her, she imagined the rocking of a deck underfoot, heard the songs of seamen raising sail, smelled the stinging brine upon the lines. Her heart skipped once and her eyelids drooped, as she slipped toward a dream of adventure in distant waters, not merely losing her existence, but casting it aside like soiled clothes.

But then from somewhere came Imago Bone's easy voice. "You should listen to him, Gaunt," Bone said. "He makes perfect sense."

With a start, Gaunt opened her eyes. Bone crawled through the passage leading to the dragon-skull's nostrils, face blue from the cliffside winds and sweaty from carrying his many pouches of esoteric tools: ironsilk lines, quicksap adhesive, a spectrum of camouflaging dyes.

As Master Salt turned, Bone sprang to the bottle sheltering the miniature *Darkfast Dreamweaver*. The thief shattered it against the table's edge.

Salt cried out.

So did the broken bottle.

The miniature ocean within the glass spilled onto the dirt floor, foaming and dwindling like a tendril of surf dying upon shore. A chorus of drowning sailors arose, dimly, like an old memory. Then water and voices were gone.

"Curse you," spat Master Salt, and the spittle boiled upon the table, and gave a sound like maddened seagulls as it vanished. He seized the thief, pressing pale blue thumbs against Bone's throat, thumbs that grew foam-white even as Bone went purple.

"Allow . . ." the thief gurgled, "allow me to introduce . . ."

"No," said Master Salt.

"Rude . . ." Bone's voice trailed off, and he flailed uselessly in Salt's grip.

Bone had saved her. Bone was friend, lover, companion on the road. Nevertheless Gaunt hesitated one moment as he suffocated; so much poetry did the the shelves of bottles hold, they might have cradled densely inked scrolls from ancient libraries.

But she knew what she must do. She shut her eyes and yanked.

The shelves toppled, shattering glass, breaking small ships, spilling the trapped substance of Master Salt. The room filled with the despairing cries of lost sailors.

Master Salt shrieked and released Bone, who crumpled, hacking saltwater. Salt knelt as well, trying to clutch the tiny oceans as they misted into nothingness. His knees crunched glass and crushed ships.

Gaunt trembled with the destruction she'd caused. But soon the sailors' voices faded to dim wailing, and she regained her voice.

"Dead sailors move you?" she asked. "Expect more. War is brewing. To prevent it, King Rainjoy will need the compassion he lost. The compassion you bear."

"You speak of compassion? You, who can do this?"

"These voices are of men already lost. But if war comes, they will seem just a drop in a surgeon's pail."

Salt lowered his head.

"I will go," he said at last. "If only to prevent your crushing more dreams."

Imago Bone rose with a look of gratitude, put his hand upon Gaunt's shoulder.

"I regret I did not arrive sooner," he whispered, then smiled ruefully. "The skeletal rooftops, they beckoned . . . ."

"We'll talk of it later," Gaunt said. "No one can help being who they are." She leaned against him, but could not bear to look at him, nor at Master Salt, who gathered broken ships, tenderly, bone by scattered bone.

II

"The first is found," sighed the man upon the ivory chair.

An older man, shuffling through the chamber of mists, stopped and coughed. "Majesty?"

"Persimmon Gaunt. And her companion thief." The voice was dim, and flat. "They have found the first. Soon, all will be well."

"The reports I bring, ah, belie such optimism." The older man scuttled closer. His robes fluttered with no regard to the drafts. "The nobles, hm, demand war with the Eldshore, if you cannot secure an alliance by marriage. I suggest you build ships, raise troops." He raised a wrinkled hand before the king's nose, then snatched at something only he could see.

He inverted the hand, revealing an *enfleshment* from the king's memory, the tiny image of a red-haired woman, proud and bejeweled. She spat in the king's direction. Her voice rose dimly: *You are cold, with no soul within you. You shall never have me.* Turning on her heel, she stalked off the palm and into nonexistence.

"Eldshore's princess will marry me," said the king, "once I am a better man. Once they make me a better man."

"Strange, mm?—that you can sense their doings while I cannot."

Mirthlessly, the king smiled. "You may have made them, sorcerer, but they belong to me."

"Do not hope for too much, my king. War is in the air."

"When you are here, Spawnsworth, the air smells of worse. Leave your reports and go."

When the older man had retreated up a staircase, the king said in a toneless voice without conviction, "I will feel again."

From the staircase descended the sounds of tortured things.

III

The journey to Lornbridge took two weeks, but they felt like two years to the thief Imago Bone.

Master Salt spoke only in grunts. Surely thousands of subjects were capable of grunting for their king; why should Rainjoy need this entity in particular?

Gaunt walked as though shouldering a treasure chest of guilt (Bone often pictured metaphorical treasure chests, feeling deprived of real ones) and there was a distance in her eyes even as she lay nights upon his shoulder.

So it was a relief, finally, to risk his neck reaching a well-guarded noblewoman noted for feathering suitors with arrows.

Seen through tall grass, the battlement looked sickly and moist in the moonlight. (Bone's cloak, after a treatment of saps and powders, matched it.) He slithered beside it, scrambled halfway up, paused for heavy bootfalls to pass, then scurried atop. Time for one gulp of manure-scented air, then he was over the other side, hurling a ball of sticky grain as he dove.

He thudded onto a haycart exactly as the pigpen filled with squealing. By the time the guards investigated, the animals would have devoured the evidence. He slipped into courtyard shadows.

This was more like it: sparks of danger against the steel of brilliant planning. A shame he wasn't stealing anything.

My beloved's doing, Bone thought as he climbed atop a stable. When they met he was a legend, perhaps the greatest second-story man of the Spiral Sea. (The higher stories went of course without question.) Though she could pay little, he'd accepted enormous risk recovering a manuscript of hers from a pair of sorcerous bibliophiles, a task that had required another book, a tome of the coldest kind of magic. That matter concluded, he'd undertaken an absurdly noble quest, the accursed tome's destruction.

Absurd nobility impressed Persimmon Gaunt.

Bone smirked, reversed his cloak to the side stained with berry juice, then leapt from the stable roof onto Duskvale Keep itself, clinging to irregularities in the russet stone. His slow corkscrew toward the highest window allowed him time to review six months of inquiries along the Spiral Sea, a process garnering nothing but scars, empty pockets, and a list of enemies who wouldn't at all mind the damnable book for themselves.

Half jesting, half desperate, Bone had proposed consulting the court wizard of Swanisle.

He'd expected scowls. Swanisle was notorious for persecuting the bards of its county Gaunt (a society of women compared to witches, and similarly treated) formerly by burning, today by exile. He'd assumed Persimmon left with her teachers, would seethe at the thought of returning. But she had assented with a strange look.

Bone should have worried more at that look.

Distracted by such thoughts, Bone froze upon hearing a bright swish. Presently, from afar, came a dim *thunk*.

Lady Duskvale was firing off correspondence.

There was not one keep at Lornbridge but two, separated by the narrow, abysmal Groangorge. Westward stood Duskvale Keep and eastward rose the sandstone tower of Mountdawn. For generations, Gaunt had explained to Bone, the youth of Duskvale and Mountdawn had swooned for each other, sighing and pining across the impassable deep.

Then, four years ago, the keeps' masters paupered themselves constructing a bridge. The fortresses became one small town. Not merely did a stone span connect the castle; dozens of hundred-foot ropes, cables, and pulleys twisted overhead with messages, squirrels, nobles' drying underwear.

Yet today the bridge was guarded, the ropes cut, the youth forbidden to mix.

Swish.

Thunk.

Bone smirked and climbed beside the topmost window.

"Oh, why does he not write me?" he heard a voice exclaim.

Bone craned his head. "Perhaps because—"

"Ay!"

An arrow shot past, a roll of paper wound upon the shaft.

This time there followed no *thunk* but a dim clatter upon the stone bridge.

"Perhaps," Bone said, heart pounding, "because he is not as good a shot as yourself. Though I am pleased even you must aim."

"Who are you?" the voice demanded.

Bone crouched upon the sill, and bowed. "Bone: acquirer of oddities."

Lady Duskvale regarded him with hawk-dark eyes framed by stern cheekbones and black rivulets of hair. "Do you plan mischief? I warn you, I will tolerate mischief with but one man, and he I fire arrows at. For you I have a knife for stabbing, and lungs for screaming."

"I have no wish for mischief, stabs, or screams."

"Are you . . . are you a messenger from Lord Mountdawn?"

"Better than that, my lady. I am Bone. I and the poet Gaunt have come to comfort Lornbridge. May I enter?"

"I would be more comforted with you outside."

"Even a footpad's foot may fall asleep."

"One moment." She nocked an arrow, drew, and aimed. Then she backed into the room. "All right."

Bone leapt inside. "I admire your caution—and more, the strength of your arm—but it is not thieves at your window you must fear. It is the embodiment of sorrow."

She raised her eyebrows, and Bone helped himself to a chair beside a small table serviceable as a shield. He drummed his fingers upon it. "Consider, my lady. In your father's day, these keeps were famous for romance. Men and women pined hopelessly from across the gulf. But that has changed."

"You mock me, thief?" Duskvale's fingers quivered upon the bowstring, as did Bone's upon the table. "Of course it has changed."

"Explain."

"Very well, though my arm grows weaker. Four years ago my father and old Lord Mountdawn, rest their souls, heard identical whispers in their sleep, imploring them to build the bridge. For a time all was glorious. Yet if there are whispers now, they implore weeping. Bravos duel for damsels, spurned paramours hurl themselves into the gorge. Only I and my love, young Lord Mountdawn, are spared these frenzies, for we are calculating and circumspect."

A carrier pigeon fluttered through the window, alighting upon a perch near Duskvale. She regarded it and Bone, then sighed and set down her bow. (Bone released a long breath.) Removing a note from the pigeon's foot, Duskvale read, "'*Soon I must fight my way across the bridge to your side. Each arrow is a caress, but I would kiss the callouses of the hand that fired it. Dear one! Alive or dead, my bloody hide arrives in the morning!*'" She looked up in vexation. "You are interrupting a private conversation, you know. Explain your purpose."

"Are you aware," Bone asked, "that your monarch was once called the Weeping King?"

"Rainjoy?" she mused. "I heard Father say as much. A sensitive boy crushed by the crown's weight, weeping at the consequences of all commands." She crushed Mountdawn's note. "Men *can* be overwrought at times. But the king has changed. Now they call him Rainjoy the Stonefaced. What does it matter?"

"Did your father speak of the Pale Council?"

"Everyone knows of them," Duskvale said impatiently. "Rainjoy's wise advisors. They came from far away and never went among the people. But the people loved them, for they counseled compassion, and kept the king's cruel wizard at bay. But they departed four years ago and this is of no consequence and my beloved is about to die for me."

"Hear this: the Council did not come from a far land, nor did they return there. One member dwells nearby."

"What?"

"They are creatures of magic, my dear, born of a bargain between Rainjoy and his wizard."

"What bargain?"

"That Rainjoy, so wracked by conscience he could not function as king, should weep but three more tears in his life. Yet those tears would be given human form, so when Rainjoy wished he could safely seek the insights of sorrow."

Duskvale fingered her bow. "Impossible."

"No, merely quite ill-advised. I've met one such tear. Another dwells here. We will need your help, and your paramour's, to snare it. Tell me, do you retain builders' plans for the bridge?"

In the end it was the sincerity in Bone's eyes, or (more likely) the desperation in Duskvale's heart, that bade her send a pointed message to Mountdawn and then summon servants to make certain preparations. Bone was relieved not to relate stealing her father's ship-in-a-bottle and rifling his memoirs. For it was Lord Duskvale who had owned the faux *Darkfast Dreamweaver*, its surging in harmony with the whispers of Lornbridge.

Soon the moonlight found the thief whistling, strolling across that great stone arch. At midpoint he squeezed a tiny sack of quicksap, which he smeared full across his gloves, then applied to his shoes.

He descended the bridge's side, enjoying the brisk mountain air, the churning murmur of the river far below, the tickle of vertigo. Presently there came a swish from the west and a thunk to the east.

At this signal Bone crawled underneath the span, hairs pointing toward watery, rocky doom. Where the plans indicated it would be, he discovered a square opening. He crawled inside.

Blue light surrounded him. "Who?" called a bleak voice, like a hollow wind through a shattered house.

The chamber was like a monk's cell, a cold stone sitting room with a few books (with such titles as *Ballad of the Poisoned Paramour* and *The Tragickal History of Violet Swoon*), some decoration (withered roses), odd mementos (lockets with strands of hair inside), and a lamp (bearing not oil but a pale blue liquid glimmering like glacial moonlight).

"I had gambled," Bone said, shedding his gloves, "you would not wish to miss the romantic play of light upon the river. I am Imago Bone," he added, changing his shoes, "and I bring greetings from the king."

The quicksap discarded, Bone gazed upon Rainjoy's tear. She resembled a spindly, large-eyed maiden in a white shift. She shimmered gently in the blue light, reflecting and echoing it. Her long white hair fluttered and frayed, blending into the chamber's dim mists.

She regarded Bone with incomprehension. "Rainjoy abandoned us."

"He would enjoy your counsel again."

"I cannot give it. I am not his anymore, a slave, nameless . . . now I am Mistress Mist. This is my home. There must be love in the world, you see. Lonely were these keeps, but I whispered of this bridge, and they are lonely no longer. Still do I whisper of love."

"You whisper of more than that. Men and women have perished."

"*I* do not slay them," Mist answered sadly. "In my presence they sense what purest love could be, and how far short they fall." She frowned at Bone. "But you—why are you here? When your true love is elsewhere, waiting and worrying. Why while your precious moments with me? Do you abandon her for me? Do you betray?"

A chill enveloped him; he could not evade those eyes.

He thought of Persimmon Gaunt. Of course he would not betray her for this apparition. And yet—was he not flippant, unheedful of her? His dallying upon the rooftops of Serpenttooth nearly caused her death. Did he not repay devotion with childish disregard? Was he not cruel?

He did not deserve her, he realized, nor life. Better to end his existence now, than risk wounding her further. Bone yearned for the abyss at his back.

But even as the impulse for annihilation took over, his old lust for living cried out. He could not prevent his leap, but he modified the angle and, falling, grasped the ironsilk strand fired by Lady Duskvale.

The thread bent, rose, bent, held. It sliced his palm, and he trembled with the urge to release it, dash himself to bits far below. Fortunately the impulse weakened away from Mist.

He saw Gaunt leaning over the bridge's side. "I am sorry . . . ."

"What?" she shouted.

He shook his head, cried instead: "Pigeon!"

Gaunt raised her arm. From the Mountdawn side of the chasm a pigeon fluttered to alight upon Bone's shoulder, a poem of Gaunt's affixed to its leg. Bone shrugged the bird upward and it fluttered into the hidden chamber. Presently Bone heard a sad voice, reading.

"Love floating skyward is earthly no longer
Braced with selfishness, ardor is stronger
On solid ground let rest love's wonder—
And so your bridge we break asunder."

"Picks!" Bone shouted, and at once there sang a chorus of metal biting stone.

"No!"

A large silvery blob, like a pool of mercury ignorant of gravity, flowed from beneath the bridge and oozed upward to the span. Blue light rose from that spot, and although Bone could not see her, he heard Mist shout, "I concede! The bridge will be mute without me. Please do not break it. Keep it, and find love if you can. I will go."

A voice like lonely seabirds answered, "They snared me likewise, sister. For we cannot destroy as they do."

"Yes, brother. They ruin themselves, and each other. We only awaken their sorrow."

"But the last tear will defeat them, sister. The last is the strongest of all."

IV

"The second is found," said the king in the room of mists.

Framing the ivory throne, twin pillars of rainwater poured from funnels and spilled into a pool with a swan's outline, wingtips catching the water, nose aimed at the throne's foot, a drain where the heart should be. Just as they believed distress strengthened the spirit, the royal house of Swanisle believed chill weather quickened the flame within a man.

The king rose, undressed, and waded in, his pensive expression unchanged.

From beside the throne his companion said carefully, "This poet is, ah, resourceful."

"Of course. She is a bard of Gaunt."

"Mm. Never forget, majesty, her ilk caused you great pain."

The king shivered in his pool. It gave him a look that resembled passion. "Great pain. And great wonder. I remember how every spider in its shimmering, dew-splattered web was an architect of genius to be cherished, not squashed. I remember a defiant spark in the eyes, a stony strength in the limbs of every maiden men declared ugly. I remember the disbelieving child in the faces of condemned men, a child whose mind might yet encompass creation, were that infinite head still upon that foreshortened neck. I remember knowing these things, Spawnsworth, but I can no longer *feel* them. But *they* will help. Soon."

"Soon," the wizard murmured, scratching his chin. His robe quivered, jerked, as though pained by needlepricks.

V

Nightswan Abbey formed the outline of a soaring bird, and although its crumbling bulk no longer suggested flight of any kind, the music pouring from its high windows did much to compensate.

A crowd of the young and elderly gathered beneath the sanctuary windows every evening to hear the sweet polyphony, as the purple sunset kissed the first of the night's stars. The sisterhood could sing only within these walls; all else would be vanity. Even so, during the last four years their music had rekindled some of Nightswan's fame, long dimmed in this age of grim, conquering kings.

It was as if those hundred mortal throats conjured the spirit of the Swan Goddess of the Night and the Stars, she who plunged into the sun, seawater glistening upon her wings, to cool its fire and make the Earth temperate and fit for life, she whose charred body fell back into the sea, to become Swanisle.

The music ceased and the listeners drifted away, murmuring to one another—all save four, who slipped among the bushes. Soon, two reemerged, one casting a line to a window, the second glancing backward. "They will not flee," Gaunt whispered. "They are contemptuous, certain their sister will humble us. I am uneasy."

Bone shrugged. "We will handle her. We've seen worse, we two."

Gaunt did not reply.

They ascended to the vast sanctuary, slipping behind the winged marble altar of the Swan. In the pews a lone nun prayed. Her white cap, cut in the outline of a swan, enhanced the rich darkness of a robe embroidered with tiny stars. The intruders made hand signals: they would pause until she departed.

Then the nun looked up, her face still shadowed by her hood, and sang in a voice sweet as any of the abbey's chorus, yet with an unexpected pain, as though a delicate aperitif were served too hot. The first stanza was muted, but her voice rose with the second:

King Stormproud fell to war's caress,
Left Swanisle to his boy,
Who had not learned to love distress:
Soft-hearted was Rainjoy.

Gaunt gave Bone a sharp look, listening.

His shivering toes just touched the floor
When he claimed his father's chair.
When the sad queen's heart would beat no more
He tore his silky hair.

The nun rose. The intruders hid themselves behind the onyx, speckled pulpit as she approached the altar, still singing.

Yet when a wizard of county Gaunt
(Spawnsworth was his name)
Tried his wicked strength to flaunt
The boy king's heart took flame.

For all Gaunt's fear, and all its horror
Marched as Rainjoy's foe.
Enfleshment was the wizard's lore—
To fashion warriors from woe.

The sister knelt where the wine was kept, the wine that symbolized the goddess's blood, shed to make all life possible. She cast a surreptitious glance over her shoulder. Her face was a pale, dimly glowing blue, growing brighter as she sang.

Rainjoy led his armies north,
Felled the work of Spawnsworth's hands,
Yet surely more would soon ride forth
Till they conquered all his lands.

Now the bards of Gaunt were rightly known
To clasp old secrets to the breast.
So the army overturned every stone
Till the king beheld the best.

The nun passed her hand over the wine vessel, and shining droplets fell into the dark liquid. They quickly dimmed, and the wine appeared as before.

"Gaunt's ancient thanes," King Rainjoy spoke,
"The very land would quick obey.
"To free it from the wizard's yoke
"I must know Gaunt as did they."

The woman said, "What you seek takes years,
"A lifetime spent in Gaunt,
"A knowledge born of woe and tears,
"Not a young man's morning jaunt."

"My father died on Eldshore's strand.
"My mother died of loss.
"A wizard makes to seize my land—
"This die I'll gladly toss."

At last Gaunt could stand waiting no more, and stepped forward. The nun ceased singing, caught her breath.

Gaunt curtsied. Meanwhile Bone leapt forward, tumbled, rolled, and stood where he blocked the nun's best retreat. He bowed low, eyes upon her.

In a hot, dusky voice more evocative of tavern than tabernacle, the nun said, "You are agents of the king, I take it?" She raised her head, showing a weary blue face and sapphire smile like a dagger-cut. "I've sensed my siblings being gathered."

"You are correct. I am Persimmon . . . of Gaunt. A poet. This is my companion, Bone. We bear Rainjoy's plea for your help. He must marry Eldshore's princess to stop a war, but she refuses. She senses Rainjoy feels no sorrow, knows no compassion."

"A wise woman." The tear laughed, one sharp, jarring note. "I am Sister Scald. You are a poet of Gaunt? Did Gaunt's bards train you, before Rainjoy exiled them?"

"They did," Gaunt said, "before exiling me."

Glimmering eyes widened. "Did you learn 'Rainjoy's Curse?'"

"Yes," Gaunt said. And she did not sing, but continued Scald's song in speech.

She led him then, where doomed ships had lunged
At cliffs where white foam churned;
To chasms where young suitors plunged;
To pyres where bards had burned.

She wooed him with rhymes of sailors drowned,
And songs of lovers dead,
And poems of bards long in the ground,
Until she wooed him to her bed.

Into a fevered dream he fell
Of the web that snares all lives—
One soul's joy breeds another's hell.
One suffers, and one thrives.

He woke to slaps: For bedding her so,
She offered jibe and taunt.
He trembled chill as she did go;
For now he knew the soul of Gaunt.

And when the nightmare horde returned,
Raised from Gaunt's old pain,
He told it, "Sleep, for I have learned:
"Let the land swallow you again."

The warriors melted into earth
And the wizard quick was seized.

Spawnsworth said, "O king of worth,
"How might you be appeased?"

Rainjoy trembled. "I feel each death.
"All paths shine slick with blood.
"I cannot bear to end your breath."
The mage swore fealty where he stood.

A king of Swanisle delights in rue
And his name's a smirking groan.
But in Rainjoy endless tears did brew
And he longed for eyes of stone.

Scald's voice bit the silence. "He has those eyes now. The bards gave him knowledge of all life's woe, but Spawnsworth tricked him out of his tears. For a time he still consulted us, but who willingly seeks out sorrow? At last he consulted us no more. He became the sort of king Spawnsworth could control."

"He senses what he's lost. Serve him again."

"I serve others now."

Bone broke in. "Indeed? Your brother served others with bottled grief, your sister with a bridge of doomed desire. We threatened these contrivances; the tears surrendered. I say good riddance."

"You mock *their* work, thief?" Scald seized Bone's chin, locked eyes with his. "I see into your soul, decrepit boy. You've begun aging at last, yet you fritter away your moments impressing this foolish girl. And *you*—" She released Bone, snatched Gaunt's ear—"you forsook the glory of voice and memory for clumsy meanderings of ink. Now you neglect even that dubious craft following this great mistake of a man." Scald stepped back, dismissing poet and thief with a wave. "What a pair you are, what a waste of wind your love! Who are *you*, to lecture me?"

Shivering, Gaunt looked away, toward the tall windows and bright stars. But she replied. "I will tell you, tear of Rainjoy. I was a girl who saw the boy king rescue county Gaunt from the creatures who tore her family to bits. I was a bard's apprentice who loved him from afar. And when my teacher *boasted* of how she granted his request by breaking his spirit, I knew I'd follow her no more."

She looked at Bone, who regarded her wonderingly. "I'd not guard secret lore in my skull, but offer my words in ink, telling of grief such that anyone could understand. I would tarry in graveyards and let tombs inspire my verse. For if the bards hoarded living song, I would peddle the dead, written word." Gaunt returned her gaze to Scald. "When Spawnsworth made an end to Rainjoy's weeping, the king's first act was to exile the bards. And how I laughed that day. Come, tear. You cannot shame me. I will repay my teachers' debt."

"You surprise me," Scald said, "but I think you will not take me. I have no bottles, no bridge to harm. My substance passes into the sacramental wine, inspiring the sisters' music. Would you destroy all grapes in the world?"

"I do not need to." Gaunt gestured toward the door.

Scald turned, saw a cluster of black, star-speckled habits underneath white swan hats.

A nun with a silver swan necklace stepped forward, old hands trembling. "We have listened, Sister Scald. Gaunt and Bone sent warning by carrier pigeon that they would seek a king's tear this night, unaware we'd knowingly given you sanctuary. I have been torn, until this moment. I might defy even Rainjoy to honor our pledge, Scald . . . . But you have meddled with our sacraments. You must go."

"*Oathbreaker*," Scald snarled. She looked right and left. "All of you—all humans are traitors, to yourselves, to others. Listen then, and understand."

And Scald sang.

This song was wordless. It was as though the earlier music was simply the white breakers of this, the churning ocean, or the moonlit fog-wisps crossing the lip of this, the crevasse. Now the cold depths were revealed. They roared the truth of human treachery, of weakness, of pain.

Before that song the humans crumpled.

"No . . . ." Gaunt whimpered, covering her face.

"Nothing . . ." whispered Bone. "I am nothing . . . not man, not boy. A waste . . ."

Somehow, Bone's anguish bestirred Gaunt to defy her own. "You are something." She wrenched each word from her throat like splinters torn from her own flesh. "You are not a waste."

The sisters knelt, some mouthing broken regretful words, some clawing for something sharp, something hard, to make an end. But Gaunt raised her head to the singer. "Scald . . ." It should have been a defiant cry, but it emerged like a child's plea. "Look what you do, to those who sheltered you. . . ."

Scald's eyes were hard, lifted ceilingward in a kind of bitter ecstasy. Yet she looked, and for a time watched the nuns cringing upon the stone floor.

She went silent.

She walked to one of the high windows. "I am no better than you," she murmured. "I sense my siblings, like me born of regret. It seems we cannot escape it." Scald removed her swan cap and lowered her head. "We will go."

Gaunt helped Bone to his feet. He clutched her shoulders as though grasping some idea rare and strange. "Why did you not tell me," he said, "of your family?"

She lowered her gaze. "When you suggested Spawnsworth might deal with that accursed tome we've locked away, Bone, I believed his skills were not appropriate and his character untrustworthy. But I realized we two might somehow repay the debt I felt to Rainjoy. It was a deception, Bone, one that deepened with time. I feared you would be angry."

He nodded. "Perhaps later. Now I am merely glad there is still a Gaunt to perhaps be angry with. It is done. For better or worse, we've recovered Rainjoy's tears."

She met his look. "Are they, Bone? Are they Rainjoy's? Or are they more like grown children? I think whatever their faults, they have seized control of their existence. I think they are people." She scowled in frustration. "I fear Scald is right; I am never consistent."

"You cannot deliver them up, now, can you?"

She shook her head. "Forgive me, Bone. We've gained nothing."

"I disagree." He leaned forward, kissed her.

Startled, she kissed him back, then pulled away. "You are changing the subject! You can never focus on one thing; you are forever a boy."

"Fair enough, but I say you are the subject, and you are what I've gained. I know you better, now. And I would rather know you better, Persimmon Gaunt, than plunder all the treasure-vaults of Brightcairn. Though I'd cheerfully do both."

She gaped at him. "Then . . . you have your wish. Whatever Scald may think of us." She gazed at the bent figure beside the window. "To risk losing you three times this journey—it makes me care nothing for how odd is our love, our life. It is ours, and precious."

"Then my dear," Bone said, "let's discuss how we'll evade the king's assassins, when we break our pledge."

"How precious . . ." Gaunt murmured, still watching Scald, and her eyebrows rose. "No, we will not break it, Bone! We will fulfill it too well."

VI

A storm frothed against King Rainjoy's palace, and the hall of mists felt like a ship deck at foggy dawn. Salt, Mist, and Scald stepped toward the ivory throne, knelt beside the swan pool. Behind the Pale Council stood Persimmon Gaunt and Imago Bone.

Upon the throne, the king studied his prodigal tears.

"So," he said.

The tears blinked back.

"Gaunt and Bone," said the wizard Spawnsworth from beside the throne, his cloak twisting as though with suppressed annoyance. "I, ah, congratulate you. You have accomplished a great deed."

"Not so difficult," Bone said easily. "Send us to fetch the morning star's shyer cousin, or the last honest man's business partner, and we might have surrendered. These three were not so well hidden." He smiled. "Anyone might have found them."

"Whatever," Spawnsworth said with a dismissive wave. "Your, um, modesty covers mighty deeds. Now, Majesty, I would examine these three in private. They have dwelled apart too long, and I fear they might be, ah, unbalanced. It might be years before I dare release them."

The tears said nothing, watching only Rainjoy.

"Yes," Rainjoy's murmured, staring back, agreeing to something Spawnsworth had not said. "Yes," I would . . . speak with them."

Before the sorcerer could object, Gaunt said, "Alas, my king, Spawnsworth's fears are quite justified. I regret where duty leads."

With that, she drew a dagger and stabbed Sister Scald where her heart ought to have been.

By then Bone had sliced the glistening throats of Master Salt and Mistress Mist.

The king's tears lost their forms, spilling at once from their robes, flowing like pale blue quicksilver into the swan pool, where they spiraled down into the drain and were lost to sight.

"What?" King Rainjoy whispered, shaking, rising to his feet. "What?"

"It was necessary, Majesty," Gaunt said. "They had become mad. They meant you harm."

"We suspected," Bone said, "that only in your presence could they die."

"Die," echoed Rainjoy. He sank back onto the throne.

Spawnsworth had gone pale, his cloak twitching in agitated spasms. But his voice was calm as he said, "I will wish to investigate the matter, of course . . . but. It seems you have done the kingdom a great, ah, service. It is not too late, I would say, to consider a reward. You sought my advice?"

Rainjoy cradled his head in his hands.

"Alas," said Gaunt, her eyes on the king, "our time with the tears has been instructive regarding your art. It is powerful, to be sure, but not suited to our problem. No offense is meant."

Spawnsworth frowned. "Then gold, perhaps? Jewels?"

Bone swallowed, but said nothing.

"My king," said the sorcerer, "what do you . . ." Then he bit his lip.

Rainjoy wept.

"My king," repeated Spawnsworth, looking more nonplused than when Salt, Mist, and Scald vanished down the drains.

It was little more than a sparkling wetness along the left eye, a sheen that had barely begun to streak. Rainjoy wiped it with a silken sleeve. "It is nothing," Rainjoy said, voice cold.

Gaunt strode around the pool and up to the throne, ignoring Spawnsworth's warning look. She touched Rainjoy's shoulder. "It is something," she said.

He stared at her wide-eyed, like a boy. "It is simply . . . I let them go for so long. I never imagined I would lose them forever. They did not obey."

"Oh my king," Gaunt said, "my dear king. Tears cannot obey. If they could, they would be saltwater only."

He held up the sleeve, dotted with a tiny wet stain. "I have tears again . . . . I do not deserve them."

"Yet here they are. Listen to them, King Rainjoy, even though these tears are mute. And never be parted from them."

The king watched as Gaunt returned to Bone's side. The poet gave the thief one nod, and Imago Bone offered the king an unexpectedly formal bow, before the two clasped hands and

"I am sad, Spawnsworth," he said, wondering. "I do not sense life's infinite sorrow. But I am sad."

But Spawnsworth did not answer, and the light in his eyes was not nascent tears but a murderous glint. He stalked up the stairs.

In his tower there twitched a menagerie of personifications: howling griefs, snarling passions, a stormy nature blustering in a crystal dome, a dark night of the soul shrouding the glass of a mirror. In places there lurked experiments that twitched and mewled. Here a flower of innocence sprouted from the forehead of a gargoyle of cynicism. There a phoenix of renewal locked eyes forever with a basilisk of stasis.

Spawnsworth arrived in this sanctum, teeth grinding, and began assembling the vials of love's betrayal and friendship's gloom, the vials he would form into an instrument of revenge upon Gaunt and Bone.

There came a cough behind him.

He whirled and beheld three shining intruders.

"We are not easily slain, as you should know," Master Salt said. He opened a cage.

"We, clearly, are more easily forgotten," said Mistress Mist. She unstoppered a flask.

"But we will see you never forget us," said Sister Scald, pushing a glass sphere to shatter against the floor. " We believe you could use our counsel. Ah, I see there are many here who agree."

As his creations swarmed toward him, it occurred to Spawnsworth that the many grates in the floor, used to drain away blood and more exotic fluids, fed the same sewers as those in the hall of mists. "You cannot do this," he hissed. "You are Rainjoy's, and he would never harm me."

"We are Rainjoy's no longer," the tears said.

He turned to flee, and felt his own cloak tremble with excitement and spill upward over his face.

Of the many voices heard from the sorcerer's tower that hour, the one most human, the palace servants agreed, was the one most frightening. When they found Spawnsworth's body in the room of empty cages, all remarked how the face was contorted with sorrow, yet the eyes were dry.

The Fantasy Writer's Assistant

ጀጋ

Jeffrey Ford

The barbarian swordsman, being such a strong iconic figure, is an easy target for parody, and writers such as George Alec Effinger, Esther M. Friesner, and Terry Pratchett have given us a lot of good laughs at the barbarian's expense. But it was somewhat surprising to discover in the course of researching this book that these parodies go back nearly fifty years—back at least to 1956, when Poul Anderson published "The Barbarian" and granted the title character the witty dialogue of saying "Duh."

But while Poul Anderson's tale of "Cronkheit the Barbarian" is amusing, this story about Glandar's creator seemed like a perfect endcap for this collection—an ironic jab at Conan's peers, to be sure, but also a gentle reminder of fantasy's place in the so-called real world. This story was first published in our February 2000 issue.

What would you expect a fantasy writer to look like? In your mind you see a man with a white Merlin beard and long lithe fingers that spark magic against the keyboard, or perhaps a plump woman with generous breasts and hair so long it spreads about the room, entwining everything like the many-tentacled spell of a witch.

Picture instead Ashmolean, my fantasy writer, the one whose employ I was in for more than a year. Whatever power of enchantment he possessed was buried behind his eyes, because his description lent itself more to thoughts of other genres. Like one of Moreau's creatures, he appeared the result of a genetic experiment run amok—a giant sloth whose DNA had been snipped, tortured together with that of a man's and then taped and stapled. His stomach was huge, his arms short and hairy, his rear end, in missing the counterweight of the tail, had improvised with a prodigious growth in width. The head was a flesh pumpkin carved with a frown. Vacant, window-like eyes were rimmed by shadows, and the scalp was as devoid of hair as was Usher's roof of shingles. Even his personality was a conundrum that might have driven Holmes to forsake his beloved cocaine for the crack pipe. The only Fantasy I noticed was when he sat at his computer. Then he pounded the keys like he was hammering nails into a wooden cross and gazed at the monitor as would the Evil Queen about to utter, "Who is the fairest of them all?"

I came to Ashmolean through an ad in the local newspaper. It said: Wanted—clerical assistant devoid of interest in literature or ideas. I was told by him at the interview that he wanted someone who would not think but merely do research. Well, I fit neither of the criteria, but being seventeen and without a college degree, I thought it might be more interesting than selling hamburgers, so I lied and acted as blank as possible. He stopped typing for a moment, which he had been doing continuously through all of his questions, turned, and looked me up and down once. "Welcome to Kreegenvale," he said.

Contrary to my job description, I had been a reader and a thinker. Even back in the lower grades, when the other children in my school would go out to the playground with their balls and bats and field hockey sticks, I would take a book and sit beneath the oak tree at the far boundary of the field where sounds from the adjacent woods would cancel that riot of competition society was desperate to inculcate me into. In high school, I suppose I could have been popular. There were boys who wanted me for my long hair and slim figure, but the only climaxes I was interested in were those offered by Cervantes and Dickens. I had a few dates, but the goings on in bowling alleys and the back seats of cars always seemed inelegant narratives, the endings of which could be predicted from the very first page.

Perhaps things couldn't have gone any differently for me, seeing as I grew up, an only child, in a house where success was measured by the majority vote of the world at large. Both of my parents had been driven to achieve in school, at work, and in their personal tastes. My father, a well-respected contract lawyer, never discussed anything but when speaking to me always closed his eyes, pulled on his left ear lobe, and held forth on some time honored strategy for defeating whatever problem I might bring to him. My mother, on the other hand, though a busy CPA, had always professed a desire to be a writer. Her favorite author could have been none other than Nabokov. In the beginning, I read to please them, and then somewhere along the way, I found I couldn't stop.

I read the greats, the near greats, the stylists, the structuralists and then I read Ashmolean. His works filled and spilled from the bookcases that lined his study. He had written short stories, long stories, novels, and even a poem or two. All of it, every word he had birthed from electrons on that computer screen, had gone toward advancing the career of *Glandar, the Sword Wielder of Kreegenvale*. Those thousands of pages contained more sword wielding than you could fit in a stadium.

That rugged thug of mountainous muscles, sinews of chain link, and spirit that was the thundering of eight and a half wild horses, had slain dragons, witches, elves, giants, talking apes, and legions of inept, one-dimensional warriors whose purpose of creation was to be mown down like so much summer hay. When Glandar wasn't wielding he was wenching, and occasionally he wenched and then wielded. He was always outnumbered yet always victorious. No one in the realm rode or drank or satisfied the alluring Sirens of Gwaten Tarn like Glandar, and no one so completely bored me to the brink of narcolepsy.

In comparison with the fiction I was used to reading, my fantasy writer's writing seemed like redundant, cliché-ridden hack-work. Say what you will of Glandar, though, his wielding pleased Ashmolean's readers no end. My fantasy writer was richer than the Pirate King of Ravdish. After his fourth novel, he could have lived comfortably for the rest of his days, existing extravagantly off the interest that Glandar's early adventures had generated. Ashmolean continued on, even though, as one unusually insightful article told, his wife had left him long ago and his children never visited. His house was falling down around him, but still, he worked incessantly, pounding on the keys with an urgent necessity as if he were instead administering CPR. It was not like anything new ever happened at Kreegenvale. Sooner or later it was a certainty there would be generous portions of wielding and then Glandar would end the affair with a phrase of Warrior wisdom. "One must retain a zest for the battle," was my favorite.

The critics raved about Glandar. "Thank god Ashmolean is alive today," one had said. About *The Ghost Snatcher of Kreegenvale*, the famous reviewer Hutton Myers wrote, "Ashmolean blurs the line separating literature and genre in a tour de force performance that leaves the reader sundered in two with the implications of a world struggling between Good and Evil." His fellow authors blurbed him with vigor, each trying to outdo the other with snippets of praise. I believe it was the writer P.N. Smenth who wrote: "I love Glandar more than my own mother."

My part in all of this was to keep Ashmolean from committing inconsistencies in his fantasy world. There was nothing he hated more than to go to a conference and have someone ask him, "How could Stribble Flap the Lewd impregnate the snapping Crone of Deffleton Marsh, in *Glandar Groans for Death*, when Glandar had lopped off the surly gnome's member in *The Unholy Battle of Holiness*?"

Ashmolean would never turn around from his computer but shout his orders to me over his shoulder. "Mary," he would say, "find out if the horse with no mane has ever been to the Land of Fog." Then I would scramble from the lawn chair in which I sat, book in hand, boning up on the past adventures, and search the shelves for the appropriate volumes that might hold this information. The horse with no mane had been to the Land of Fog on two separate occasions—once while accompanying Glandar's idiot first cousin, Blandar, and the second instance as a part of that cavalry of the famous skeleton warrior, Bone Eye.

This process was rather tortuous at first, as I struggled to learn the world of Kreegenvale the way a new cabbie learns the layout of a foreign city. After a time, though, by taking books home to peruse at night and with the speed I had accrued as a well-practiced reader, I had been over almost every inch of the mythical realm and probably knew better than Ashmolean where to get the best roasted shank of Yellow Flarion in the Kingdom or the going price of a shrinking potion.

The one thing I didn't know at all after so much time had passed was Ashmolean himself. He was always brusque with his demands and would offer not so much as a thank-you no matter how obscure the tidbit I dredged up for him. When he would rise from his throne at the computer to go to the bathroom (he drank coffee one cup after another), he would pass by me without even a nod. On payday, the second and fourth Monday of every month, my money would be sitting for me in an envelope on the seat of the lawn chair at the back of his office. It was a paltry sum, but when I would try to broach the subject of a raise, he would call out, "Silence, Kreegenvale hangs in the balance." The surreal nature of my employment was the thing that kept me returning Monday through Saturday for such a long stretch of time.

When I would leave in the afternoon, I often wondered what Ashmolean did when he wasn't writing. There was no television in his house as far as I could see, and no one save his agent ever called him. He hid from his fans for the most part except when there was a conference, and then I had read that he would not sign books and would not hold conversations once he had stepped down from the podium.

It was a puzzle as to when he shopped or did his laundry or any of the other mundanities that the rest of us take for granted. He seemed somewhat less than human, merely an instrument through which Glandar could let this world know of his exploits. The one clue that he was actually alive in the physical sense was when he would break wind. After each of these long, flabby explosions, which prompted me to begin thinking again of the merits of selling hamburgers, he would stop typing for only a moment to murmur Glandar's famous battle cry, "Death to the unbeliever."

You couldn't find two greater unbelievers than my parents during this time. They wondered why I hadn't raced off to college what with my excellent grades. "How about a boyfriend?" my mother kept asking me. "It's time, you know," she would say. My father insisted I was wasting my life, and I needed a real job, something with benefits. All I could tell them was what I felt. I wasn't quite ready to do any of that, although I was sure some day it would happen. Working for my fantasy writer was the closest I could get to that feeling of sitting at the boundary of the field by myself, away from the riot, and still pretend to be doing something useful.

Then one day, a year and a half into my employment, Ashmolean was hammering the keys in service of his latest work, *Glandar, the Butcher of Malfeasance*, and I was in my lawn chair, skimming through a novella entitled, "Dream Fountain of Kreegenvale," which had appeared in the March 1994 issue of *Startling Realms of Illusion*, when the typing abruptly stopped. That sudden silence drew my attention more completely than if he had taken a revolver from his file drawer and fired it at the ceiling. I looked up to see Ashmolean's hands covering his face.

"Oh, my god," I heard him whisper.

"What is it?" I asked.

He spun his chair around, and still wearing that finger mask, said, "I'm blind."

Out of habit, I moved toward the bookshelves, initially thinking some scrap of research would ameliorate his problem. Then the weight of his words struck me, and I could feel myself begin to panic. "Should I call an ambulance?" I asked, taking a step toward him.

"No, no," he said, removing his hands from his face. "I'm blind to Kreegenvale. I can't see what Glandar will do next. The entire world has been obliterated." He stared at me, directly into my eyes for the first time. Through that look I could feel the weight of his fear. All at once, I remembered that I had read his real name was, of course, not Ashmolean but Leonard Finch.

"Maybe you just need to rest," I said.

He nodded, hunched over in his chair, looking like a lost child in a shopping mall.

"Go home," he said.

"I'll be back tomorrow," I said.

He waved his hands at me as if my words worsened his condition. I wanted to ask him if I would still be paid for the rest of the day, but I didn't have the courage to disturb him.

On the four-block walk back to my parents' house, I had metaphorical visions of Ashmolean as an abandoned mine, a tapped-out beer keg, a coin-operated drivel dispenser long since dropped from the supplier's route. He had plumbed the depths of vapid writing and actually found the mythical bottom. As the day wore on into evening, though, I had a change of heart. I don't know why, but after dinner as I was sitting alone in my room, making poor progress with Camus's *Myth of Sisyphus*, I suddenly had a vision of the defeated Leonard Finch still sitting in his office with his hands covering his face. I threw down the weight of Camus and went to tell my mother I was going for a ride.

I went everywhere on my bike, hoping people would think me a health nut instead of realizing the embarrassing fact that I had not yet tested for my driver's license. It was early autumn and the night was cool with a Kreegenvale moon—like the blade of a scimitar—as Ashmolean would have it time and again. I covered the four blocks to his house in minutes, and, as I pulled into his driveway, I noticed that all the lights were out. For the longest time I sat there, trying to decide if I should knock on the door. I think what finally made me get off my bike and go up the steps was that same desire that always drove me onward with any story I was reading. I wanted to find out how it ended.

For all my innate curiosity, I knocked very softly and took a step backward in case, for some reason, I had to run. I waited a few minutes and was about to leave when a light suddenly went on inside. The door slowly pulled back halfway and then Ashmolean's head appeared from behind it.

"Mary," he said and actually smiled. He pulled the door open wider. "Come in."

I was more than a little taken aback by his good humor, unable to remember ever having seen him smile before. Also, in that moment, I realized there was something very different about him. All of that frustrated energy that released itself daily in his punishment of the keyboard now seemed to have vanished, leaving behind a meek doppelgänger of my fantasy writer. I was reminded of his novella "Soul Eaters of the Ocean Cave," and momentarily hesitated before stepping inside.

"One second," he said and left me there in the foyer. I wondered what he had been doing in the dark. He soon returned with a manuscript box in his hands.

"Take two days and read this. On the third day, come to work. I will pay you for the time," he said.

I took the box from him and just stood there not knowing if I was to leave or not. He looked to me as if he needed someone to talk to, but I was mistaken. That vacuous demeanor that had put me off on my arrival now crumbled before my eyes. The redness returned to his face, the arch to his eyebrows. He stooped forward and, with true Ashmolean fury, blurted out, "Go."

I did, quickly. By the time I was on my bike, the lights had again been extinguished inside the house. There was no question in my mind that he was a maniac; what bothered me more was his obsession for creative honesty. He truly could not continue unless he saw for sure inside his head what would happen next in Kreegenvale. This was a practice I had always associated with writers of a different caliber than my fantasy writer. It was with this in mind that I began that night to read *The Butcher of Malfeasance*, and, for the first time, I found I cared about Glandar.

When Ashmolean wrote a novel, it was always a door stopper, and *Malfeasance* was no exception. It was different in one respect, though. For the first time in any of Glandar's adventures, the hero had begun to show his age. There was a particular passage early on, following the beheading of an onerous dwarf, where he even complained of back pain. Also, while lying with the beautiful Heretica Florita, green woman of the whispering wood, he opted for long conversation before vegetable love. Moments of contemplation, little corkscrew worms of uncertainty, had burrowed into the perfect fruit of wielding and wenching that had been Kreegenvale.

I thought perhaps these changes had come because of the nature of the story. In this adventure, Glandar's enemy was a product of himself. It had been well established way back in *A Flaming Sword in the Nether Region* that the Gods of Good smiled upon Glandar for his heroic deeds. To keep him healthy and able to work their positive will against the forces of evil in the world of men, they would send the black bird, Kreekaw, to him at night. The bird would snatch his nightmares from him as he dreamed them and then fly with them to the Astral Grotto where they would be incinerated by Manck, the celestial blacksmith, in his essential furnace.

In the new novel, Stribble Flap the Lewd seeks revenge for having had his member lopped off in an earlier book. Taking his bow, he waits outside the palace at Kreegenvale one night, and as the black bird leaves Glandar's window with a beak full of nightmares, he shoots at it and slays it with an arrow to its heart. The bird plummets into Deffleton Marsh, releasing the nightmares, which coalesce in the rancorous bottom mud and form, through a whirling, swirling, glimmering, and shimmering mumbo-jumbo reminiscent of Virginia Woolf, the monster Malfeasance, a twelve-foot giant with an amorphous rippling body and a shaggy head the size of seven horses' rumps set side by side. This horror begins to roam the countryside spreading its ill will. Glandar avoids a confrontation with it until he learns that it has killed Heretica Florita and sloppily devoured her green heart.

On the third day, I returned to Ashmolean. He was waiting for me in his office, looking again rather pale and meek. I was surprised to find my lawn chair had been moved up next to his writer's throne. He greeted me by name again, and motioned for me to sit beside him.

As I handed him the manuscript box, he asked me if I had read it.

I told him I had.

I thought he would ask me what I thought of it, but I should have known better. Instead, he said, "Did you see it? In your mind, like a movie? Were you there?"

I told him I was there, and I had been. Although the writing was Ashmolean's usual halting, obvious, subject/verb, subject/verb style, the whole adventure, right up to the end where the final battle was about to take place, had truly been more vivid than life.

"Please," he said, and then paused for a moment.

"Please?" I said to myself.

"Just as you would find on the shelves those instances from the history of Kreegenvale I required, now I need you to find something for me in the future of the realm."

I knew what he was asking, but still I shook my head.

"Yes," he said. "You must. There is no one else who knows the saga as well as you. I chose you for this. I have slowly been losing my vision of Kreegenvale for the last two books. I hired you because I knew you were bright. I could see you were a dreamer, a loner. What kind of girl as pretty as you would apply for a stupid job like this? I knew the day would come when I would go completely blind to the story."

"You want me to write the end of the book?" I asked.

"You don't have to write it," he said. "Just tell me what you see. Tell me in as much detail as possible what Glandar does in his final battle with the Malfeasance. Not just how he slays it, but how he moves the sword, how he dodges the monster's acid belches, what kind of oaths he showers upon it."

"How?" I asked.

"Close your eyes," he said.

I did.

"See it here," he said, and I felt his finger touch my forehead between my eyes. "Go back to the adventure. See it step by step. What did they look like? How did they sound? What was the exact shade of green of Heretica's flesh? When you fall into the story, when you are there, follow what they do. Speak it to me, and I will write it down."

"I'll try," I said. At first it was hard to get to the story, because all I could think about was his telling me he knew all along I was bright and why would a pretty girl like me want such a stupid job.

"One must retain a zest for the battle," I heard him whisper, more, it seemed, to himself than to me. Like a shard of glass this phrase made a small tear in my thoughts of me, and the light from Kreegenvale shone through. With great concentration, I widened the hole in the fabric and eventually struggled free into the realm of Glandar.

The beginning of the story played itself out before my eyes like a video on fast forward. I was everywhere I had to be, like an actual subject of the realm, in order to see the key moments of the story speed by. I watched Stribble Flap fire his arrow, saw the dwarf's head roll onto the ground with a gush of blood, and turned away as Heretica reached toward Glandar's loin cloth at the end of their lengthy dialogue. When I looked back, I was standing beside the hero himself. The wind was blowing fiercely, the sky was, of course, cerulean blue, and we were very near the edge of the cliff that overlooks the ocean.

Glandar held his sword, the mighty Eliminator, in his left hand. In his right, he clutched the octagonal shield, Providence, given to him by his dying father. Sweat glistened on his tan, muscled body. His long black hair was tied back with a vine of Heretica's hair; all that was left of her. Fifty feet away, near the very edge of the cliff stood the Malfeasance, its towering blob of a body birthing faces here and there that called insults to the king of Kreegenvale. The head of the monster was like an enormous clod of earth come to life. Its yellow mane hung down in a tangled greasy mess, stained with blood and spleen. Its mouth opened wide enough to swallow a cow, displaying numerous rows of jagged teeth.

"Smell my bile, the perfume of your own night terrors," it bellowed, licking its lack of lips with a boil-ridden whale tongue.

The Malfeasance released a ball of gas, a miniature violet sun, that sailed on the breeze toward Glandar. He lifted his shield and held it up to block the bomb of acid breath. I watched as the noxious blast bubbled the paint that had been the heraldic design of Kreegenvale. Glandar grunted and fell to his knees.

"I think that burnt the hair in my nose," he whispered from where he knelt on the ground. Then he looked up and right at me. I saw a glimmer of recognition in his eyes as if he was actually seeing me standing there. He smiled at me and slowly stood up.

"Hold up, Mal," he called to the monster. "She's here."

As the hero walked toward me, I saw other characters from Kreegenvale come out of hiding from behind the rocks and trees that were about fifty yards behind us.

"Somebody give me a drink," called the monster, "I've got to get this taste out of my mouth."

"Everybody take a break," called Glandar over his shoulder.

He shoved his sword into the ground and dropped his shield.

"What's happening?" I asked.

"Mary, right?" he asked.

I nodded.

"We've been waiting for you."

The others, all of whom I recognized from other stories, gathered around him. The Malfeasance was now leaning over us, swaying in the wind.

"Hello, darling," the monster said to me, reaching down with an arm that grew from its side for a wine skin from Stribble Flap.

"Mary," said Glandar, "there's not much time. I'll explain. We had Heretica put a spell on Ashmolean a few books back so that he would eventually lose touch with our world. It took a while to work, because he's so powerful. I mean, he's god, if you know what I mean. At first we thought he might just give up on us, but then, when he hired you, we realized what his plan was."

"You mean, to finish the book?" I asked.

"Right," said a woman to my left. I turned and saw the beautiful green face of Heretica Florita.

"I thought you had been devoured?" I said.

The Malfeasance laughed. "We made up a woman out of grass and sticks and such and I ate that in her place. How could I really eat her?" he asked.

"Don't ask," said Glandar. The assembled characters started laughing and Heretica leaned over to punch the hero in the arm.

"Why are you telling me this?" I asked.

Glandar waved the others away. "Let us have a moment, here," he said. They all took a few steps back, and sat down on the ground. In seconds, what appeared to be flagons of wine and mead were making the rounds. The Malfeasance was sipping from its wine skin and letting the children use its back as a slide. Every time one of the little ones laughed, so did the creature with a wheezing cough.

Glandar led me away toward the edge of the cliff. When we were out of earshot of the others, he turned to me and said, "It's got to be over, Mary. I can't take any more of this."

"You miss Ashmolean?" I asked.

"No, not at all. I thought you would understand. What I'm telling you is I can't go on. If I have to kill one more thing, I don't care if it's a mosquito, I'm going to lose my mind."

"You are unhappy with Ashmolean," I said.

"Some of the others call him Ash-holean. I have more respect for him than that, but I've been with him from the first page. There were times in the beginning where it was all very exhilarating, but now, man, life in Kreegenvale is a tedious thing. There's nothing new here. I know, when every adventure begins, that I'm going to be killing. Imagine waking up every day and knowing you are going to have to kill something or someone, maybe a whole army of men you have no quarrel with."

"But there are other aspects to Kreegenvale than the killing," I reminded him.

"I'm not a drinker. Every time Ashmolean has me quaff flagons, I'm sick as a dog for the next fifty pages. All that wenching too—sickening. You'd think the guy never saw a woman with normal size breasts. All I ever wanted was a few minutes of love, but that's more exotic to the big man than the three-faced cat-boy of Ghost City."

"Do you want me to make him write love into the plot?" I asked.

"It's too late for that. I just want to help free the others now. I want an end to it, so that they can go back to the lives they had before I happened to them."

"I used to feel the same way about Kreegenvale when I first started reading about you," I said. "But now, I don't think I've ever read anything that has been so alive to me."

"Ashmolean would be a sham if not for one thing. He truly feels it. That's a miraculous thing. I'm doing this because I want to help him out as much as the others."

"You want me to sacrifice you to the Malfeasance, don't you?" I asked. He nodded and I could see tears in his eyes. "That's what heroes are for," he said.

"I don't know if I can do that. He probably won't let me," I said.

"He will," said Glandar. "He can't prevent it. You're too powerful."

"Too powerful?" I said.

"Please," said Glandar and his voice went through an odd transformation into Ashmolean's. "Do you see it?" asked my fantasy writer.

I looked to my left and there he was, fingers poised above the keyboard, ready to start hammering. I turned back to my right and saw Glandar and the Malfeasance in their battle positions by the edge of the cliff.

I could feel the power that Glandar had mentioned welling up inside of me. "Okay," I said, "get ready." My words came forth with an energy of their own, flowing straight up from my solar plexus, colored with vivid description, crackling with metaphor and simile. I spoke without hesitation the battle of

Glandar and the Malfeasance, monster, born of the hero's own ill thoughts.

The Eliminator flashed in the sunlight, and there was rolling and running and gasping for air. Wounds blossomed, blood ran, bones shattered. Great chunks of the monster's amoebic body flew on the ocean wind. And the invective was brilliant: "May you burn in Manck's essential furnace until the scimitar moon sews your soul to eternity." Acid breath and biting steel, the two fought on and on—now one getting the upper hand, now the other.

To my left, Ashmolean was white hot, typing faster than the computer could announce the words that jumped from me to his fingers. "Death to the unbeliever," he murmured under his labored breath.

In the end, Glandar, so brutally wounded that he was beyond recovery, gave one final suicide charge forward, burying himself in the viscous flesh of the monster, forcing both of them over the edge of the cliff.

Ashmolean cried out, "It can't be," as I described them falling, yet his fingers continued typing.

"No," he moaned as they hit the rocks hundreds of feet below, but the action on the keyboard never slowed.

He wept as the ocean waves washed over them. After he hit the final period, he turned away from me to cover his face again with his hands. With that last dot, Kreegenvale went out like a light in my own mind. I pushed back the lawn chair and stood up. Ashmolean's body was heaving, but all of his grief was silent now. Saying nothing, I left the room, left the house, and never went back.

As devastating as the death of Glandar might have been for Ashmolean, it left me with a sense of determination about my own life that even the sword wielder had never exhibited. When thinking what to do next, I remembered Leonard Finch putting his finger on my forehead and saying, "See it here." In rapid succession, I took the job at Burgerama and registered to begin taking classes at the local college. I often thought about what I had done to my fantasy writer, but reconciled it by telling myself it was the best for everyone.

Still, memories of Kreegenvale would sometimes blow through my mind, especially when I sat in the literature lectures and the profs would fall into theoretical obscurity. Then I prayed Glandar would kick in the door and start wielding. For the most part, though, I loved learning again. I took a lot of English courses, but I knew I didn't want to teach. As for the job, it was greasy and hot for little pay, and when I'd slide those horse fat sandwiches across the counter to the eager customers, I'd whisper, "Death to the unbeliever." For all the Gwatan Tarn horrors of Burgerama, it was fun getting to know the other workers who were my age.

Things were going very well, and my parents were pleased with my progress, but for me, there was something missing. I realized one night that what I wanted was to be a writer. Even to be back in Ashmolean's study, where words breathed life into the impossible, would have sufficed. I bought a notebook and began trying to tell a story, but from some lack of courage or an overabundance of self-criticism, I never got further than the first few lines. "If only Kreekaw would come," I thought, "and snatch this frustration from my troubled sleep."

I was into my second semester of college and succeeding in the time-honored tradition, when one day a package for me was delivered UPS to my parents' house. My mother called me, and I came downstairs, rubbing the sleep out of my eyes. I had been up late reading Swift's *Battle of the Books* for an exam. She handed me the brown parcel, planted a dry kiss on my cheek, and then left for work.

Opening the mailer, I slipped out the contents—a brand new fat hardcover book. A thrill ran through me when I saw that it was a copy of *The Butcher of Malfeasance*. Of course, I dropped the mailer and paged frantically to the end of the novel, to the part I had been responsible for. Five pages from the end, I picked up the narrative where Glandar faces off against the monster by the edge of the cliff. Reading it was an experience I will never forget, for Ashmolean had used my exact words. I ran my fingers over the print on the page and when it didn't brush away, I thought to myself, "I created this."

I saw the battle take place before my eyes just as I had seen it in Ashmolean's office the day I dictated it to him. The oaths and all were there, perfectly rendered. But when I read to where the ocean came and washed the fallen bodies out to sea, there was another whole page of writing.

Puzzled, I continued to find that Glandar returns that night to Kreegenvale. Soaking wet, with urchins in his hair and seaweed wrapped around his neck, he steps into a room of mourners. They rejoice, the flagons are passed, and he tells how the elastic body of the Malfeasance saved him from the fall. Although he almost drowned, he managed to fight the current and come ashore three miles down the coast. Then the novel ends on a high note, promising more drinking, wenching, and wielding to come.

"What the hell is this?" I said aloud. A few minutes later, after reinspecting the mailer, I found my answer. In my rush to see my words in print, I had missed the letter from Ashmolean that was addressed to me.

Dear Mary:

I'm sorry, but I had to change your ending a little. Think of all the future royalties I would have lost had I let Glandar die. I'm not ready to kill him off just yet—everyone needs a fantasy. He sends his best and apologizes for his part in the fiction I created for you. I knew from the day I met you that you were smart and that you loved books and ideas. I would have realized that even if I hadn't made a phone call to your school before you even came to the interview. They told me about your place on the edge of the field. I know that place. There are other places you need to go as well. Sometimes an act of destruction can be an act of creation. I felt you needed that to begin your journey. I believe that as your obsessed, blinded fantasy writer, I was the best character I ever created. What good is the illusion of fiction if it cannot show us a way to become the people we need to be? Glandar says, "Be courageous, squeeze every ounce out of life, and live with honor." Simple but still not a bad message to sometimes remember in this complex world. I did this because I knew someday you might become a writer, but that you needed a little help. Glad to be of assistance.

Ashmolean

At first I was confused, but I read the letter again and laughed like a believer. I never took my test on Swift that day, but instead went to the kitchen and made a pot of coffee. Then, I returned to my room and over the course of two days, my mother and father calling to me from the other side of the locked door, I wrote this story.

Acknowledgment is made for permission to print the following material:

"The Hall of the Dead" by Robert E. Howard and L. Sprague de Camp. Copyright © 1966 Conan Properties International LLC. First published in *The Magazine of Fantasy & Science Fiction*, Vol. 32, No.2, February 1967. Reprinted by permission of Conan Properties International LLC.

"A Hedge Against Alchemy" by John Morressy. Copyright © 1981 by Mercury Press, Inc. First published in *The Magazine of Fantasy & Science Fiction*, April 1981.

"Ill Met in Lankhmar" by Fritz Leiber. Copyright © 1970, 1995 by Fritz Leiber. First published in *The Magazine of Fantasy & Science Fiction*, April 1970. Reprinted by permission of the Richard Curtis Associates, Inc.

"Counting the Shapes" by Yoon Ha Lee. Copyright © 2001 by Spilogale, Inc. First published in *The Magazine of Fantasy & Science Fiction*, June 2001.

"Firebird" by R. Garcia y Robertson. Copyright © 2001 by Spilogale, Inc. First published in *The Magazine of Fantasy & Science Fiction*, May 2001.

"Dragon's Gate" by Pat Murphy. Copyright © 2003 by Spilogale, Inc. First published in *The Magazine of Fantasy & Science Fiction*, August 2003.

"After the Gaud Chrysalis" by Charles Coleman Finlay. Copyright © 2004 by Spilogale, Inc. First published in *The Magazine of Fantasy & Science Fiction*, June 2004.

"The Swordsman Whose Name Was Not Death" by Ellen Kushner. Copyright © 1991 by Ellen Kushner. First published in *The Magazine of Fantasy & Science Fiction*, Sept. 1991.

"The Island in the Lake" by Phyllis Eisenstein. Copyright © 1998 by Phyllis Eisenstein. First published in *The Magazine of Fantasy & Science Fiction*, December 1998.

"Darkrose and Diamond" by Ursula K. Le Guin. Copyright © 1999 by Mercury Press, Inc. First published in *The Magazine of Fantasy & Science Fiction*, October/November 1999.

"King Rainjoy's Tears" by Chris Willrich. Copyright © 2002 by Spilogale, Inc. First published in *The Magazine of Fantasy & Science Fiction*, July 2002.

"The Fantasy Writer's Assistant" by Jeffrey Ford. Copyright © 2000 by Mercury Press, Inc. First published in *The Magazine of Fantasy & Science Fiction*, February 2000.